SPIRIT OF THE GARGOYLES

GARGOYLE GUARDIAN CHRONICLES
BOOK 5

REBECCA CHASTAIN

M
Y
M

Mind Your Muse Books
PO Box 374
Rocklin, CA 95677

ALSO BY REBECCA CHASTAIN

THE MADISON FOX ADVENTURES

A Fistful of Evil

A Fistful of Fire

A Fistful of Flirtation

A Fistful of Frost

Madison Fox Novella Box Set

NEVER MISS ANY NOVEL NEWS: Join Rebecca's newsletter today!

Visit RebeccaChastain.com

CONTENT WARNINGS

As with all books in the Gargoyle Guardian Chronicles, this novel is action-packed and intense, and it will ultimately end positively. However, if you like to know the kinds of negative themes you might encounter along the way, this book includes: magical violence and harm to animals (gargoyles).

Never fear, though; Mika won't rest until every gargoyle is safe.

For Cody, guardian of my spirit.
You are my world.

Constructive Elements

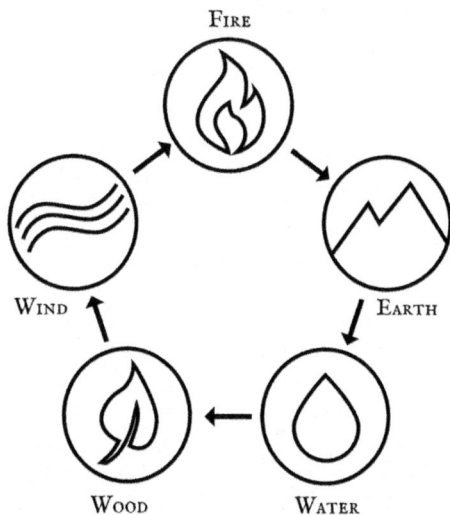

Fire

Wind

Earth

Wood

Water

Destructive Elements

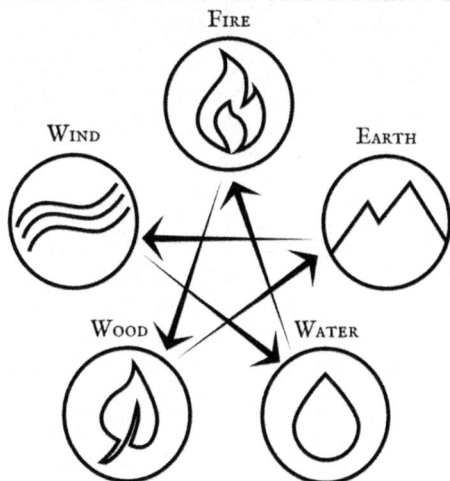

Fire

Wind

Earth

Wood

Water

1

I blinked blearily at the shadowed ceiling, wondering what had woken me. The street below my open windows was silent, and not even the flap of pegasus wings or the drone of a dirigible's propulsion spells disturbed the hush. Kicking free of my tangled sheets, I checked the horizon. This time of year, the sun rose directly through the bay windows of the room I rented in Ms. Zuberrie's Victorian house. I groaned with relief to find the sky a deep indigo. Sunrise was another hour away. Maybe by then, I would feel rested.

A warm breeze tickled strands of hair across my forehead as I resettled myself. Footsteps thumped across the roof, making the rafters pop. One of my gargoyles was repositioning themselves. Maybe their movements had woken me.

Yawning, I checked my mental map. Five beacons glowed in my mind, each correlating with a gargoyle perched atop the Victorian's peaked roof. I hadn't always been able to detect gargoyles in this manner—the same way gargoyles sensed each other. It was a new gift I treasured, even if the uniform nature of the beacons made it impossible to differentiate one gargoyle from another.

Oddly, all five gargoyle siblings were clumped together along the front eaves. Normally, they distributed their weight more judiciously—

A sixth beacon careened into my sensory range far to the east. The gargoyle flew erratically, bobbing and weaving as if battling their way through a hurricane instead of the tranquil night sky.

I leapt to my feet—and promptly stubbed my toes on a bag of quartz I had stupidly left in the middle of the floor. Clutching my throbbing foot, I staggered across my room. My hip slammed into my worktable. It screeched several inches across the hardwood floor, dumping a cascade of loose paperwork off the side. Cringing, I rubbed my aching hip and limped the last two feet to the window.

Clutching the sill, I searched the horizon. Although my room was on the second floor, it felt more like the third, since the front yard sloped away from the house. The incoming gargoyle hadn't slowed, and their flight hadn't gotten smoother. Above the treetops, I caught a blur of movement only because I knew exactly where to look.

The gargoyle was small, barely bigger than the average house cat or gryphonette. From this distance it was impossible to tell if they were a baby or an adult, and the zigzagging beacon on my mental map gave me no answers, either. All I could determine was they were in trouble.

The gargoyle's right wing dipped, and they canted, their stone body spiraling toward a brick chimney. My heart lurched. Disoriented flapping spun the gargoyle in a loose circle, then they reoriented on the Victorian—on *me*—and bumbled into a higher flight.

I seized the elements. Magic roared to me, amplified by

the power of five gargoyles' boosts. A flick of fire, and a thumb-sized glowball popped into existence in the center of my room. After only moonlight, I squinted against the glare of the fiery light, but it made locating my bag without tripping over it much easier. I hefted a strap, staggering under the weight of fifteen pounds of raw seed crystal.

A gargoyle beacon dropped from the roof to the balcony railing, then my balcony door popped open. Oliver thrust his head into my room. Carnelian from nose to tail, with a sinuous Chinese dragon body, he stretched nearly from my door to Kylie's on the opposite side of the balcony. With his wings folded, Oliver had to squeeze to fit through my doorway, but he only thrust his square muzzle across the threshold. In the light of my glowball, the contours of his mane looked like living flame, and his wide, orange-flecked eyes were embers glowing with worry.

"A gargoyle needs you, Mika," Oliver shout-whispered.

"I know. I'm coming."

I lurched across my room and into the hallway. My door bounced off the wall with a bang, but I no longer cared if I interrupted my housemates' sleep. Fear pushed me faster. The incoming gargoyle's beacon swayed dizzyingly, their flight uncoordinated and dangerously uncontrolled.

Grabbing the stair railing, I threw myself down the steps, taking them two at a time. My bag pounded against my spine, seed crystals clacking. Recklessly, I jumped the last three steps, landed hard on the first floor, and thundered barefoot across the foyer to yank open the front door. Cool wood planks slapped against my feet, and distant pain echoed from my soles as I pounded down the porch stairs.

Five gargoyles launched from the Victorian, sweeping overhead, but my attention remained locked on the beacon of the unknown gargoyle careening over the treetops.

I spun air element into a dense net. The stone walkway flashed past. I leapt the sidewalk and sprinted into the empty cobblestone street, stuttering to a halt.

Above my own heavy breathing, I could hear the erratic clatter of stone feathers and the softer susurrus of my gargoyles' wings. I squinted at the night sky, my view obscured by the cottonwoods lining the street and my night vision ruined by the street lanterns' light reflecting off the undersides of their leaves. The beacons in my head swirled around the unknown gargoyle, and snatches of their words filtered down to me.

"Get beneath—"

"—can't catch—"

A flash of orange-red wings and a sinuous carnelian body swerved between trees five houses away before the shadows swallowed Oliver again. Seconds later, Quinn swept into view, his huge citrine lion body and long wings glinting like gold in the lantern lights. Anya swooped in behind him, flying close enough for her dark blue dumortierite and green aventurine panther body and wings to be mistaken for Quinn's shadow. Both dove toward me with heart-stopping speed, but the smaller bundle of jasper quartz plummeted faster.

They were all too close together for the spell I intended. Before I could modify it, the unknown gargoyle collided with Quinn. The smack of their stone bodies resounded like a thunderclap in the still air. The small gargoyle bounced, skipping off Quinn's slick back. Claws scrabbled and caught, briefly, on Anya's wing. Then the gargoyle tore free. Legs and wings flailing, they hurtled straight toward me. I locked eyes with the terrified gargoyle, registering an impression of tiny paws and a pointed muzzle before I flung myself out of their path.

"—going to hit—"

I whipped around, magic already extended. My net of thickened air closed around the gargoyle inches before they crashed into the cobblestones. If my spell had been built with my strength alone, it would have shattered, but enhanced by five gargoyles, the net held. The gargoyle landed with a muffled *clop* and slid, cocooned in the pillowy spell.

"Mika, *duck*," Quinn shouted.

Twin beacons speared toward me from behind. With a squeak, I dropped to a crouch, bracing my hands against the cold cobblestones. Quinn, then Anya, whooshed past, dodging to either side, wing tips slicing the air above my head. My loose hair whipped into my face, stinging my eyes. The gargoyles landed, quartz feline paws hammering the cobblestones more deafeningly than a herd of galloping centaurs.

The bobbing flight of Oliver's beacon warned me a second before he landed behind me. In two loping strides, he fell in beside me as I bolted for the distressed gargoyle. They were trying to rise, but I couldn't make out what kept causing them to stumble, not with Quinn and Anya hovering over them.

"Easy, easy. Let me through." I touched Quinn's flared wing, then Anya's rump, and they shifted aside for me. Oliver pushed his way forward, too, so the four of us ringed the newcomer. I refined fire element into a glowball the size of my fist and floated it above our heads.

Twin honey-ginger eyes blinked at the light, unfocused but bright with pain. The little gargoyle had a raccoon's face, with striations of vivid-vermilion, creamy-orange, and parchment-white sardonyx mimicking the markings of his furred counterpart. Ruddy jasper fur covered his petite feline body, transitioning back into a fluffy ringed-sardonyx tail. His head was proportional to his smaller feline body, his tail long enough to arch over his entire back and his paws barely as wide as Quinn's individual toes. Even his orange-and-rust calico wings were small, barely larger than a crow's. Despite his diminutive size, though, I thought he was full grown.

I cataloged his wounds: a deep scrape down his right cheek bleeding multicolored quartz dust, half an ear missing, scratches along one shoulder and the opposite hip, and several clipped feathers. None accounted for the gargoyle's perilous, uncontrolled flight.

Distantly, I sensed Lydia land, the large lion-footed goose managing the quietest touchdown yet. Herbert circled our heads, then winged toward the Victorian. Doubtlessly, the entire household was awake, but I didn't check. The sick gargoyle held all my attention.

And it was clear now that he *was* sick. His calico wings flared and flapped for balance against an unseen force, and his long stone tail whipped as if he walked a swaying tightrope. He staggered half a step and collapsed.

I dropped to my knees and cupped my hands over his shoulder and hip, gently anchoring him against the ground.

"It's all right. I've got you."

At the sound of my voice, the gargoyle let his head loll to the cobblestones. His gaze continued to rove aimlessly.

"Lowell?" Oliver asked, snaking his head in front of the raccoon gargoyle's.

It didn't surprise me that Oliver knew the sick gargoyle. He made it his mission to speak to every gargoyle in Terra Haven about me. As the city's sole gargoyle guardian, I had the same goal; however, without wings, it was taking me much longer to meet every gargoyle. I had never laid eyes on Lowell before tonight.

"Dizzy. Need healer," Lowell slurred.

"He was healthy the last time I saw him," Oliver said, wings hunched in confusion.

"I'm here, Lowell. I'm going to help you. Try to hold still."

Forming a test pentagram, I tuned it to the unique balance of a living-quartz gargoyle and eased it into Lowell. Pain radiated back to me. The fiery agony of Lowell's sheared-off ear was the worst, but every ache and pang of abused muscles and abraded flesh drilled into me. I quested deeper, searching for the root of his sickness.

A wave of discordant energy surged through Lowell. It bludgeoned my delicate magic, distorting it. Fire flared hotter. Earth compressed. I fought for control, stabilizing my magic just in time to be struck by a second wave. The elements hiccupped in my grip, flaring and ebbing nauseously.

I released my magic and jerked my hands from the little gargoyle, catching my balance against the cobblestones rather than Lowell's wounded side when the street tipped sideways.

"Mika?" Quinn braced my shoulder with his wing. "Are you all right?"

"Just caught off guard." And confused.

Typically, gargoyles were as steady as quartz beneath my elemental touch. I had never encountered a gargoyle with free-floating, chaotic energy inside him like Lowell.

Steeling myself, I quested a new bundle of healing elements into the little gargoyle. Lowell's pain barely registered before the first inharmonious surge bowled into me. My magic stretched, unraveling around the edges. Vertigo buffeted me. I clung tighter to the elements, my groan mingling with Lowell's. Distantly, I felt my elbows buckle. Quinn caught me on the left, Oliver on the right, holding me when I would have fallen.

Working from instinct, I countered the next wave of fluctuations in Lowell, making minute adjustments to the elements I held. The discordant wave unraveled into blessed serenity. Then the next jagged burst skittered through him. I countered it again, chasing the vibrations toward their source. Three more times, I flattened the baffling fluctuations within Lowell, pressing deeper into his body each time.

My confusion grew. This wasn't an imbalance from enhancing too much of one element. I recognized those symptoms well, and they were easy to fix. This was something I had never encountered before.

My breath caught when I pinpointed the origin of the misaligned energy. It wasn't within Lowell's body; it was pulsing from his spirit.

I held my magic at the periphery of Lowell's innermost being, weighing my options against my foreboding. Healing a spirit was risky, because it required me to use my own as a conduit. Untethering my spirit—even a small portion of it— could leave me permanently unbalanced and weak, both physically and mentally, if any part of the process went wrong.

But I had done it before. I had sat outside a gargoyles' birthing cavern—a cynosure baetyl—dying gargoyles all around me, and I had dived my spirit into each one so deep I inhabited more of their bodies than my own . . .

A whisper of the baetyl's powers ghosted through my mind. My breath rasped out. I never expected to delve this deep into a gargoyle again. I shouldn't—

Harsh energy welled from Lowell's spirit, threatening to tear my magic apart. I countered it. Another nauseous wave built behind it, and I abandoned caution. I couldn't heal Lowell by healing his body. I had to go deeper.

Shifting my spirit was not something anyone taught me. It wasn't common magic—it was too dangerous. I had chanced upon it by accident and perfected it in desperation. Now, it took only a moment to locate that center, core piece of myself. It took longer and more concentration to separate a portion of it from my body.

Cautiously, I quested the spark of my spirit deeper into the little gargoyle, savoring the harmony between us. *This* connection, this alignment of our core selves, was what made me a gargoyle guardian, far more than my affinity for quartz-tuned earth element. For all that splitting my spirit scared me, I reveled in the privilege of being a perfect match for these incredible beings.

Like magnets drawn together, my spirit zinged to Lowell's. I sailed effortlessly through his body, until he filled my vision, a brilliant golden feline figure with a raccoon face, bushy tail, and soft wings folded against his body. We floated together in a space that didn't exist in any one place inside Lowell but permeated every cell of his body. This golden figure wasn't real, either. It was my mind's interpretation of the part of Lowell that made him *him*—his consciousness, his personality, his *aliveness*. His spirit. Here, Lowell existed in his purist form. Here, he should be safe, untouchable.

Instead, Lowell's radiant spirit self quaked like a struck gong.

Tentatively, I stroked my magic like a phantom hand along Lowell's glowing form, borrowing from the stillness of my own spirit. The baetyl's song hummed at the edge of my awareness, more emotional resonance than memory. For a brief time, I had been intimately linked with the baetyl's unfathomable intelligence and unspeakable power. I had known every note of the song of life, the elemental fusion of creation. I had possessed the power to *make* gargoyles.

But my brain was too fragile, my body too finite. Maintaining a connection with the baetyl would have destroyed me. Severing my link with it nearly killed me. Now, all I retained of the baetyl's wisdom were these rare glimpses.

Careful not to focus on the baetyl's song too closely and risk losing it, I tuned the elements to harmonize with its faint notes and infused my magic with the love radiating from my spirit. Gently, I wrapped everything over the glowing form of Lowell. With uncanny precision, my magic countered his quivering. Lowell stabilized.

I rested in the peaceful, infinite space inside the tiny gargoyle. Then I retreated, drawing my spirit and magic outward.

The pain of Lowell's physical wounds assaulted me when I surfaced, but they emanated from a steady, stable body. My grip on the elements quivered, and I let my magic dissipate. My spirit pinged back to my body along a gossamer thread, snapping into place with an electric jolt. I forced out a shaky breath, then another, grounding myself in my own body and in the feel of Oliver and Quinn on either side.

Lowell stirred, quartz paws grating against cobblestones. I opened my eyes to check on him. He twisted to sit on his haunches, his raccoon nose inches from mine. Soft orange eyes focused on me, and when he smiled, sharp canines peeked past his lips.

"Guardian," Lowell breathed, reverence and relief in his whispered word.

"Hi, Lowell," I said.

I stroked a hand down his uninjured side, surprised when the simple motion took effort. Despite Oliver's and Quinn's support, I sagged over my knees.

Footsteps slapped down the Victorian's porch stairs and raced toward us.

"Mika, how can I help? Herbert said there's a sick gargoyle . . ." Kylie trailed off, skidding to a stop behind Anya. Unlike me, my best friend looked ready for work, not as if she had been woken minutes earlier. Only the misaligned buttons of her blouse and the snarls in her white-blond hair betrayed the haste in which she had dressed. She took in Lowell, then my slumped posture, and dropped to her knees beside me. A swirl of heated air spun around me, chasing away the morning's chill.

"Thank you. I need to finish heal—" I cut off, twisting toward the sound of running footsteps approaching the end of the street. The tree-lined lane spun in my vision, and I blindly grasped Oliver's shoulder to steady myself.

A tall figure skidded to a halt in the distant intersection, silhouetted against the dawn's light. I couldn't make out his features, just that his hair was short and dark, he had a lanky build—and he wore a Terra Haven guard uniform.

Oliver crowded closer, his wings flaring. "Who's that?" he asked.

"Looks like a guard," Kylie said. A subtle ward sprang up around our group, twists of soft air ready to be hardened into a protective barrier. I relaxed marginally. If all the gargoyles were enhancing Kylie like they were me, my powerful friend's shield would be able to withstand an explosive phoenix hatching, if necessary.

"Trouble?" I asked. I surveyed the street, but I didn't spot anything dangerous enough to bring a guard running. "Or one of your informants?"

Kylie's eyes narrowed. "Maybe." As a journalist for the *Terra Haven Chronicle*, Kylie nurtured relationships with people around the city to ensure she learned about story-worthy events in time to report on them.

"I don't recognize him, but I'll go check." Running her hands through her hair, then straightening her shirt, Kylie dropped her ward and started down the street. Quinn fell in beside her. They made it two steps before the guard pivoted on a heel and jogged back the way he had come.

"Or not," she muttered, drawing up short. "How odd."

"Was that guard chasing you?" Oliver asked Lowell.

The small gargoyle shook his head, then hissed, crimping an injured paw to his side.

"Here, let me heal that." I reached for my bag of raw quartz, surprised to spot it several feet behind me. In the excitement of Lowell's crash-landing, I didn't remember dropping it.

I shoved to my feet, only to bend back in half when my head tried to float from my body and gray spots danced in my vision. Oliver butted his forehead beneath my palm. I wrapped my fingers around the stone ruff of his mane. Equilibrium restored, I thanked him as I straightened.

"Ladies," Josephine Zuberrie called from the top of the porch steps. Command laced my landlady's voice. "Why don't you come inside?"

"I need to heal Lowell first." I plodded toward my bag, my steps clomping as if I wore weights on my feet.

"In that case, I suspect Mr. Higgins will have a happier morning than he anticipated."

I jerked around, spotting gray-haired Finch Higgins ogling me from his porch steps three doors down. He wasn't the only neighbor clutching robes or weapons in their front yards, their attention rapt on the gargoyles. And on me.

The dawn breeze slid across my thighs and fluttered the hem of my nightgown—my threadbare summer-weight nightgown. Embarrassment choked my dismayed curse to a squeak.

Kylie spun toward me, her blue eyes widening as she took in my scanty apparel in the growing daylight. A tinted cloak of air sprang into existence around my shoulders. The subtle weight of it was lighter than a robe but far more effective. Planting her hands on her hips, Kylie shot a glare at Mr. Higgins. The old man waved.

"Pervert," she muttered.

Cheeks burning, I slung my bag over my shoulder and scurried back to Lowell. He urgently needed healing. So did Quinn. I could see ragged chips in his feathers where Lowell had crashed into him. But I desperately wanted to escape the weight of my neighbors' curious stares.

"I think Josephine is right; we should get off the street." Kylie cast another puzzled glance after the mysterious guard, then turned to Lowell. "May I carry you behind our house wards before Mika finishes healing you?"

The phrasing of her question reminded me we didn't know what had made Lowell sick, or what had drawn the guard's notice. Prudence dictated we relocate somewhere with better protection until we had answers.

It didn't hurt that the decision spared my modesty, too.

"Are you Quinn's journalist?" Lowell asked, perking up.

She grinned. "Yes. My name is Kylie."

With Lowell's assent, she scooped him up in a soft cup of air and floated the gargoyle toward our house. Oliver and his siblings launched into flight, using the open street to gain altitude, then soaring over the Victorian to land in the backyard.

Dew-drenched grass chilled my bare toes as I followed Kylie across the front yard and around the side of the house. I yanked the side gate closed behind us, shielding us from our neighbors' curious stares, and Kylie let the shadow cloak dissipate.

I peeked down at my body. The burn in my cheeks intensified. When I purchased my nightgown years ago, it had been red, but many washings had faded it to pink. It was also worn thin enough to add no heat to a summer night. Up until today, that had been the quality I most appreciated about the gown. Of course, I never expected to show off my sleepwear to the entire neighborhood. I needed to purchase something more socially appropriate in case—

In case another dizzy-sick gargoyle shows up in the middle of the night?

A shiver climbed my spine, cooling my embarrassment. I would run into the street naked if it meant saving Lowell or another gargoyle from crash-landing. But I would rather make sure another gargoyle didn't suffer the same sickness in the first place.

Lowell swung his head, taking in the backyard and the well-timed sequential landing of Oliver, Quinn, Anya, and Lydia. Lowell's eyes were clear and curious now, but the memory of his stuttering spirit made me rush to ease my magic beneath his skin the moment Kylie set Lowell on the flagstones. Although pain assaulted me, I breathed easier when I confirmed his energy remained stable.

"Do you want me to grab you shoes?" Kylie asked.

"And a coat, please," I said, shivering as I knelt on the damp stones beside Lowell. I let my bag drop beside me, relieved to be free of its oppressive weight.

"Do you have a preference what I heal first?" I asked Lowell, reaching into my bag for a seed crystal.

"My feet."

I examined his paws, wincing to see that more than his claws were broken off. Lowell must have clipped both front paws on something hard during his haphazard flight. A similar blow to a human would have broken bones but otherwise left the digits attached. However, for gargoyles, forceful impacts tended to shear off body parts rather than break them internally. Perhaps because gargoyles didn't have bones. They might resemble stone versions of flesh-and-blood animals and even move like them, but their internal structures were pure living quartz—for which I was incredibly grateful. I could do something human healers could only dream of: I could use raw source material to regrow missing body parts.

Sinking magic into Lowell, I began the delicate process of connecting inert crystal with his complex quartz tissue. As I replaced missing toes and claws, the gargoyle's body guided me, defining the shape and texture of the digits. Another seed crystal regrew Lowell's ear, and two more soothed the raw patches scraped into his shoulder and hip.

At some point, Kylie returned and draped my coat over my hunched body. I wasn't sure if I thanked her out loud or only thought it. I didn't dare pause. This level of healing took effort, but it didn't usually exhaust me. Stabilizing Lowell's spirit had sapped more energy than I realized. By the time I finished regrowing the tips of his broken feathers and soothing quartz into his scraped muzzle, I drew heavily on Oliver's and his siblings' enhancements to keep my magic steady.

Releasing the elements brought my fatigue crashing

down on me, and I slid off my heels to sit on my butt on the flagstones.

Lowell stood, then stretched. Sunlight glinted on the clear patches in his calico wings and glistened across his muzzle. It would take days for his body to fully absorb and transform the new quartz into his natural sardonyx and jasper, but eventually it would be impossible to tell he had ever been injured.

The little gargoyle pranced in place tentatively, then with more force, his small paws clacking gleefully against the stone. With a flap of his wings, he lifted off the ground, then landed. Grinning wide enough to display every sharp tooth in his mouth, Lowell sat and planted a paw on my knee.

"Thank you, Guardian."

"You're welcome, Lowell." I clamped my teeth together to repress a shiver and tugged my coat tighter around my body. "What can you t-tell me about wh-what happened to you?"

"Just a minute, healer," Ms. Zuberrie interrupted, exasperation heavy in her voice. "There's time to take care of yourself first. You'll be no good as a healer if you neglect your own needs too long."

I blinked, glancing around at the audience I had half forgotten existed. Oliver sat on my left, close enough to lean on if I needed him. Lydia and Anya lay on the lawn, and Quinn sat across from me. Kylie stood beside him, her hand resting on his citrine mane. Herbert perched on a nearby table. With his armadillo body and toucan head, he was the only gargoyle sibling small enough to sit on furniture without breaking it.

Ms. Zuberrie crossed the patio to loom over me. Only a

peek of her nightgown's lacy collar and the tips of her thin lavender slippers dared to hint that she wasn't wearing proper attire beneath the heavy robe cinched around her slender frame. A bonnet encased her white hair. I hadn't seen anyone except my grandmother use a sleep bonnet, and while my landlady was more than old enough to be my mother, she wasn't *that* old. She was, however, a stickler for propriety.

"If you keep sitting on the ground in that slip of a gown, you're going to catch a cold," Ms. Zuberrie said.

I allowed myself to be herded to a chair, taking time to put my arms through the sleeves of my coat and slide my feet into my boots. Damp skin against cold leather wasn't the most comfortable sensation, but it was warmer. Ms. Zuberrie disappeared inside and returned with a blanket to wrap around my legs.

I gave her hand a grateful squeeze, shocked by the warmth of her fingers in mine. A year ago, Ms. Zuberrie would have been more likely to berate me for drawing trouble to her house than she was to coddle me. Having five gargoyles in residence had gone a long way toward softening her attitude. That, and her nosy nature. Between Ms. Zuberrie and Kylie, I couldn't tell who waited with the least patience for me to get settled before turning their attention back to Lowell.

"What happened to make you sick?" Oliver asked before I could.

"I don't know. I felt fine yesterday."

With the deceptive ease of felines everywhere, Lowell leapt to the tabletop, landing softly on all four feet in front of me. The wooden boards groaned. Herbert clacked his beak in greeting and fluttered to the opposite end of the table. Both gargoyles were small, but they were also solid rock. The table could hold twice their weight, but not if it was all concentrated in one place.

"The dizziness is new?" I asked once Lowell settled.

He nodded.

"Where do you live? Maybe it was something in the air," Kylie said, taking the seat next to me.

"I live above Leaf and Loom, next door to the Blue Lotus. But I didn't smell anything out of place."

I didn't know of Leaf and Loom, but the Blue Lotus was an iconic florist shop famous as much for its gorgeous bouquets as it was for its massive greenhouse—the largest in the city. The florist was nestled in the Cambium District, an area populated by wood elementals and plant-based businesses. I couldn't picture a section of the city with cleaner air.

"Plants are the source of most poisons," Ms. Zuberrie said, as if reading my mind. Among us, she had the most extensive knowledge of plants. Her skills with wood element and flora-nourishing spells were responsible for the backyard's emerald lawn, the fecund garden that produced enough fruits and vegetables to share with everyone on the street, and the proliferation of decorative flowering plants around the yard's perimeter.

"And floral scents can mask all kinds of dangerous toxins," she added.

I nodded, following her logic. The Blue Lotus took up an entire city block, and the fragrant aromas wafting from the high greenhouse windows permeated the air three streets in every direction. More, if the breeze was just right.

"Do you think it was poison?" Kylie asked me.

"I don't know." I had never encountered a gargoyle suffering from an ingested or inhaled poison. Or maybe one suffering from an allergy? "Lowell, has this ever happened before?"

"Not to me, and not to any gargoyle I know."

"So you suddenly got dizzy—"

"Not suddenly," Lowell corrected. "It came on slowly. I didn't really notice it until I tried to fly. That's when . . ." He lifted his paw, studying the clear quartz of his new toes. "That's when I fell from my perch."

My stomach squeezed at the thought of Lowell plummeting helplessly from a rooftop. "Do you feel anything like that now?"

Lowell shook his head.

"Anyone else?"

Oliver and his siblings assured me they felt fine.

Worry continued to eat at me while I healed Quinn's minor injuries. I hated not having the answer for Lowell's illness. As a healer and guardian of gargoyles, I should be well-versed in all potential hazards to their health. If nothing else, I should be able to trace a sickness to its root cause. Yet, as much as I wracked my brain, I couldn't fathom a reason why Lowell's spirit had stuttered out of sync with his body.

Unable to do anything else, I sent Lowell home, promising to check in with him later. Anya volunteered to accompany him. I was pleased to see Lowell's flight hold as level and steady as a crow's—or as a creature with crow wings—on my mental map. Anya's beacon gliding protectively at his side was another reassurance that our new friend would make it home safe.

When Lowell's and Anya's beacons vanished as they flew out of range, I pushed from my chair. Oliver rose at the same time, and the other gargoyles stretched and stood. I realized they must have been monitoring Lowell's progress, too. I wasn't the only one worried about the raccoon gargoyle.

"That was almost creepy," Kylie said.

"What was?"

"You were all so still, then you all moved at the exact same time. The gargoyles are rubbing off on you, Mika." Kylie tossed the words out like a joke, but her tone fell flat. Her speculative gaze flicked to the scars on the backs of my hands.

I left my palms on the table, pretending I failed to notice the connection my friend's glance inferred. I had never given Kylie an explanation for the new trail of hexagonal amethyst that marched from the base of my pinkies to my wrists. Each stamp of purple flesh was as glossy and flexible as the living quartz of a gargoyle, because that's exactly what it was. It shouldn't have been possible, though. No human could meld flesh and quartz so seamlessly—but a baetyl could.

"That's a wonderful compliment," I said, forcing a nonchalant yawn that became all too real. I couldn't discuss my baetyl-granted ability to sense gargoyles for the same reason I couldn't explain my scars: Cynosure baetyls were gargoyle birthing grounds, sacred and secret. To even mention one would mean breaking the trust of every gargoyle alive.

Kylie scrutinized my face, questions filling her blue eyes. "Do you have any idea what made Lowell sick?" she finally asked.

I let out a soft breath and shook my head, glad I didn't need to lie to my best friend today.

"I don't have a clue, but I intend to find out."

———

2

I stumbled into my room and let my bag drop. Bracing a hand against the wall, I toed off my boots, then clung to the vertical surface when a yawn nearly toppled me. Oliver had flown over the house in the time it took me to trudge up the stairs, and he opened the balcony door with a practiced hook of a claw before I could do it for him. Squeezing into the room, he reared onto his hind legs to peer at my worktable.

"My everlasting seed?" I asked, suspecting we both hoped the magical souvenir would have an answer for Lowell's sickness.

"You don't have it on you, do you?"

"I wasn't planning to need it while I slept." The words came out unintentionally snide. I gave Oliver an apologetic smile and gestured to the table. "It's there somewhere."

I tossed my coat on my rumpled bed and edged between Oliver's wing and a pile of dirty laundry to peer blearily at my worktable. The scarred surface was buried under the muddled topography of my new life as a gargoyle guardian: Mountains of books and newspapers caged avalanches of mail, with buttes of glass inkwells and makeshift quartz paperweights submerged under a sea of loose-leaf documents. I patted various stacks, feeling for a palm-sized lump. After I stabbed my finger on a broken pen nub, I took more care unearthing an abandoned prasiolite figurine of Herbert, another of Oliver in amethyst, and a twisted lump of tigereye slated for a wind chime I no longer had time to design. Oliver rifled through a heap of old newspapers, examining each pen, candle, and wax stamp as if he had never seen each before. Neither of us voiced our hope that my everlasting seed wouldn't be instantly recognizable because it had evolved into a new shape. Instead, I tested each small item with a touch of magic before setting them aside.

Something beneath the fabric of an ink-stained blot cloth scraped across the table. I pinched the cloth between my fingers and lifted it, revealing my everlasting seed.

My shoulders slumped. "It's the same."

Everlasting trees bloomed once a generation, and during that magical moment, anyone present could ask a question of the enchanted tree and be granted an answer in the form of a seed. No two seeds were alike in shape or texture, resembling anything from glass to metal to fabric—but each was a clue. If the recipient deciphered the meaning of the clue and took appropriate action, the seed evolved into the next clue. The number of times a seed metamorphosed varied from person to person, but eventually, it would transform into a concrete answer.

When I risked my life flying to the everlasting tree weeks earlier, I believed I had found a loophole in the everlasting tree's magic, one I could harness to my advantage. After careful deliberation, I asked the everlasting tree, *How can I best fulfill my role as a gargoyle guardian every day for the rest of my life?*

My strategy was simple: While everyone else sought an answer, I was only interested in the clues. I thought I could trick the everlasting tree into giving me a seed that would continually evolve, endlessly illuminating new ways to be a better guardian, providing a ceaseless sequence of clues to follow.

Instead, I got a dud seed.

Stalking to the bathroom, I retrieved a wet cloth, then I slouched on the edge of my bed and scrubbed the grime from my knees. Pain flared like fire beneath my vigorous swipes. I hissed, jerking the cloth away. I wasn't bleeding, but both knees bore bright-pink abrasions from the rough cobblestones.

"I think you're wrong," Oliver said. "The raised part is different. Look." Grasping my seed between his claws, he played sunlight across its surface.

From where I sat, the seed looked exactly the same, like a milky-quartz disc with a rough and unrefined rim and irregular flecks of clear quartz and pearlescent striations bisecting the glossy planes. If I didn't know better, I would dismiss it as a crude spell-hewn drink coaster: sloppy around the edges, lumpy in the middle, and sized too small for a standard mug.

The subtle protrusions in the middle were the seed's most frustrating details. Partially formed and difficult to discern, the bumps might have been important, but their vagueness made it impossible to tell. Not for the first time, I wondered if the everlasting tree had made a mistake. Had it given me an unfinished seed? Or one with faulty magic?

Oliver scratched a claw across the surface. "It's definitely changed. Slightly."

"Slightly," I repeated, dubious. Everlasting seeds didn't undergo minor alterations. They remained static until they evolved into something completely new.

"Feel." Oliver thrust the seed at me.

I closed my fingers around the disc. It fit neatly into my palm, as if made for my hand—a fact I once found comforting. Squinting at the surface, I looked for the faint projection of three overlapping rings that had taunted me for weeks. Instead, a cluster of narrower protrusions teased across the surface.

I ran my thumb over the disc. My finger bumped across a glossy, half-formed star, the lines gracefully curved. A single, thin ring connected the star's points, the circle rough, as if eroded or sanded.

Canting the seed toward the sun, I spotted new white fracture lines in the quartz. They radiated from the center in three geometric arcs, as if the seed had absorbed the earlier partially raised rings, transforming them into flaws in the quartz.

"That's . . . That's not possible," I said. My seed didn't look so much like it had evolved as it had changed its mind. This wasn't how Kylie's everlasting seed had worked, or Quinn's. Or anyone's in written history.

"What about yours, Oliver?"

Oliver lifted a wing and tugged loose a pouch tied to his foreleg near his shoulder joint. Using a claw, he untied the drawstring, then spilled his seed onto his upturned paw.

If similarities could be drawn between my seed and Oliver's, it was only in their mineral appearance. Oliver's everlasting seed was a perfect icosahedron seemingly carved from a see-through stone several shades more orange than citrine quartz. Precise amber lines branched through the seed in a network too complicated to trace. Rolling the seed didn't help. No matter which way the twenty-sided seed faced, the lines always appeared to start closest to the observer and flare toward the far sides.

"No change," Oliver said, his brows drooping in disappointment. "I hoped Lowell coming here would be enough to activate it."

Oliver's question to the everlasting tree had been a cleverly worded request for guidance in increasing the flow of information between gargoyles. Since Lowell knew to come to me for healing and help, it showed that Oliver's tireless drive to improve communication among Terra Haven's gargoyles was already working. That could easily have been enough to prompt his seed to evolve into the next clue.

"Did Lowell say anything to spark a new idea about your seed?" I asked.

Oliver shook his head.

I ran my thumb over the embossing on my seed again. "This isn't quite a pentagram. And nothing about it seems related to Lowell or his mystery illness." I bounced my seed on my palm. "I wish I knew what this tiny alteration means." *Or if this everlasting seed offers any guidance at all.* I didn't voice the last thought out loud. Oliver didn't need to be further disheartened by my pessimism.

"We must be getting closer to activating your seed, or it wouldn't have changed, right, Mika?"

"We must be," I said, but I couldn't fake any conviction. When Oliver's shoulders slumped and his soulful eyes slid from mine, I wanted to kick myself. "Hey. Seeds or no seeds, we're still going to do our best to help all of Terra Haven's gargoyles. Nothing's going to stop us from that, right?"

Oliver sighed. "Right."

"Starting with Lowell. We'll figure out what made him sick, so it doesn't affect another gargoyle."

"Right," he said, more firmly this time.

A yawn eclipsed my smile, and I resumed scrubbing my feet. I didn't need my seed to guide me; I was a gargoyle guardian, and I would figure this out on my own.

————

WEIGHT TIPPED THE BED, AND A COOL STONE EXHALE FANNED across my face.

"Mika, wake up," Oliver said.

I blinked at him. His square chin rested on his paw inches from my face.

"Did I fall asleep?"

"We both did," Oliver said.

I frowned at the sunbeam slanting across the floor beside Oliver. It was midmorning? Memory flashed— Lowell's frantic arrival, healing him, my neighbors' stares . . . and curling under my comforter to warm up. I never intended to fall to sleep.

"Marcus is here," Oliver said.

"Here? Now?" Alarm splashed cold water on my sleepy thoughts, and I jolted upright. Surprised, Oliver lurched backward and knocked into the table. Seed crystals bounced to the floor.

A muffled knock reverberated through the floorboards, then the unmistakable rumble of Marcus's deep voice carried up the stairs. My heart did a cheerful twirl, and my stomach dove toward my toes. I ran a hand through my snarled hair and decided my stomach had the right response. My relationship with Marcus was new and exciting, and it was far, far too soon for him to see my haggard, early-morning state.

"What is he doing here this early?"

"Isn't it a good thing?" Confusion knitted Oliver's expressive brows. "We can tell him about Lowell. Maybe he knows what's going on."

"We could have done that later." This evening. When we had dinner plans. I was supposed to have an entire day to get stuff done before Marcus arrived. For starters, I had planned to tidy up my room so it looked less like a hurricane had spun through it. Or better yet, to meet him downstairs.

I lurched to my feet, then froze, torn between cleaning my room and myself. The raggedy state of my sleepwear decided for me. I had embarrassed myself in front of enough people today. I would not open the door to Marcus wearing a threadbare nightgown smudged with dirt.

Yanking the gown over my head, I tossed it to the floor of my closet and grabbed a pair of sage-green pants and a lightweight cream-and-rose checkered top. Both were well worn but decent. Darting to the bathroom, I splashed water on my face, gave my teeth the fastest brushing of my life, and cinched my hair into a ponytail.

Footsteps climbed the stairs too fast and heavy to be Ms. Zuberrie. I tugged my comforter over my unmade bed and closed the door of my disheveled closet. I stared at the rest of my room in despair. Another hour wouldn't be enough to make it presentable.

Marcus rapped softly on my door. "Mika?"

"Coming." Grabbing my boots from where I had discarded them in the center of the room, I lined them up at the end of the bed, then skirted an amused Oliver and opened the door.

"Marcus, I, ah . . ." I took him in, and my thoughts scattered.

Marcus Velasquez was built like a minotaur, with

massive shoulders, trim hips, and enough muscle to lift Oliver with his bare hands. In his gray Federal Pentagon Defense uniform, he looked part warrior, part protector, and wholly delicious.

My insides performed a giddy somersault when he smiled wide enough to display his dimples. I still couldn't believe I got to call this man my boyfriend.

"I love it when you do that," he said, his voice a soft rumble against my chest.

I didn't remember stepping into his embrace, and I didn't try to extricate myself.

"Do what?" I asked, wrapping an arm around his neck to steady myself as I went up on my tiptoes for a kiss.

"Forget what you're saying when you look at me." Marcus gave me a cocky smile and waggled an eyebrow, holding himself an inch out of reach.

"I didn't notice you saying anything at all. Does that mean you were awestruck?" I cringed even as the words left my mouth, regretting drawing attention to my rumpled appearance.

"Every time I see you," Marcus murmured against my lips, easing my self-doubt.

I pressed into him, savoring the hard planes of his body against mine. When he finally kissed me, heat and happiness suffused me.

Marcus backed me up a step, then another, and swung the door shut behind him. Prudent, given Ms. Zuberrie's penchant for popping upstairs after his arrival. My fingers curled into Marcus's hair. It was just long enough to get tangled in, and I loved the silky texture of it. Marcus groaned, his tongue teasing me, his hands steady on my hips, supporting me.

A throat cleared behind me. I smiled against Marcus's

lips and sank down to my heels. Marcus gave me one more kiss, then eased his hold on me.

"Hi, Marcus," Oliver said. His nails clicked against the hardwood floor as he scrunched to one side of the room to make space.

"Hi, Oliver." Marcus gave the gargoyle a fond smile. His gaze started to shift back to me but snagged on my work-table, then bounced around the room, taking in every messy detail.

"You're here a lot earlier than I expected," I said, and I flushed when it came out accusatory rather than curious. Nudging a pair of dirty socks beneath my bed with my toes, I rushed on. "Not that I'm not delighted to see you, of course."

"The squad is being called out of town. We're not going to return until after nightfall, so I need to postpone tonight's dinner."

"Oh." Disappointment flashed through me, followed by guilty relief. I had a lot to do today, and I had already wasted half the morning with my unplanned nap. "I understand. The job comes first."

"Mika . . ." Marcus waited until I met his baffled gaze. "Ms. Zuberrie said you had an incident at the house this morning. Did it happen in here?"

"No. I've just been . . . busy." I hustled to my table and fussed with the nearest pile. It warped beneath my touch, sprawling into a larger mess. Several envelopes slid to the floor, and I stooped to grab them.

"Mika healed a sick gargoyle this morning," Oliver said. "Lowell. He was so dizzy he could hardly fly."

"Sick from what?" Marcus asked without taking his eyes from me.

"We're not sure," Oliver said. "He crash-landed in the street. We barely got there in time."

Oliver recounted our morning adventure while I shuffled items on my table, hyperaware of Marcus's scrutiny. Humiliation clawed hot fingers through my chest. When it was just Oliver and me, I could pretend I was making a dent in the shocking amount of paperwork that came with being a gargoyle guardian. But seeing it through Marcus's eyes forced me to recognize how much I was failing. How much I was a failure.

I could only imagine what Marcus thought.

"It's good you and your siblings were there to help Mika," Marcus said.

His tone didn't match his words, and I peeked at his expression. A scowl bunched his thick eyebrows as he watched me fidget. My stomach knotted, reading disapproval in his shuttered gaze. Hastily, I rounded the table, grabbed my seed, and thrust it into Marcus's hand.

"I'm going to confirm Lowell's still feeling well in a bit, but check out my seed. It changed, sort of." I was talking too fast, but I needed to redirect Marcus's attention. Tugging out my chair, I sat, trying not to squirm under Marcus's unwavering stare. "Have you ever seen anything like it?"

Marcus didn't move. I dropped my gaze to study my hands. A fresh nick scarred my thumbnail and dried blood crusted a cuticle. *Look at the seed, Marcus,* I urged, feeling like I was crumbling beneath his regard and getting angry about it.

Finally Marcus sat on the edge of my bed. He braced his forearms on his legs and held the seed between us. When Oliver sat beside me, Marcus tipped the seed so he could see it, too.

"You didn't do anything with rings when you healed Lowell?" Marcus asked.

I thought about the vibratory feeling inside the raccoon gargoyle. Could the overlapping circles have symbolized that? I scrunched up my face and shook my head. Nothing about his sickness had felt as well defined as those rings.

"Does this new shape mean anything to you?" I asked.

"It could be a dirigible propeller."

I shuddered at the thought.

Marcus's frown deepened, and he scraped a nail over the faint design. "It could also be a flower. Or a pinwheel. It's too vague to tell."

I accepted my seed back and tried to keep my disappointment from showing.

"My seed didn't change, either," Oliver said, his glum tone reminding me how easily he caught my mood.

"If it helps, mine hasn't changed, either." Marcus gave Oliver a fond pat, and my friend perked up a little.

"Can I see yours again?" Oliver asked.

"Sure." Marcus retrieved his seed from a bulky pouch at his waist and held out his hand.

We all peered at the adorable maroon-and-white crocheted baby octopus curled in his callused palm. I couldn't help myself; I ran a finger down the precise stitching. The seed felt like soft wool. Every detail was perfect, from the tiny suckers on its baby tentacles to its comically large eyes. If I saw Marcus's seed sitting on a shelf, I would assume it was a kid's toy.

He had asked the everlasting tree to help him locate a family heirloom that had been missing for longer than he had been alive. I didn't understand how the octopus related to the missing heirloom, but I was deeply envious of it. Marcus's seed looked like a real object. It was cute. It was a specific and obvious clue, even if Marcus didn't know what the clue meant yet.

"Does anyone in town sell anything like this?" I asked.

Marcus shook his head. When Oliver reached for the octopus, Marcus gave it to him. The woolen seed flexed between Oliver's claws.

"Mika." The seriousness in Marcus's tone made my stomach knot. "I thought you said you've been resting."

"I have."

"Resting implies taking it easy. Slowing down."

"I *am* going slow. Too slowly sometimes." I didn't look at the tabletop behind me. It spoke for itself. Every page and envelope represented a gargoyle—one who knew I existed or didn't, one who might be injured or in need of my help, all of them waiting for me to reach out. Knowing my lagging progress meant gargoyles endured unnecessary suffering haunted me.

"You didn't give yourself time to fully recover from every-thing you've been through: Focal Park, the ba—"

Oliver's head whipped up, his eyes locking with Marcus's. My boyfriend had been about to say *the baetyl*, as in the secret hatching grounds of gargoyles. Marcus and I only knew of the existence of baetyls because of a gargoyle emergency. It was a secret I guarded with my life, and Marcus did, too. Baetyls weren't mentioned in casual conversation, especially not by name.

"That was a strenuous experience," I agreed, glossing past the actual word, "but I'm feeling good."

"What about our trip to the everlasting tree? That thing you did with the quartz was—"

"It was quartz. I work with quartz all the time."

"Mika . . ."

I shook my head. I didn't want to think about the flight

to the everlasting tree, especially not *that* moment, when I hadn't been sure we would live or die. I had done something with magic in *that* moment that I still couldn't explain. It had been a fluke of desperation and luck and blind instinct, and just thinking about it made my palms clammy.

Marcus closed his hand over my interlaced fists, engulfing them. "I'm just saying, you've been pushing yourself hard, and your energy was already depleted. Or do you not remember how I practically had to carry you when we returned from the tree?"

"Because I hadn't slept in days. But now I'm here every night. It's amazing what a lot of sleep can do." Or some sleep. *Enough* sleep. I smiled at Marcus, which was hard to do through gritted teeth. "I'm taking care of myself."

"Is that why your boot soles are worn through?"

"Ha, ha," I deadpanned, but I surreptitiously checked to confirm Marcus couldn't see how worn my boots were from where he sat.

"And now it looks like you're running either a postal service or working as a scribe on the side."

I crossed then uncrossed my arms, struggling not to take offense. "This is me figuring out how to be a guardian. Not the healing part—all the other stuff."

"What other stuff?"

"Finding gargoyles. Educating people about gargoyle needs. Letting people and gargoyles know I exist and am here for them." That didn't count my side business of making quartz art, which helped pay my bills. Or it used to. I hadn't had time to create anything worth selling lately. Shrugging, I waved dismissively at the table. "This is the mundane stuff, like figuring out expenses with such a fluctuating income."

"Are you having trouble with money?"

"No. I just—" Embarrassment heated my neck. I didn't want Marcus offering me money. That would be disastrous. Gathering my wits, I pasted on a cheerful smile. "I know it's messy right now, but I'm figuring it out."

"You won't be able to help *any* gargoyles if you run yourself ragged. You need to take care of yourself."

I took a deep breath and clung to my patience. Marcus meant well, but he wasn't responsible for every gargoyle in the city and beyond. He didn't see gargoyles who had suffered for years with wounds dulled by erosion but still aching. Gargoyles who had no one to heal them *except me*. If anything, I needed to work harder and squeeze more out of every day.

"I heard back from the friend I told you about," Marcus said. "She's ex-FPD and takes in those of us who need time away from the job. She thinks her place would be a good fit for you, and I agree. I think you'll like her, and Mandrake Valley."

"Mandrake Valley? Isn't that near the coast?"

"A bit inland—"

"That's a fifteen-day trip from Terra Haven!"

"More like six days. But time away from the city—away from all the demands on you here—would be good for you. Just until you're fully refreshed."

"I can't leave Terra Haven. Not now." My work loomed behind me, the phantom weight as heavy as a granite overcoat. If I left, it would only grow. When I returned, it would crush me.

"You don't have to fly. You can take a train. It only extends the travel time by a day or two."

"Be gone even longer?"

Marcus smiled tentatively. Placatingly. "I'm not saying

you should leave immediately. You can wrap things up and leave at the end of the week."

My hands clenched, and I fought to keep my expression neutral. Wrap things up in a week? It wasn't like I had a set number of tasks, and once they were completed, I could take a vacation. Being a guardian was a full-time, lifelong job.

"Thank you for thinking of me," I said, trying to be polite. "And thank you for asking your friend if I could stay with her, but I feel fine. Besides, I need to figure out what happened to Lowell and make sure it doesn't happen to him or another gargoyle again." I had the horrible image of sick gargoyles crashing down around the Victorian and me lazing about in Mandrake Valley, out of reach and out of touch. I couldn't leave the gargoyles to suffer.

"I have no doubt you'll figure it out." Marcus collected my hands again, straightening my tense fingers. "I'm only asking that you think about taking time to recenter yourself. *After* you get to the root of Lowell's sickness. I think you could learn a lot from my friend."

"I'll think about it," I said. As soon as I finished the other 194 items on my to-do lists.

"Thank you." Marcus leaned in.

Our first kiss was stilted, but by the third brush of his lips, I was practically in his lap.

A whistle pierced the air. I jumped and Marcus growled.

"That would be Winnigan," he said, referring to his squadmate. He stood with obvious reluctance. "I'll see you tomorrow morning?"

"I can't wait." I stole one more kiss, then watched Marcus leave, my fingers pressed to my tingling lips.

It wasn't until the sound of his footsteps faded that I realized I hadn't thought to ask about the assignment taking him out of town. A last-minute summons of his squad could only mean a catastrophic threat—one Marcus and his team would throw themselves in front of. And instead of being concerned for my boyfriend's well-being, I had been self-conscious and defensive.

Sighing, I closed my bedroom door. Tomorrow, I would make it up to Marcus.

My gaze returned to my overflowing worktable, and I sighed again. Why couldn't Marcus see I had way too much to do right here in Terra Haven to leave any time soon?

3

T hirty minutes later, I staggered out of the stuffy
confines of a packed airbus and dragged in a
breath of fresh air. Heat radiated from the ocher
cobblestones through the soles of my boots, and I hustled
into the shade of the elm-lined sidewalk as I got my
bearings.

I could sense four gargoyles. Two were located in the
wrong direction: Sebastian a block north and Maya even
farther away. I met them both over a week ago; Sebastian
had only minor cuts and scrapes, but Maya had lived with a
broken tail for years. A third gargoyle's beacon bobbed
between them, the wave pattern of the gargoyle's flight
confirming it was Oliver. I took comfort in his lack of
urgency. If he found another sick gargoyle, he would race to
get me.

The fourth gargoyle in the heart of Cambium District
had to be Lowell. Anya had assured us he made it home
without incident, but I needed to confirm nothing in
Lowell's environment would sicken him again.

The airbus nosed into traffic, its heavy-duty propulsion

spells kicking up a dust cloud. Holding my breath, I hurried in the opposite direction, my bag of seed crystals clacking against my spine. Once I turned off the main thoroughfare, the ambient temperature dropped several degrees. Towering bigleaf maples and box elders provided shade from one side of the lane to the other, gardens spilled into the sidewalk, and foot traffic meandered through flowering arches, the vines supported by nothing more than the plants' own thick, twisting stalks. Living-wood buildings nestled among stone and brick neighbors seemed to defy gravity, with walls that bent and twisted around the trunks of trees older than Terra Haven itself.

No one hurried along these canopied lanes, not the pedestrians, not the aproned merchants, and not even the horse-drawn carriages or more maneuverable flying carpets. No one but me. I wove through the ambling shoppers, my ponytail swishing against my neck as I scrutinized the street for toxins or airborne contaminant sources that could have sickened Lowell.

Dodging around yet another lallygagging group clogging the walkway, I bitterly wished for a flying carpet of my own. With one, I could have made the trip from my house to Lowell in fifteen minutes. A flying carpet would make *every* trip faster—and I could go farther, increasing the number of gargoyles I could contact every day. More importantly, I could reach injured gargoyles quicker.

However, my income fluctuated unpredictably. So far, I had managed to pay my bills and rent on time, but I never knew when I would receive my next payment or how much it would be. I shuddered at the thought of overextending myself and being forced to rely—even temporarily—on Ms. Zuberrie's generosity. No, buying a flying carpet now wasn't prudent.

I shifted my bag, grimacing when my sweat-soaked shirt stuck to my back. Levitating the bag would have been cooler, but maintaining the spell without Oliver's boost took too much energy. Laughter filtered through a nearby restaurant's open patio doors, overpowering the cheerful flute music coming from inside. I skirted around a cluster of wrought-iron tables crowded with patrons enjoying late breakfasts. My stomach growled. The apple and cheese I wolfed down on the airbus had been more of a snack than a meal, but they had been convenient and quick. Making up for the time lost to my nap was more important than a hot meal.

My stomach didn't agree. Neither did my mouth, judging by how much I was salivating over the omelet and biscuit a server carried out on a tray. When the woman caught me staring, I picked up my pace.

The fragrant scents of lilacs and roses, jasmines and honeysuckles perfumed the air by the time the Blue Lotus came into view. Its towering glass-walled greenhouse jutted above the surrounding trees and vine-engulfed buildings like a diamond among the verdant scenery, the upper windows canted open to release humidity and the heady aromas of its interior. Bees buzzed in and out through the openings, winging between the cornucopia of flowers and their hives atop an abutting honey shop.

From afar, the Blue Lotus appeared serene and self-contained. It was only as I drew closer that I spotted the crowd milling in front of the florist, spilling from the sidewalk into the street. The flurry of elemental messages zipping through their ranks, the people's agitated air, and the way they pointed into the Blue Lotus's windowed storefront spurred my steps faster. My stomach knotted when it became clear Lowell's beacon wasn't beyond the florist, atop

Leaf and Loom, where he lived; he was inside the Blue Lotus.

"What happened?" I asked a group of women at the crowd's edge.

"Thieves! Right here on our quiet street," the nearest said, giving the strings of her apron a firm tug. "I've pulled out extra chamomile and valerian root, because everyone's nerves are going to need them today. You should pop in. Half price until the street clears." Her kindly pat on my arm included a subtle nudge toward the Sweetfern Tea House across the street, the name of which was embroidered in red across her apron.

"Think beyond today's profits for once, Cecile," admonished her lithe companion. She clutched a fold of yellow fabric to her chest, her fingers fretting over an unfinished spell woven through the cloth. "You know Mo keeps that shop warded tighter than a spellworks studio. If thieves bypassed his defenses, none of our businesses are safe." Her worried glance darted to a boutique clothier at the corner.

The florist was robbed on the same night Lowell got sick? Dread wormed into my gut. That couldn't be a coincidence. Which meant Lowell's sickness wasn't random. Something more nefarious had occurred. Frowning, I squeezed past the women, pushing through the press of people for a better look inside the Blue Lotus.

The florist's showroom sat in front of the greenhouse, its pale wooden walls and five round windows a pristine canvas for the riot of color inside. I could point directly to Lowell, but where he perched at about hip height was blocked from view by obnoxiously large display bouquets. Straining on tiptoes only allowed me to see the florist's name across the back wall, crafted entirely out of living flowers.

". . . why we need more guards," groused an elderly man near my elbow. "More patrols. They've gotten too lax."

"Used to be I could leave the Edmonia Wildfires out front and never worry about a passerby getting a sideways thought about them," another man said. He crossed his arms and nodded firmly, setting his many chins waggling.

A gray-haired woman swatted his arm. "Hogwash, Rupert. We've kept the Wildfire sculptures behind the counter since we opened. You never put anything pricier than apprentice work out front, and you ward it twice."

"Twice? Now who's stretching the truth?" Rupert asked, but his tone lost its righteous edge.

"Wouldn't need to ward it *once* if we had more patrols," the first man said.

"Sorry. Excuse me." I ducked around them, repeating the words like a mantra as I threaded through the onlookers. Finally, I caught a glimpse of people inside. They clustered near the back counter—around Lowell, according to his beacon. My pulse quickened. Were they surrounding him because he was sick again?

I shoved toward the closed front door, but my plan of rushing inside was thwarted by the guard on the threshold. Three feet of empty space curved in front of her, as if she held an invisible ward, though it was purely the weathered woman's steely gaze that kept people back.

"Excuse me," I said to get her attention. "I'm here to speak with the gargoyle inside."

"No one enters."

"Could you let the gargoyle know I'm outside, then?" Lowell should be able to sense me at the door, but he might not be in any condition to reach me.

The guard's eyes drilled into me, flicking from my sweaty

face and scraggly ponytail down my body to my scuffed boots.

"Do I look like a messenger?" she asked.

My spine stiffened. "Of course not, but—"

"Good. Back up."

"Wait, I—"

"Back. Up."

I retreated, but a hand on my spine brought me up short.

"If you were hoping for a little friendly goodwill, or even civility, you're not going to find it here," said the woman who had stopped me before I trampled her toes. She was shorter than me and a year or two older, wearing wire-rimmed glasses and an atrocious puffy-sleeved beige dress that looked less like apparel and more like a rumpled cotton worm in the process of swallowing her. Yet it was the wicker hat perched on her mousy brown hair that drew my eye. An excess of colorful cloth flowers weighted the rim, and twin vertical sprays of garish pink-and-purple feathers bedecked the sides, giving the impression that the woman possessed avian-inspired donkey ears.

"Lucy Fishburne," she said, thrusting her hand toward me, revealing a cheap metallic bracelet on her wrist. "Junior agent for the Society of Amicable Trade and Trust."

"Ah, Mika Stillwater." I tore my gaze from her hat and gave her delicate hand a shake. "Gargoyle healer."

"A healer? Interesting. But Ms. Loomswell isn't going to care," Lucy said, speaking to me but facing the guard. "I've been telling her it's my job to speak with the proprietor after a theft like this, but she won't budge."

"I don't need to get inside. I just need to check on Lowell, the gargoyle right there." I pointed to the door as if I could see Lowell on the other side. In a way, I could.

"And like I said, you need to back up," the guard said, straightening to her full height.

Loomswell, indeed, I thought, taking a half step back.

"How much longer—?" Electric alarm choked me, and I spun to face the gargoyle beacon diving toward me.

Oliver speared over the far rooftop as if a wyvern were on his tail, his wings a fiery blur. I searched the sky behind him, the afterimage of his carnelian body pulsing in my vision. A dirigible soared in the distance, and a flock of pigeons burst from a roof two streets away, but nothing visibly threatened my friend.

Oliver dove for me. A scream pierced the air, then curses and exclamations. Dozens of wards flashed into existence. I grabbed the elements. Magic surged to me, heavy with Oliver's and Lowell's boosts. Seizing Lucy's arm, I dragged her back with the rest of the crowd as Oliver dropped between me and the guard. He landed hard on all four feet, his massive eagle wings cupped to avoid clipping anyone. I winced at the painful clap of his quartz paws against the limestone walkway.

"Oliver, what's wrong?" I couldn't find any cause for his alarm, not in the sky, the street, nor among the frightened, silent crowd cowering under their protective spells.

"Is Lowell sick again?" he asked, his gaze fixated on Loomswell.

"I don't know. Is something chasing you?"

Oliver shook his head. His sides heaved from exertion, and he hadn't fully folded his wings. "I saw something. It's not important. Why is there a crowd and why are you out here?"

I let out a shaky breath. He had been worried about me. We were both on edge, and I tried to reassure him with a hand on his wing, but neither of us relaxed. Loomswell remained half crouched, one hand on the doorknob, the other brandishing a wooden club. A bright shield of air and earth flared around her, connecting with the building on either side.

I took a step, drawing the guard's attention. "Oliver is my gargoyle companion," I said, emphasizing *gargoyle* and giving her shield a questioning eyebrow raise. I gave the club an outright glare.

Loomswell's gaze darted toward the crowd. In the reflection of the windows, I saw most had dropped their wards. Conversation resumed, loud and excited. Gargoyles didn't typically arrive so dramatically, and no one—especially not city guards—had anything to fear from a gargoyle.

After a beat too long, Loomswell thrust her club through a loop at her belt and let her shield drop.

Oliver shifted his wings, rasping his quartz feathers against each other. He stood tall on all four stubby legs, his square muzzle tilted to glare at the guard. When I tried to step around his cupped wing, he flared it higher to keep himself between me and Loomswell.

"Why haven't you gone inside?" Oliver asked.

"I was trying to get Loo—to get this guard to let us inside," I said. "Or to let Lowell out."

"You're holding a gargoyle captive?" Oliver reared to snarl down at the guard, his sinuous body elongating so he towered over Loomswell. He planted both wings' tips on either side of his slender body in a shocking display of intimidation, caging the guard.

My pulse raced. My usually amiable companion looked ready to rip out Loomswell's throat. Unnerved but trusting Oliver, I stepped up beside him.

"No one is a captive," Loomswell said, regaining her hands-on-hips posture. She couldn't muster the same level of authority she possessed earlier, not with her neck kinked to trade glares with Oliver.

"Mika is a gargoyle guardian," Oliver announced. "She is allowed anywhere there is a gargoyle."

"Um, right," I said weakly, warmed by his defense but leery of the guard's darkening expression.

"Mika is also a healer, and Lowell was sick this morning," Oliver continued, snaking his muzzle into Loomswell's personal space. "She will check him now. You will move aside."

Ruddiness climbed Loomswell's weathered neck. If her spine stiffened any further, she would splinter. Out of the corner of my eye, I saw the crowd lean forward as if with one body. A few murmurs came from those in the back, but everyone else was silent, riveted by the scene we were making.

"Gargoyle or gargoyle guardian, neither of you have authority here. Clear the threshold." Loomswell swept out an arm, curtailing the motion just short of bopping Oliver on the nose.

"Oliver, maybe we should—"

The door behind Loomswell jerked open, and a guard with salt-and-pepper hair and red-rimmed eyes peered out. Silver pentagrams on the collar of her olive-green top designated her a captain. She gave a small start at the sight of Oliver looming over her subordinate, then leaned out beyond the other woman's shoulder.

"Is there a Mika Guardian out here?" she shouted loud enough to be heard a block away.

"Here." I raised my hand, my muscles stiff with so many eyes on me. Sweat trickled down my sides. "It's, ah, Mika Stillwater."

Like Loomswell, the captain took in every detail about

me with a flick of her gaze. I locked my jaw, prepared to be denied entry yet again.

"You're being asked for, and this will go faster if you come inside," the captain said.

Tension loosened from my shoulders. Oliver dropped to all fours and stepped forward.

"The gargoyle, too, Captain Rojas?" Loomswell asked, not moving.

"Yes, yes, the gargoyle, too. Just leave the door open. Ward it for sound, but give us some flaming fresh air." The captain disappeared into the flower shop, muttering about olfactory assaults.

Loomswell finally stepped aside. I rushed forward. Even so, Oliver managed to enter the florist first *and* last, his head and wings preceding me, his tail following. He snapped the long tip at Loomswell, not quite threateningly, but not friendly. I frowned at his antics, but I didn't say anything.

The noise of the crowd swelled with fresh speculation, but Lucy's protests drowned them out. "Hey, if she gets to go in, I should, too. I'm here to provide a much-needed service to the proprietor, and you're infringing—"

A soundproof ward dropped into place over the open doorway, cutting off all noise from outside. The silence rang in my ears, and Oliver's footsteps on the marble tiles seemed amplified.

My gaze zeroed in on Lowell. The raccoon gargoyle sat on a white marble counter at the back of the shop, near Captain Rojas and a stout man in an eye-catching yellow shirt. When Lowell lifted his head toward me, his eyes were clear. He waved.

The sight of the gargoyle at ease snapped my brain back into gear. I let the elements go, feeling foolish. If Lowell were dizzy again, he wouldn't have been able to enhance my magic. Whatever had happened here, it wasn't affecting Lowell—at least not now.

As urgency bled from my limbs, self-consciousness roared in to replace it. I hadn't anticipated interacting with a city guard captain when I left my house, and I hoped it wasn't too late to make a good impression. Taking a deep breath of the cool, spell-tempered air saturated with the shop's heady aromas, I blotted sweat from my upper lip and attempted to fix my mussed appearance without being obvious. Dozens of tables dotted the showroom floor, each tiered with gravity-defying bouquets, with cannisters of loose-cut flowers crowded beneath. Living walls of greenery and small white flowers flanked the showroom, and even the vaulted ceiling was covered in a riot of colorful petals, though those were painted. Chandeliers caging dozens of tiny glowballs hung from the ceiling, their light eclipsed by the sunlight spilling through the five large porthole windows at the front of the shop. A dozen people were pressed to the glass, hands cupped around their eyes to stare inside—at Oliver and me. Behind them, the crowd seemed to have grown larger.

Oliver strode toward Lowell, and I paused to let him go first. If we tried to walk side by side, we would knock over one of the expensive displays. Even single file, Oliver's bunching gait made navigating the narrow gaps between tables difficult.

"Careful, careful," cautioned the man standing near Lowell, all his attention on Oliver. He was stocky, with black hair, a thin goatee, and an even thinner mustache. On the street, his saffron-and-silver floral-print pants and sunshine-yellow shirt would have been garish. In here, he fit right in among the blooms.

"Watch your wings. Those are Middlemist imports." The

man's hands fluttered ineffectually at Oliver, displaying a pinkie ring with an emerald half the size of a seed crystal.

Oliver skirted a table laden with mauve blossoms. The shimmy of his truncated footsteps set the quartz bracelets around his ankles chiming. The bands were Oliver's idea, each loop made from clear seed crystals. Purely functional, they allowed Oliver to carry extra raw quartz. We hadn't yet encountered a situation where I needed more crystal than fit in my bag, but Oliver was right: Having spare quartz close at hand never hurt.

When Oliver safely cleared the last of the display tables, the man's sigh of relief stirred the waxed ends of his mustache, and he sank dramatically backward to rest a hip on the counter.

"Thank you for letting me in, Captain," I said, stopping beside Oliver. Turning to include the man in my thanks, I belatedly added, "I, uh, I'm Mika Stillwater, and this is Oliver."

The man twitched, hesitated, then extended his hand. "Oliver and, um, Ms. Mika, I'm Mo Almasi, owner of the Blue Lotus."

I shook Mo's hand. His gaze flicked down my shirt and pants, a there-and-gone moue of disapproval pinching the corners of his mouth.

Ah. My clothing said I couldn't afford anything more pricey than the plainest bouquet on the discount table, yet I was accompanied by Oliver. Typically, gargoyles befriended full-spectrum—and therefore wealthy—people. Hence, Mo's conundrum: Was I worth his time or not?

Captain Rojas cocked a hip against the marble counter next to Lowell and flipped open her notebook, drawing everyone's attention.

"Ms. Stillwater, why are you . . ." She paused to press a

finger against the base of her nose. With impressive effort, she staved off a sneeze. "Why are you here?"

"Lowell came to me sick this morning. I healed him, and I wanted to check on him."

"I feel fantastic," Lowell said, giving his wings a fluff that highlighted the glossy perfection of his orange, brown, and white sardonyx feathers liberally mixed with new, clear quartz.

My smile died when I caught the captain's impatient, bloodshot stare.

"Are you going to confirm his statement, healer?" she asked.

I frowned. I took Lowell at his word, and the captain should do the same. It took a second to realize it wasn't Lowell's honesty she doubted; it was mine. The captain wanted proof I was a gargoyle healer. Again, she should have taken Lowell's word.

Trying not to show my irritation, I formed a quartz-tuned test pentagram and tweaked the elements to resonate with Lowell's physiology. With Lowell's permission, I sank my magic into him. Harmonious health radiated back through my magic.

"Well?" Captain Rojas squinted at me, then at Lowell. I wasn't sure if her expression indicated suspicion or if her allergies were making it difficult to see.

"Lowell's earlier sickness hasn't returned."

"And what—"

"Can we return to the crisis at hand?" Mo asked, interrupting the captain. "What are you going to do about this break-in?" He jabbed a finger toward the side wall, the tips of his mustache trembling with the vigor of his gesture.

An open doorway exposed a pristine office with cream walls, an ornate pale-wood desk and matching cabinets, and plush ivory chairs. A single porcelain vase holding a sprig of snowy myrtle blossoms adorned the desk.

In all that white, the square hole in the wall stood out like a shout. The wall safe's door hung ajar, the shadowy interior empty. Beneath it, an oil painting of a blue lotus leaned against the wall, waiting to be rehung after the safe was closed.

"Your ward is unbroken—as we proved." Captain Rojas held up a pink fingertip, one that looked as if she had touched it to a hot kettle.

"I warned—"

"No one could have gotten into your safe except you," the captain continued.

"Yet, *clearly*, someone did."

"So you claim—"

"I *never* leave my safe open. I'm not an idiot." Mo's tone implied the intelligence of other people in the room was up for debate.

"Yet, *clearly*," Captain Rojas muttered, rubbing her temples. Before Mo could sputter a response, she turned to yell at the guard at the door. "Jaffer, where's that fresh air?"

Loomswell—Jaffer—stood an arm's length from the doorway, addressing the crowd. With the soundproof spell in place, we couldn't hear what she said, and she couldn't hear the captain's shout. Grumbling under her breath, Captain Rojas yanked a handkerchief from her pocket and dabbed her nose.

"Captain," I said, drawing her glare, "the sickness Lowell had, it was something I haven't seen before. It came on him last night."

"I've noted the possible connection between the gargoyle's sickness and Mr. Almasi's alleged theft, but it doesn't seem likely."

"But . . ." I protested, trailing off when I couldn't offer any real argument to back up instinct.

Captain Rojas gave me a sympathetic look. Or maybe her eyes were simply watery. Her voice was firm when she said, "Often what looks like coincidence at first glance is mere correlation. A pattern we try to create, not a real clue. You say you've never seen his sickness before?"

I shook my head.

She consulted her notebook, then bellowed, "Haubner."

I jumped. So did Mo, though he tried to cover it by brushing nonexistent lint from his pants.

Twisting to project her voice over her shoulder, Captain Rojas yelled, "Haubner, report."

We all peered toward the back, where twin doors opened into the enormous greenhouse. A crushed-gravel walkway spiraled deeper into the glass-walled paradise, wending between lush floral beds and exotic greenery. Birds chirped merrily just out of sight, and an orange-winged butterfly flitted in and out of view. I could see why the Blue Lotus had a reputation as a great date spot, especially in the winter. In the summer, sweating in the greenhouse's humid air likely diminished the romance.

A guard strode along the path. He was vaguely familiar: tall, lean, and fit, like many younger guards. His olive-green shirt bore the standard cluster of elemental symbols on the left breast, but otherwise, he had no special rank. The six embossed in the gold-and-silver star on his hat marked him as a guard from the same house as Captain Rojas.

At the captain's second shout, he broke into a jog, passing from the sunny greenhouse into the shadowed interior. For two steps, he was silhouetted against the bright backdrop, and a jolt of recognition shot through me: Haubner was the guard who chased Lowell to our house this morning—and who bolted before Kylie could talk to him.

I checked Oliver to be sure. He had gone stiff beneath my fingertips. The shift in him was minor, a gargoyle's stillness gaining tension, but it was all the confirmation I needed.

"The doors were locked," Haubner said. "I had to break the ward to get in, just like the others—"

"Thank you, Haubner," Captain Rojas interrupted.

Haubner's eyes narrowed when they landed on me, then Oliver. I returned his mistrustful assessment with one of my own. What had this guard been doing all the way over in my neighborhood when he was stationed at the sixth house?

Mo harrumphed. "Like I said, I didn't know I had been robbed until I got to my office."

"To confirm, the missing items are this week's payroll, a pocket watch—"

"A gold-and-ruby Breguet pocket watch," Mo corrected.

"That will be easier to track down than the . . ." Captain Rojas dabbed her nose with her handkerchief as she consulted her notebook. "Than the vial of Lady Baret and Daughters' Never Wilt Water you say is missing, or the packets of sunstone ivy seeds, the tea caddies, and the two— sorry, *three* bouquets."

"The bundles of lavender and feverfew are inconsequential. But the same cannot be said for the silver-inlaid rosewood caddies filled with Lapsang souchong and bouquets of premium saffron crocus." Mo ran a hand through his hair. "And I don't *say* they're missing. They *are* missing. That's a substantial monetary loss for me, and it all happened under your nose."

Captain Rojas stared at Mo. Her puffy eyes and red-tipped nose should have detracted from the quiet challenge in her gaze, but it was Mo who looked away first, a flush creeping up his dark cheeks. Pressing his lips together, Mo reached for Lowell, absently petting the gargoyle. Lowell leaned into his touch.

"Captain," Mo said, having regained his composure, "I was home all night with my sick kid. She had a fever and threw up twice. I barely got any sleep. Then I show up, and this—"

"No, you were here last night," Lowell said. "I boosted you."

Everyone turned to stare at Lowell.

"You boosted Mr. Almasi?" Captain Rojas asked. "You're certain?"

Lowell nodded.

"What time was this?"

Lowell's eyes darted from the captain to me, and I nodded encouragingly. "After midnight but before Baker Lainie fired her ovens."

Mo shook his head, confusion filling his eyes. "I wasn't here last night. You couldn't have boosted me. You must be mistaken."

"Or the gargoyle is lying," Haubner said.

I gasped at the accusation. The guard stood to one side, his arms crossed. His suspicious gaze flicked between Lowell and me. Lowell looked stunned, his large eyes unblinking, his muzzle slightly agape.

"That's absurd," I said, furious on Lowell's behalf. "Gargoyles don't lie."

"Ever?" Captain Rojas raised her eyebrows skeptically.

"Never," I huffed. "Lowell is Mo's friend. He has no reason to lie, and to accuse him of doing so is outrageous."

Oliver exerted gentle pressure on my foot, stopping me from advancing on Haubner. Belatedly, I lowered my hand

and the finger I had jabbed at the odious guard. Lowell cowered on the marble counter, his puffy tail tucked tight to his body. My anger burned hotter to see the gargoyle's forlorn glance toward Mo. The florist had retracted his hand, no longer offering Lowell soothing pets.

"I don't think Lowell would lie, either," Mo said, his tone guarded. "But he's mistaken. I wasn't here."

"I could help clear things up," a woman said from the doorway.

Lucy Fishburne, the overeager insurance saleswoman, stood on the threshold, her head poking through the sound-proof ward. Absorbed in a vigorous argument with another bystander, Guard Jaffer remained oblivious to Lucy's trespassing.

Captain Rojas's exasperated exhale stirred the lilies at the end of the counter. "And you are?"

Lucy took the question as an invitation, and she stepped fully into the florist. With exuberant strides that set the feathered ears of her hat quivering, she navigated the maze of bouquets, a hand extended.

"Lucy Fishburne, junior agent with the Society of Amicable Trade and Trust." She pumped Captain Rojas's hand, not seeming to notice that the other woman didn't partake in the handshake. Spinning on a low heel, she grasped Mo's hand before he could recoil and gave it a firm shake. "This is a devastating time for you, Mr. Almasi. Truly devastating. The nerve of these terrible, no-good criminals to come into such a fine, beautiful, oh my, such an elegant shop as this and *abscond* with your goods. It's insulting. It's infuriating. And my bosses want to make sure it never happens again." She smiled and pushed her wire-frame glasses up her nose.

"I don't have a policy with Amicable Trade," Mo said,

reclaiming his hand and crossing his arms. "I don't see how you—"

"That's the second tragedy, isn't it?" Lucy interrupted. "If you were covered by my company, a representative would already be here investigating alongside the guards. Not me, of course. My bosses don't send junior agents to established clients. Only senior agents. Someone with superb investigative expertise, who can devote their *full* attention to finding your lost goods. And Amicable Trade and Trust would make sure you were compensated for any losses in the meantime."

Lucy smiled again, and this time Mo tentatively smiled with her.

"Yet somehow Mr. Almasi must muddle on with a mere guard captain at the helm of the investigation," Captain Rojas said, deadpan.

Mo cleared his throat, but his gaze lifted to the open safe, then drifted back to Lucy.

"Not *merely* with your help," Lucy said, oblivious to the captain's darkening expression. "I have this." She fumbled a hand into a bag at her hip. The excessive fabric of her sleeve temporarily thwarted her, then she freed an object and lifted it with a dramatic flair. Mo gasped, and Captain Rojas straightened, suddenly alert. I stared, puzzled.

Lucy held a plum-sized ceramic replica of a pipsissewa flower. Five round pink petals created a soft cup, with two sets of stamens protruding from the center of each petal. A polished jade pistil protruded from the center of the flower.

Real pipsissewa blossoms were tiny, barely as large as my thumbnail, but powerful. Their many stamens dispersed clumped elements, passively diluting dangerous build-ups that could otherwise destabilize local magic. Their usefulness made pipsissewas ubiquitous across Terra Haven, from private gardens to public roadways. Even the Blue Lotus likely grew pipsissewas in the greenhouse to help cleanse the elements.

Although Lucy's artistic replica was beautiful, I failed to see why it excited the others. Even Haubner had finally stopped squinting at me in lieu of squinting at the pipsissewa.

"What is that?" Oliver asked before I could.

"This is the answer to everyone's questions," Lucy said. "With this, I can read the magical signature of any spell created—or the signature of any tricky spell used to circumvent a ward. I can tell you who broke into your store, Mr. Almasi."

Captain Rojas folded her arms across her chest. "*You* have a signature analyzer."

"Yep." Lucy beamed at the pipsissewa, rocking it to play the light off its pink petals.

"I've been trying to get one for our guard house, but it hasn't been in the budget. How did *you* get your hands on such an expensive device, Junior Agent Fishburne?"

Lucy smiled, showing an impressive number of teeth. "The Society of Amicable Trade and Trust is well funded. Only the best for us, or so Grandma says. She should know. She's worked for the firm so long she practically runs the place." She pivoted to face Mo, who hadn't taken his eyes from the analyzer. "Mr. Almasi, if you will allow, I can test the spell on your safe. Once we know who broke in, Amicable Trade would be happy to help track down your stolen items, for a small finder's fee, of course."

"Of course," Mo said.

"Your claim is as absurd as it is implausible," Haubner said, pushing past the captain. "An analyzer *might* identify the signature of whoever broke Mr. Almasi's safe ward, but it won't lead you to the culprit. How exactly do you plan to track anyone with that?"

"How do I . . . ?" Lucy adjusted her glasses, peering at Haubner as if he were speaking gibberish. "*I* won't track down anyone. I'm just here to get the ball rolling. Once we have a magical signature, I'll bring a senior agent in to take over the investigation. At Amicable Trade, we have an eighty-five percent recovery rate. We're highly motivated, because we don't get paid until we find our client's missing property." Lucy bit her lip, then leaned closer to Haubner and whispered, "Or do you need tips on how to conduct a criminal investigation? I'm sure my boss would be happy to talk with you." She rummaged through her bag with her free hand. "I have his trade card here somewhere."

A red flush crept up Haubner's neck, but his retort was cut short by Mo.

"Ms. Fishburne, let's give your device a try."

"Really?" Lucy's head popped up, and she graced Mo with a dazzling smile. "You won't regret it, sir."

"Captain, you can't allow this," Haubner said.

Captain Rojas shook her head. "Mr. Almasi can get into business with whoever he chooses. Besides, I want to see this analyzer in action."

Haubner looked as if he wanted to protest further, but a sharp glance from the captain shut him up. Crossing his arms, he glared at Lucy. And the analyzer. And me.

"I'll need to test your magic first," Lucy told Mo.

He floated a basic five-element pentagram above the spell analyzer. Lucy held the pipsissewa steady beneath it, her bottom lip clenched between her teeth. A delicate flux of elements twined from the pipsissewa's stamens to brush against Mo's spell. Lucy closed her eyes and nodded to herself.

"Got it." Sidling between Haubner and Captain Rojas, she beelined for Mo's office.

Mo disbanded his magic and followed, the captain on his heels. Haubner planted himself in front of Oliver and me, as if to prevent us from accompanying them. I ignored him, stepping closer to Lowell. Oliver's carnelian paws clacked against the marble tiles, his quartz bracelets a soft echo, as he joined me.

"I'm not a liar," Lowell said.

"I know." I ran my fingers along the stone fur of his back, then traced his wings, keeping my movements slow and soothing. "When did you learn the florist had been robbed?"

Haubner's boots squeaked when he twisted to hear Lowell's answer.

"When Mo burst out onto the street and yelled for the guard. I flew in to see if I could help. I never . . . I don't understand." Lowell cast a forlorn glance in Mo's direction.

"You didn't see anyone last night?" Oliver asked.

"I should have been paying more attention." Lowell stared at his feline paws, his toes clenched. "I could swear—"

"What do you mean you only sense me?" Mo bellowed. "You must not be using the analyzer correctly."

"I can only tell you what it tells me," Lucy said. She scurried out of the office, Mo hot on her heels. "No one broke your safe's ward, not with magic."

"Well, it didn't open itself." Mo's cheeks flushed an unhealthy, florid shade. He glanced at Captain Rojas. She stood in his office doorway, her arms crossed, watching him with an unreadable expression. "And *I* didn't open it. How many times do I have to say it? I'm a respectable business owner. I did *not* steal from myself."

"But, sir, the analyzer can't be fooled. No magic but yours has touched the safe—" Lucy cut off with a squeak when Mo advanced on her. He flung a hand toward the door, and she flinched as if she expected to be struck.

"Out. Take your faulty equipment and get *out*!"

Lucy shrank into her oversized dress. With a trembling hand, she stuffed the pipsissewa into her bag, then fled.

"Don't darken my doorstep again," Mo shouted after her.

The pound of Lucy's footsteps cut off as she leapt through the soundproof ward. Mo's harsh breathing filled the silence.

Captain Rojas snapped her notebook closed and tucked it into a pocket. "Haubner, I'm going to get some fresh air. Finish up here and meet me outside."

"Captain, you can't think—" Mo tried to stop Captain Rojas, only to find Haubner in his path.

"Mr. Almasi, are you positive you wish to submit a criminal report?" Haubner asked.

"Of course. I've been *robbed*."

4

ound assaulted me when I exited the Blue Lotus—
frustrated carriage drivers shouting at people clogging the street, enterprising vendors hawking cold
drinks and ready-made lunches with spell-enhanced cries,
and everyone else yelling questions at Captain Rojas. Lowell
hunkered on the threshold, ears flattened and eyes rounded
at the cacophony.

"Do you want to come with us?" I asked him.

He shook his head. "I need to think. Alone."

My chest felt tight. I knelt to check the gargoyle's expression, then I gave him a soft pat. "Promise me you'll find me if
you feel even a twinge of dizziness."

Lowell agreed, then darted into the air, angling for the
serenity of Leaf and Loom's roof. I watched him go, frustrated I didn't have answers for him. The burglary had to be
connected to Lowell's sickness, but I couldn't see how. I
wasn't even certain Mo *had* been burgled. Why would the
florist lie about not being here last night? It made him look
guilty, and disproving his claims of a break-in was too easy
for the guards, even without Lucy's fancy device. Yet,

without Lowell's testimony, Mo's vehement denials might have convinced the captain he was telling the truth. None of it made sense.

"Move along," Loomswell—Guard Jaffer—ordered.

Oliver snaked his head around me to glare at Jaffer. I patted his wing, then stepped out of the doorway before he and the guard got locked in a staring match. Hoisting my bag to a more comfortable position, I headed in the opposite direction as Captain Rojas. Ahead, I spotted the familiar pyramid-tipped brick turrets of Terra Haven's largest book-store, Vanderlei's Books and Fine Goods Emporium. Envisioning the hushed, spacious interior, I hastened my steps. The spell-cooled bookstore would make the perfect refuge while I collected my thoughts. Oliver loped to catch up, his stone steps barely audible beneath the clamor.

"There's something—" he started to say, but the crowd's questions swelled in volume, drowning him out.

"Hang on." I dodged a fruit stand and threaded between worried clusters of shop owners.

"A crime has been committed here," Captain Rojas said, her booming voice hushing the crowd. Just as loud, she continued. "I assure you, my team of investigators and I will find the culprit. The best thing you can all do is return to your normal lives."

The crowd erupted in questions. Almost everyone was focused on the captain, but a woman at the edge of the crowd wearing a press badge spotted me, or more likely, spotted Oliver. The journalist nudged her neighbor and pointed in my direction. I ducked my head and quickened my steps. Sweat broke across my forehead. I didn't relish being interrogated by reporters, especially when I had no answers.

We rounded the corner, and the hubbub faded. Oliver's

quartz footsteps created a pleasant four-beat chime against the stone sidewalk, and I slowed to allow him to catch up.

"Let's duck into the Emporium—"

A woman called my name. I didn't recognize her voice, and I hunched my shoulders, pretending not to have heard.

"Should we stop?" Oliver asked, shooting a glance over his shoulder.

Footsteps drew closer, the clack of a woman's heels pounding louder than Oliver's carnelian paws.

"Ms. Stillwater? Mika? I'd like to ask you a few questions."

"I can't talk right now," I said, not bothering to turn around. I didn't have much experience being hounded by reporters, but Kylie told me the easiest way to avoid giving a bad quote was to avoid giving a quote at all. Except to her, of course. "Captain Rojas can answer your questions."

"This is about a gargoyle," the woman said.

I wanted to keep going, but her words arrested me as if they were a lasso spell. Crossing my arms, I spun on a heel to face the stranger.

She was plump and pale, with impeccably styled honey-blond hair beneath a tasteful floral hat. Her pink-and-cream-striped summer dress looked hand tailored, the wealth of spells woven into its seams and bodice barely noticeable. Even without the glint of gold and tourmaline in her earrings and necklace, I would have known she wasn't a reporter. No journalist could afford to look so effortlessly put together. That required money.

"Pardon my imposition. I saw you earlier, and—" She paused to catch her breath. A tendril of magic spiraled through her bodice, and a cool breeze scented with euca-lyptus wafted from her gown. Composure reinstated, she extended a manicured hand for me to shake. "Ms. Stillwater,

I am Amelia Vanderlei. I am interested in hiring your services."

"I, ah . . ." The brush-off I had prepared dried up in my throat.

Even before my role as a guardian made it prudent to learn the names and faces of local full spectrums—the people and families most likely to attract a gargoyle—I had known of Amelia Vanderlei. It was safe to say everyone in the country knew of the Vanderleis. The full-spectrum family had a reputation for championing knowledge, and all Vanderleis were involved in one form of print or another. In addition to the Vanderlei's Books and Fine Goods Emporiums stores located across the country, the family owned a newspaper or two, several book publishing houses, and a cartography company. I couldn't remember who was in charge of what, but given the proximity of the Emporium, I suspected Amelia was the local bookseller, if such a quaint title could be given to someone wealthy enough to walk into the Blue Lotus and buy every plant, bouquet, knickknack, and the building itself with her pocket money.

"Um, pleased to meet you," I said after my mouth had hung open for what felt like a full minute but was hopefully only a rude second or two. I released her hand, intensely conscious of the dampness of my palm and the sweat beading my upper lip. I fought the urge to brush my hands down my pants or over my hair. Neither action would make me look more presentable and would only draw attention to the stains on the knees of my pants and the flyaways that had escaped my haphazard ponytail.

Irritated by my urge to preen for a full spectrum—even if she was *Amelia Vanderlei*—I firmed my jaw and said, "This is Oliver."

"Hi," Oliver said.

"Hello, Oliver." Amelia smiled warmly at my friend. "Forgive my brazenness. I don't normally chase people down the street."

I studied her expression, searching for censure. "I don't imagine you do," I murmured. No one in their right mind made *Amelia Vanderlei* chase them.

She gave me a rueful smile. "I try to avoid places where journalists congregate, but I saw your breathtaking arrival, Oliver, and I learned you, Ms. Stillwater, were inside Mo's shop. I've been meaning to talk with you. I waited at the corner, but you move fast."

I blinked, knowing I looked as dumbfounded as I felt. "*You've* been meaning to talk with *me*?"

"I planned to approach you in a more formal manner, but this seemed like a good opportunity. Unless you need to rush off on gargoyle business?"

"We, ah, were only rushing to avoid getting cornered by journalists ourselves," I said, my words slow as my brain struggled to comprehend the situation. Amelia was leagues above me in elemental power and social standing, yet she was behaving as if she were an inconvenience for me. It wasn't the attitude I expected—or received—from full spectrums. More importantly, she knew to link me to "gargoyle business."

"Reporters are equal-opportunity pests, aren't they?" Amelia said easily.

I nodded, as if the two of us had anything in common. "You said you needed to talk to me about a gargoyle?"

"Yes, I believe my Greta could use your unique skills."

"Greta is a gargoyle?" My heart hammered. "Is she sick?" Was this entitled full spectrum downplaying a gargoyle's suffering?

I twisted to check the rooftops, then spun to peer toward

Amelia's enormous bookstore. An erratic beacon—or any new gargoyle beacon—should have been obvious on my mental map, but maybe I had been too preoccupied—

"No, nothing like that, thank goodness." Amelia patted my arm, her motherly reassurance snapping me out of my panic. "My apologies. I didn't mean to alarm you, Ms. Stillwater."

I dropped to my heels and released the death grip I didn't remember taking on Oliver's wing.

"I don't know a Greta," Oliver said.

"She's been staying at my residence. In the country."

"Because she's too unwell to fly?" I asked.

Amelia smiled and shook her head. "She enjoys the quiet. We've heard rumors of you, though. What, exactly, is a gargoyle guardian?"

I savored a zing of triumph. If *Amelia Vanderlei* had heard of me, maybe it meant Oliver's and my ceaseless efforts to raise awareness of my services was working.

"Mostly it means I heal gargoyles from whatever ails them: cuts and nicks, missing limbs, or sickness."

"Mika protects us, too," Oliver said. "She saved my life when I was a cub. And she stopped that cruel woman from killing Rourke in Focal Park a couple months ago."

"That was you?" Amelia's pale brows disappeared under the brim of her hat.

I flushed. "I only assisted Terra Haven's FPD squad."

Amelia's smile returned. "I do believe you thought that would make you sound less impressive."

When I began to stammer, she chuckled. "You *should* be bragging about such wonderful accomplishments. I would appreciate it if I could book some of your time for Greta. I have done what I can to mend her scrapes over the years, but I believe you could help her more."

"I can come out to your house," I said, mentally rearranging my day. Lowell was fine, for now. Paperwork could wait. So could the gargoyles I planned to introduce myself to today. As much as I worried that someone might be suffering because of my ignorance, I had to prioritize gargoyles who I knew needed me. The issue would be transportation. Airbuses didn't leave the city limits, and Amelia said she lived in the country. That meant renting a horse or a flying carpet—

"I'm sure you're busy. Please, allow me to bring Greta to you."

I hesitated. According to our societal standings, Amelia's time was worth much more than mine. She ran an impressive business, one with dozens of employees—hundreds, if I tallied the staff of all the Emporium locations. I should be falling over myself to make our interaction more convenient for her.

But if Greta came with her to the city, it would save me an entire day of travel, not to mention the expenses. Amelia could afford to travel back and forth to the country every day. Bringing Greta with her wouldn't be an imposition.

"Greta would be all right with that?" I asked.

"She's eager to meet you."

Emboldened, I set up a meeting for the next morning and fished a trade card from my bag, relieved to find it pristine. On the front, a stylized drawing of Oliver glowed against a creamy backdrop, and on the back, my business information and address were printed in an elegant font. I could already picture Ms. Zuberrie's delight. Having such a prominent Terra Haven citizen on her doorstep would make her the talk of the neighborhood for a week.

Amelia departed, her stride graceful and confident. I

remained flatfooted, my insides a jumble of pride and embarrassment.

I caught my reflection in a nearby window, and embarrassment won out. Sweat dampened my shirt's armpits and collar, and my pants were rumpled from the airbus ride. I didn't look like someone who did business with the likes of Amelia Vanderlei. I looked like I was on break from a job chiseling quartz at the quarry.

I don't care about impressing full spectrums with fancy attire, I reminded myself. *All I want to do is heal gargoyles.*

Irritated with myself, I jammed my hands into my pockets. My fingers scraped my everlasting seed. A tingle of hope made me pull it out, but the faint stylized pentagram bulging from the disc remained unchanged.

"That's what I wanted to talk to you about," Oliver said, indicating the seed in my hand. "I spotted something from the air that made me think of it."

"Really? Oh, that's right," I said, recalling Oliver's rushed words after his dramatic landing at the florist. "You said you saw something. Is that why you were flying so fast?"

"Until I saw the crowd and realized you weren't with Lowell."

My lips thinned with residual irritation at Guard Jaffer, but I brushed it aside in light of Oliver's revelation. "So what did you see?"

"It'll be easier to show you. Follow me."

———

FIFTEEN MINUTES LATER, WE STEPPED INTO A NARROW ALLEY choked with climbing hydrangeas. The vines crisscrossed the brick walls to either side and stretched across the gap, forcing us to shove branches aside to pass. Four strides beyond the alley's opening, I lost sight of the sidewalk behind us.

"I remember this place." I took a deep breath of the sweet air and pressed a hand to the cool bricks on either side. I didn't need to fully extend my arms to span the narrow gap. Ahead, the passage ended with a free-standing granite arch.

Oliver peered at me over his shoulder. "You've been here before?"

"Years ago."

Oliver's footsteps and the jangle of his quartz bracelets echoed too loudly in the tight corridor for a longer explanation.

Sunlight glinted beyond the arch's opening. I blinked, shielding my eyes with a hand as I shoved past the last of the hydrangeas into a neglected courtyard. Two- and three-story buildings surrounded us, leaving a gap over thirty paces across. In the center lay a circular stone dais twice again as wide as Oliver's wingspan. Weather-worn writing rimmed the flat parchment-hued quartzite. Three interlocking rings, just like the ones on my everlasting seed—or the ones that *had* been on my seed—curved from the dais's surface.

I was an idiot. I should have made the connection sooner.

"What is this place?" Oliver asked. He traced a faded petroglyph with a claw, his gaze roving over the plant detritus littering the ground. Weeds and a lone cottonwood grew in the corners.

"It's a remnant of an ancient culture, the Stone Sworn. It might be a temple or a power focus. Here. Let me show you."

I set my bag in the dirt, then stepped onto the stone dais.

Weight lifted from my shoulders, and it had nothing to do with dropping pounds of seed crystals. I opened myself to earth element and hummed with satisfaction.

Oliver hopped up beside me, and his pupils flared round. "The elements," he gasped.

I grinned. "They're different here."

"Smoother," Oliver agreed. "Earth feels like it's everywhere. Like I could roll around in it." He took another bunching step and spread his wings. "It's like an earth bath. But the other elements, they feel . . . off."

"Muted?"

"Like they're linked or knotted in a pattern I can't see."

"It feels like an earth-element hug to me."

"But how's it work?"

"I don't know." With enough time and gargoyle enhancement, I could create a replica of the rings and dais, but I didn't know where to start to duplicate the elemental texture in the air. "This was made a long, long time ago by people who believed earth, fire, and water were dominant elements, and air and wood were lesser."

Oliver peered at the ruins with open fascination, gently fanning his wings. I walked around him to examine the interlocking rings more closely. They lay canted on their sides, half protruding, half sunk into the quartzite disc. No rim was taller than my knee, and none were deeper than a handspan. A single rock type formed each ring: pin-striped gray schist, speckled gray-and-black amphibolite, and pale gneiss banded with soft black and rusty yellow. Where the rings overlapped, they wove over and under each other. Despite the rough nature of gneiss, amphibolite, and schist, the rings were smooth as water to the touch.

All three rocks were common. I could delve into the ground anywhere around Terra Haven and find them within easy reach, as well as quartzite. The Stone Sworn creators hadn't imported any of these rocks; they had pulled them straight from the soil and shaped them with impressive skill.

"Why did you come here before?" Oliver asked. He folded his wings and stepped into the gneiss ring. He had to curl his tail to fit.

"Kylie brought me a couple months after I moved to Terra Haven." I stepped into the schist ring. The earth element I held altered slightly, but not in a way I could define. "I found the city overwhelming after my small hometown. This place helped me relax. It grounded me." Terra Haven life no longer felt too fast or too crowded, but I still found the rings' energy soothing. "I returned a couple of times, but then I got busy with work, and I forgot about this place."

I tugged my seed from my pocket and laid it flat on my palm. The white quartz glistened in the sunlight, a froth of milky fractures looping away from the center. The geometric imperfections roughly resembled the interlocking rings, but their shape was hard to see with the partially formed star and circle overlaying them.

Feeling glum, I showed my unchanged seed to Oliver.

"Maybe you haven't done whatever you're supposed to do here," he said.

Maybe it was too late.

Trying to stay positive, I looked around. On my mental map, I could sense two gargoyles. One was Lowell, but he was too far away to boost me. If I had visited the ruins earlier, before he got sick, would I have sensed something different about him? Would it have strengthened the seed's shape and given me a real clue?

"That's Sebastian, right?" I asked, pointing in the direction of the other gargoyle I sensed.

"Yes."

"And he's fine?"

"Yep. He said he's never heard of a gargoyle getting sick like Lowell did."

That should have made me feel better. Sebastian was decades older than Oliver. If he had no knowledge of Lowell's sickness, the disease wasn't common. But it also meant another dead end in the mystery of the illness's source.

I tried to remember if any gargoyles lived near the ruins the last time I visited. Back then, I wasn't a guardian. I hadn't yet healed a gargoyle. I hadn't even spoken with a gargoyle, let alone been enhanced by one. If a gargoyle had perched atop one of the nearby buildings, I wouldn't have known.

"Maybe it's not about a gargoyle, not yet," Oliver said, each word less convincing than the last. "Maybe it's something about this place that you're supposed to see. Or do?"

Holding my seed in front of me, I roamed around the ruins. I stood in each ring, then in every overlapping section, and finally in the center. Each area provided its own sensation of peace, and the center was especially harmonious. My seed didn't change.

I cleaned dead leaves and dirt from the ruins, then selected some seed crystals from my bag and sat in the center. A triangle of gneiss, schist, and amphibolite defined the space, with quartzite beneath me. Sun beat down on my scalp and heat radiated through my thin pants from the quartzite. Earth element slid through my senses like whipped butter, soft and silky. Tuning it to quartz made it hum with a different harmony. It wasn't so much sound as vibration, one keyed to my spirit. If I hadn't been inside a baetyl, privy to its powers, I would have said earth element couldn't feel better than this.

Idly, I flipped my hands over. In the sunlight, the amethyst hexagons on the back of my hands glistened like gems. I flexed and fluttered my fingers, and the amethyst stretched like gargoyle skin. Some days, the scars reminded me of my humanity and how close I had come to losing it. Other days, they made me long for what could have been if I had allowed the baetyl to fully reshape me.

I fancied I could feel the sun's rays soak through my shirt to warm the long carnelian hexagonal slashes down my shoulder blades. I missed my wings. Even though they had never fully formed, I mourned their loss.

"Mika, would you like some shade?" Oliver lifted a wing, holding it like a sail above me. A shadow fell across my hands.

I blinked. The afterimage of bright hexagons glowed against my eyelids.

"Thank you," I said, my reply several beats too late to sound natural.

I gave my shoulders a shake. Pretending I didn't see the worry in Oliver's eyes, I balanced my everlasting seed on my knee. Then I focused magic on a seed crystal. Reshaping it into a tiny clear-quartz version of Lowell took mere minutes.

"Pretty," Oliver said.

We both checked my everlasting seed. No change.

Over the next half hour, I worked with every type of quartz in my bag. Some I shaped into gargoyle figurines, others into poppies, irises, and tulips, drawing inspiration from Mo's shop. I made a palm-sized replica of the ruins with tigereye, chalcedony, and aventurine on a clear crystal base. I worked quartz in every section of the overlapping rings, then from the dirt. I dug handfuls of schist, gneiss, and amphibolite from the soil and used the elements to reshape them, too. Those weren't half as refined as my quartz creations, but they were passable.

Through it all, my seed didn't alter in the slightest way. Oliver-enhanced or working solo or not doing anything at all with the elements, nothing affected my everlasting seed.

"This isn't working." Surprisingly, I wasn't tired from manipulating so much quartz, but I was hot. And disappointed. Trudging to the cottonwood's shade, I plopped down. Oliver curled next to me, careful not to touch me with wings still scorching hot from the sun.

"Do you think we are too late?" he asked.

"It looks that way."

The thought was depressing enough to make a knot form in my throat, but I swallowed it down.

"Could it have been pointing toward what made Lowell sick?" Oliver asked after a long silence.

"Maybe. We need to find out more about the theft. I can't shake the feeling they're connected."

"Do you think Mo hurt him?"

I let my head fall back against the tree, eyes closed. I could picture Mo's affection for Lowell—and his shock when Lowell revealed his lie. "I don't think so. Do you?"

Oliver shook his head. "More likely Haubner did."

"He didn't seem to like us." I opened one eye to check Oliver's expression. "Did you notice how he didn't want Lucy to use the signature analyzer?"

"Everything about him is suspicious."

I nodded, though my friend seemed to possess a conviction I lacked. The guard's behavior was puzzling, and his accusing looks grated on my nerves, but I couldn't fathom anything Haubner would gain by making Lowell sick.

"We need to find out why he was chasing Lowell last night," I said.

"And we need more information about the other thefts."

"What?" I sat up. "What other thefts?"

"Haubner let it slip. He said he had to break the wards on the florist's doors, 'just like the others.' The captain cut him off, but I think he was referring to other burglaries."

I had been so distracted by Haubner's arrival, I had completely missed it.

Rolling to my feet, I shoved my useless everlasting seed into my pocket. I had wasted enough time puzzling over what might have been. It was time to focus on the present, and that started with getting to the bottom of the mystery of Lowell's sickness before it afflicted another gargoyle.

I knew just where to start, too.

5

I hopped on the first airbus toward downtown while Oliver flew ahead and confirmed Quinn—and, therefore, Kylie—was at the *Terra Haven Chronicle* headquarters. Pleased that I wouldn't need to wait until tonight to talk with my well-informed friend, I disembarked at the stop closest to the newspaper. Before Oliver and I could cross the street, Kylie and Quinn burst out of the building and raced to meet us on the sidewalk.

"Is it another sick gargoyle?" Kylie asked, worry brimming in her bright blue eyes and her hands outstretched toward me. "How can we help? What can we do?"

"It's not that. I need information."

"Oh." Kylie straightened and took a visible breath to calm herself.

"I told you Oliver wasn't alarmed," Quinn said.

Kylie gave him a rueful smile. "I let my imagination get the best of me. Just a talk, then? Here." Gesturing, she guided us out of the flow of foot traffic and down a side street.

Instantly, the noise of the main thoroughfare faded, as

did the number of curious eyes on us. The sight of Oliver or Quinn walking with one of us always drew attention, and the two of them together tended to stop people in their tracks to ogle. I hadn't noticed how tense my shoulders were until we reached the relative seclusion of a pocket park tucked between two shops. A tidy pentagram of flowerbeds covered the narrow lot, with a central tiered fountain and a metal bench tucked beneath a pruned willow tree.

"What sort of information are you looking for?" Kylie asked as we sat, Oliver and Quinn flanking us. Even in the dappled shade, Quinn glistened like gold, and Oliver was no less beautiful, his feathers shimmering like frozen fire. It was no wonder people couldn't help but stare at my gargoyle friends.

I gave Kylie a brief recounting of meeting Lowell at the florist and the alleged theft, as well as our introduction to Haubner.

"And the florist, Mo, he insisted he wasn't there last night?" Kylie asked. "He called Lowell a liar?" She shared a bewildered glance with Quinn. Like me, Kylie knew gargoyles didn't lie. I thought *everyone* knew gargoyles didn't lie.

"They used a signature analyzer to prove no one but Mo had been near his safe's wards," I said.

"They shouldn't have needed to prove anything." Oliver's wings rustled with renewed irritation.

"Wait, go back," Kylie said. "This guard captain had a signature analyzer? Are you sure?"

"It looked like a giant pipsissewa and it read magic. But it wasn't Captain Rojas's. It was Lucy's. Lucy Fish-something. A junior insurance agent trying to drum up business, but that imploded when Mo kicked her out."

"I wish I had seen it." Kylie stared into the middle

distance, one hand sliding to rest on her camera bag. "I can't believe her company let a junior agent run around with a real analyzer."

"I got the impression Lucy enjoys a bit of nepotism," I said, bemused by Kylie's dreamy expression. "Is a signature analyzer really that impressive?"

"They are notoriously difficult to make, which is why they are exorbitantly priced. The mold is pipsissewa resin embedded with living pipsissewa petals. To keep the flowers' properties intact after they're picked takes meticulously specific wood-element control, kind of like you with earth and quartz. It's a rare specialty not many can achieve."

"Well, no matter how expensive or special the device, it was useless. We're no closer to figuring out what made Lowell ill, but my gut tells me it's linked to the theft. Which is where I'm hoping you can help me. Do you know of any recent burglaries? Haubner alluded to some, but— What?" I asked when Kylie stiffened.

"You haven't seen this morning's paper, have you?" When I shook my head, Kylie pulled a copy from her bag. "The Gilded Hammer was burgled two nights ago. The thief got away with money and some spare silver."

I skimmed the article Kylie indicated. "It says the smithy is located near Paradise Row and West Parkside." I closed my eyes, picturing a map of Terra Haven. "I can't think of any gargoyles near there."

"Me either," Oliver confirmed.

"We'll check it out, just in case."

"And I'll talk with Hannah," Kylie said, tapping the byline to indicate the journalist who wrote the piece. "If she hasn't heard of other thefts, I'll check around. Maybe there's a larger story someone's working on that I don't know about."

"Thank you."

"Show Kylie and Quinn your seed," Oliver said. "It changed. Sort of."

"Sort of?" Kylie asked.

I fished my everlasting seed out of my pocket and handed it to her.

"This is so strange." She leaned forward, holding the white quartz out for Quinn to see, too. "It's like this new shape pushed the rings outward." She licked her finger, then rubbed the moisture across the disc. It didn't do much to highlight the new, unfinished stylized star. "In all the interviews I've done with people who returned with seeds from the everlasting tree, I've never encountered another person with a seed so . . ."

"Vague?" I offered.

"Or one that partially changes. You didn't do anything to make this happen?" Kylie handed my seed to Quinn, who held it cupped in his lion's paw.

"It was like this after I healed Lowell."

"Shouldn't it have taken a new shape, like ours did?" Quinn asked.

I shrugged. "I don't think healing Lowell was the catalyst to an evolution. A *real* evolution."

"Maybe it would have been, if we'd found the rings sooner," Oliver said.

"Sooner?" Kylie perked up. "What did you find?"

"Remember the Stone Sworn ruins in the Cambium District?"

"Off Old Spruce Way! Why didn't I think of that sooner? You went there today? What happened?"

"Nothing." I rattled off every trick I tried, and Oliver filled in the ones I forgot. When we wound down, Kylie sat back in a slump.

"It sounds like you did everything I would have." She gave herself a shake. "But that doesn't mean we're at a dead end. We'll figure out this next clue soon."

I managed a smile at her *we*. Curiosity might drive Kylie, but it was always fortified by a genuine desire to be helpful.

"If the clue has a time limit, I wish the seed included a timer," I said.

"Maybe it does. Maybe that's why this new shape is so undefined. The time to reach it might already be waning."

"In that case, I feel like I'm being set up for failure."

Kylie squeezed my hand in sympathy. Taking the seed back from Quinn, she created a passable magnifying glass with a twist of water and air elements and examined it more closely.

"Does this look like a logo to you? The way it's in the circle like that . . . Almost like a badge, but not quite . . ." She bolted upright. "The LTs! This looks like their logo."

"What are el teas?"

"The Terra Haven League of Tradeswomen. The LTs. They're a social club for businesswomen. My mom's a member. So are most of the entrepreneurial women of the city, or at least the, ah, bigger ones."

Her hesitation over word choices made me grimace. She had stopped herself from saying either *elite* or *full spectrum*. Those were two groups of people whom I went out of my way to avoid, or I did before I became a guardian. *Elite* was code for *wealthy*, or in my experience, for people more preoccupied with money than manners. Full spectrums were among the most magically powerful people in society, and predictably pretentious about it. Personal experience— repeated humiliation and belittlement by schoolmates and business owners in both categories—made it hard to trust anyone in either group.

Except for Marcus, I silently amended. *And the rest of his squad.*

And maybe Amelia Vanderlei.

"How could a pompous social club possibly be important for my seed?"

Kylie shot me a knowing look through her eyelashes, but she said nothing about the whine in my tone or my word choice. We both knew the answer to my question. Gargoyles gravitated toward full spectrums; belonging to a social club full of *elite* women increased my chances of meeting new gargoyles.

Even so, the thought made me cringe. It would be much easier if gargoyles formed their own social clubs and I could skip interacting with their human friends entirely.

"Well, it could also be the propeller logo for Sultry Skies," Kylie hedged, angling my everlasting seed toward the sun.

"Do I want to ask?"

"It's an all-woman airship organization. They put on shows and races. It's a lot of fun—" Kylie caught my expression and closed her mouth.

A land-bound social club suddenly looked more appealing.

"Are you sure it's not something else?"

"You asked the tree how you can help gargoyles, right? What was your exact wording?"

"I asked, 'How can I best fulfill my role as a gargoyle guardian today and every day for the rest of my life?'" And then I broke the tree, because clearly I had asked for too much.

I tried to picture myself taking the airbus across town to lounge in a fancy dining room or parlor, reading about the latest fashions or gossiping with powerful women. Even in my imagination, I couldn't get through the club's front door. These societies weren't free to join, and I had even less money to waste than I had time to idle about.

"Something at one of those locations is bound to trigger your seed," Kylie said, her unflagging optimism making me grit my teeth. "You won't know until you go there."

"I'll add it to my to-do list." Right at the bottom.

———

A GENTLE SHAKE OF MY SHOULDER WOKE ME. I CRACKED ONE weighted eyelid.

Kylie knelt beside my bed, her blond hair gleaming in the soft orange light of a fingernail-sized glowball. Behind her, the windows were dark. A field of stars filled the sky.

"There's been another theft," Kylie whispered.

I pushed my face into my pillow. "Tell me later." Whatever Kylie had learned from her fellow journalists, it could wait until sunrise.

Yesterday, Oliver and I had walked all the way to the Fussy Fox and the Alcott Sisters' Trading Post, two merchants who sold my art. Gratifyingly, both had space for the new figurines I had made in the Stone Sworn ruins and money for me from sold items—enough to cover my portion of the grocery expenses without needing to dip into my savings. Afterward, we looped northwest of downtown to check on three gargoyles in the area. None had heard of a sickness like Lowell's, but all needed minor healing. I missed the last airbus of the evening and plodded three miles home on foot. As much as I had longed to drop straight into bed, a shocking amount of mail had arrived in response to my latest ad touting my gargoyle-healing services in the *Terra Haven Chronicle*. As the city's official gargoyle ambassador, it was up to me to educate the public about their needs. The more people who knew how to contact me if they spotted a gargoyle in distress, the better. Which meant every letter required a response, even those from people who were merely curious.

At least, that's how I felt in the daylight. Right now, all those letters could blow out the window if it meant I could get another half hour of sleep.

Kylie flipped the covers off my head. Cool air cut through the thin layer of my nightgown.

"Mika, a guard—one of my informants—she's at a store that's been burgled. She said the resident gargoyle's in bad shape."

Ice plunged into my gut. I bolted upright. "Where was the theft?"

"At the Wandering Crane General Store. Off Bridgeway and—"

"I know it. Nimoy lives there." I stood too fast and had to grab a bedpost to steady myself. "Is he here?"

A frantic check of my mental map answered my question: No gargoyles flew outside, erratically or otherwise. The only beacons I sensed belonged our five gargoyles—Oliver in the balcony doorway, and his four siblings on the roof.

Kylie straightened from her crouch. "My informant said he can't fly."

"We need to go—"

Kylie grabbed my arm, halting my spin. "First, get dressed. Try not to wake Josephine."

I nodded. Waking our landlady would only slow us down.

Kylie departed on tiptoes, squeezing past Oliver and disappearing into her room. For the first time, I realized she was still in her pajamas. She must have rushed straight to me when she heard the guard's message.

I hooked a glowball into the ceiling lantern, feeding a candle's amount of fire into the spell. I didn't need a brighter light to locate yesterday's pants. My nightgown got tossed to my rumpled bed, and I wasted precious seconds aligning the buttons of my shirt. Kylie returned while I hunted through the mess on my table for a hair tie. She was dressed, her bag and shoes in hand.

"You don't have to—"

Her disbelieving snort cut me off. "Do you really think you're going running off to help a hurt gargoyle—and toward an interesting story—and I'm going to, what, fall back to sleep?"

"Right." I finished tugging my hair into a high ponytail and squatted to restock my bag with seed crystals. Kylie muffled the sharp clacks of the stones with a dome of dense air.

"Let's go."

"Wait. I need my bracelets," Oliver said.

I hesitated. He didn't need to carry quartz for me, not for an emergency run like this. If healing Nimoy required more seed crystals than fit in my bag, I would bring him home. It made sense for Oliver to cart around extra raw material only on longer excursions, when we didn't know how many gargoyles in need of healing we would encounter.

However, Oliver's determined expression stayed my denial. Maybe he saw a reason my sleep-slow brain wasn't grasping.

"Step forward," I said.

Oliver gingerly crossed the threshold. The hardwood planks creaked. In the quiet night, with the house suspended in slumber, the shift of the floorboards sounded as loud as hand claps.

Four curved bars of raw quartz lay beside the door, yesterday's bracelets removed and discarded. Working fast, I reshaped one around each of Oliver's ankles. All five gargoyles' enhancements flooded me with magic, and it took more effort to refine it to the trickle of earth element I needed than it did to manipulate the quartz and seal each band to itself. It didn't matter if the four seams looked as if they were molded by toddlers, only that they didn't pinch or chafe Oliver's legs when he ran.

Despite the care I took, the chime of the bracelets still rang like church bells against Oliver's carnelian limbs when he leapt to the railing, then to the roof.

"Do you want Quinn to wear quartz, too?" Kylie asked, confused.

"No." I grabbed a lightweight coat and boots, but Kylie beat me to my bag, levitating the heavy satchel with bands of air.

We ran on tiptoes down the stairs and slipped out the front door. After a frustrating pause at the base of the porch steps to put on our boots, we sprinted down the sidewalk. Behind us, two gargoyle beacons dropped silently from the roof, then flapped higher to clear the treetops.

One empty street after the next, Kylie and I ran side by side. With each step, my boots landed harder, my feet growing heavier. The initial rush of adrenaline faded, and the fatigue of a long day and little sleep dragged on my legs. The Wandering Crane wasn't far—an airbus could have made the trip in less than ten minutes, but public transportation didn't begin circulating for hours yet. On foot, we had to zigzag through neighborhoods, navigating hills that multiplied and bloated in the darkness. I cursed when the road sloped upward yet again and the burn in my thighs intensified.

"Two more blocks," Kylie encouraged, less out of breath than me despite the added burden of levitating my heavy bag. The glow of a streetlight illuminated a sheen of sweat on her forehead, but overall, my friend looked far better than I felt.

I really needed more sleep. Or a flying carpet.

Both seemed equally improbable.

When I spotted the cluster of people outside the Wandering Crane, I started to slow. Three women knelt in the middle of the street. They were as different from each other as possible, one a young guard with short-cropped black hair, another a matron in a white robe embroidered with eye-popping yolteohuia parrots, and the third a stocky woman in chef's green-and-white houndstooth check pants and a billowy white shirt. A man as dark as a shadow and dressed to match stood behind the older woman, his attention divided between the general store behind him and the blanket laid out between the women.

I searched my mental map for Nimoy's beacon, locating it at the same time I spotted a glint of blue dumortierite and orange carnelian on the blanket. My frantically beating heart stuttered.

Reaching deep, I pushed fresh speed into my legs. Surprised faces jerked around, and the guard started to raise a hand—and likely a ward—but let it drop when she looked past my shoulder. *At Kylie,* a distant part of me realized. *She must be Kylie's informant.*

Then I was on my knees in front of Nimoy, and the rest didn't matter.

He lay on a thick quilted bedspread. It hadn't been here when he landed. When he fell.

Nimoy was the size of a large fox or a small coyote, with a fluffy tail and skinny, fawn-like legs ending in delicate canine paws. With a gargoyle's characteristic proportional harmony, his elephant head was perfectly sized to match his small body, his slender trunk an echo of his graceful legs. His bladelike wings lay crumpled against his sides.

Cornflower-blue dumortierite and honey-gold carnelian swirled through his trunk, head, and soft ears, darkening to ink-flecked indigo dumortierite along his body. His legs and paws were pure carnelian, fiery orange along their length, deepening to scarlet through his paws. In the harsh light of the glowball suspended over the gargoyle, with one delicate leg badly broken and the others fractured, he resembled carelessly dropped cooling glass.

"Oh, Nimoy." The sandpaper of my throat turned my voice into a stranger's.

The gargoyle's legs weren't his only injuries. Cracks ran through Nimoy's trunk, the skin badly scraped along half its length. One tusk ended in a jagged break after a mere inch. His wings were mangled. Soft bands of air held him in a cocoon, but he trembled and shifted restlessly. His visible eye, glassy and unfocused, drifted aimlessly.

"Guardian?" Nimoy whispered.

"I'm here." Fury and anguish choked my already labored breathing.

Two thefts. Two sick gargoyles. This wasn't a coincidence; it was intentional.

6

I locked eyes with the guard. "There was a theft here?"

Her chin jerked in a nod, then her lips thinned, as if she hadn't meant to answer me.

"Only at the general store?"

The woman gave me her best stony-faced stare. "Who are you—?"

I stopped listening. People moved inside the Wandering Crane, and lights blazed from the interior. In this neighborhood, shopkeepers lived above their businesses. Lantern light glowed in the windows of several second-story apartments, and a smattering of proprietors clustered in the doorways of their shops. None of the other stores had a guard presence, though.

I located Kylie standing discreetly to one side, assessing the situation.

"Find out what happened here," I ordered.

Her blue eyes widened, and she gave me a brisk nod.

The guard tried to question me again, but the clatter of quartz paws on cobblestones drowned her out. The cacophony doubled when Oliver landed closer, slowing more easily than his heavier brother. Both had circled the neighborhood in opposite directions before honing in on us. I suspected they had been searching for a cause to Nimoy's sickness, but neither looked to have any answers. Quinn trotted to Kylie, but Oliver loped up behind me, not stopping until he peered over my shoulder at Nimoy. His soft moan of distress harmonized with Nimoy's.

"Quinn," I called.

The lion gargoyle shifted directions, padding up to our group.

"Check every gargoyle in the area." I could sense four gargoyles, and I knew of a fifth to the east. "I need to know if anyone else is sick. But stay in range; I might need you. Visual inspection only, and if you feel at all odd, return *immediately*."

Quinn's brows bunched with worry. "I'll be quick."

Cobblestones squeaked beneath his hind paws when he spun. In a deafening rush, he galloped three strides down the empty street, then launched. His wing beats receded, and in my mind's eye, his beacon spiraled overhead in a tight climb.

"So dizzy," Nimoy murmured, his words slurred around his broken tusk. "I can't . . . I tried . . ."

"Shh. Steady." I placed my hands on Nimoy's sides, careful to touch only glossy, uninjured fur. The bands of air hugging the gargoyle shifted to accommodate me.

"Are you FPD?" the standing man asked.

"She's not FPD," said the woman in the bright robe.

"How can you tell? She barks orders like a Fed."

"She's a gargoyle person. Nimoy knows her."

I gathered magic, pulling the elements through Oliver's and Quinn's boosts, readying myself.

"Hold me steady?" I asked Oliver.

He stepped up to my left side and wrapped a wing around my shoulders. Anchored in his solid, familiar embrace, I eased magic into Nimoy.

Pain hammered me, spiking through the magic connecting us. It battered me from every direction, from Nimoy's feet and ankles, from his trunk and mouth. Teeth clenched, I fed more magic into the mangled gargoyle.

Nimoy's internal stability stuttered. My magic stretched agonizingly, then contracted as the gargoyle's essence wavered. Nausea chased dread up my spine, my fear confirmed: Nimoy suffered the same spirit-quaking sickness that had struck Lowell.

Another wave of discord tore at my magic, then another, without rhythm and from disparate directions. I fought to maintain my hold on the elements as every overlapping collision of jagged palpitations increased Nimoy's unrelenting pain.

The gargoyle slipped and skittered sideways in my jangled vision. I closed my eyes. Knowing I experienced only an echo of Nimoy's misery, I pressed gently down on his side, holding him in place—anchoring him as Oliver anchored me. Then I reached inward, pulling the core of myself into my magic. My spirit split with surprising ease, my recent practice with Lowell speeding the process.

"Careful. Not too much," Oliver murmured.

My spirit slid into Nimoy, ghosting along the pathway laid by my magic. My awareness went with it, until I lost track of my body. Only Nimoy mattered.

I countered each vibration with the elements, sinking deeper into Nimoy even as I stitched together his natural harmony. He was a living-quartz gargoyle, and I knew the pattern of him—of all gargoyles—intimately. That pattern was part of me. It lived in the amethyst on my hands and the carnelian on my shoulder blades.

The sensation of being drawn deep into Nimoy became a free-fall as I surrendered to the gargoyle's need. Tumbling through waves of pain, I clung to control of the elements by my mental fingernails and dropped through the last of Nimoy's barriers. Golden light engulfed me. At the center of this intangible space stood Nimoy, uninjured and ethereal.

His glowing form quivered, his edges blurry with noxious vibrations. Nimoy tossed his head, and his whole body shook. Here, at the core of himself, he should have been safe. Instead, someone had hurt this gargoyle so badly they sickened his spirit.

As part of the theft? As a distraction?

Both thoughts fueled my fury. My concentration faltered; my grip on my spirit and my magic wavered.

The baetyl pounced.

One second, it was just me and Nimoy. The next, raw power of an infinite sentience surged inside me. Its song swelled within the confines of my spirit, as if the baetyl's immense power twined within me once more—as loud as it had when I nearly died crash-landing a doomed airship.

I flashed on the memory of a quartz wave rising from a field, toppling trees and shifting boulders as if they weighed no more than seed crystals. Fear had consumed me and guided me. It had saved me. This was different. I wasn't afraid for my life; I was afraid for Nimoy's.

My righteous anger fueled my anguish—and the baetyl's power.

No. This was a mirage. This wasn't the real baetyl. It wasn't the sentience that built gargoyle nesting grounds and incubated gargoyle eggs. It was an imprint. A memory. But it felt as if it would drown me. As if it would drown Nimoy and me both.

I couldn't let that happen.

I tamped down my anger; Nimoy didn't deserve it. Reaching out with a phantom hand, I gingerly soothed baetyl-tuned magic down Nimoy. This precious gargoyle deserved only love.

My awareness of the baetyl's energy imploded like an indrawn breath, and the song quieted on an exhale of love. This deep inside Nimoy, where more of myself existed within the gargoyle than did within my own body, maybe the entire presence of the baetyl was my imagination, just my brain's way of making sense of the impalpable process.

I released my confusion and focused on engulfing Nimoy's spirit in another magic-enhanced wave of love. The golden elephant canine steadied. The last of his vibrations calmed, restoring his innate gargoyle stillness.

A breath passed. Another. Time had no meaning here. We were safe, cocooned together in perfect harmony. Nimoy's smile curved around his tusks. I smiled back.

Reluctantly, I retracted my spirit. It felt like running full tilt into a quartz wall. The gargoyle's pain lanced through me, white hot and omnipresent.

Gasping, I reeled in my spirit, retreating to my body and letting my magic dissipate. Guilty relief flooded me as the agony vanished.

Oliver's wing dug into my shoulder, pinching me to his side. My arms were wet sand, heavy and ready to crumble. Without Oliver's support, I would have been facedown atop Nimoy.

I hung limp in my friend's embrace as my eyes regained focus. Nimoy wasn't shaking. The restless twitches of his trunk had subsided. The women eased their protective bands of air away from Nimoy, and he remained motionless, watching me with one big elephant eye. Pain, not dizziness, filled his gaze.

"I'm going to heal you now, if you're ready," I croaked, my throat scratchy.

Nimoy gave me a fraction of a nod, the smallest movement of consent he could manage. Anything more would add to his suffering.

I forced myself to sit on my heels without Oliver's support. Twisting, I spotted my bag two feet away. Before I could summon the energy to reach for it, the robed woman slid it toward me with a band of wood-laced air.

"Thank you."

I reached for seed crystals and fell off my heels to my hip. Oliver caught me before I pitched fully to the cobblestones.

"Careful," someone said.

"Eilidh, some pizazzies."

Footsteps pounded away from us. I blinked black flecks from my vision and rearranged myself into a cross-legged position. My thighs burned as knotted muscles stretched, and needling pain assaulted my toes. Blindly, I fumbled for a seed crystal.

"Wait, child." A cool hand settled on mine, and it took a moment to connect it with the robed woman. She glanced up the street. The baker was hurrying back to us, a glass and platter in hand.

"Your friend said you'd need this," the baker said with a heavy Scottish accent. She thrust a glass of water into my hand. "And some food."

I downed the water. The cool liquid slid like a balm

down my parched throat. The baker reclaimed the empty glass and thrust a platter of pastries in front of me.

I waved them away. "I need to concentrate—"

"You need energy," the baker insisted.

Oliver rumbled his agreement.

I tested my grip on the elements, then grabbed a pastry, chewing it by rote.

"We'd like to link with you," the woman in the robe said.

"We insist," the baker said.

"We need to help. This—" The older woman waved a frustrated arm over the blanket, perhaps indicating the disbanded cocoon of air, too. "This wasn't enough."

I wouldn't need the help of linked magic once I collected myself, not with Oliver and Quinn boosting me. However, I appreciated these strangers' concern for Nimoy, and I sympathized with how helpless they must have felt watching him suffer, unable to do anything useful.

I swallowed the last of the pastry and nodded. "I'm Mika."

"A gargoyle guardian," Oliver added.

The others quickly introduced themselves and handed me balances of elements, all of us eager to ease Nimoy's suffering. The baker, Eilidh McClosky, possessed a fitting magical signature of a warm hearth on a cool morning. Shelly Spiro-Pia was the robed woman and owner of the Wandering Crane. Her husband, Lee, startled me when he rumbled his name and thrust magic at me; I had forgotten about him standing guard behind Shelly. Both Spiro-Pias were wood elementals, his signature carrying the sensation of deep roots curled into the grooves of a granite boulder, hers the gentle brush of rain across a blooming marmalade tree. The guard moved to stand halfway between our group and the general store, her attention on a message spell sailing over the roof. I looked for Kylie but couldn't find her.

"Oliver, please tell Kylie that Quinn can extend his range." I didn't have to glance up to know Quinn hadn't widened his gliding circle more than a few blocks. Like most gargoyles, he had excellent vision, but I would feel better if he more closely examined the nearby gargoyles. Plus, with Oliver enhancing me *and* the three people in our link, I no longer needed Quinn's boost.

Oliver touched his nose to the tip of Nimoy's snout, then trundled away to find Kylie. I pulled a handful of seed crystals from my bag. Shelly leaned forward and Lee crouched as I reshaped the raw quartz. Magic flowed to me with surprising ease that had nothing to do with the link. I paused, taking an internal assessment. I felt . . . refreshed?

Seeing my confusion, Eilidh grinned.

"It's my pick-me-up pizzazzies," she said, gesturing to the platter of remaining pastries. "My morning customers say they can't get by without them."

I could see why. With a belated thanks, I pulled harder on the elements and began layering numbing magic through Nimoy's wounds. Shelly gasped when I applied the first threads of quartz to Nimoy's broken leg. After that, I didn't have any spare awareness for my audience. All my focus went toward healing, first Nimoy's leg, then his trunk. Rebuilding his tusk took longer.

"Mika, you should eat," Oliver said.

I startled, not having felt or even heard his return. Blinking to clear the bleariness from my vision, I only noticed the sluggishness of my magic when I let it go. Nimoy curled and uncurled his trunk, flexing the long appendage without pain. He couldn't yet stand, but he wasn't in agony.

He looked more tired than anything. Using raw quartz to replace missing body parts still required the gargoyle's energy to assist in his healing. I wasn't close to overtaxing Nimoy's body yet, but a breather wasn't a bad idea, either.

Eilidh offered me the pastry platter once more, and I selected two. Shelly and Lee also each took a pastry. I shoved the second pizazzy in my mouth before everyone finished their first. Already, I was more alert. Still chewing the last bite, I reached for magic again. I didn't know how long the pizazzies' energetic boost would last, and I didn't want to waste a moment.

After Quinn returned, confirming every gargoyle in the area was healthy, I sank deeper into the painstaking reconstruction of Nimoy's wings. Conversations murmured in the distance, but I didn't try to follow them. Kylie or Oliver would relay any important information I missed.

I soothed the last fracture from Nimoy's back leg, then threaded delicate, assessing magic through him. His wings were more clear quartz than blue dumortierite. His trunk the same. His tusks were mismatched, and one ear had a new clear rim. But he was whole and pain-free. Finally, I sat back and disbanded the link, letting the unused seed crystals roll from my cramped fingers.

"Incredible. Simply incredible," Shelly said on a sigh. Eilidh nodded and petted Nimoy's side, tracing fingers reverently along his healed wings.

"How's the gargoyle?"

I startled at the familiar voice, surprised to find Captain Rojas standing at the edge of our circle. Kylie observed all of us, a notebook in hand.

"Better, thanks to Mika," Shelly said.

The captain appeared to have recovered from the

florist's. The whites of her eyes were clear, the red puffiness gone from the tip of her nose. In the harsh glowball light, deep wrinkles underscored her eyes and lined her tanned cheeks. Despite the late hour, her gray hair was contained in a smooth braid identical to yesterday's and her uniform was pristine.

Nimoy curled his trunk around my ankle. I rested a hand on his cheek and reached for Oliver with the other. My friend placed his paw in my hand, and I tipped to lean my head against his, letting my eyes close.

". . . all finished inside," Captain Rojas said, and I realized I had missed some of the conversation. "The thief made off with money from the till and safe, a complete Aunt Clara's Wardrobe Whirl spell kit, two pocket lanterns, three bottles of wine, possibly some ginger, and all your chocolate bars."

Kylie double-checked her notebook, nodding along with the captain's list. Thankfully, she was fully alert.

Thinking of the walk home, I reached for the remaining pizazzy. For the first time, I actually tasted the rich chocolate at the heart of the vanilla-sweet pastry. It wasn't until I swallowed that I noticed the faint green-tea aftertaste of the stimulant.

"Do you think this was a prank?" Kylie asked. "Or a dare? The items taken, other than the money, all read like an indulgent shopping trip."

"Or gifts I might get from a date," the other guard said.

"That doesn't account for the *how*," Captain Rojas said, not looking away from Lee and Shelly. "It appears the chocolate was temperature-spelled by you, Mr. Spiro-Pia. The property wards were created by your wife. Is that correct?"

"Shelly is stronger at wards than me," Lee said. "It was the backlash from the broken cooling spell on the chocolate that woke me."

"You're certain it wasn't the smashed lock on the front door that woke you first?" Captain Rojas asked.

"Such a small sound? Why would it? Our ward was still intact," Shelly said, frowning.

"Indeed." The captain's eyes landed on me. "This is a pattern we've seen too often lately."

"Like at the florist, right? Could it be a doppelganger spell?" Kylie asked.

It was a good theory. A doppelganger spell was a high-level illusion designed to mimic a person's appearance and voice well enough to trick their own mother—or the mother of the person whose identity had been stolen. The spell was illegal, of course, but that wouldn't stop a thief from using it. I wasn't sure it would trick a gargoyle—*two* gargoyles, counting Lowell.

"Like *what* florist?" Shelly asked.

"Who would use such a complicated spell to get through our wards?" Lee asked on top of her.

Captain Rojas's lips thinned, and she gave Kylie a brief glare before shaking her head. "They wouldn't. Considering what was stolen, they wouldn't be able to make a profit using a doppelganger spell. They would need ten times what was in your safe to buy one."

"And they'd need a different doppelganger for each place they burgle," Kylie said, tapping her pencil against her notepad.

Captain Rojas nodded grudgingly.

"Multiple doppelganger spells and multiple thieves?" Kylie asked.

"Even less likely."

"Then what?" Lee stared toward his store, his fingers curled into fists. "Do you have any idea who did this? Or how?"

Captain Rojas ignored the questions, shifting to crouch beside me. Oliver swiveled to face her, his exhales tickling the hair at the base of my neck.

"Is he awake?" she asked of Nimoy.

The gargoyle lay with his legs folded, his head resting on his curled trunk. If we weren't here, he would be asleep, but he valiantly opened bleary eyes when I ran a hand down the flap of his ear.

"Who did you believe you were enhancing?" the captain asked.

"Shelly." Nimoy turned toward the shopkeeper, his glossy eyes bright with anxiety. "I'm sorry. I didn't know it wasn't you."

"Shh, none of that," Shelly said, though she looked shocked by the gargoyle's mistake. When she reached for him, Nimoy curled his trunk around her wrist, and she petted his forehead. "I'm just glad you're all right, dear."

"You couldn't tell the difference between the thief and Ms. Spiro-Pia?" the captain pressed. When Nimoy shook his head, she sat back on her heels. "Then the florist wasn't lying."

"Neither was Lowell," I said.

"The gargoyle? I never thought he was."

I reined in my temper. Would it have hurt her to say as much at the florist?

Captain Rojas stood, her expression troubled. "I suspect we're dealing with a person who is deranged. Or someone unaware of the dangerous magic they've stumbled into."

"So it's true?" asked the other guard. "We have a genuine spirit-shifting thief on our hands?"

Surprise stiffened my spine. Spirit shifting wasn't normal magic. It wasn't common, either. Most people didn't even know how to do it.

But I did—to heal gargoyles. How was someone using the same means to steal?

7

T he captain's lips compressed, her glare for the younger guard sharp enough to prod the woman back a step. Rojas swept her gaze over the rest of us, and her nostrils flared in annoyance.

"Spirit shifting is a theory," she said curtly. "A *working* theory, and one that shouldn't be repeated. By anyone."

A flying carpet rounded the far end of the block, the man atop it dressed in a familiar olive-green guard uniform. My shoulders tensed when I recognized him. I had hoped never to see Haubner again after leaving the Blue Lotus.

"Him again," Kylie muttered.

"He better not accuse Nimoy of lying, too," I growled, standing.

"He wouldn't," Kylie said, though she didn't sound certain. Her fingers curled around my bicep in a soft grip. Did she think I would attack the odious man?

I stuffed my hands in my pockets, surprised I had to relax clenched fists so they would fit.

Haubner halted his carpet several lengths from our group. His assessing gaze swept everyone clustered around

Nimoy before resting on me. And Oliver. My friend noticeably bristled, and my spine tried to do the same.

Leaving the carpet floating, Haubner hopped to the cobblestones and approached. He addressed Captain Rojas, but his loud words were clearly meant for me. "How curious to find Ms. Stillwater here. Out for an early-morning stroll? Interesting how it took her right past the last place the thief struck."

"I don't find the thief 'interesting.' I find him infuriating," I said, the memory of Nimoy's pain buzzing beneath my skin.

"Yes, interrupted plans can be infuriating," Haubner murmured, his tone implying something nefarious. "Were you able to get what you needed from this gargoyle?"

"What *I* needed? I'm here because Nimoy was grievously injured. I healed him."

"Chambers sent for her through a mutual friend," the captain said, her eyes cutting meaningfully to Kylie.

Haubner's hooded gaze swung to Guard Chambers, then to Kylie, taking in the notebook my friend clutched in her free hand.

"I would have sent a plea straight to the guardian if I had known of her," Eilidh said, crossing her thick forearms. "Nimoy was suffering something terrible."

Guilt welled in the pit of my stomach. *If* she had known of me. Despite all the ads I ran in the *Terra Haven Chronicle* and the hours I spent writing letters to business owners and full-spectrum families, too few people knew of my existence.

"Do we have a problem I don't know about?" Captain Rojas asked mildly.

Haubner twitched in her direction, but his hot gaze returned to me. "No, ma'am," he said.

What was the man's issue with me?

"Then I assume you have an explanation for your delay," Rojas said, a thread of warning in her voice now.

Haubner flinched and finally gave the captain his full attention. "There was a fire," he said. He snapped a sound-proof ward around himself and Captain Rojas, cutting off the rest of his explanation.

I tried to be logical—information shared among guards often required discretion—but I suspected Haubner was simply being insulting. The way Guard Chambers drummed her fingers against her thigh, clearly irked, all but confirmed Haubner's rudeness.

"Do you two have history?" Shelly asked me, studying Haubner. The way her gaze roamed down his body, then speculatively over my face made my cheeks heat.

I unclenched my jaw with effort. "I met him only yester-day. I can't take credit for his charm."

Eilidh snorted.

Nimoy shifted on the blanket, drawing our attention. Bracing his curled trunk against the ground, he climbed to his feet, unsteady with fatigue but graceful. I knelt, ready with bands of air element to catch him as he tested each long leg.

"Any pain?" I asked.

"None." He high-stepped off the quilt, his crystalline claws catching at the fabric. Turning in a slow circle, he examined his body and his repaired wings.

While Shelly and Eilidh fussed over Nimoy, admiring his glossy fur, I searched him for any minor injuries I might have missed. My heart hurt for the sheer amount of clear crystal covering the gargoyle. Nimoy had nearly died from his fall. When the spirit-shifting thief struck again, would the next gargoyle survive?

"Let me get this straight," Kylie said. Her gaze flicked to the soundproof ward around the captain and Haubner, making sure they couldn't hear her. "Your spirit *is* your magical signature. It's who you are. So the captain is saying someone is changing their *spirit* to another's, and therefore mimicking their signature?"

"And doing it well enough to walk right through their spells," Chambers agreed.

"I thought that was impossible," Kylie said.

So did I, at least in the way they were talking about.

At the most basic level, a person's spirit dictated their elemental abilities. The shape of Kylie's spirit enabled her to perform complex spells with air, but she would never work quartz with the same skill as me, and vice versa. Also, just as no one could pick up a glass without leaving behind a fingerprint, no one could work the elements without leaving behind their magical signature—the metaphysical fingerprint of their spirit. Every magical signature was as original as a personality and equally impossible to imitate perfectly.

And yet, my spirit was uniquely compatible with all gargoyles' spirits. This was my greatest strength and what elevated me from a healer to a guardian. This similitude enabled me to flood a gargoyle with so much of my magic, and therefore so much of my spirit, that I could shift my spirit *inside* a gargoyle. Which was exactly what I had done to save Nimoy and Lowell. But even having shifted my spirit multiple times into different gargoyles, I was clueless how to replicate another human's signature.

"It's rare, not impossible," Chambers said.

"You're saying that with enough practice, I could match my magic so closely to another's it would *shift* my spirit?" Kylie asked, incredulous.

"It takes more than mimicking another's magic to shift a spirit," Captain Rojas said.

Chambers jumped, a guilty flush staining her cheeks.

Haubner had dropped his ward, and now he stood next to the captain, his stance wide and his arms crossed. The cut of his uniform added breadth to his shoulders, but he was more lean than muscled. If he was trying to be intimidating, he failed. At best, he looked angry. I found the captain's stony expression and the way she clasped her hands behind her back as she contemplated Kylie more formidable.

Shelly stood, her hand going to her husband's. "We should not talk of this. Spirit shifting is vile magic. Intolerable."

I flinched and pivoted toward Captain Rojas, struggling to keep my voice neutral. "The thief isn't shifting their spirit into anyone else? They're somehow *altering* it? Within themselves?"

The hairs on the back of my neck tried to stand on end when everyone's attention locked on to me.

"'Into' someone?" Kylie asked.

"What do you know about it?" Captain Rojas asked.

"Only theory." I fought not to squirm. My mouth was too dry to swallow, and licking my lips didn't help moisten them. "I've never seen it done. But it sounds like the kind of magic that would make a gargoyle sick."

Kylie shot me a *we'll talk later* look and directed her next comment to Captain Rojas. "Maybe if you explain how spirit shifting is done—"

"It's safer for you if you don't know," the captain interrupted. Her gaze lingered on me, and I forced myself not to look away.

"So how do you stop the thief?" Kylie asked.

"If they keep it up, I won't have to worry about it. Anyone

messing with shifting their spirit is gambling with their life. One shift or a dozen, eventually, it will kill them."

I broke eye contact first after all. Flexing blood back into fingers that had been squeezed tight around Oliver's folded wing, I bent to gather scattered seed crystals, hiding my face from the captain's penetrating gaze.

"For now, I need everyone to keep this theory to themselves," Captain Rojas said. She pointed at Kylie. "Nothing about it in print, you've got that?"

I couldn't believe what I was hearing. Lowell's illness and Nimoy's was no longer a mystery. Somehow, enhancing the spirit-shifted thief disrupted the gargoyles' spirits, dangerously sickening them. Not for the first time, gargoyles were being harmed by someone intent on their own selfish profits. It was disgusting and cruel, and I wouldn't stand by and let it happen.

"We can't keep this a secret."

Captain Rojas pinned me with the full weight of her authoritative gaze. "Ms. Stillwater, we want to catch this thief, not tip him off. We need to proceed cautiously."

"You mean slowly."

"I mean methodically."

"Can you identify a person who has shifted their spirit?"

"I have methods."

"Like waiting for this person to kill themselves?"

"The captain does not need to explain herself to you," Haubner said.

I ignored him. "Vague promises aren't enough. This thief is endangering lives. You saw Nimoy. He was so dizzy he crashed into the street. And he was lucky. People were around to help him. The next gargoyle might not be so fortunate." The thought made me sick. "We need to warn the gargoyles. *Every* gargoyle."

"*We?* How would you have me inform all of them, Guardian?" Captain Rojas asked. "I can't tune messages to gargoyles. They don't read newspapers. Should I set up town criers on every corner? Or should my guards neglect their duties so they can run around, personally delivering messages?"

Nothing she said wasn't true, but I heard my own ineptitude in her questions. I was the guardian. I should have an easy way to spread information among gargoyles. In Rojas's mouth, my title became a taunt, and embarrassment heated my cheeks.

"I'll do it," Oliver said. "I'll tell every gargoyle in the city not to enhance anyone, even those they know, unless they can see them."

"Especially at night," I said, thinking of the thief's habits.

"I'll help," Quinn said.

Captain Rojas planted her hands on her narrow hips. "That will cause problems. High-traffic centers and businesses rely on gargoyles' boosts to keep everything running smoothly."

"They'll have to manage," Shelly said, surprising me. "No other gargoyle should go through what Nimoy did."

The captain glanced at the gargoyles, then at me, and she huffed out an aggrieved sigh. "Tell the gargoyles if you must, but tell them it's a secret, too. Help me catch whoever is doing this."

I gave her a tight nod, irritated that she thought I wanted anything less. The thief must be stopped immediately—for the gargoyles' sake as well as my own. So long as the thief continued to shift their spirit to steal, I had to shift my spirit to heal.

It has to be different, I told myself. What the thief did was dangerous, but I was helping. What I did had to be safe.

Right?

With a final warning to Kylie not to publish anything that would harm the investigation, Captain Rojas stalked away to retrieve a crumpled flying carpet from up against the Spiro-Pias' general store. Guard Chambers trotted to catch up with her. I hoisted my bag onto my shoulder, swaying under the weight despite how much lighter it was after healing Nimoy. The sun had crept over the horizon while I wasn't paying attention, and more people crowded the shop doorways and windows, curious stares fixed on our small group. No matter what Captain Rojas wanted, rumors and speculation would run rampant from this theft.

Before I could leave, Shelly and Eilidh bade me to wait. In minutes, they bustled back from their respective shops. Shelly thrust a pouch of coins in my hands.

"Please take this," she said. "Eilidh and I pitched in for Nimoy's healing, Guardian."

"Oh, I couldn't—"

She pulled me into a hug that cut off my oxygen supply. Whispering her thanks again, she let me go.

"And here, take these," Eilidh said, pressing a cloth pouch with two more pizazzy pastries into my hands.

Those, I accepted gratefully.

Nimoy had fallen asleep on his feet in the middle of the street, and the women turned their attention to him, gently encouraging him toward the sidewalk.

"Looks like the Spiro-Pias got robbed twice tonight," Haubner said, watching from atop his floating carpet.

"What?"

"First the thief wipes out their safe, and now you charged them to heal a gargoyle that isn't even part of their family." Haubner gave the pouch of coins I clutched in my fist a significant look.

"They insisted," I said, but guilt made my words sullen. He was right. I should have been firmer in refusing Shelly's and Eilidh's money. It wasn't their fault Nimoy had been hurt. But I had thought about how many seed crystals the coins would buy, and my protest had been weak.

"Every healer has a right to compensation," Kylie said, shoving between me and Haubner. "The money was freely given and none of your business."

Oliver crowded behind me, his soft growl vibrating against my thigh. Quartz footsteps sounded on the left as Quinn drew closer.

"I imagine the thief believed they were getting their just 'compensation,' too," Haubner said, undaunted.

"What are you saying?" Kylie demanded.

The guard arched an eyebrow, his head cocked to look around my friend at me. "I'm saying thieves come in all shapes and sizes."

When Haubner's gaze drifted to Oliver, I was too flabbergasted to form a response. With a smirk, the guard flew away.

Seething, I spun in the opposite direction as Haubner. Kylie, Oliver, and Quinn fell in beside me, indignation and anger shading everyone's expressions.

"I'm not leaving this investigation to *him* or Captain Rojas." I couldn't, not when it endangered gargoyles. "I'm going to hunt down the thief before he can hurt anyone else, and I'm going to do it *with* the help of gargoyles, not by keeping them in the dark."

"Good. I'll help," Kylie said.

"How? Are you going to publish about the spirit shifting?"

"No. I agree with the captain: Publishing the theory would probably do more harm than good. We need more information about the thief first. I got a few leads yesterday after we talked, and I'll follow up on them."

We made plans to meet at home for lunch, then Kylie and Quinn left for the *Chronicle*. Oliver and I continued toward the nearest gargoyle with the hope they had seen something Nimoy missed. At the very least, we could start spreading our warning.

I couldn't escape the queasy suspicion that no matter how quickly we worked, we wouldn't be fast enough to spare the next gargoyle. For weeks, I had devoted my days to contacting gargoyles, and still I hadn't set foot in entire sections of the city. We needed to spread our warning faster. Granted, passing on information would take less time than healing, but even so, I didn't see how we could warn all the city's gargoyles in less than a week. The thought of another seven nights during which gargoyles would be vulnerable to the thief's noxious magic made me sick.

"We have to split up," I told Oliver. Separately, we could cover more ground and reach more gargoyles—especially Oliver.

Reluctantly, he agreed. He would talk with the nearby gargoyles, then head north, where others lived farther apart; I would circle toward the inner city and the cluster of gargoyles who lived within walking distance of each other. At noon, we would regroup at home and hear what Kylie and Quinn learned.

I was two hours and six warned gargoyles into my plodding journey when a message spell dropped in front of my face. Rocking on my toes, I managed to stop before bungling into it. I recognized Ms. Zuberrie's signature. She wouldn't contact me like this unless—

My stomach dropped. *Amelia Vanderlei*. I completely forgot about our appointment today.

When I activated the spell, Ms. Zuberrie's crisp voice, full of annoyance, spilled out.

"Do you know who is cooling her heels in our parlor this morning, Mika? You don't make a woman like this wait. Nor do I appreciate being put in the position of entertaining a *Vanderlei* without notice. Get home. Now, girl."

I sprinted for the nearest airbus stop before the last notes of Ms. Zuberrie's voice faded.

The entire glacial airbus ride home, I rehearsed my apology, my guilt and anxiety leapfrogging off each other. Ms. Zuberrie was right; women like Amelia didn't wait on others. They certainly weren't forgotten by people who made plans with them. Worse still, I had hoped meeting with Amelia would open doors to other full spectrums, giving me fast, easy access to gargoyles who lived among high-society families. Now, those gargoyles would suffer longer all because I made a social blunder.

I had to fix this.

Oliver caught up with the airbus before I was halfway home, landing on the roof. He must have seen my beacon's path and recognized a deviation from our plan. At the first stop, he dropped down to stand below my window, his neck stretched high to talk to me.

"Where are we going?" he asked.

Mindful of the curious passengers listening raptly and leaning out the window to stare at Oliver, I said only, "Amelia."

Oliver's eyes widened, and his head whipped in the direction of our house, still a ten-minute ride away.

"I forgot," he whispered.

"Me too."

Oliver resumed his perch on the roof, and given the pleased exclamation of the driver, must have opened his boost to the woman. Not that it did any good. An airbus could crawl only so fast through streets clogged with horse-drawn and air-propelled carts. By the time my stop arrived, my stomach was in knots.

I burst from the airbus and sprinted down the sidewalk, my bag bouncing bruises into my back. I couldn't see the Victorian from here, but I could count the gargoyle beacons clustered at its location: only three. Quinn would be with Kylie, hopefully chasing down a solid lead. That meant the beacons either belonged to Lydia, Anya, and Herbert, or one of my gargoyles had flown elsewhere and the third was Greta, Amelia's gargoyle friend.

Please let Anya or Lydia be out exploring. It was possible. Herbert rarely left home, but his siblings often ventured into the city.

Oliver soared from the airbus and landed in the street, then veered toward me once he folded his wings. I gave him a tight smile and hugged the inside of the sidewalk to give him room. I didn't have the spare breath to ask why he was loping beside me when flying would be easier. I suspected I knew the answer: He was showing his solidarity. We would arrive together and face the consequences together, too.

Please let Amelia Vanderlei be a rare magnanimous full spectrum.

My initial burst of speed slowed to a jog, varying degrees of pain radiating from my thighs, back, shoulders, and feet. Somewhere in the last hour, the boost of Eilidh's pizazzy pastries had worn off, and my legs felt twice as heavy as normal. My breaths rasped loud enough to be audible over the clatter of Oliver's quartz paws. By the time I staggered up to the Victorian, sweat dripped down my temples and plastered my shirt to my sides. I cringed to think how I must smell.

Ms. Zuberrie stood at the top of the porch stairs. Her pale hair was coiled in a loose bun, soft strands framing her scowl. Silver buttons marched up the front of her lavender-and-gray linen dress. More dotted the cuffs. A wide belt cinched her waist, with spells scrolled along its length. It was the kind of dress a woman wore to an upscale function, not around the house. Even for Ms. Zuberrie, who typically dressed one step fancier than necessary, this was too much.

Or maybe it was exactly the sort of outfit a person wore when one of the wealthiest women in the city made an early-morning house call.

I glanced down at my grubby pants and sweat-stained shirt. A cleansing spell would help, but it wouldn't transform my work attire into something classy. Self-consciously, my hand went to my hair. My ponytail hung limp, and I didn't need a mirror to know the escaped strands resembled the frizz it was, not an intentional stylistic effect.

I stopped at the base of the stairs, bracing my hands on my knees to catch my breath. Gathering the elements, I prepped the strongest cleansing spell I knew.

"Don't bother," Ms. Zuberrie said. "Ms. Vanderlei left a half hour ago."

I straightened and crimped a hand around the stitch in my side. A glance at the roof where Lydia, Anya, and Herbert leaned over the edge confirmed my landlady's statement. I had well and truly messed this up.

"Maybe you should be thankful Ms. Vanderlei isn't here." Ms. Zuberrie's cool blue eyes scanned me, her mouth pinched. "You look like you spent the morning mucking a cerberi kennel. Mika, you're not a mere artisan anymore. You're a healer, and your duties require you to work with people in a different social tier. A higher one. You need to rise to meet them, or they will never respect you."

Shame heated my cheeks. "I know," I mumbled.

"I've been lenient, letting you conduct your affairs out of my *home*. But I am not your secretary or in your employ. You need to respect my time and my house."

"Of course. I'm sorry. It won't happen again."

Hardly waiting for me to finish my apology, Ms. Zuberrie whisked into the house. The screen door slapped against the frame with extra force. I flinched and let out a pent-up breath.

"She looked really mad," Oliver whispered.

"She has every reason to be."

I slumped up the stairs, the weight of all my failings dragging on me. A string of self-recriminations blinded me to my surroundings, and I was nearly to the top step when I spotted Marcus. He sat in a porch chair, where he had watched the whole embarrassing confrontation in silence.

8

"What are you doing—" I started, then wished I could take the words back when Marcus stiffened. Our postponed date. Another commitment I had completely forgotten about.

"Marcus, I'm sorry. I should have sent a message." My emotions pinged from humiliation with an extra helping of guilt to defensive as he took in my bedraggled appearance. I climbed the last step and crossed my arms over my chest. I could read his disapproval clearly: He was disappointed to find me out, not home. Not *resting*.

"Another gargoyle was sick this morning. He fell and broke nearly every limb in his body."

Oliver slumped up the stairs behind me, greeting Marcus with a subdued, "Hello."

Marcus's gaze finally shifted off me. I almost sagged against the porch railing, but I didn't want to give him an excuse to scold me about not taking care of myself. I was doing the best I could, damn it, even if it didn't look like it this morning.

Marcus said hi to Oliver, then stood and walked toward me, stopping halfway. "Want to tell me about it?"

One question, and my defenses melted. I stumbled to Marcus and wrapped my arms around him. He was solid and warm and smelled so much better than I did. Just when my self-consciousness flared to life, reminding me I shouldn't get sweat all over my boyfriend, Marcus's arms slid around me. I snuggled into his embrace, nuzzling my nose against his throat.

Marcus took a deep breath, and I mirrored him. He smelled like sun and man and safety. I took another deep breath. My bag pulled on my shoulders and my feet hummed with distant pain. The need to sleep stalked behind my eyes like a physical creature, waiting to pounce. But none of it could compete with the contented serenity of being held by Marcus. Our breathing synced. His heart pounded beneath my ear, steady and reassuring, and mine gradually slowed to match.

"Here, let me take this." Marcus eased the burden of my bag with a cup of air.

I sighed and unwound my arms from him so I could slide them free of the straps.

"Are you hurt anywhere?" he asked.

I shook my head. I could list my body's complaints from head to toe, but none qualified as an injury. Just overused muscles and a need to get in better shape.

"This morning was rough," I said, hobbling to a chair. My voice scratched my dry throat, and I swallowed hard.

"Wait."

Marcus disappeared inside, returning with two tall glasses of water. I accepted one gratefully and downed it. Marcus placed the other one on the table near my elbow, then chose the seat closest to me. Oliver assumed a position between us and leaned into Marcus. Apparently we both needed his emotional support this morning.

"Here." Marcus handed me a cloth sack that had been sitting beside his chair.

Delicious aromas of cinnamon and sugar wafted from the bag. I peeked inside at a cinnamon roll bigger than my hand nestled in a warming spell. Inhaling deeply, I closed my eyes. My stomach growled. In my rush to leave this morning, I hadn't grabbed food or money. After healing Nimoy, I hadn't wanted to waste time returning home for either, relying on the pizzazzies to get me through until lunch.

If only I had listened to my stomach.

"You must be starving," I said, trying to gauge how long Marcus had been waiting for me. I pulled the cinnamon roll out and started to split it in half.

"I've eaten."

"Oh. I'm sor—"

"Don't apologize again. Please."

I peeked at Marcus through my lashes, unable to decipher his tone. He looked so rigid.

"Thank you. For breakfast. I should have—"

"Mika."

"I—" I wanted to tell him I had been looking forward to eating breakfast together, but it would be true only in the abstract: I always looked forward to seeing Marcus, but I also hadn't thought about him once this morning. If he hadn't waited for me, how long would it have taken me to remember yesterday's plans?

Eyes downcast, I peeled off the outer rim of the cinnamon roll and stuffed it into my mouth. "Thank you," I mumbled around the delicious treat.

"Just tell me what happened."

Between bites, I described our alarmed wake-up, the theft at the Wandering Crane General Store and Nimoy's terrible condition, and finally Captain Rojas's theory of a spirit-shifting culprit. By the time I finished, Marcus's scowl should have bored straight through the porch floorboards. When his eyes finally lifted, his gaze lingered on my face, and not in a flattering way.

"I know what you're thinking," I said, licking the last of the frosting off my fingertips. "I need rest. But this is an emergency; it's vital that Oliver and I warn every Terra Haven gargoyle about the thief."

"Even at the expense of your own health?" Marcus asked.

My molars clenched, and I forced myself to take a slow breath. "I can't stop being a guardian just because I'm tired. You heard Ms. Zuberrie. I have responsibilities, and I need to work harder to meet them."

"Or you're taking on too much."

Who else is going to do it? I wanted to ask. Who else is going to heal gargoyles who have injured spirits? Who else is going to look out for them?

I pinched my lips together, not letting the words escape. Marcus wanted me to be safe, healthy, and happy—in that order. I wanted to be a gargoyle guardian worthy of the title. The gargoyles needed me. If that meant pushing myself, so be it.

"Do you know who might be behind the thefts?" Oliver asked after the silence stretched uncomfortably long.

Marcus dragged his hand down his face. "I don't know anything about this investigation, other than what you've told me."

"You haven't heard anything? Seen anything like this before?" I asked.

"Nonhazardous thefts are a guard-level issue, not something the FPD gets involved in. Terra Haven guards are smart. They'll find the thief. Let them do their jobs."

"I'm not standing in their way. I'm focused on the affected gargoyles. We hoped you could help us with your FPD experience and knowledge." A flush of color rushed up Marcus's neck, and I hurried on before he could speak. "Spirit shifting is hard, right? The thief shifted his spirit two nights in a row—that we know about. Maybe more. Signature swapping, or spirit shifting, is an unusual skill. Maybe you know something the guards don't."

Marcus stopped petting Oliver, and his tone, when he spoke, simmered with suppressed emotion. "Spirit shifting is not a 'skill.' It's an idiot's tool. Few are stupid enough to attempt it. If they do, they never try it twice, because it's so obviously dangerous." His voice lowered, and his eyes searched mine as if he were trying to see inside my skull. "You know this. You know how much it takes out of you, because you've done it. More than once."

I glanced away, afraid of what he would see in my expression. Marcus wasn't referring to my recent spirit-deep healing of Lowell and Nimoy. I hadn't told him about that part. He was talking about the comatose gargoyles I helped inside the baetyl. That was different, though. I knew my limits now.

"I've never done anything like this. *This* type of spirit shifting is harmful," I said.

Marcus blew out a breath. "There are no 'types' of spirit shifting. It's not like a spell. It's either done or not done."

I shook my head. I didn't have the energy for this argument, but Marcus was wrong. What I did to heal gargoyles didn't change the shape or texture of my spirit. When I shifted my spirit, it had a safe place to land, whole, inside a gargoyle.

"How many times can the thief shift his spirit before it harms him?" I asked, hitting the pronouns hard to emphasize we weren't talking about me.

"I don't know. Probably several more times. But the guards should catch him soon," Marcus said, engulfing my knee with his hand and giving me a reassuring squeeze. "They're trained to catch lawbreakers."

"But not to heal gargoyles hurt in the meantime."

"Mika . . ." Marcus swallowed whatever he planned to say when Oliver and I lifted our heads in unison to check the sky. The gargoyle beacon flying leisurely in our direction veered toward the house. A glint of citrine-gold confirmed the specific gargoyle.

"It's Quinn," Oliver said.

"Good. Kylie won't be far behind."

Marcus grumbled something under his breath that sounded a lot like *nosy reporter* and *death wish*. I patted his hand. I wasn't sure if I was warning him or reassuring him. A bit of both. Kylie was my best friend. She was brave, impulsive, and curious—all traits that made her an excellent reporter *and* a magnet for trouble. The first, Marcus could overlook, if grudgingly. The second was the problem. Marcus hadn't forgiven Kylie for being the reason a dangerous predator attacked our home, even though it hadn't been her fault. Pointing out I hadn't been hurt hadn't helped. I trusted he would come to see all the good in Kylie that I did. He just needed time.

Quinn landed at the base of the walkway and waited for Kylie before they climbed the stairs together. The porch boards groaned under the large quartz lion's paws, but they held, thanks to recent carpentry upgrades and reinforcing wood spells. Somehow, despite being up as long as me, Kylie still had a bounce in her step. Her clothes were clean. Her white-blond hair was woven into a neat braid. Ms. Zuberrie would find no fault with her appearance, and neither would a full spectrum like Amelia Vanderlei.

A stab of envy made me shift in my chair. I wasn't jealous of my friend, just of her spell repertoire. And her energy.

"What happened?" Kylie asked. Her footsteps slowed when she spotted Marcus, her gaze zipping between him, me, and Oliver. "You're here earlier than I expected. Is everyone all right? Grant? And you both?"

"I'm fine. We're fine. Grant is fine."

I quirked an eyebrow at Marcus for confirmation. Grant Monaghan was his FPD squad captain and a powerful air elemental. Personally, I thought it would take an aerie of wyverns to put a scratch on Grant, but he was Kylie's fiancé, and I understood her worries.

"Grant is fine," Marcus said.

"I missed my appointment with Amelia," I said.

"Oh no!"

"But Marcus came by for breakfast," I rushed to add before Kylie could commiserate. Anything she said, no matter how kind, would only make me feel worse. "He brought me a cinnamon roll from Dragon's Hearth Bakery. The very best." I gave Marcus a smile, trying to convey an apology he didn't want to hear with my gratitude. The roll hadn't given me the energy rush of Eilidh's pastries, but it had been delicious and filling.

"Since you're here earlier than expected, does that mean you learned something useful at the *Chronicle*?" I asked.

Kylie smiled and dropped into a chair across from Marcus and me. Quinn sat next to her.

"I read through every article regarding thefts in the last three months," she said. "Then I made a list of every burgled location and what was taken, and I noted each—in order of theft—on a map."

I could have hugged Kylie. She just saved me hours of research, and I had no doubt that her findings would be more thorough than mine. Kylie was a natural-born researcher, with an uncanny eye for the details that would make an article sing. Or in this case, that might lead us to the culprit.

"I'm sure the guards have already made lists, maps, and plans to capture the thief," Marcus said.

"I hope so," Kylie agreed easily. "But I don't have any guards working for me. Though it's not for lack of trying. At least Cham— Ah, at least my informant came through for us last night, or Mika might not have known Nimoy was hurt and needed her."

"Chaim? Who is Chaim? Is that a guard?" Marcus rocked forward on his chair, as if he were contemplating grabbing Kylie and giving her a shake. "Which house does he work at?"

Kylie met my boyfriend's demands with a faint raise of her eyebrows. "I think we should focus on the thefts."

"So you have the name of the criminal?" Marcus asked, his demeanor shifting suspiciously fast.

Kylie frowned. "No."

"A description?"

"No."

"His whereabouts?"

"Not yet."

"Then everything else you have to say can wait until Mika gets some rest."

I bristled. I wasn't a child to be sent to her room when an adult decided she needed a nap.

"I want to hear what Kylie has to say."

Marcus's expression turned stony. I pretended not to notice.

"Yes. Well." Kylie ducked her head, avoiding both of our gazes as she retrieved her notebook from her bag and unfolded a map of Terra Haven. The map was the size of a newssheet, and the paper was a similar rough quality. Familiar lines defined major roadways and large buildings, though neighborhoods like ours were roughly sketched and incomplete. A series of circled numbers dotted the map, drawn in Kylie's neat handwriting.

"That's a lot more burglaries than I realized," I said, overwhelmed.

"They might not all be connected to the same thief. Here." Kylie spread the map on the porch between us, and Oliver and Quinn anchored the edges. I studied the numbers. They were scattered across the whole city.

"I don't see a pattern. Do you?" I directed the question at Marcus and received a grunt in response.

"I didn't see a pattern at first, either. But look. The thief is getting bolder." Kylie consulted her notebook, laying it open next to the map for us to view, too. Three columns of information scrawled down the page, one with dates in descending order, the next with names of businesses, and the last detailing a shocking number of stolen items and money.

"See? The first six don't really fit, but then a pattern emerges. These four are all small businesses. None have more than two workers and limited nighttime security. It's despicable to think about it this way, but if you're trying to steal without getting caught, these shops are good places to start. Though the thief didn't make off with much. So he moved on to bigger businesses. Places that tend to have larger profits, though that backfired on him at the Fletcher's Mark and at Tinker's Traded Trinkets. Both are struggling financially. Actually, they're my next stops after I grab a bite. I'm hoping a bit of press will help them, otherwise, having all their on-hand cash stolen might be enough to put them out of business."

"That's terrible, but I don't think that's what the thief intended." I hated to be so cynical about someone losing their livelihood, but I had to focus on relevant details. "What do we know that will help predict where the thief will strike next?"

"Right." Kylie pointed at me enthusiastically. "We need to know his motive."

Marcus sat back in his chair and crossed his arms. "His motive is clear: money. Cash or what can be sold easily."

"That's why we need to examine the smaller items taken." Kylie leaned over her map and notebook, missing or oblivious to the glare Marcus directed toward her scalp. "Aunt Clara's Wardrobe Whirls from the Spiro-Pias' general store tonight. Feverfew and lavender from the Blue Lotus. An embroidered coin pouch and tins of crystallized ginger wafers from Silverleaf Sundries. And a pound or so of Gruyère taken from Von Bergen Crèmerie."

"Those items are all commonplace," I said. "Some aren't even expensive."

"Exactly. They speak to the thief's personality. What type of person grabs these particular items after stealing the store's cash? Who stops to filch ginger wafers after they pocket"—Kylie consulted her notebook—"the store's entire case of dragon-scale brooches and two complete chess sets of basilisk-petrified beetles?"

"Ew," Oliver said.

Kylie chuckled. "It sounds gross, but collecting the beetles in basilisk territories is dangerous, and that makes them one of the most expensive burgled items on the list."

"So if we assume all the pricey items were taken for their resell value, everything left means . . ." I scanned the list. "We're looking for someone with clean clothes, who smells like lavender and likes to eat ginger and cheese?"

"That could describe either of you, or Ms. Zuberrie," Marcus said.

"Well, I wouldn't eat ginger and cheese *together*." Kylie gave Marcus a smile that didn't reach her eyes. "Let's consider gargoyles, though. Lowell's location, or the Blue Lotus, was the fourteenth robbery but probably only the eighth or ninth target of this thief, at least the way I'm reading the trends. Before the Blue Lotus, did any burgled place have a gargoyle nearby?"

"Oh!" I should have thought of that immediately.

Oliver and I bent closer to the map. If I had been more alert, it would have been easier to concentrate. While I labored over pulling up a mental image of the first location, then identifying nearby gargoyles, Oliver raced ahead.

"Nettie might be within boost range of number eight, but she prefers enhancing people in the square, not in the businesses. And Bernard is picky. He's here." Oliver pointed a claw toward the number six location. "He doesn't boost outside his family."

"So the thief wouldn't have encountered a gargoyle until the Blue Lotus," Kylie said, waiting for Oliver's nod before continuing. "I think that was intentional. He started small, and he's been escalating every time he doesn't get caught—taking more, robbing more public places, and then finally striking a place where a gargoyle resides."

"All thieves take more risks the longer they escape being caught," Marcus said. "The guards know this. It's all part of their plan to catch this guy."

"What plan?" Kylie asked.

"I don't know. I'm not a guard. But I know they're not sitting around waiting for a journalist and her friend to tell them how to do their jobs. In fact, I guarantee they would react quite poorly to that."

Kylie lifted her chin. "But did the guards notice that tonight's theft didn't fit the pattern?"

"In what way?" I asked, skimming the list of items stolen from the Spiro-Pias once again. The mixture of expensive and ordinary items taken seemed similar to the other thefts to me.

"The Wandering Crane is a profitable general store but relatively small. It was never going to have as much money as, say, a general store closer to the Copper District. But what it did have was a gargoyle. I think the thief realized how useful it was to have a gargoyle's boost when he burgled the Blue Lotus, and he intentionally sought one out tonight."

"He targeted Nimoy?" Anger sharpened my words. Oliver's tail lashed across the porch boards, then stilled. I reached for him, soothing a hand down his wing.

"Not necessarily Nimoy. The thief just needed *a* gargoyle." Kylie looked like she wanted to give me a hug, but it didn't stop her from finishing her point. "Working with a gargoyle's boost always makes spells easier. Faster. The thief could target a business with the owners literally upstairs, and get away. He found an advantage when he used Lowell, and he exploited it last night."

My pulse throbbed in my temples. This wasn't the first time someone cruel and selfish had abused a gargoyle.

Sadly, it wouldn't be the last. Too many horrid people cate-
gorized gargoyles as tools, things to be used for their
magical enhancement and discarded, not as the kind, intel-
ligent individuals they were. It was the reason I worked so
tirelessly. The gargoyles deserved a champion to protect
them from the dregs of the human species.

"But . . . knowledge is power." Kylie tapped her notebook. "With this, we can predict where the thief will strike
next. In fact, I think your see—"

"No, you can't," Marcus cut in with a growl of frustration.
"If writing a list and figuring out that the thief wants *money*
were enough, the guards would have caught the bastard
already. Kylie, look at Mika. She's spreading herself too thin
as it is, and you're prodding her with false hope. You don't
have a strategy. You have busywork. Because that's what
attempting to anticipate the actions of a madman will be: a
waste of time. And Mika will do it, because it might, *might*
help a gargoyle. Just . . ." Marcus dropped his hands, and
they hit his thighs with a clap. "Just let Mika rest."

By the time Marcus finished, Kylie had wilted into her
chair, her blue eyes pools of hurt.

"So we should do nothing?" I said, rounding on Marcus.
I held on to Oliver when the chair felt as if it were tipping
out from under me. Sitting—stopping moving—had been a
mistake. It had given me time to realize how tired I was, but
I wasn't about to let it show, not after Marcus's tirade. "That's
all you want me to do, right? Just sit up in my room and *rest*.
At least Kylie is helping me."

"I'm sure she thinks she is. That's the problem. But the
guards have this under control. They have actual training in
apprehending thieves and real information to guide their
investigation." *Unlike you.*

Marcus left the last unspoken, but he might as well have

shouted the words. He stood, hands stiff at his sides. After a moment's hesitation, he leaned to brush a kiss across my cheek. Oliver got a fond pet, but he didn't take his eyes off me. "I have to go, Mika. My squad is waiting. Try to . . ." He shook his head. "Take care of Oliver."

He didn't give me a chance to respond. In two quick strides, he crossed the porch, then clattered down the stairs. I didn't call out after him. I was done with this argument. It was almost a relief to watch him walk away. Almost.

"Maybe he's right," Kylie said. She carefully folded up her map and closed her notebook. "This morning was rough. I saw how much healing Nimoy took out of you—"

"What were you going to say about my seed?" I interrupted.

Kylie's eyes flew to meet mine. I heard my tone of voice, and it wasn't kind, but I couldn't bring myself to apologize. I was fully capable of judging my own stamina. What I didn't need was another person pointing out my weaknesses.

Whatever she read in my gaze made Kylie straighten her spine and unfold the map again. She flipped to a new page in her notebook, revealing one additional entry.

"Number sixteen. It's the League of Tradeswomen. They were burgled early this morning. I didn't find out until I reached the *Chronicle*, but I'm certain that was the news that irritating guard shared with Captain Rojas."

That had been hours ago. I peered at the map. The tradeswomen operated in a part of town I hadn't yet visited.

"Are there any hurt gargoyles?" If there were, Captain Rojas should have sent for me. Immediately. "Wait, didn't Haubner mention a fire?"

"Exactly. It didn't fit the pattern. There was a theft, but the thief set the building on fire to make his escape. That's why I didn't lead with this. But your seed might be pointing to the LTs, so . . ."

"I need to go there sooner rather than later," I finished.

"Carmen lives there," Oliver said.

"Where? At the league's building?"

"Yes."

"Carmen is a gargoyle?" Kylie asked.

Oliver nodded.

I shoved to my feet. Finally my seed and the thief's actions overlapped. Maybe this time the seed's lackluster clue would be useful.

"Let's go."

9

O liver and I had to run to catch the next airbus. It wasn't until I was panting in my seat that I remembered to check my everlasting seed. I slumped toward the window. The half-formed flower-propeller and rough circle no longer protruded from the milky quartz. The stone disc had absorbed them, flattening their shapes into crystalline fractures in the stone's surface. Remnants of the original three overlapping rings, now disjointed geometric curves, hugged the edge of the disc, pushed outward by the flower.

A new shape bulged from the center of the seed, frustratingly indistinct. Again. When had it changed? Before or after I healed Nimoy? When the thief set the fire? Or had it changed after I decided to check on Carmen? I should have looked earlier. I was floundering, and the clues were disappearing faster than I could figure them out. I was failing: failing the test set by the everlasting tree. Failing the gargoyles who needed me to be smarter than the spirit-shifting thief.

Failing as a guardian.

Pushing the bleak thoughts down, I twisted the seed toward the sun. A thumbprint-sized spiral partially protruded from the center of the disc. Five tiny bulges dotted the spiral's outer edge. If the bumps had been closer together, the relief would resemble a paw print. I ran my finger across the disc. Maybe some protrusions were missing and the whole spiral should be ringed with bumps.

"Maybe the bumps mean nothing," I muttered.

My knuckles whitened, my grip tight with leashed frustration. This incomplete form could represent a location on a topographical map, the shape of a spell I was supposed to master, or the markings on an animal I needed to find. Or none of the above.

I thought getting an everlasting tree seed would keep me one step ahead of gargoyle problems, not leave me chasing after them. I could chase problems without a seed.

Shoving the useless disc back into my pocket, I tried to silence my doubts, utterly failing. Was something preventing my seed from completing its natural evolution? Was I the reason every clue was unfinished? Was I doing something wrong?

The stop-and-go trek across the city lasted an eternity, giving me plenty of time to wallow in my misery. Finally, I disembarked near the Polished Bit, one of the city's larger horse stables. A steady flow of equine traffic bustled through the open wrought-iron gates, and a chaotic array of carriages, horses, and handlers filled the stables' deep courtyard. Amid the clangor of farriers' hammers and the clatter of hooves and wooden wheels, Oliver's leap from the airbus to the cobblestones was barely audible.

Rather than shout, I gestured toward a coach pulled by four dappled-gray geldings, and we jogged in its wake until we could cut up a side street away from the hubbub. The fragrant aroma of horse and hay lingered, gradually over-powered by the acrid scent of smoke.

I navigated by gargoyle beacon rather than stopping to ask directions, but I could just as easily have followed the crowds. A buzz of speculation about the fire ran through every conversation around me, and half the city's residents suddenly had a pressing errand that required going past the League of Tradeswomen's building.

"Do we go around or push through?" Oliver asked, eyeing the crush of people on the sidewalk and the confu-sion of wagons and carts clogging the street. Even people on nimble flying carpets weren't moving faster than those of us on foot.

"Every nearby street probably looks like this. I'll squeeze through. You fly ahead and make sure Carmen is all right."

Oliver retreated to the intersection, where he could open his wings without hurting anyone. He launched with a tremendous jump and a clatter of quartz feathers, lifting himself vertical in an impressive maneuver that startled horses and humans alike and set a team of cerberi howling. I clapped my hands to my ears as the three-headed dogs' deep baying echoed and redoubled against the brick build-ings to either side.

Tracking Oliver's beacon as he sailed over the rooftops and out of sight, I fought my way forward through an increasingly sweltering and fragrant mass of people and animals. Oliver dropped down next to Carmen, close enough that their beacons overlapped, which meant she, at least, wasn't stuck in the midst of a mob. It took another ten minutes before I squeezed through the bottleneck at the intersection. Fresh air hit my face, cooling my sweat-matted scalp. I almost stopped to take in the corralled chaos of the wide boulevard, but the stomp of hooves at my back and the irritated curses peppering the air propelled me forward.

Traffic crawled to the left, funneled down a narrow lane partitioned along one side of the boulevard by a series of shouting guards and judiciously placed wards. Beyond them, it looked as if a palace had vomited its contents onto the road, sidewalk, and water-logged lawn. Humans and minotaurs swarmed among the displaced finery like bees in search of a missing queen. Spells flashed and messages pinged in every direction. A stately two-story pink granite building towered in the background, seemingly forgotten in the hubbub. Soot blackened the fascia above its gaping front doors, and matching ugly smudges flared above shattered windows on the second floor. Despite the clear blue sky, water ran in gray rivulets down the granite walls—a silent testament to the spells used earlier to extinguish the fire. A controlled cyclone of air and water element funneled the residual smoke out through the roof, presumably through a *hole* in the roof.

Like most people stumbling along the boulevard, I gaped at the building, but not because of the fire damage. I couldn't take my eyes off the high relief carving above the front doors. It was an exact replica of my everlasting seed's previous shape. Well, *exact* if my seed's shape had been more pronounced. Five stone petals of a flower—a forget-me-not or a cinquefoil—flared inside a ring of text: *Terra Haven League of Tradeswomen.*

This was where my seed had been pointing me. Toward Carmen? If so, why had it changed before I met her?

I dodged around a mule laden with packs and got my first clear sight of Oliver. He sat halfway down the street next to a large silvery gargoyle. Oliver appeared calm, with his scarlet wings folded and his head tilted down, but he shot an anxious glance over his shoulder at me. I quickened my steps, cutting between wards and veering across the street toward my friend. Miraculously, the guards let me pass—either because I was female, as were the majority of humans and minotaurs on this side of the barricade, or because I moved with the same intensity of purpose as those cleaning up after the fire.

Up close, it was easier to spot order among the mare's nest of furniture and carts and trampled shrubbery. A cluster of women gathered around a high table with singed legs, drafting a letter on creamy stationery. Closer to the road, on the outskirts of the disarray, others oversaw an impromptu breakfast station, complete with sandwiches, pastries, tea, and coffee for weary volunteers. Most women, though, performed heavy labor. With muscles and magic, they sorted and organized oak tables and chairs, mahogany desks, brass lamps and crystal chandeliers, soot-stained paintings, and other fine goods into orderly piles along the sidewalk. Elemental specialists walked among the items, directing some toward waiting carts and personally applying their restorative skills to others.

Then I got my first good look at Carmen, and surprise blotted out everything else. Her beacon was the same as every other gargoyle's in size and shape, but Carmen herself was not: She was a kraken.

Iris agate dotted the smoky quartz of her conical squid body and triangular fins, and the suckers on her arms and tentacles were glass smooth, but she was a sea monster—in miniature. Carmen couldn't have been longer than ten feet from the top of her mantle to the tips of her arms—tiny for a kraken but enormous for a gargoyle. Her shape should have looked top heavy and cumbersome on land, but the shimmery clear-quartz wings flaring from her mantle gave her an ethereal grace. The membranes weren't feathered; instead they were textured more like fish fins. If gargoyle flight relied on muscles, those gossamer-thin appendages wouldn't have been good for more than a gentle breeze, but I suspected Carmen flew as well as any other gargoyle when she felt well. Right now, she clung to a lamppost with three arms, her body swaying as if she were aboard a ship at sea. A familiar daze clouded her eyes.

A middle-aged woman with a halo of frizzy auburn curls stood beside Carmen, a freckled hand resting on the gargoyle's mantle. Soot stained her loose overalls and plain pink blouse.

"Are you Ms. Stillwater?" she asked.

"One moment, please." I stepped over Carmen's splayed arms and knelt close to her body, setting my bag beside me. "Carmen, I'm Guardian Mika. I'm here to help."

"Young Oliver was just telling me about you," Carmen said. Her mouth faced the ground, but she used her grip on the lamppost to cant her body so the sidewalk gave her melodious voice a sonorous quality.

The clarity of her words surprised me, and I reassessed her eyes. They were large and flat, vaguely fishlike, and their iridescent irises bounced slightly when she focused on me.

"Are you dizzy?"

"Not as much as earlier. When the fire started, I crawled down the building rather than risk flying."

"You were afraid you would crash?"

Her free arms performed a coordinated wave that resembled a shrug. "I'm big, but I was afraid the ladies wouldn't see me in all the confusion, and I would accidentally hurt them."

Of course Carmen had thought of others' well-being before her own; she was a gargoyle.

"May I heal you?"

"I would be honored."

I gathered a gargoyle-tuned balance of elements and added tweaks of smoky and iris quartz to the mix. The redhead leaned closer to watch as I eased the elements into Carmen.

A subtle ache resonated through my magic, but nothing like Nimoy's pain. All of Carmen's injuries were minor. Her body, however, was vast. I was still questing magic along her mantle, learning her shape, when the first wave of disharmony assaulted me. The jagged pulse was mild, but it bombarded me from nine different directions. Disoriented, half lost in the varied pathways of Carmen's multitude of arms and tentacles, I struggled to maintain elemental cohesion. The next disjointed energy wave split and split again, spinning me. Its reverberations blindsided me, stretching my magic. I fumbled for control, pouring more magic—more of myself—into Carmen.

The baetyl swelled toward the surface of my consciousness, omnipresent and incomprehensible. Its siren call hummed at the edge of my awareness, inviting me to remember it fully—and to allow myself to be consumed.

I had anticipated this sensation. I thought being prepared would make me immune to the baetyl's innate ability to enthrall, but I grossly underestimated the baetyl's allure.

My momentum stalled. The baetyl's song intensified. I hummed the notes with it, gratefully stretching magic along its familiar pathways. Down and deeper. All I needed to do was surrender—

"Mika." Cool quartz breath puffed against my face.

The baetyl's song unraveled into a hundred different sounds—my heart pounding against my eardrums, the harsh rasp of my breath, Carmen's surprised murmur and the clatter of her arms against the metal post, Oliver's long exhale. Even the redhead's gawking presence contained the baetyl's music.

Oliver loomed in my vision. Behind him, the burned roof of the tradeswomen's building spun in a stuttering circle, then dipped in the opposite direction. I slammed my eyelids shut.

Regrouping my magic, I sank back into the gargoyle, keeping my elemental touch delicate but strong. Discordant vibrations assaulted me. I soothed what I could but pushed deeper before the dizzy energy entangled me. The baetyl's power progressed ahead of me, a shadow I couldn't quite catch, a shape I couldn't fully make out. Chasing it, I tumbled into the golden cocoon at the core of Carmen. The kraken gargoyle floated in the warm light, a fine quiver blurring the outline of her spirit.

As I had with Nimoy and Lowell, I soothed Carmen with my spirit, petting baetyl-tuned magic from her triangle-finned mantle to the tips of her long tentacles. Gradually, Carmen stabilized.

Pivoting in this vast, impossible place, she faced me. Large round eyes studied me. Carmen's squid face was too foreign for me to read, but I felt no fear when she curled a tentacle around my shoulder, stroking a shorter arm down my cheek. I had no body and neither did she, but it didn't matter. I could feel the soft polished-quartz texture of each sucker on her arm and the comforting weight of the tentacle hugging me. Her finlike wings undulated serenely. Gratitude filled me, the emotion rising from outside myself and pouring inward. Then Carmen braced all eight arms against my chest and shoved.

I soared, weightless. *Like a gargoyle in flight.* Then I fell. Fear and denial burst through me. I wanted to fly—

I collided with my own body. Air filled my lungs, the relief in my chest as profound as if I had surfaced after being underwater too long. Muzzily, I blinked at the sky. Thin white clouds drifted across an expanse of blue . . . that should have been gold?

"Mika." Oliver pushed his muzzle into my view. He was upside down and too close to focus on.

"Oliver, did you hear it?"

Worry scrunched his face. "What took so long?"

I shook my head. Healing Carmen hadn't taken much time at all.

Ribbed carnelian feathers brushed my cheek. More stretched beneath my palm. With a start, I sat up. My ankle twinged as I straightened it, painful tingles igniting across the top of my foot and spreading toward my toes. At some point, I had tipped backward, and Oliver had caught me with his wing.

I shivered. I hadn't felt myself collapse. I hadn't sensed the impact of my back or head against Oliver's cupped wing. I hadn't felt my body at all.

"Thank you, Oliver."

Carmen flexed her arms, slithering them along either side of my legs. She peered at me with one clear iridescent eye. "A true guardian. I never thought I would live to see one."

"I couldn't quite tell what you did there, but Carmen looks much better," the redhead said. She beamed at Carmen, then me. Leaning forward, she extended a hand. "Hi, I'm Deidre Brehany, lead craftswoman and design artisan of Ivory Blossom Porcelain Studio. Or just Deidre. Siphiwe says we should always introduce ourselves like that, but it seems silly with the LT building in shambles and us on the street and me looking like this."

Her monologue gave me time to recover my equilibrium, and I belatedly shook her hand and introduced myself—including my title at Deidre's prompting. Her eyes lit up.

"A gargoyle guardian. How marvelous! Are you an LT?"

I shook my head, fishing a pair of seed crystals out of my bag. Oliver crowded close, as if he were afraid I would tip over again. I took comfort from his solid weight at my back, but I wished I hadn't worried him.

"What a terrible day to make a first impression. Tomorrow would have been better. It's the annual craft show. Or it was going to be."

Deidre's morose gaze swept down the sidewalk, where a surprising number of artistic glass, wood, clay, and stone pieces lay atop soggy rugs on the sidewalk, fretted over by women in varying degrees of finery. Deidre's frown lingered on a precarious pile of ceramics protected by a domed ward. Even from a distance, I could see the fine craftsmanship in the eclectic mix of flutes, writing boxes, jars, and teapots.

"The arsonist couldn't have struck at a worse time," she said. "We had all the inventory on hand for the sale. So much got ruined."

"Or stolen?" Oliver asked. "We heard—"

When Oliver went stone stiff, I looked up. Following his line of sight, I spotted Captain Rojas conferring with two statuesque minotaurs. Guard Haubner stood behind the wiry captain, observing but not part of her conversation.

"There was a theft?" Deidre looked shocked. "Who would steal from us?"

Haubner spotted me. His spine jerked straight. He took a half step toward us, then stopped.

I glowered at the guard, then turned back to Carmen.

She was more important than engaging in a staring match with an idiot.

Without the distraction of fluctuating magic, it was easy to spot Carmen's injuries. Some were fresh, like the chipped-off sucker cups on several of her arms. Most wounds were old abrasions and scrapes that had been worn almost smooth but still radiated individual aches.

"May I?" I asked, reaching for Carmen's closest arm. She obligingly twisted the agile limb to expose the hurt bits.

While I grafted new quartz to her body, Oliver and I asked about last night, and Deidre knelt to listen in. Unfortunately, Carmen didn't have much to share. From her perch atop the roof, she hadn't seen anyone suspicious enter or exit the building. The tradeswomen kept odd hours, especially the week before the craft show. Carmen had been enhancing several familiar signatures when she noticed her dizziness. By then, the building was on fire and she had to flee.

"I couldn't boost anyone when they needed it most," she said mournfully. "I was too disoriented. All I could do was get to safety."

"You did the right thing," Deidre said, giving the gargoyle a hug.

"What time did you start feeling dizzy?" Oliver asked.

"I'm not certain. An hour before dawn, maybe."

"Was the fire what made you sick?" Deidre asked.

Carmen bobbed her mantle side to side. "It shouldn't have."

I shared a look with Oliver, but we had promised not to talk about the spirit-shifting thief with humans, so we kept our mouths shut.

Sealing the last of Carmen's wounds with a thin line of fresh quartz, I sat back and blotted sweat from my forehead.

While I had worked, so had the women and minotaurs bustling around the league's grounds. All the large pieces of salvaged furniture and office paraphernalia had been stowed on carts. Cleanup crews were being organized and the crowds were dispersing.

"Do you see Captain Rojas?" I asked. She needed to know Carmen had been sickened just like Nimoy and Lowell—proof that all three thefts had been committed by the same person.

"There." Oliver pointed.

The captain stood at the far end of the street, her hands on her hips as she listened to a group of women.

"This is incredible," Deidre said, admiring the clear quartz edging Carmen's long tentacle. "You really must talk with Siphiwe."

"It'll have to wait—" I cut myself off, realizing Deidre was already gone. Turning to Carmen, I said, "Please convey my apologies to Deidre. Maybe another . . ." I started to stand but fell back to my butt when my vision darkened and I lost track of my feet.

"Guardian?" Carmen's arms curled around my hips to support me, and Oliver's paw braced my upper back.

"I think . . ." I blinked black flecks from my vision. "I think I need some water." I retrieved a small jug from my bag, silently thanking Kylie for insisting I delay long enough for her to pack it for me. The water helped, but I wished for one—or five—of Eilidh's pastries.

A pair of guards roamed past, gesturing toward the burned building. Oliver watched them with narrowed eyes and a distinct sneer to his lips. I frowned.

"Oliver, what do you have against guards?"

"Nothing."

I placed the tip of my finger under Oliver's square jaw, and he let me turn his head until his eyes met mine.

"Nothing?"

It wasn't just Haubner who raised Oliver's hackles lately. My friend had never met the two guards walking by, but he looked like he was contemplating how they might taste. Yesterday, he had been ready to go to battle against the guard who barred us from the Blue Lotus. Even Captain Rojas got glares from my normally affable companion. I could dismiss Oliver's hostility toward Haubner, but not the others.

"They don't know what they're doing," Oliver finally said. "If they did, they would have found the person hurting gargoyles by now."

I sighed. "I wish it were that easy, but they're following clues just like us."

"Are they?" he asked with uncharacteristic petulance.

"Of course they are. You saw how much information Kylie put together in twenty-four hours. Marcus was right: The guards probably know a lot more. They're working in ways we don't—"

"I don't trust them," Oliver burst out.

I rocked back, surprised. "You don't?"

"I haven't since—" His wings slumped, his head dipping until he stared at my boots.

"Since?"

"Since Walter."

"Oh."

Walter had kidnapped Oliver and his siblings when they were mere cubs. Oliver had suffered immensely at the hands of that evil man. Quinn and Herbert had nearly died. I had forgotten Walter initially tricked Oliver and his siblings into trusting him by wearing a guard's uniform.

My heart hurt for Oliver. He had recovered physically, and his compassionate spirit testified to his mental resilience. I hadn't realized the dreadful experience continued to plague him, though I should have.

"Walter wasn't a guard," I said softly.

Oliver drooped further. "I know. But . . ."

"Not every person who puts on a guard's uniform is bad."

"I know that, too." Oliver peeked at me. "But what if every person who puts on a guard's uniform isn't good?"

"Like Haubner?"

"Exactly."

"What's so bad about this Haubner?" Carmen asked. "And who is Walter?"

Oliver explained both men, starting with Walter. Carmen hissed and writhed in commiserative fury, the metal lamppost to which she clung creaking alarmingly. With an eye on the glass lantern swaying above our heads, Oliver quickly moved on.

"A foolish man, indeed," Carmen proclaimed when Oliver recounted Haubner's accusations against Lowell and me, though she relaxed her arms around the lamppost. "But what he did was nothing like Walter, young Oliver. You cannot judge one as if he wears the other's skin."

Her wording was strange, but her sentiment was sound. Oliver, however, didn't agree.

"Lowell, Nimoy, and now you, Carmen, have all gotten sick from spirit-shifted magic," he said.

Carmen emitted a clack of surprise, but then she bobbed her head in agreement. She had felt my spirit against hers. She knew how I healed her, and she accepted Oliver's explanation of how her spirit had gotten out of balance.

"Every time a gargoyle has been spirit-shifted, Haubner has been involved," Oliver continued. "When Lowell was sick, Haubner chased him to our house, and then ran away before we could talk to him. The florist didn't notify the guards of the robbery until the morning. So how did Haubner know about Lowell hours earlier?"

"That's . . ." I ran through the timeline in my head. "That's a really good question. But he wasn't near Nimoy when he was sickened."

"Captain Rojas expected him to be, though. Remember? She asked why he was late."

"He was here. At the fire. That's my point. He might have been near Carmen, but he wasn't near Nimoy."

Oliver shifted, his claws scratching against the sidewalk. "Yes, but most of the guards here are wearing uniforms from house number eleven."

"That's the local guard house," Carmen said.

"What does the guard house number have to do with Haubner?" I asked.

"Haubner works out of guard house six. That's several districts away, closer to the center of the city." Oliver swept a paw to indicate the whole lot. "No other guard here is from that far away. So why would Haubner be way over here last night?"

Carmen clacked her beak. "Suspicious, suspicious."

"Maybe there's a reasonable explanation," I said.

Oliver glanced around to make sure no one was close enough to hear, then said, "The one explanation that fits is that Haubner is the thief."

I shook my head in a knee-jerk denial even as I ran through Oliver's logic. At the Blue Lotus, Haubner had been the one to check the locks. It was his word that proclaimed them untouched. Plus, he must have seen the recognition on

Oliver's face and mine when he walked in on us talking with Captain Rojas and Mo. We knew he had chased Lowell. He hadn't given us a chance to say anything, though. Instead, he redirected suspicion from himself by accusing Lowell of lying. And now Haubner was here, far outside of his patrol range, at the location of another sick gargoyle and another theft.

"How do you explain Nimoy?" I asked, then answered myself: "A flying carpet."

"Exactly. Haubner could have robbed the Wandering Crane." Oliver scratched a line into the sidewalk. "Then flown here." Another scratch produced a line two feet away from the first. "He had time to rob the league and set the fire, then rush back to meet up with Captain Rojas."

"Barely," I said, but I wasn't disagreeing with my friend, only trying to maintain objectivity. Haubner was prejudiced against gargoyles, which made him easy to distrust. I wanted to make sure we weren't allowing our emotions to pollute our logic. "What is his reason for breaking in to all these places?"

Oliver shrugged. "Money?"

"Humans have a peculiar obsession with possessions," Carmen said.

I couldn't refute that.

"Captain Rojas trusts Haubner." I left unspoken that my instincts told me to trust the captain.

"What if she's wrong?" Oliver asked.

The possibility sat like a granite boulder in my stomach.

10

W̶e needed proof. Splitting up made the most
sense. I could talk to Captain Rojas to learn
the exact time the fire started and what was
stolen. Meanwhile, Oliver could fly to Nimoy, pinpoint the
time the Spiro-Pias were robbed, and ask if Nimoy had seen
Haubner beforehand. Along the way, he could drop in on
Lowell and ask him about the suspicious guard, too. When
we reunited, we could compare timelines and either reinforce or debunk our theory about Haubner's guilt.

Oliver, however, didn't want to leave me alone when
Haubner was lurking among the tradeswomen.

"I won't be alone. Look at all these people."

Oliver's gaze roved over the diminishing crowd, his lips
compressed with unease. Ultimately, urgency won out. The
sooner we could identify the culprit, the safer it would be
for the city's gargoyles—and, selfishly, for me. Neither of us
mentioned my collapse while healing Carmen, but I knew
Oliver hadn't forgotten.

I tried to pretend otherwise, but healing Carmen had
scared me. So had healing Nimoy. When I restored their

shifted spirits, I got lost inside them. Each time, the baetyl came closer to overpowering me. I didn't know what would happen if I had to heal another gargoyle's shifted spirit.

The all-consuming nature of the baetyl wasn't inherently inimical. It wasn't benevolent, either. It was sentient magic with a monomaniacal compulsion to craft gargoyles according to its design. Or to restore them to the design the baetyl found pleasing.

Within the crystalline cave that housed the baetyl's vast power, it ruled like a god. If the merest wisp of its power remained in me, it would be more than enough to destroy me.

If I wasn't imagining things.

I wasn't the same woman who entered the baetyl, but I'd thought I surrendered all connection to the baetyl's power when I left.

Shaking off my doubts, I sank to a crouch in front of Oliver.

"Before you go, let me remove your bracelets."

He pranced back a step. The clear quartz chimed against the tops of his paws. "I should keep them."

I frowned. He wore extra quartz in case I needed more than I could carry. If I wasn't going with him, he didn't need the superfluous weight.

"I'll put it in my bag. I have room."

"But you're tired," he said.

"And you aren't?" Before he could argue further, I split the bracelets and straightened the raw quartz. Compared to the complex elemental weaves it took to heal a gargoyle, reshaping the inert quartz was effortless. I slid the clear bars into my bag, then stood and hoisted it to my shoulder. My bag felt twice as heavy as normal, but I was careful not to let the strain show. I didn't want Oliver to worry. Especially not because I *should* be stronger. After weeks of carting around pounds of seed crystals on daily treks around the city, my stamina should have increased. Instead, I was getting weaker.

I mentally scoffed at myself. I had healed two spirit-shifted gargoyles today—and after only a few hours' sleep. I wasn't getting weaker. I was just tired. So tired.

"After I check with the captain, I'll head home." By airbus, not foot. I wouldn't make it out of the district on my weary feet.

"I'll find you," Oliver promised.

I wouldn't be hard for him to locate me. Like me, Oliver could sense nearby gargoyles as beacons in his mind's eye. It was an innate ability all gargoyles possessed. Since I returned from the baetyl, every gargoyle could sense me in the same way, and Oliver claimed my beacon looked slightly different from a normal gargoyle's light. Even if it didn't, all Oliver would have to do is look for the one beacon traveling slow and close to the ground, and he would know it was me.

Oliver departed, pushing himself hard. I watched him disappear over the rooftops, then vanish from my mental map, wishing I could caution him to go easier on himself. Later, I would make sure he hadn't strained his wing muscles. Preventing Haubner from harming another gargoyle was vital, but it wouldn't help matters if Oliver injured himself in the process.

Giving myself a shake, I looked around for Captain Rojas. I would have to word my questions carefully, but I needed to learn why Haubner had been here this morning, what the captain's opinion of him was, and how long he had been with the Terra Haven guards. Any of those details could help pin proof on Haubner's guilt.

Or exonerate him, I reminded myself. Though the more I

considered the timeline of events, the more suspicious I became of the obnoxious guard.

I startled hard enough to rattle the seed crystals in my bag when a hand clamped down on my arm.

"All finished, Mika?" Deidre asked, peering at Carmen, me, then the air, presumably looking for Oliver.

"Yes, and I need—"

"Good! Siphiwe's over here."

Deidre took off across the soggy lawn, keeping one hand clamped on my arm. For such a tiny woman, she had a grip like a gryphon. I staggered in her wake, doing my best to avoid knocking into anyone we passed, afraid if I didn't keep up, she would pull my arm from its socket.

"Here she is, Siphiwe," Deidre said, halting in front of a statuesque minotaur with a roan bovine head and large liquid-brown eyes framed by a fan of black lashes. "This is Mika, the woman who helped Carmen."

Deidre finally released me, and I tried to subtly rub the woman's red handprint off my arm.

"Hello," I said.

Siphiwe shimmered with wealth. Gems glinted on her fingertips, a conch shell cameo of mirror-image minotaur profiles graced her throat, and an engraved silver pocket watch was looped on a golden chain through her vest's third button. A multitude of spells wove through the fabric of her black pin-striped suit, all so well integrated they were only noticeable because of the outfit's immaculate appearance among the mud and smoke. For the second time today, I felt gauche and grubby, and I took meager consolation in Deidre's presence and her work-worn attire.

Siphiwe managed to scrutinize me without dipping her muzzle, despite being over a head taller than me. After a fraction of a pause, she grasped my hand, her warm grip just shy of painful.

"Siphiwe Yadav, master cameo carver and engraver for Herd Yadav Designs and president of the Terra Haven League of Tradeswomen."

My eyebrows jumped. It wasn't every day I met such a prominent artisan. The women of Herd Yadav Designs were known throughout the nation for their exquisite jewelry— beautiful, one-of-a-kind pieces with correspondingly singular prices.

I was still formulating an appropriate response, unsure whether to address her position as president or as an elite craftswoman, when Siphiwe said, "And you are with the guards."

"Oh, no, I'm a gargoyle guardian." I pointed self-consciously with my free hand toward Carmen, only to freeze halfway through the gesture. Captain Rojas stood beside the gargoyle, leaning close, obviously questioning her. This was the perfect time to get my answers, too. "I'm sorry. I need to—"

"You're not a guard," Siphiwe said, her tone implying restrained patience. She caged my right hand between hers and waited.

"No . . ." I drew out the word, unsure what else needed to be said. Deidre made a subtle rolling motion with her hand.

"Oh. Um, I'm Gargoyle Guardian Mika Stillwater."

Deidre made the rolling motion again. Across the lawn, Captain Rojas wrapped up her conversation with Carmen and disappeared behind a cart.

"Uh, healer and, ah, protector of gargoyles." I winced when my voice lifted at the end of the sentence, as if it were a question, not a statement.

The captain reappeared next to a stack of flying carpets.

Selecting one from the pile, she activated its levitation spell and zipped out of sight.

Glumly, I turned back to the minotaur.

"Right, we can work on that," Siphiwe said, releasing me.

"Ah, thank you?"

"A gargoyle guardian is a unique trade. And seeing what you did for Carmen, I can tell it's important. I would be interested in hearing more about what you do."

"It's fairly straightforward. I heal injured gargoyles and look out for their welfare. Here, I have a card." I dug into my bag and pulled out trade cards, handing one each to Siphiwe and Deidre.

Was this why my seed pointed me toward the League of Tradeswomen? To meet Siphiwe Yadav? As the president of a large social club, the minotaur could quickly spread the word of my existence to more gargoyles. Her status among the Yadav herd marked her as a full spectrum, too, which meant she likely knew gargoyles—or knew people who did. Through Siphiwe's connections, I might be able to reach more gargoyles in a day than I could on my own in a week.

"Please tell any gargoyles you meet about me, and any... one . . ."

A trim black-haired guard wove through the crowd, headed straight for the burned building's gaping doorway. Haubner. He was still here.

"Anyone?" Siphiwe prompted.

"Ah, anyone who might know a gargoyle, please put them in contact with me."

Haubner peered into the empty building. He glanced around to see who was watching, then ducked into the shadowed opening.

Alone.

Without any supervision or witnesses.

Had he left behind incriminating evidence when he set the fire? Was he sneaking back inside to get rid of it?

"Excu—"

"I am not a message board, Ms. Stillwater."

Siphiwe's tone froze me in place. Her ears flicked back against her scalp. They didn't stay pinned, but the flare of her nostrils spoke of suppressed irritation.

Alarm constricted my breath. For the sake of gargoyles yet unmet, I had to salvage this conversation.

"I apologize, Ms. Yadav. I didn't mean any rudeness by it." I kept my eyes on Siphiwe, though I itched to check the doorway for Haubner. "I ask everyone I meet to do the same: to tell gargoyles and those who know gargoyles about me. I learned about Carmen's sickness hours late, and only because I have a friend at the *Chronicle*. If more people knew to contact me when gargoyles were in distress—if *you* had known to contact me—I could have been here sooner."

Siphiwe regarded me for a long moment before her ebony ears relaxed. Her muzzle lowered a fraction so I no longer had to crane my neck quite so painfully to maintain eye contact.

"Perhaps. But it doesn't do to rely on others to build your business," she said.

Before I could correct her—she made it sound as if I was trying to drum up sales, not rescue suffering gargoyles—she turned away from me.

Speaking over her shoulder, she added, "Come to the club. Talk with Charissa Bloom, our member coordinator. You would benefit from the League of Tradeswomen's tutelage. Deidre speaks highly of you, Ms. Stillwater. I would like to do the same."

I rocked back on my heels, feeling like a scolded child. Siphiwe didn't glance back again. She glided toward a group

of aimless-looking women, giving orders. A flurry of organized activity shaped itself in her wake.

"Sorry about that." Deidre patted my shoulder. "Siphiwe
is . . . stern on a good day, and today has been anything but.
That was actually a decent interaction. She doesn't invite
everyone to join the LTs, and you should. We're a good
group."

"I'll think about it," I said, but I couldn't envision finding
the free time.

I turned away from Deidre's hopeful smile in time to
catch Haubner exiting the burned building, brushing his
palms together. Wiping evidence from his hands? Or was
that an unconscious gesture of a man pleased about getting
away with yet another crime? I couldn't read his expression
from here, not closely enough to see if he was smirking or
shifty-eyed. His scowl, though, was easy to spot when a
woman wearing a familiar pink-and-purple feather-eared
hat bobbed through the crowd and planted herself in front
of him, ruining any plans Haubner had of skulking away.

"It was nice to meet you, Deidre," I said, talking fast. "I
see a friend who needs help. Excuse me."

"Your vulturelike behavior is crass, Ms. Fishburne,"
Haubner said, loud enough to be heard from several strides
away. "You should be ashamed of yourself."

"What's there to be ashamed of? Vultures serve an
important purpose." Lucy planted her hands on her hips.
Her puffy sleeves made a valiant effort to engulf her neck.

I didn't think it was possible, but Lucy had found a dress
even less flattering than yesterday's, this one equally as oversized but made entirely out of a sickly yellow fabric and
wrinkled enough to have been slept in. I wondered if Lucy
would have an easier time getting clients for her firm if she
dressed better, then I immediately felt bad for judging her

by her appearance. Lucy was dogged enough for two insurance agents. What she wore shouldn't matter.

"Can you imagine all the rotting animal corpses that would be lying around, stinking the place up, if there were no vultures? Now that would be something to be ashamed of."

Haubner's scowl darkened, possibly from Lucy's graphic imagery but more likely because we had made eye contact. I stopped beside Lucy, but she continued, oblivious to my presence.

"But you're wrong about the League of Tradeswomen, my good guard. They're not dead. Far from it. Look at this street. The LTs will go on, stronger than ever, and I want to help them."

"You want to profit from their tragedy," Haubner said.

"I want to help them rebuild. Now if you would kindly point me toward the, well, for a social club, they don't have a proprietor, do they? Toward the property owner, then."

"There," Haubner said, pointing vaguely toward the bustling street. "Somewhere out there."

"I can point out the league's president to you," I said. "I'm sure she'll be more helpful."

Lucy spun, holding a startled hand to her chest. "Flaming frog legs! Don't go sneaking up on people . . . Mika? The gargoyle guardian, right? Oh no! Does that mean there's another sick gargoyle?" Lucy clutched my forearm, alarm widening her brown eyes behind the wire frames of her glasses.

"Unfortunately, but she's healed now."

"Another sick gargoyle at yet another robbery location," Haubner said. "I wondered how long it would take you to show your face, Ms. Stillwater."

Lucy gasped. "Robbery? I thought this was just an

arsonist targeting successful women; you know how the bigots can be. But if they're getting robbed, too, the league is going to want extra insurance coverage."

I blinked at Lucy's offhand dismissal of the criminal's motive for torching the establishment. What sort of horrors had she become accustomed to in her short career as an insurance agent?

"What was stolen?" Lucy asked.

"The usual sort of things." Haubner tried his glare on Lucy once more, but she remained impervious.

"They couldn't have made off with much." Lucy cast her gaze over the street, tapping a finger against her chin. "I saw the piles earlier. So many ruined and damaged treasures! It makes my heart hurt. We have excellent restoration specialists on staff—but back to the thief. Even a centaur couldn't have made off with that heavy stuff. They must have taken smaller items. Thefts of opportunity, my gran calls them. Unless—" She pivoted to face Haubner again. "Unless this was staged."

"That's a cynical thought," Haubner said.

"I don't understand."

"Mika, my dear, you should see what I've seen," Lucy said, giving me a pat on the arm like she was a grandmother, not a woman close to my own age. "People do the most shocking things for money, like set their own properties on fire to claim the insurance payout. Or pretend they've been robbed so they can collect a paycheck from good companies like mine. Maybe this isn't a partnership the Society of Amicable Trade and Trust should be pursuing."

I tried to picture the moneyed Siphiwe Yadav setting her social club on fire to defraud her insurance company. My imagination came up blank.

"This was a real crime, Lucy. Trust me."

Haubner's eyes sharpened on me. "I agree with the healer. Everything stolen was small enough to be carried out. Even a slim woman like yourself, Ms. Stillwater, wouldn't have trouble transporting any of the items taken."

I pasted on a false smile. "Anything small enough to be taken by a woman could also have been taken by a man."

"Or lifted with magic." Lucy smiled at both of us, oblivious to the palpable tension in the air. "I know just how to determine *that*, too." With a dramatic flourish, she tugged the signature analyzer from her bag.

"We don't need that," Haubner said, but his gaze clung to the oversized glassy pipsissewa.

"Help me out, Guard Haubner. Let's test the spells used inside by the alleged thieves. If the women of the social club committed fraud, you'll know who to arrest, and I can save my boss the embarrassment of doing business with crooks. If it's not them, you'll still know who to arrest."

"I'm sure Captain Rojas would approve," I said. "She'd probably insist on it."

Haubner's eyes narrowed, uncertainty warring with arrogance as he studied me. I lifted my chin. If he was innocent, he had no reason to turn down Lucy's offer.

"You can test out here," he said finally.

"Out here? There's nothing to test out here. The crimes happened inside, if any of this really is a crime and not an elaborate hoax." Lucy said the last loud enough to turn heads, including those of nearby guards and minotaurs.

"This is not a hoax," Haubner said through gritted teeth. He waved aside a fellow guard's offer of assistance and turned his full glare on Lucy. "Fine. We'll go inside. And I'm using the analyzer."

"I can't let you . . . Aaand he's not even listening," Lucy

muttered, glaring at Haubner's back as the guard stomped into the burned building.

"Quick. Before he changes his mind." I grabbed Lucy's elbow, hustling her after Haubner. Impulsively, I leaned close to whisper, "Watch him. I don't trust him."

Lucy's big eyes widened, and she gave me a nod.

The air-cleansing spell nearly cost Lucy her hat and blew my hair into my face as we crossed the threshold. I windmilled an arm for balance when one booted foot slid across the mud-slick marble foyer. Haubner split his sneer generously between Lucy and me. Propelled by the wind, we stumbled into the main room. I stepped closer to the wall to escape the elemental current and sucked in a breath that tasted like a chimney flue.

Ash coated the huge room, thick as tar across the back wall, gritty as granite dust against the front windows. Mounds of charred wood and crumbled plaster swelled beneath gaping holes in the vaulted ceiling. Alarmingly, I could see into the rooms above us, where pictures hung askew, plants wilted among spilled dirt and pottery shards, and a desk smoldered. Judging from the slant of sunlight across the wet walls, I thought I could see straight up to the sky if I ventured closer to the hole in the ceiling.

I stayed where I was.

The building groaned. An internal beam shifted, releasing a cascade of droplets from the water-beaded ceiling. Wood-and-earth elemental braces bolstered damaged pillars and patched the plaster of the far wall—temporary stopgap measures against the second floor's ultimate collapse. I reached for magic. Holding the elements didn't settle my nerves, but it helped.

"What did the arsonist use? Is there a spell for lava?" Lucy asked, goggling at the nearest hole in the ceiling.

"What does the analyzer tell you?" Haubner asked.

Lucy waved the pipsissewa around without moving her feet. "Too many signatures in here to tell much of anything."

"Especially from there."

Lucy shot Haubner a glare. "The fire didn't start in this room. It started over there." She pointed to the blackest section of the far wall, where the fire damage was the worst around an arched opening. "Can we get closer?"

Rather than march across the open room, Haubner hugged the side wall and led the way deeper into the building through a narrow doorway. Single file, we entered a gloomy hallway, bumbling in the miserly light of Haubner's minuscule glowball. Something cold tapped my forehead. Swiping frantically, I snapped a glowball into being, one as large as two fists and as bright as a bonfire.

Heat washed over me from the spell, and sinister shadows bounced across the walls. I shoved the glowball higher, revealing a jagged crack in the ceiling. Water trickled along the broken plaster, coalescing into erratic drips. The next droplet hit my cheek. I wiped it away with one finger, then examined the smear of ash on my fingertip. Lucy stared at my finger, then squeaked in dismay. A second later, a flimsy air shield protected her ugly hat.

I bit off a curse when I spotted safety spells coating the walls—and how close my glowball was to burning through them. Diminishing my spell to little more than a candle flame, I scurried after Haubner's retreating form. Lucy gripped my arm with one hand while using the other to wave the analyzer about. Every time the pipsissewa passed close to a spell, delicate tendrils of magic lifted from the woven elements and disappeared into the oversized stamens. Lucy even sampled my glowball. I didn't feel a change in the spell as the pipsissewa drew particles from the fiery light and siphoned them through its complex analytical magic. Lucy made soft *hmm* sounds to herself, but she didn't elaborate.

A ward blocked us from approaching the location of the fire's origin. Through the spell's wavering earthen lines, I could make out a curved staircase. Half the landing was missing. Had the arsonist started the fire *on* the stairs? I shivered. Anyone upstairs would have been trapped inside the burning building. The thief couldn't have known how many women were upstairs or how quickly they would be rescued. People could have died. For what?

"He's disappeared," Lucy whispered.

I whipped around. Haubner had already passed through the room next to us and vanished out the far side. I rushed after him, mincing through a ransacked office, where scattered papers, spilled inkwells, and abandoned chairs were all that remained.

"Was anything taken from this room?" Lucy asked. "We should stop to examine—"

"Keep up," Haubner called from out of sight ahead of us.

He didn't stop until he reached an immense kitchen, then he gestured for us to enter it first. Keeping half an eye on the guard, I sent my glowball questing into the space without crossing the threshold, looking for a trap.

Luxurious gray-veined white marble counters anchored three walls, inset with cast-iron ovens and deep sinks. A matching island bisected the room, its white surface jarring after the state of the rest of the building.

The fire hadn't touched the kitchen, but it looked as if a dozen rabid thieves had ransacked the room. Every cupboard door hung open, every drawer yawned wide. A hodgepodge of items remained: earthenware jugs and wooden spoons, dried goods in tin cannisters and cloth napkins spilling from a drawer, and a dented brass kettle on the stove.

Glass crunched underfoot when I eased into the room, and I froze. Dozens of delicate bottles lay shattered from the island to the door, a small fortune of spices and herbs scattered among the shards. I minced around the mess, and Lucy followed. The rich aroma of crushed oregano and basil blossomed into the air, momentarily overpowering the stench of smoke.

"No silverware in the drawer, no clock above the stove, no wine decanters. No knives, not even paring knives," Lucy said. "The only spelled items left are those bolted down—unless you count that sad kettle. Everything of value has been taken."

"By the thief?" I asked.

"Or the tradeswomen." She looked to Haubner for confirmation. "Do you have a list of what they claim was taken?"

"I do." He stalked into the room and extended a hand to Lucy.

She stared at his empty palm. "Are you going to show us this list?"

"No. Hand it over, Ms. Fishburne. I'm ready to test your analyzer."

"As I tried to tell you out front, I can't do that. This analyzer looks like a pretty bit of art, but it's very, very expensive, and I'm not supposed to let anyone else touch it. My gran—*my boss*—was adamant about it." She waggled a finger at someone not present and dropped her voice, mimicking a more cultured accent. "'Pipsissewa flowers are common, but signature analyzers aren't. They're a lot harder to replace than junior agents.'"

"I won't break it. I'm a city guard. If you can't trust me, who can you trust?"

Lucy's eyes darted to mine and away, but not so fast that Haubner didn't catch the exchange. His lips flattened.

"Or we can walk back out front, and I can tell the president of the League of Tradeswomen that you think she's a thief and a fraud. We'll see how well that works out for your career in this city."

Lucy swallowed audibly. When she passed the analyzer to Haubner, her hand trembled. "Be careful. Please."

I crossed my arms and glared at Haubner. He strode around the far side of the island to an iron chest deep enough to fit Lucy's hat and twice as wide. I stalked after him, stopping just outside of his reach. Lucy trod close enough behind me to clip my heel.

"What's that?" I asked. With its hinged lid and three drawers, it reminded me of a jewelry box, though I doubted anything so fanciful—or incongruous—was stored in the heavy-duty box bolted to the marble with spell-reinforced screws.

"It's a lockbox," Lucy said when Haubner didn't respond. "This is where the kitchen keeps"—she paused to go up on her toes and peer into the open drawers—"*kept* the money."

"Why would the kitchen need to keep money?"

"To pay vendors. Sometimes management uses lockboxes to hide valuables they don't want visible to the general public." Lucy gave Haubner a pointed look and raised her voice slightly. "Its contents are the first thing a cook would grab in a fire."

"The kitchen was empty when the fire started," Haubner said, "and the box was empty by the time the fire was put out."

"That doesn't exonerate the tradeswomen. You should

see how crafty people get when enacting their fraudulent schemes. More creative than thieves, in my experience. Gran always says you have to watch the client as closely as the riffraff."

I only half listened to Lucy. It was Haubner I needed to keep an eye on. He took his time examining the signature analyzer, inspecting each stamen of the mock-pipsissewa, then each petal. Once satisfied, he turned the petals toward the lockbox. Individual earth-and-fire locks spelled the lid and drawers, and Haubner tested each, his frown deepening. Clearly, the spells had failed—the drawers were empty, and the upper compartment held only stained trade cards from local food vendors—yet the elemental locks remained intact.

Circling the kitchen, Haubner tested the spell on the wine cabinet, the kettle's quick-boil spell, the proofing bin's warming spell, and every piece of magic on the multiple ovens. Lucy fluttered behind him, cautioning him to be careful, her hands darting forward and back, as if she thought Haubner would drop the pipsissewa and she would be fast enough to physically catch it.

Haubner completed his circuit by marching up to me and thrusting the analyzer beneath my glowball. I jerked the light away from him, but not before the pipsissewa absorbed particles of my spell.

"This analyzer is useless." He slapped it into Lucy's hands, and she clutched it convulsively to her chest.

"No, it's not. You're using it wrong."

"It doesn't tell me anything I didn't know."

"Maybe you don't know what to look for," Lucy shot back.

"Can I try?" I asked.

"You?" Lucy looked surprised. "Why?"

I couldn't very well tell her I wanted to make sure Haubner wasn't hiding something, not with him listening. Nor could I explain my Haubner-is-a-thief theory. That one I wouldn't share without proof.

"I want to see if anyone made a recent spell with Carmen's boost," I said.

"You can tell that?" Lucy's wide-eyed gaze focused on me with penetrating intensity.

"I won't know until I try."

Lucy nibbled the inside of her lip, then handed over the analyzer.

I closed my fingers gingerly around the expensive tool. Its shape was deceptively simple, the five petals curved so the back of the flower fit comfortably into my cupped palm. Like a living pipsissewa, two garnet-purple stamens curled from the base of each petal toward the center of the device. The whole analyzer—every petal, every stamen, and even the jade-green pistil—was composed of hardened resin. Layers and layers of pressed pink and magenta pipsissewa petals filled the clear resin flower, and the stamens contained feather tines, gravel, pale splinters, water drops, and tiny sparks in their depths. Given a week or two, I could replicate the analyzer, replacing resin with quartz, though it would be twice as heavy. The spells imbued within the resin-frozen materials were another matter. I doubted I could recreate them even if I devoted a lifetime to studying the labyrinthine magic.

A brass ring lay flat against the back of the analyzer, attached by a hinge. I gave it an experimental tug, and the ring swung perpendicular to the flower, creating a handhold.

"Oh, you don't need to use that," Lucy said.

I slid my middle finger through the ring, giving Lucy a smile. "I don't want to take any chances."

I cradled my hand close to my body, painfully aware that I couldn't afford to replace the expensive analyzer if I broke it. Just thinking of the debt made my skin prickle.

Stepping around Lucy, I edged unnecessarily close to Haubner. He arched a dark brow at me, then snorted when I swiped the signature analyzer beneath his glowball.

I expected to need to use magic to activate the pipsissewa, but it required no help. The analyzer breathed in Haubner's magical signature and slid it along my senses as intimately as if I had initiated a magical link with the guard. My awareness of the room receded, replaced with the impression of a deep, tranquil pool surrounded by soft grass. A single willow tree shaded the bank, its long, supple branches stirring in a gentle breeze.

I blinked, feeling as if I were returning to my body after floating in that pool. With effort, I stopped myself from swaying in synchronization with the willow tree. Haubner watched me with open suspicion. I squinted right back at him, then thought better of getting into a staring match with a potential criminal and turned toward the lockbox.

I tripped over my own foot. Flinging out my free hand, I caught my balance against the counter. Lucy's soft gasp made me blush.

"I'm not usually this clumsy," I muttered.

"It can be a lot to take in. Maybe you should give the analyzer back to me."

I nodded but held the pipsissewa up to the lockbox first. I had to prove Haubner tampered with the spells. I had to stop him from hurting another gargoyle.

Fresh sensations spiraled through the pipsissewa's stamens, submerging me in hot steam caged by lava rocks and delicate red spidery flowers. I yanked my hand back, irrationally afraid I would be burned, before logic kicked in. Embarrassed, I fiddled with the drawer. The heavy iron slid easily home but resisted my attempt to reopen it. When it sprang free, I staggered a half step back.

Lucy materialized at my side, both hands cupped around mine to encase the pipsissewa. I blinked at the cheap metal bracelets cutting into her wrists, struggling to focus my tired eyes. Disappointment simmered in my gut. The signature on the lockbox was the polar opposite of Haubner's. If he had shifted his spirit to match the steamy signature that spelled the box, he had done so well enough to open the locks without leaving a trace of his own magic.

"Here, let me take that," Lucy said, sliding the signature analyzer from my finger. She nestled the expensive device into her bag and cinched the top closed.

I twisted to check on Haubner, not liking him at my back. He stood with a hip cocked against the island. I couldn't read his expression, because after I stopped moving, the room continued to tilt. I rocked against the counter, curling my fingers into the marble lip on either side of my hips to hold myself stable. The dimness of the room alarmed me until I realized I wasn't losing consciousness; my glowball had dissipated, leaving only Haubner's to light the kitchen. I didn't remember extinguishing my spell, which was frightening. Healing Carmen had exhausted me far more than I realized if I was losing track of active magic.

"Did you learn anything useful?" Lucy asked, her eyes darting back and forth between mine.

I shook my head. The room spun in my periphery, blocky shadows sliding across each other at the edge of my vision only to snap into place when I looked directly at them. "Maybe I'm not the right person to handle such expensive equipment."

"The first time using an analyzer can be disorienting," she said.

Haubner snorted. "Your acting skills need work."

Lucy flinched on my behalf. I didn't have a comeback.

"It's past time for you two to leave," Haubner said. "Come on."

A gargoyle beacon dropped from the sky dizzyingly fast, spearing toward me as if they would plow right through the building. I gasped and spun toward the empty doorway. My feet tangled on each other, and I banged my hip on the island. Grabbing the marble with both hands, I willed strength into my legs.

The gargoyle landed in a crash of quartz. They were close, within the building. Their speed spoke of urgency or danger—and the undulating bob of the beacon's light was intimately familiar. I staggered toward the door.

"Oliver!"

11

"Mika!" Oliver careened off the door frame as he burst into the kitchen. The ceiling groaned, and a flurry of powdered plaster rained down behind him.

Oliver's head whipped back and forth, then his eyes locked on to Haubner. His expression twisted into a frightening snarl. Lucy screamed. Oliver bounded to me, his quartz steps deafening, glass shards pinging in a dozen directions. Whipping around in a screech of claws, he planted the tip of his wing and flared the bulk around me like a carnelian cape, crowding me with his long body. He splayed his other wing, and I dropped instinctively to my knees. Oliver's wings closed overhead, cocooning us in darkness and the heady aroma of crushed oregano.

"What? What's wrong?" My heart beat in my throat, adding a quaver to my words. I grabbed for the elements, but they slid from my exhausted grip. I needed light. I stretched again for magic, but I couldn't focus. "Is something after you? Are you all right?"

Oliver's side heaved against mine, his breaths rasping in

the ringing silence. "You," he panted. "What did"—*gasp*—"he do"—*gasp*—"to you?"

"*Me?* Oliver, are you hurt?"

"No. Are you?"

"No." I ran my hand down Oliver's neck, over his shoulders, back up to his face, blindly reassuring him and checking him for injuries. Pain nipped at my fingers, but it was mine, not his.

"So theatrical," Haubner said. "Like guardian, like gargoyle."

A low growl rumbled up Oliver's throat. I leaned into him, resting my forehead on his cool scales, breathing in his familiar, mineral scent. I had a dozen questions for Oliver, but they could wait until we were alone.

"We should get up," I said.

Oliver twisted, his exhales blowing my hair from my face.

"You're not sick?" he asked.

"No."

"Your— You looked unwell when I first spotted you."

"We probably all looked unwell when you burst in here like an enraged kludde," Haubner muttered.

I ignored him. Oliver wasn't referring to when he saw me with his eyes. I must have been more drained than I thought if it was affecting the brightness of my beacon.

Finally, Oliver dropped his wings. In the feeble light, I could make out rough gouges in his carnelian feathers from the door frame. My instinct was to heal Oliver immediately, but seeing the animosity on my companion's face when he locked eyes with Haubner, I changed my mind. Not that I had a choice; the elements still eluded me.

I gave Oliver's cheek a fond stroke, redirecting his attention. "I'm all right. Just tired." My panic must have burned up the last of my energy reserves, because I was having a hard time getting to my feet.

"It's been a long morning, hasn't it?" Lucy said, a touch breathless.

"And a longer night. Too bad all this thieving keeps interfering with our rest." Haubner shot me an irritated glare, deflecting blame toward me once again.

Lucy started to nod, then gave the guard a side-eyed look. Belatedly, she dispersed a clumsy ward. The fragile barrier wouldn't have been enough to deflect an enthusiastic puppy, let alone Oliver's full weight if he had crashed into her. Haubner let his protective ward dissipate, too. Interestingly, the guard had encompassed Lucy in his spell, but not me. Nothing about his magic had been feeble, either.

Oliver helped me to my feet, keeping his body between me and Haubner. I bent to brush my knees clean, hissing when pain flared in my palms. Turning them toward the light, I stared in stupefaction at the clear sparkles amid the bright red scratches.

"You're cut," Oliver said.

Which made more sense than my first thought: that I had inadvertently grafted carnelian to my flesh. I twisted my right hand over to examine the amethyst hexagons on the back. Nothing about fusing quartz to my hands had been accidental. It had required the concentrated power of the baetyl working through me. I couldn't have done it to myself if I wanted to.

"Oh dear." Lucy fluttered closer, though she didn't breach the implied ward Oliver created around me with the curve of his tail. "I don't have any healing skills."

"I do."

I peered at Haubner in the gloom. His glower remained,

and he made no move to approach me. He didn't even expend the effort of increasing the size of his glowball to provide more light.

The nearest healer hall was four airbus stops away. The cuts were minor. I could wait. But *knowing* glass was embedded in my flesh made it sting all that much more. Haubner might be a thief, but he also had guard training, which included a basic education in healing spells.

"If you can remove the glass, I can see a healer," I said, compromising with myself.

Oliver huffed through slitted nostrils. Turning in a tight circle, glass squeaking and pulverizing beneath his paws, he faced the guard. I wanted to soothe him, but I couldn't touch him without hurting myself.

Haubner assessed Oliver for several beats before he finally stepped forward. When he reached for me, I hesitated, then shoved my hands toward Haubner. Oliver snaked his head between us, his bright eyes locked on the guard. Haubner ignored him.

"Hold still." The guard swept cool air and water magic across my palms, the pattern of his spell as delicate as it was complex. Blessed numbness tingled across my skin. As if my sigh of relief were a signal, Haubner's magic flowed faster. In three quick swipes, he removed every shard and speck of crushed glass.

"Thank—"

Heat licked my palm, a blend of all five elements woven into a practiced spell too fast to follow. The minor cuts and scrapes healed before my eyes, until only wet smears of blood remained.

"Thank—" I tried again.

"Time to go," Haubner said, cutting off my grudging

gratitude. "Watch where you step. I don't need you two or the gargoyle bringing the roof down on my head."

Lucy gave Oliver a wary look but hurried to take my elbow. "Come. Let's get out of here."

I tested a step. My legs were wobbly, but they would hold. I urged Oliver to lead the way. I didn't want Haubner at my back, but it was better than leaving Oliver close to him. Despite Haubner's charitable healing, I still didn't trust the guard. However, I didn't think he would attempt to harm me. Not with two witnesses. Oliver in his current mood was the unpredictable one.

The reverse trek through the ruined building took twice as long as I concentrated on not tripping and dragging Lucy down with me while doing my best to ignore the hostile man stalking behind us. Lucy dealt with her nerves the way she dealt with all of her emotions: by talking incessantly.

"Healing gargoyles must take a lot of magic. I tried healing a cut once. I ended up hurting myself more than helping. I couldn't find the right balance of elements. But gargoyles? That's not the same as healing a human, right? Not the same at all. All that quartz. Oh, I have no affinity for earth. But here you healed a *whole* gargoyle. That's something. Plus those cuts. I know they were minor, but healing always saps the vigor right out of you. No wonder you're swaying on your feet. Let me take you out for some food. I'm sure a nibble will help you feel better, and I'd love a chance to talk with you."

Lucy paused, and it took me several steps to realize she was waiting for my response, not just taking a breath. It was on the tip of my tongue to decline, but the flick of her gaze to indicate Haubner and the way she emphasized *talk* had me agreeing despite how badly I longed to find the nearest airbus home.

Lucy hustled me out the gaping front doors into the sunlight, not pausing before making a right turn and heading up the sidewalk. Oliver fell in beside me. All three of us drew in deep breaths of clean air.

"I'll be keeping an eye on you," Haubner shouted after us.

I glanced over my shoulder. The guard stood with his hands braced on his hips, his scowl locked on me.

"I'm sure you will, you ninny," Lucy muttered. "I hate the ones like that, all full of themselves for no reason. Did you see that ward he made? Like he thought your gargoyle—Oliver, right? Like he thought Oliver was going to harm him. How ridiculous. Gargoyles don't hurt people."

I didn't point out that Lucy had made a protective ward of her own. If I hadn't known it was Oliver thundering through the burned building, I would have been alarmed, too. I didn't correct her assumption that gargoyles didn't harm people, either. Normally, I would have agreed wholeheartedly with the statement. But with his ears pinned to his stone mane and his wings hunched, Oliver didn't look like he had peaceful intentions toward Haubner.

While we were inside, the street had cleared. The guards' wards no longer partitioned the boulevard, and traffic moved unimpeded. Pedestrians still clustered across the street, ogling the burned building, of course. A few pointed in our direction when we exited, and I picked up my pace in case they were reporters.

Carmen was easy to place, even without her beacon to guide me. The massive gargoyle curled atop a coffee shop across the street, the iridescent iris agate spots along her squid mantle shimmering in the sun. Several women sat on the roof with her, which made me smile. The tradeswomen seemed like the kind of people I wanted to associate with—as soon as I found an hour to spare.

I waited until we were down the side street, well clear of Haubner's line of sight, before pulling Lucy to a halt.

"Oliver, let me heal you."

"I can wait. Lucy is right; you should eat first."

"You think I can enjoy food while you're injured?"

"It's not that bad."

I sat down on the sidewalk. "Come here."

Oliver curled around my legs, so close he would be in my lap if he leaned. I let my bag slide to the ground and scooped a handful of seed crystals into my palm. It was more quartz than Oliver's minor injuries needed, but something about holding the seeds helped.

"Is there anything I can do?" Lucy asked, shuffling to one side.

"Thank you, but no."

I reached for the elements. Earth came first, slowly. Grudgingly. I reshaped it, tuning it to quartz. The familiar texture of the magic soothed my weary mental muscles, and the other elements trickled to me. Only once I held all five elements did I open myself to Oliver's boost. Relying on his enhancement for strength, I gently cleaned his injuries, then guided raw quartz into the scrapes on his wings and paws. It didn't take a full seed crystal to fill his wounds, but it was worrisome how much the simple healing took from Oliver's limited reserves. His fatigue couldn't be blamed on one rushed flight across the city, either. It was accumulative from weeks of flights, running communications for me among all the city's gargoyles.

I eased my magic from Oliver and silently vowed that as soon as we stopped the spirit-shifting thief, we would take a day off. Maybe two. And I would make sure Oliver truly rested. Besides, I had plenty I could accomplish from my worktable.

My friend studied me, head tilted. "You look better," he proclaimed.

"I feel better." I didn't let on how badly my eyelids wanted to droop closed. "Do we need to . . . ?" I trailed off, not sure how to ask what he had learned about Haubner without saying too much in front of Lucy.

Oliver shook his head, his mouth pinched into a frown. I wanted to dig deeper, but Lucy reached a hand down to help me stand.

"All done?" she asked.

With one last glance at Oliver, I nodded. "Done, and starving."

Lucy grinned and led the way to a street-front kitchen. The tiny restaurant had no indoor seating, just a walk-up bar and four tiny sidewalk tables barely large enough for two plates and cups. However, the smells emanating from the twin stoves set my mouth watering. Minutes later, I dug into a plate towering with eggs, bacon, and pancakes drenched in syrup, and it was even better than it smelled. Lucy ate hunched over her poached eggs on toast, for once silent. I wondered how terrible I looked, because she kept sneaking glances at me like she thought I would fall off the rickety chair. Oliver sat beside me, his chin level with the tabletop.

"What happened in there?" Oliver asked.

"Lucy let me try the signature analyzer. I tested Haubner's signature—"

"Surprisingly weak-willed, don't you think?" Lucy asked. "All bendy, with no solid backbone."

I paused with my fork halfway to my mouth. That hadn't been my interpretation. Haubner's signature was tranquil in a way that made me wary of hidden depths, and nothing about the man or his signature implied *spineless* to me. Thankfully, Lucy went on without waiting for a response.

"Yours, though, is something else. I mean, quartz is so fitting for you, but it's like you're a core of it, with fire breathing through you and wood more of a support than a detriment."

"Huh," I said intelligently, and stuffed the bite of pancakes into my mouth.

Feeling the texture of your own signature was impossible even with a device as sophisticated as the pipsissewa analyzer. It would be like trying to taste my own tongue or to describe the voice that gave silent sound to my thoughts. Signatures were detectable only to others, and no one sensed another person's signature exactly the same way as anyone else. We each perceived signatures through our own perspectives, likes, and dislikes. Kylie said I felt like stability in magical form, a warm, glowing rainbow quartz spire vined in white clematis, softened by mist. Marcus saw a sphere of iridescent quartz warmed from the inside by fire, snuggled in a nest of white clematis, the surface of the sphere wet with a recent rain. Lucy appeared to sense my signature as something harder and hotter. I wasn't sure what that said about her. Or about me.

"Was Haubner's signature on anything?" Oliver asked.

I shook my head. "Not on anything I tested."

"Me, either," Lucy said. She searched my eyes. "You suspect him? The guard?"

I shared a glance with Oliver, then nodded. I'd already told Lucy I didn't trust Haubner. Her conclusion wasn't a stretch.

Lucy tapped her chin, eyes unfocused. "A guard as a thief. A thief as a guard. It could work." Her sudden smile was sharp. "That would be terrible of him, but what a perfect cover. No wonder you don't trust him. I mean, I don't trust him, either. There's something about him. I can't quite put my finger on it. He's so . . . so . . . belligerent."

"Unfortunately, we need more than that to go to his captain with. I hoped using your analyzer might help," I said. "You tested the safe at the Blue Lotus and the lockbox here. Was the same signature used on both?"

Lucy gave me a puzzled frown. "You mean, did Mo Almasi break in here and steal the tradeswomen's money after pretend-stealing his own? No. Not unless he's got two signatures."

I stiffened. The nagging feeling in the back of my mind finally crystallized. "I am such a fool. We were never going to find Haubner's signature in that kitchen or anywhere else in the LTs' building. If he's shifting his spirit to break in without setting off alarms or fracturing wards, his signature wouldn't be anywhere on the premises."

Lucy jolted, dropping her fork. It bounced off her plate and clattered to the cobblestones.

"*Spirit shifting?* How do you know he's doing that?"

Mentally cursing my loose tongue, I leaned in to whisper, "I don't know that *Haubner* is shifting his spirit, but we know the thief is. I wasn't supposed to share that, though, so please keep it to yourself."

"Of course," Lucy said weakly. "My boss would have a fit if she knew. You can't insure against someone just—" She mimed reaching her hand went through an invisible door and grabbing something. Glancing around for anyone who might be listening, she hissed, "Are you *sure*? Spirit shifting is so dangerous! And how?" Her eyes darted back and forth between mine. "How does someone change something so fundamental about themselves?"

I shrugged. "Captain Rojas seemed to know, but she refused to explain it." I turned hopefully to Oliver. Figuring that with everything I had blabbed, it no longer mattered if Lucy heard Oliver's findings, I asked, "Did you learn anything?"

"Lowell saw Haubner a few times, he thinks." Oliver released a frustrated puff. "He didn't bother identifying one guard from another until yesterday."

"And Nimoy?"

"He recognized Haubner. He's boosted him in the past, but he doesn't remember seeing anyone on the street last night."

Neither statement was proof that Haubner was innocent. He could have worn a disguise or sneaked past sleeping gargoyles. But without anything definite from the gargoyles, we were back to empty speculation.

"You reiterated to both of them that no one boosts anyone they can't see, right?" I asked.

Oliver nodded sharply.

Lucy blinked wide eyes at me. "The gargoyles all report to *you*? That's quite a network of spies."

"We're just sharing information," I protested.

Lucy didn't seem to hear me. Her fingers drummed the tabletop. "Gargoyles are so quiet and unobtrusive. They must know so much . . ." Her vacant gaze sharpened on me, and she grinned. "Mika Stillwater, any chance you want a job at the Society of Amicable Trade and Trust?"

———

I TRUDGED HOME FROM THE AIRBUS, STICKY WITH SWEAT AND bone weary. Head down, Oliver plodded at my side. A daze of heat muffled the neighborhood, the streets empty and quiet except for our footsteps and the drone of insects. The treetops stirred with a faint breeze, but it failed to filter down to the muggy air near the sidewalk. I considered cobbling together a cooling spell, but assembling the elements was too much effort.

When I turned up the walkway to the Victorian's porch stairs, Oliver hung back, gathering himself to launch toward the roof, where Anya and Herbert perched. He flared his wings, then froze.

"Is that Marcus?" he asked.

A lone flying carpet coasted down the street three feet above the ground, my boyfriend's unmistakable figure surfing it with enviable ease. My breath hitched. Wind ruffled Marcus's short black hair and pressed his gray FPD uniform to his body, emphasizing every delicious ridge of muscle in his torso. His gaze pinged from Oliver to me, and his expression turned guarded.

My stomach flipped. I fought to keep my face neutral, hating the sudden churn of trepidation in my gut.

Marcus slowed and lowered the flying carpet, stepping to the sidewalk in a fluid motion without glancing down. The carpet drifted deeper into the yard, but he didn't take his eyes off me.

I tilted my chin up and slid one hand into a pocket. Casual. Confident. At least that's how Kylie looked when she held this pose. I curled the fingers of my free hand around my bag's strap. My grip spasmed when Marcus's gaze skimmed from my toes to my head, noting every flaw in my appearance, before settling on my face. He didn't speak. He didn't need to. I could read his disappointment in the furrow of his brow and the tension of his jaw.

"Is something wrong?" Oliver asked.

Marcus finally looked away, and I let out a breath I

hadn't been consciously holding. Walking back to the side-walk, I stopped with Oliver between us.

"I have something I wanted to share with you," Marcus said. His lapis lazuli eyes flicked to mine and held. "I took a chance that you would be awake, but apparently you never went to sleep. Did you go out?"

Irritation flashed through me, hot and fresh.

"The thief struck again, and another gargoyle needed healing." *And I'm a gargoyle guardian; I don't have to run my activities past my boyfriend before I leave the house.* Unable to help myself, I added, "I thought that was more important than 'resting.'"

"Are you . . . ?" Hesitation wasn't Marcus's style, and I could tell he was choosing his words carefully. "Are you feeling all right?"

"I feel fine." I wouldn't admit to my exhaustion, not even if my legs gave out. I refused to listen to another lecture on how I was pushing myself too hard. I also wasn't going to waste my breath attempting to explain once again why I couldn't lounge around while gargoyles suffered.

"You look . . ." Again, he hesitated. It made me feel like I was a monster he had to approach cautiously. As if I were irrational and in need of soothing.

"I'm hot," I snapped. "The gargoyle was at the League of Tradeswomen's building. It was a long, sweltering airbus ride. I might look a mess, but I just need a cold shower. I'm fine."

Marcus worked his jaw. Taking a deep breath, he turned away to retrieve his carpet from the bushes and deactivate its spells. With practiced motions, he rolled it up and tucked it beneath his arm. By the time he finished, his expression was unreadable again.

"Did you learn anything new?"

"There's a guard, Haubner, who's been nearby every sick gargoyle," Oliver said. "We think he's—"

"A jerk," I cut in. As much as I longed to, I couldn't give Marcus a target to lock that scowl on, not until I was certain of Haubner's guilt.

"Definitely that," Oliver grumbled, but he caught my subtle head shake and didn't say more.

Marcus glanced between Oliver and me. The carpet creaked beneath his arm.

"The gargoyle is healthy now?" he asked.

"Yes."

"Do you have any idea where the thief will strike next?"

I thought of my unhelpful, partially changed everlasting seed. "Not a clue."

The words burned, but not as much as the flash of relief that brightened Marcus's eyes. I wanted him to be angry on my behalf, furious with the thief, and ready to tear the town apart with me to find him.

"Don't you . . . ?" I trailed off, pride closing my throat even as I finished the question in my head: *Don't you want to help me?*

"I care, Mika," Marcus said, hearing the wrong unspoken words. "I care about your safety, yours and Oliver's. I don't want any more gargoyles to be hurt. I'm sure the guards are going to catch the thief soon. Maybe even today." He brushed a lock of hair behind my ear, and I tried to see affection in his touch, not patronization.

"Did you talk with Grant about the thief? Is the FPD going to step in?"

Marcus started shaking his head before I finished the question. "Not unless the thief escalates his attacks." His gaze dropped to a smear of blood on my pants, his mouth tight. "His magic has been foolhardy but nothing city guards can't handle."

"Gargoyles are getting hurt. Isn't that big and important enough to warrant the FPD's attention?" *Isn't it enough to warrant* your *attention?* I wanted to shout.

"Mika, if I could—" Marcus shoved his fingers through his black hair with enough force that I was surprised he didn't pull out fistfuls. "It's not that simple. Yesterday, we hunted a trio of wendigos threatening the Tok'kwa centaur herd. Today, we defused fourteen kinds of illegal spells in a confiscated airship at North Haven Port. I haven't encountered magic that sophisticated or violent since I left the military."

"I didn't . . ." I closed my mouth. Saying *I didn't know* would only make me sound stupid and self-absorbed. Marcus tackled the worst magics and the deadliest creatures plaguing the area. He was a federal warrior; it was in his job description. But I hadn't bothered to ask about his latest assignments, and I hadn't thought to worry about his well-being, either. Maybe it made me a terrible girlfriend, but I had to put the needs of gargoyles first. I had to be a guardian first.

"I'm not telling you this to make you feel bad or to make excuses. It's just . . ." Marcus glanced down at Oliver's round eyes, then back at me. "I hate saying it, but this thief is too small scale for us."

The memory of Nimoy's broken limbs flashed to the forefront of my mind. *Too small scale.* My stomach knotted around the words, and my guilt evaporated.

"I trust the guards to handle this. They want to find the thief as much as you do." Marcus slid his palm down my arm to grip my limp hand in his. "I'm sorry; I can't help. Not this time."

I rocked on my heels. I thought of myself as independent and self-reliant. It was how I had built up my quartz artisan business. It was how I was building my guardian business. But Marcus's quiet words hit like a punch. He couldn't help me—*not this time.* Not like he had when Walter kidnapped the baby gargoyles. Not like he had in Focal Park. Not like he had with the baetyl or on the harrowing trip to the everlasting tree.

And now, I was doing it again, hoping Marcus would step in and protect me when everything got dangerous.

A small voice in the back of my mind protested. *I* saved Oliver and his siblings when they were babies. *I* rescued the comatose gargoyles. *I* connected with the baetyl, not Marcus. But he had been beside me for every challenge of my guardianship.

Except this time.

Had I relied on Marcus too much? Was I a guardian without him to prop me up?

"I miss you, Mika," Marcus said. "Every time I see you lately, it feels like a status update. I want more. I want a real date. It's been too long."

"I know." We had returned from the everlasting tree weeks ago, yet I could count our dates on one hand. I wouldn't need all my fingers, either. Guilt burgeoned once more. I wanted to spend more time with Marcus. I loved him. But I had been so busy helping gargoyles that all I had left for him were snatches of time, stolen moments between tasks. It wasn't fair to Marcus. Plus, even that—even an hour here or there spent enjoying Marcus's company—made my conscience squirm. It wasn't fair for me to be having a good time while a gargoyle might be suffering. I had to ensure every gargoyle was healthy and happy before I could truly enjoy my own pleasurable pursuits.

"I know," I repeated. "I just need some rest first."

I was a coward, but if I tried to explain, it would come out all wrong.

Marcus's eyes softened, and he squeezed my hand. "You must be exhausted. Why don't I come back this evening?"

"I, ah, I meant I need a couple of days." A couple of weeks seemed more likely, but I was too selfish to go that long without seeing him. I just needed a few more days to find the thief, then I could relax my duties, at least for an hour or two.

Marcus's smile slipped. His expression blanked.

"Days," he said.

"To rest." The knot in my stomach morphed into solid granite.

"Genuine rest, or the sort you've been doing lately?"

"I can't stop everything—"

"Right." He dropped my hand. "I get it."

Frustration and distress warred within me. I was so tired of this argument, but I hated the way he had closed down. It felt dangerous. Final.

"This isn't coming out right, Marcus. Maybe I can be more coherent"—*more persuasive*, I mentally amended—"after a nap."

"I'm not confused. I'm . . ." Marcus's gaze lifted over my head.

A message spell arced over the trees and dropped down next to us. It took me a beat to realize it was keyed to my magical signature, not Marcus's.

"Go ahead," Marcus said when I hesitated.

I activated the spell, and Amelia Vanderlei's cultured voice rolled out.

"Ms. Stillwater, Greta and I will be at the bookshop for

the next few hours. If this is a good time for you, please drop by. I look forward to your reply."

"Oh." I snatched at the dissipating threads of the spell, parsing Amelia's signature from the elements: curls of steam rising from a hot spring surrounded by blooming umbrella magnolia trees. Somehow, she embodied heat and elegance in equal portions.

I formed the shell of a message spell to reply. My first attempt fell apart when I yawned and miscalculated the level of air. Of course I had to flub a routine spell when Marcus was watching.

"I hope you're planning to tell her you're busy," he said.

"I'm not busy." I cast a glance toward my bedroom windows. My bed would be there when I got back. I could go a bit longer without sleep. Especially if I emptied some of the seed crystals from my bag to lighten the load before I left.

I glanced at Oliver and received a firm nod in response: He was ready to go back out, too.

"That didn't sound urgent," Marcus said, his scowl deepening.

I ground my teeth. "I already missed my first appointment with Greta."

"You don't have to jump to fit into Amelia's schedule. You can wait for a day when you're more rested."

I almost laughed, but I didn't want to unleash the ugly, bitter sound. "Greta needs healing. I'm not going to make her wait."

I turned away from him and spoke into my message spell, letting Amelia know I would be there within the hour. The spell rocketed away with the boost of three gargoyles behind it.

"So when you said you needed rest, it only pertained to

spending time with me," Marcus said, his jaw tight. "Now that Amelia called on you, you're full of energy?"

My guilt shattered into a dozen piercing shards, each slicing phantom, white-hot pain through my midsection. "How is that any different than you? You canceled our date yesterday to rush off to your job. You left earlier *for your job*. Well, *this* is my job. I'm a gargoyle guardian. I heal gargoyles. I can't spend all my time resting in my room so I can be fresh whenever you make time for me."

I wanted the diatribe back as soon as I finished it. I had twisted Marcus's words and warped his intentions to suit my needs. But I didn't apologize, because too much truth resided in my rant.

Marcus snapped open his carpet and activated the levitation spell. It floated beside him, but he didn't get on it. His blue eyes shone with a forge's molten heat.

"You're doing it again, you know," he said, and only a hint of a growl in his voice betrayed his anger.

"Doing what? Working? I have to work."

"You're pretending you *are* your work. That's a pretty narrow definition of yourself."

I wanted to shout, but I managed a civil volume. "I *am* a gargoyle guardian."

"That's exactly my point, Mika."

With an infuriating shake of his head, Marcus said goodbye to Oliver, stepped onto his carpet, and flew away.

12

I glared at Marcus's back until he was out of sight. Why couldn't he see I was trying hard? Why couldn't he understand that I had to put all my energy into being a gargoyle guardian, because I was the only one? Just me. And when I asked for his help—

"He seemed angry," Oliver said, his voice small. "Angry with us."

"Definitely not with you. Wait here. I'll be right back." If we had to run for the airbus again, I needed to empty my bag of some weight.

I stomped up the walkway. If anyone was going to be angry—if anyone had a *right* to be angry—it was me. Marcus and his squad of highly trained warriors weren't going to step in to protect the city's gargoyles from the thief. The guards were floundering. It was up to me to prevent another gargoyle from suffering at the thief's hands. Why couldn't Marcus see that?

"The rest of my guardian duties don't cease because I had a rough night." I grumbled the words under my breath, but in my head, I was standing toe-to-toe with Marcus, speaking loud enough to get him to really hear me. "The least you could do is be *encouraging*."

The screen door slapped against the house, and Ms. Zuberrie marched to the top of the porch steps. She planted her hands on her waist.

"You had best not be considering meeting a Vanderlei looking like that, Mika Stillwater."

It didn't surprise me that Ms. Zuberrie had listened to my conversation with Marcus from the living room and had heard Amelia's message, too. It would have surprised me if my busybody landlady *hadn't* eavesdropped.

I glanced down at my outfit and dusted soot from the front of my shirt. It was damp with sweat, but if I tucked it in, it would be presentable. I could cover the bloodstain on my pants with my bag.

"Is *that* how you believe a gargoyle guardian, a representative of all gargoyles, should present herself?"

My shoulders slumped. When Ms. Zuberrie put it that way . . . "I don't have much time."

"Then hurry, girl, and leave your bag with me. I'll clean it while you change."

I heaved myself up the porch steps, stopping to hand off my dusty bag to Ms. Zuberrie. She took it with one hand and a brace of air element. With her other hand, she reached for my face, cupping my cheek gently as she examined me. Her pale blue eyes softened.

"He's right, you know. You're pushing yourself too hard. No, no, you don't need to explain. I understand why you do it, but that doesn't make him wrong."

I managed a small nod of agreement, surprised at the lump in my throat. My emotions were too near the surface.

"Thank you," I said, gesturing to my bag.

"Of course, dear. Now hurry." She waited until I opened

the screen door before adding softly, "Mika, if you keep on the path you're following, you're going to find yourself walking it alone soon. Mr. Velasquez has more patience than I would have credited him with, but even someone like him has limits."

Her soft words hit like a sucker-punch to my gut. I took a deep breath, blinking back fresh tears.

"I have limits, too," I whispered and let the door ease shut behind me.

————

OLIVER AND I RUSHED THROUGH THE BACK ALLEYS OF THE Cambium District, avoiding the cooler tree-shaded lanes crowded with ambling pedestrians. Making myself presentable—according to Ms. Zuberrie's standards—had eaten up more time than I anticipated. My feet throbbed at the punishing pace I set, but I didn't dare slow. After having missed my first appointment with Amelia Vanderlei, I cringed at the thought of being late the second time. I needed to repair my reputation. As Ms. Zuberrie reminded me, my behavior reflected on gargoyles and impacted my ability to help them.

I flapped the front of my shirt, trying to generate a cool breeze. My fresh pants and shirt were unwrinkled, thanks to the application of Ms. Zuberrie's temporary supple wood-and-air spell, but not even my skilled landlady could weave sophisticated heat-deflecting spells in the limited time available. Instead, she had directed her magic toward caging my hair in a bun, with a copious application of air weaves to smother any wayward frizz.

A sunburn stung the back of my neck by the time the multistory Vanderlei Books & Fine Goods Emporium came into view. I could sense Lowell's beacon behind us, near the Blue Lotus, though I had passed beyond the range of his freely offered boost. Only one unidentified beacon glowed on my inner map, hovering motionless about thirty feet above the ground directly in line with the bookstore. That had to be Greta.

I swiped sweat from my jaw. Slowing to clamp a hand to the crimp in my side, I caught sight of my reflection in a nearby window and grimaced. My cheeks were so red that my wrinkle-free clothes looked as if they had been ironed with me in them, and the floral print of my shirt couldn't disguise the damp sweat rings radiating from beneath my bag's straps.

"So much for making a good impression," I grumbled.

"Mika! Oliver!"

I jerked around. Amelia Vanderlei stood outside the bookstore's tall double doors, waving frantically. A thrill of alarm shot through me. I double-checked Greta's beacon. It didn't look dim or flickering, but that didn't mean she wasn't hurt in a way the identifying light couldn't discern.

Appearance forgotten, I broke into a run. Oliver thundered at my side. The pounding of his paws startled everyone on the sidewalk, and people rushed to clear a path.

"Ms. Vanderlei, is Greta hurt? I brought supplies, and—" My lungs gave out, and I bent in half around my aching side, gasping for breath. Through the floor-to-ceiling display windows, I could see deep into the bookstore's interior. I skimmed a blur of shoppers and bookcases, searching for the stairs. Greta was above us—not quite as high as the roof, thankfully. Closer, on the second floor.

"Hurt? No, no, dear. Oh my. I can see . . ." Amelia patted at her chest as if soothing her heart. "You gave me a fright, Ms. Stillwater, but I think I did the same for you."

"Greta is fine? But I saw you gesturing, and—"

Amelia gripped my forearm, compelling me to look at her. "Greta is unharmed. She spotted Oliver, so I came down to greet you. I should have realized my waving could be misinterpreted."

"Oh. *Oh.*" Heat scalded my cheeks. She had hailed me like a normal person, and I had charged her like an idiot. "I'm so sorry for startling you, Ms. Vanderlei. I jumped to the wrong conclusion."

"It's quite all right. I barely know you, but I can see you're a passionate woman. Here, come inside. And please, call me Amelia." She swung the bookstore's door open, holding it for me.

"Ah, yes, and, um, call me Mika." Flustered, I hurried through the doorway, not wanting to keep her waiting. I could feel the curious eyes of people on the street, and I was eager to escape the weight of those gazes, too.

"Should I fly up?" Oliver asked.

I pivoted on the threshold, a denial on the tip of my tongue. Where I went, Oliver went.

Amelia beat me to it. "The shop is designed to be friendly to four-legged folks as well as two-legged. You shouldn't have a problem navigating inside. Come with us. Unless you prefer to stay outside, of course."

With a pleased smile, Oliver trotted into the bookstore on my heels.

Cool air engulfed me. I inhaled the pleasant, dusty-vanilla scent of books and blinked sun blindness from my eyes. Elaborate spell-lit chandeliers cast a warm glow over rows of blackwood bookcases filled to bursting with a fortune of books. Cozy sitting areas invited patrons to peruse titles and socialize, but the true genius of the empo-rium were niches of home goods. Replica parlors, mock bathrooms, and faux solariums peppered the floor, each decorated with gorgeous purchasable goods. Dozens of humans, minotaurs, and centaurs crowded the aisles, and the vast bookstore hummed with conversation and laughter.

I stepped into a pocket of silence as those near the entrance strained to see who the illustrious Amelia Vanderlei personally welcomed into her store. Covertly blotting sweat from my upper lip, I shuffled to the side and willed my ragged breathing to normalize. Luckily, Oliver drew most of the attention. He twisted and turned to take in every detail of the Emporium, his carnelian scales shimmering in the multitude of lights. With an excited exhale, he loped across the carpeted floor to an artful display of delicate glass vases and spelled scent diffusers shaped like roses, carnations, lavender, and lilies.

"Mika, you should sell your pieces here," he said.

"Oh, I couldn't—"

"What do you create?" Amelia asked, taking my elbow and guiding me deeper into the store.

"Quartz objects, mainly figurines," I mumbled, feeling my blush climb toward my hairline. I hoped she didn't think I had put Oliver up to saying that. Even when being a quartz artisan had been my main goal, I hadn't dreamed of selling my work in a renowned Vanderlei Emporium.

"Mika can make anything out of quartz," Oliver said. "Earrings, glowball lanterns, kitchen stuff. But she's best at figurines, especially of gargoyles. The ones of me sell really well at the Fussy Fox."

"Really? I would love to see your work another time, Mika."

I smiled weakly, certain she was merely being polite.

Strolling unhurriedly, Amelia escorted us through the bookcases and up a ramp against the back wall to the second floor. I worried it wasn't designed to handle a gargoyle's impressive weight—especially one as large as Oliver—until we passed a pair of centaurs going down.

Oliver maintained a steady prattle, adorably intrigued by everything and unafraid to ask questions. Amelia was a gracious host and chatted with him like they were old friends. I trailed behind, self-consciously fluffing my damp shirt. I almost wished Amelia were more haughty. Then, I could pretend I wasn't bothered by how homely I felt next to the wealthy woman. Where I plodded, Amelia glided. Her golden hair haloed her peaches-and-cream complexion in a soft updo unmarred by sweat or wind. Her navy skirt was laced with delicate spells, as was her checkered top—both of which probably cost more than my entire wardrobe. Even if we exchanged clothes, I suspected the full spectrum would make my plain attire look regal, whereas I would look like a girl playing dress-up in Amelia's ensemble.

We met Greta in Amelia's personal office, an elegant room with a surprisingly small footprint. The gargoyle perched atop a wooden pillar obviously designed for her. She was small but healthy, with a sturdy lizard body and a cute, bearlike head, which Amelia later explained resembled a small marsupial called a wombat. Her entire body swirled with striated orange agate that contrasted beautifully against the office's green-and-cream-striped wallpaper.

Oliver loped into the room ahead of me, positioning himself next to Greta's perch. Seated, he was nearly eye level with Greta, his head half the size of her entire body. Yet his posture spoke of his deference to Greta, an acknowledgment of her age.

"G'day, young Oliver," Greta said.

I blinked in surprise. Greta was the first gargoyle I had met with an accent.

She leaned forward to touch noses with my friend before pivoting to me. "Guardian Mika. Thank you for coming."

"Hello, Greta. I'm sorry I missed our appointment yesterday. I hope you haven't experienced too much discomfort while you've waited."

"None at all."

I half expected—half hoped—Amelia would disappear to conduct her important bookshop magnate duties now that she had shown us to Greta. Instead, she asked to link with me.

"I want to be able to heal Greta myself, in case she's hurt when we're away from Terra Haven," Amelia said, fondly petting Greta's curved forehead.

I wondered if she wanted to keep an eye on me, too. Both things could be true.

I set my bag on the floor, then accepted Amelia's balance of elements. The warmth of her magical signature filled the link. It would have been soothing if I hadn't been so self-conscious of the disparity in our elemental strengths. Amelia was as strong as Marcus, as strong as anyone on his elite squad. I peeked at Amelia, wondering if she was shocked by my midlevel strength. She studied me with candid curiosity, and try as I might, I could find no pity or condescension in her open gaze.

Swallowing my insecurity, I accepted Oliver's boost, then felt Amelia do the same. A flood of magic bloomed within me. Once, this influx of power would have disoriented me. Now, all it took to ground me was a deep breath.

With Greta's assent, I twisted the elements into a perfect match for her orange agate body and slid the magic into her. Dull pain radiated back through the link, originating from two severed claws on a front paw and a time-worn notch in her blunt nose. Reshaping a seed crystal, I delicately grafted it onto Greta, replacing her missing parts with clear quartz her body would slowly absorb into orange agate. With another pass, I soothed scrapes and scratches from her paws and belly. All in all, Greta's healing took less time than the airbus trip across town.

When I extracted my magic from Greta, the gargoyle stretched and flapped her wings. Peering at her new, clear claws, she grinned, exposing rabbitlike front teeth.

Amelia snorted. "Well, there goes my plan to be useful in the future."

"What do you mean?"

"That twist you did to earth element at the beginning, I *might* be able to replicate, but then you tuned it to Greta herself. I didn't know that was possible."

"Mika is a guardian," Oliver said, the statement a verbal shrug and an explanation rolled into one.

This time, Amelia laughed outright. "Honestly, I have no idea why I thought healing would be simple."

Even sheepish looked refined on Amelia.

She insisted I stay for afternoon tea, as if I were an invited guest, not someone paid for her services—and tipped extravagantly, despite my protests. When I sat across from Amelia, my spine melted into the criminally comfortable wingback chair, and I strangled a groan. The throbbing in my feet faded. I stifled a yawn. Standing back up might take more willpower than I had in reserve.

Amelia produced slices of cinnamon-dusted peaches and zesty lemon crinkle cookies, with cold-brewed green tea served in frosted glasses. I ate carefully, afraid I would get crumbs or juice on the pristine furniture. Amelia and Oliver carried the conversation. I let my attention drift around the room, noting a second perch on Amelia's desk, a handle shaped for a small paw on the inside *and* outside of the window, and a miniature door cut into the wall above a bookcase.

"It's important that you don't boost anyone you can't see," Oliver finished, having filled Greta—and therefore, Amelia—in about the dangerous thief. "At least until we catch him. I think we're getting closer." He gave me a small nod, letting me know he wouldn't divulge our suspicions about Haubner. Investigating the guard was our duty, not Greta's, and certainly not Amelia's.

"The thief is shifting his spirit?" Amelia shook her head. "That's devious, if shortsighted."

"And heartless," I growled. I would have said more, but I was forced to hide a yawn behind my teacup.

"Healing the sickened gargoyles takes a lot out of Mika," Oliver said with entirely too much candor.

"Nothing I can't handle," I protested.

"I was wondering, but that explains why . . ." Magic unspooled from Amelia in a soft wave, engulfing me. Cool and refreshing, the spell cascaded down my scalp, across my shoulders, and dove toward my fingertips and toes in a tingling rush.

I dropped my teacup. A band of air caught it before liquid splashed my shins or the carpet. Amelia leapt out of her seat, a hand to her mouth.

"Oh, Mika! I'm so sorry. That was too forward of me. I shouldn't have done that. Not without your permission."

I stared at my fingers in shock. Every scrape and cut was missing, replaced by perfectly healed flesh. The soreness in my shoulders and feet had vanished. Without looking, I knew my knees were no longer bruised.

I extended a hand to show Oliver, who rushed to my

chair. My amethyst scars sparkled against my unblemished skin.

"That was . . . incredible." Meeting Amelia's worried gaze, I smiled to show her I wasn't offended. Maybe I didn't understand the intricacies of high society, but someone generously granting skillful healing seemed like something to be grateful for. "You startled me is all. Thank you."

"I just, I . . ." Amelia collapsed into her chair and patted her flushed cheeks. "You remind me of my sister so much, and well . . ." The full spectrum shot me an abashed glance. "I thought if I *did* ask if you needed healing, you would refuse."

"I, ah, it wouldn't have been right."

Amelia chuckled. "You are such a match for your magical signature. And that's a compliment."

I blushed and picked at imaginary lint on my pants. Amelia kept defying my expectations of an elite full spectrum. She was oddly relatable, unpretentious, and open-hearted. I found myself thinking she would get along great with Kylie, and probably Ms. Zuberrie, too.

"It's time I had a talk with Randall," Amelia said, thankfully changing subjects.

"Who's that?"

"Randall Hollinger, Terra Haven's chief of guards. He needs to understand the seriousness of this situation and put his best people on this case. The thief must be caught before he harms another gargoyle." A thread of steel edged her voice.

"Ah, Captain Rojas asked us not to spread around the theory about the spirit shifting."

"Except telling gargoyles," Oliver said.

"Is it still just a theory?" Amelia asked.

I hesitated, then shook my head.

"Then Randall needs to know. As someone with a gargoyle family member, I don't feel such important information should be kept quiet. Not from gargoyles, and not from those of us who love them."

This sort of highhanded full-spectrum mentality usually riled my moral sensibilities, but this time, I found myself nodding along with Amelia. Finally, someone other than me was championing gargoyles. It didn't even annoy me that the words would have more impact coming from Amelia than me.

"There's one thing I don't understand," Amelia said. "If you already performed two healings today, why did you agree to meet with us now?"

I frowned, not understanding the question. "Because Greta needed healing."

Amelia and Greta shared a look I couldn't interpret.

"We are both grateful for what you did for Greta," Amelia said, and Greta nodded vigorously. "But it could have waited. Another day—another week—wouldn't have been so bad, would it, Greta?"

"Of course not."

"If a gargoyle is suffering from injuries, any delay is too long," I protested.

Greta clicked her teeth twice. "Guardian, we are not fragile."

"But the pain—"

"It was an annoyance, easily ignored."

"And you were so tired," Amelia said. "I know; I felt it in our link. My sister used to work herself to the same state of exhaustion. I recognized the signs. And I was right, because the elements just poured into you. I'm going to need more than this snack to recover. You, too."

I stared blankly at Amelia, casting my awareness inward.

I had been so discombobulated by the full spectrum's kind but surprising healing spell I hadn't noticed the absence of fatigue permeating my muscles. The urge to yawn was gone, too. I felt energized, as if I had feasted on two or three of Eilidh's pick-me-up pizazzies. I would pay for it later, of course. All healing burned through the body's energy, but for now, the elements bolstered me.

"I, um, I'm sorry." I wasn't sure if it was the right thing to say, so I added, "Thank you."

Amelia waved off both statements.

"Mika, if running a business has taught me anything, it's that you have to set boundaries. Only you know how full your schedule is, and only you can judge how much energy you have. Listen to your body. Tell people no whenever you get a chance. It's very freeing."

I folded my fingers together, not quite meeting Amelia's gaze. It was easy for her to say no to others: She had social and elemental power. People already respected her. She also ran a bookstore—a huge enterprise that employed countless people, but still just a shop. My business was different. I couldn't say no, not when it meant a gargoyle would suffer.

"Ah, see, so much like my sister," Amelia said to Greta.

The gargoyle nodded. "Stubborn. A good quality in a guardian."

"So long as it doesn't become a point of pride."

Greta nodded. So did Oliver!

Just when I was starting to feel ganged up on, Amelia smiled at me. "Even guardians need their own champions. Please, think about what I said. It's important you take care of yourself. A lot of gargoyles are depending on it."

I let out a pent-up sigh and nodded. "I'll do my best."

13

My best involved a hasty meal followed by hours at my worktable, reading correspondences and drafting responses. The words gradually grew blurry, and my handwriting became choppy. When the exhaustion lurking behind Amelia's revitalizing spell caught up with me, it swallowed me whole, dragging me mercilessly into sleep.

I woke to a dull pain throbbing in my neck, a page of my notebook stuck to my face. Clumsily, I peeled myself free and sat up. I was at my worktable. My room was dark, the treetops out my window illuminated by silvery moonbeams. Kylie's windows were open, the faint silhouette of her sleeping form visible in her bed. Five gargoyle beacons rested around the house: three on the roof, one—Herbert— on the worktable in front of me, and Oliver on the balcony railing.

I must have groaned, or maybe it was the loud pop of my neck that woke Herbert. He opened one eye, yawned, and closed it. I reached to pet him, but stopped short when I found my everlasting seed fisted in my palm. Uncurling my fingers hurt. The imprint of the milky-quartz disc's rough edge looked like a bruise in the dim light. I ran my thumb over the soft bumps on the seed's surface. I hadn't woken up sprawled across my paper-strewn worktop, quartz clutched in my hand this often since I studied for the quarry test—

I lurched to my feet. The chair toppled, and I caught it with a flail of air before it could wake the house.

Oliver pushed through the doorway, eyes wide with alarm.

I held a finger to my lips, indicating Herbert, who had fallen back to sleep. Then, grinning, I whispered, "Meet me downstairs. I recognize my seed's clue."

I tiptoed downstairs, my seed-crystal-stuffed bag in one hand, my boots in the other. I stopped in the kitchen long enough to fill a canteen with water. Then I slipped from the silent house.

Oliver waited for me on the sidewalk.

"It's another business logo, this time for Earthspire Studio," I explained while I laced up my boots. "It's a stoneworks shop. I went there once to take a test before I got a job at the quarry. I haven't thought of the place since." I told him the location, an easy few minutes' flight for him, a forty-minute hike for me.

Neither of us suggested waiting until daylight. Twice, I had been too late to take advantage of my everlasting seed's clues. I couldn't—*wouldn't*—miss this one, too.

"I'll stay close," Oliver said.

I set out at a fast walk when I wanted to run. Urgency and excitement lent me energy, but I couldn't sprint the whole way. Even a continuous jog was beyond me. Yesterday's healings—the gargoyles' and my own—had wiped out my energy reserves, and the little sleep I had gotten wasn't enough to reinvigorate me.

Oliver flew ahead, the rustle of his wings softer than his footsteps. He landed on the rooftop at the end of the block, then soared to the next corner when I approached.

When I reached the intersection, I broke into a modest jog, my bag rattling and clacking against my back. I kept it up for a block, then walked the next. Using Oliver's boost, I cobbled together a crude cushion of air to help support the weight of my bag, but I refrained from a full levitation spell. My mental muscles were as tired as my physical muscles, and I didn't want to chance wearing myself out magically when a hurt gargoyle might be ahead. Impatience thrummed in my veins. *Would* I find an injured gargoyle at the stoneworks studio? Or was my seed pointing toward a key to capturing the thief? Or toward a different problem entirely?

I cut across the outskirts of downtown. This early, the only other people out were lamplighters, an occasional baker or wardminder headed to work, and guards. None but the guards paid me any mind. I studied them as closely as they scrutinized me, searching for Haubner among them.

I passed in range of gargoyles Cosimo, Roslyn, and Jenji, and each offered me a boost from afar. Now that I could sense gargoyle beacons, the freely given influxes of magic no longer caught me off guard. However, the gargoyles' generosity and trust never failed to humble me.

Oliver paused to chat with each gargoyle, but I tossed waves and kept moving. Every so often, I pulled my ever-lasting seed from my pocket to check its surface. It remained unchanged, which only added to my urgency.

As I neared Earthspire, I cut down Orchardlace Lane, a narrow, garden-like road flanked by high-end shops. Dogwoods graced either side of the lane, the undersides of their interwoven branches lit by the spelled streetlights.

Exuberant floral vines climbed the brick and stucco store fronts, with blooming plants overflowing serpentine planter boxes beneath their display windows. During the day, this pedestrian-only pathway would be clogged with wealthy customers and dreamy-eyed window-shoppers, but in the morning twilight, I had the street to myself. I slowed, gulping down air flavored with the sweet scent of gardenias.

A beacon glowed on my inner map, positioned atop the roof on the right—Daphne, a part-fox, part-otter gargoyle, whom I met weeks earlier. She hadn't bonded with a particular business owner or family; instead, she considered Orchardlace and all its shopkeepers her family.

Puzzled, I slowed further. I was within Daphne's range, but she hadn't offered me an elemental boost.

Shielding my eyes, I shuffled to the side, trying to see past the illuminated foliage to the night-cloaked rooftop where Daphne perched. Even without the tree branches in the way, I thought she was too far back to see from the street.

A shadow twisted in the doorway two shops away. I froze. The shape moved again, forming the silhouette of a man dressed in all black. A matching cloth covered his nose and mouth, leaving only his eyes and short black hair visible. He stood outside an open door, his back to me, his face turned away from the nearest light. Another step, and he would trigger the ward across the doorway.

Painted gold letters identified the shop as Traipsing Through Stardust, a goldsmith. The interior was dark, but enough streetlight shone through the front window to outline the blocky shapes of display stands and cases—and another masked figure clad in all black. They skulked past the ornate cash register to a warded cabinet at the rear of the shop, swaying as they grasped the handle.

A shock jolted through me. They were thieves! *The* thieves? Different thieves? Should I—

Daphne shifted. Her foot or tail or wing smacked something solid and wooden, and a scramble of quartz claws followed, shattering the silence. Her beacon flickered all too familiarly.

The man in the doorway twisted to glare at the roof. The person inside spun around. Our gazes collided.

For a heartbeat, neither of us moved. Then the thief bolted for the door with a distinctly feminine shout. I yanked hard on the elements. Oliver had veered toward a distant gargoyle, but he was still in range, and magic flooded me through his enhancement. Before I could formulate a spell, the male thief whipped around to face me. Menace radiated from his shadowed eyes.

Fear locked my knees. The man was tall and lean. His hair was the right shade and length. Was it Haubner?

When I hesitated, he attacked. Shards of ice sliced through the air. I shoved a quartz-hard shield into existence just in time to deflect the elemental razor blades.

The woman darted through the doorway as the man flung his next attack. Prepared for a frontal assault, I was caught flatfooted when the volley of ice blades flew high, then dove over my shield. Pain sliced the top of my shoulder and down my back. One strap on my bag snapped, staggering me. Dropping to a crouch, I yanked my shield into a solid dome around me. A flurry of baneful shards lambasted me from multiple directions, chipping at my protection.

I glared at the pair of thieves through my ward, cursing my earlier hesitation. These were *the* thieves. Daphne failing to boost me had been my first clue. Her clumsiness my second. Now I could tell by her beacon that she was dizzy and disoriented, her spirit vibrating inside her body. Because of these two. No ordinary thief struck a goldsmith, either. They were notoriously impenetrable—unless, of course, the thief could shift her spirit to match the gold-smith's.

Fury and helplessness warred inside me. The culprits were less than ten feet away, but I was powerless, trapped behind my own ward. If I faced only one thief, I could have chanced dropping my ward for a counterattack. With Oliver's boost, I might be able to overpower a single person, but not two. As it was, I could barely move within the confines of my magic, but I didn't dare expand my ward and risk weakening it.

The man charged. I braced myself, fingers digging into the gritty cobblestones, my bag dragging awkwardly on one arm. I tore open the top of the bag, spilling quartz seeds, knowing I would be too slow to create a weapon from them, but I had to try.

The woman lurched after the man, grabbing his arm and dragging him to a halt. She said something harsh, the words lost beneath the roar of blood in my ears. He jerked his arm from her grip. Magic wove at the ends of his fingers. Water leapt from a nearby fountain into the air in front of him. The melon-sized globe divided into five long spikes. They were pure liquid, but the elements encasing them made their edges gleam like steel. His initial attacks had been hasty, designed to scare and distract me. These weapons were crossbow bolts calculated to punch through my ward—and through me.

The woman made another grab for her partner.

"Don't," she hissed. "You'll kill her, and we need—"

The man launched the spikes. I lunged aside, dragging my magical protection with me. Quartz seeds bounced like marbles around me, sliding underfoot. A second too slow and far too weakly, the woman shoved a countercurrent of air at the blades. Three spikes flew wide. Two hit my ward dead-on, the twin punches hammering deep in my mind. Teeth gritted, I clung to my ward. Behind me, glass shattered. The low wail of a triggered ward swelled in volume.

The woman slapped her partner. Even with the cloth covering his cheek, the blow landed loud enough to be heard above the shrill alarm. The man staggered, then spun toward the woman with a fist cocked. She yelled and pointed to the air above my head.

In my mind, a shining beacon shot across the rooftops toward us. With the underside of the trees lit up and the night sky an inky backdrop, I doubted the thieves could see Oliver. But they could hear his frantic wing beats.

As one, they spun and sprinted away from me.

"Hey! Stop!" I collapsed my ward, losing precious seconds as the backwash of magic staggered me. Abandoning my bag, I surged to my feet, cursing as I slid on seed crystals.

The woman twisted, raising a hand. Frozen sparks glistened in her palm, small and bright. I dove behind a planter and tented a shield above my head. Golden drops of fire arced through the air, hit the storefront opposite me, and scattered.

I braced for an explosion.

A defensive ward flashed, but no flames followed.

The woman canted her arm, aiming for me. I ducked. A hail of yellow sparks pelted my ward, bouncing and skittering across the cobblestones. The building's ward next to me erupted with a shriek louder than a harpy.

I clapped my hands over my ears and risked a peek. The woman was racing after her partner, escaping.

Oliver crashed through the trees, landing hard on the cobblestones beside me in a rain of broken branches just as the goldsmith's compromised ward shot a blazing beacon into the sky. I squinted against the glare, dropping my ward.

"It's the thieves," I shouted, pointing up the street.

The woman tossed another handful of sparks, setting off more wards. Her partner was barely visible in the distance, a shadow sprinting into the night. I tore free of a tangle of vines and gave chase. Oliver pounded behind me, the clamor of his quartz paws lost beneath the cacophony of alarms.

Sprinting, I willed my feet even faster. I couldn't let the thieves escape to harm another gargoyle.

Magic hummed inside me. I formed a blast of air and shoved it ahead of me, hoping to knock the woman off her feet. Wind roared down the tight corridor. Plants flattened in their boxes and trees bent under the force of the air. My elemental blast caught the thief's next toss of golden shards and catapulted them back at her. Before she could be struck by her own weapon, the woman darted around a corner. My magic hurtled uselessly past the intersection, carrying a cloud of torn foliage, dirt, and bright sparks down the lane.

Oliver launched, punching a new hole in the dogwoods to climb over the buildings. I prepped a spell to rip cobblestones from their beds, praying I had the strength. I wouldn't get another chance to stop the thief. If she got much farther ahead, I would lose her. Already, my legs felt like shale, my breaths fiery rasps.

Leaning into the turn, I sprinted around the corner into a dark alley. Invisible claws snatched my torso, lifting me from the ground, knocking the wind from my lungs. My feet churned empty air. Gasping breathlessly, I lashed out with a flurry of earth element.

A nullification spell engulfed me, thick as quicksand. The elements vanished. Black dots danced in my vision as I flailed. I couldn't touch magic. I couldn't twitch so much as a finger. Panic spiraled up my spine, icy and disorienting.

"Hold her until we can question—"

"She's going to pass out."

Something firm pounded my back, once, twice. Air sucked into my starved lungs.

Oliver's beacon dove through the buildings, a blur inside my mind.

"Whoa! Stand back!"

The snap of quartz wings ricocheted down the alley. Carnelian feathers suddenly filled my vision.

"Let her go," Oliver yelled.

"Grab it."

"But it's a gargoyle."

"Do you want to explain it to Hollinger if this gargoyle is part of that mess?"

Oliver's startled squawk transformed into a roar as his claws screeched across the cobblestones. Thick bands of air forcefully pulled him away from me. Earth pinched his wings, pinning them to his sides, caging him to the ground. I screamed, straining for magic so intensely my skull felt as if it would split open. I couldn't let the thieves—

A glowball floated into sight, illuminating the shadowy alley. Three unfamiliar city guards circled me. All were magically linked. I craned my head to look behind us. Two more guards—also part of the link—filled out the squad. Incredulously, they controlled the nullification spell neutering my magic, not the thieves. These supposed protectors of Terra Haven's citizens were the ones holding me captive and pinning my friend's jaw to the cobblestones as if he were a rabid wyvern, not a beloved gargoyle.

"Release him—"

A muzzle of air slapped over my mouth. Another silenced Oliver. Fury burned hot enough to choke me, despair a scalding chaser.

The thieves were gone. I had been so close, and I had failed.

14

The guards held us until Captain Rojas arrived. Only then did they allow my feet to touch the ground. Only then did they allow Oliver to lift his head. A dull headache pounded behind my eyes, compliments of the null spell cutting me off from the elements. Or maybe it was the outrage burning in my veins hot enough to melt quartz.

The captain threaded between her people, planting herself in front of me, ignoring Oliver. He looked furious but unharmed. I sliced an impotent glare across the guards, memorizing their faces. I could forgive their mistaken detainment of me, but not of Oliver.

The captain gestured to the shortest guard, and the muzzle of air vanished from my mouth. Oliver remained silenced. I ground my teeth.

"Captain, Oliver's done *nothing* to deserve this treatment. He's a gargoyle. Why is he—?"

"Ms. Stillwater." Captain Rojas clasped her hands behind her back. She stood close enough for me to map the wrinkles on her face, and every crease delineated her displeasure. "You better have a damn fine explanation for tonight."

"Another gargoyle is sick. Spirit shifted." I spat the last like a challenge. I wouldn't keep the theory quiet—because it was true, and because I wouldn't perform favors for a woman who allowed those under her to cage gargoyles.

"I suppose you want to run and tell Chief Hollinger about it."

I almost asked, *Who?* But with a sinking feeling, I remember Amelia telling us he was the chief of Terra Haven's guards.

"You don't need to trouble yourself. I'm sure he already knows," Captain Rojas said, her mild tone at odds with the tension in her crossed arms. "Your friend, the chief, and I had a talk today. He's under the impression that my investigative skills have been deficient."

"I never said—"

"'Lax' was the term Chief Hollinger used."

It was her people who let the thieves escape. *Inept* would have been a better descriptor. I bit my lip, though, because as satisfactory as the retort might be, it wouldn't free Oliver or me.

"Apparently a young guardian whined in her high-society friend's ears, and now I get to report directly to the chief at the end of every shift. My private theory is now public knowledge. All the traps I had planned might as well be smoke for all the good they'll do now. But I'm sure you'll appreciate that your friend Hollinger ordered increased force to be used on *anyone* suspicious until the thief is caught." The captain arched a brow at me, then at Oliver. "So I repeat, why were you here tonight, Ms. Stillwater? Or would you prefer to have this conversation at a guard house?"

I ran my tongue over my teeth, swallowing several barbed responses. I didn't regret Amelia interceding on behalf of the city's gargoyles. I could shrug off the captain's attempt to guilt me for her failings, too. But her implication that I was to blame for the guards' barbaric treatment of Oliver made me want to growl. I suppressed the urge. Oliver was doing enough growling for the both of us.

"I'm here because of my everlasting seed," I ground out, choosing expediency over righteousness.

Captain Rojas scoffed. "You asked the tree about criminal activity in Terra Haven?"

"I asked the tree how I could help gargoyles. My seed pointed me here."

"Here? Right here?" The captain pointed at the ground.

Her perverse insistence on mincing words made me want to scream. The longer this explanation took, the longer Daphne suffered.

"If you allow me to show you, I have my seed in my pocket."

Captain Rojas nodded, and the spell binding me unraveled with an unnecessary shove. I staggered to catch my balance. Oliver's growl escalated in pitch, but the guard holding the link appeared oblivious.

My hand closed on my seed, and my heart flip-flopped in my chest. The seed was round. With trepidation, I held it out on the flat of my palm.

My everlasting seed had evolved. Instead of a milky-white disc, it was a pale-yellow glass sphere. Exquisitely detailed knotted ivy and trumpet-shaped flowers formed the outer shell. A partially formed animal bulged in the center, its four stubby legs and lumpy head potentially the beginnings of anything from a panther to a pegasus.

When Captain Rojas reached for my seed, I closed my

fist around it, hiding it. She raised her eyebrows in silent rebuke and reached for my seed again. Reluctantly, I let her pluck it from my hand.

"This told you to come here tonight?" she asked, skepticism lacing every word.

"Captain, that's just like—"

A flick of her gaze shut the guard's mouth on whatever he had been about to say.

"It didn't look like that earlier," I said. "It looked like the Earthspire Studio logo."

Captain Rojas glanced in the direction of the studio, two streets away, then back at me. "What a remarkable coincidence that you decided to come through this street at this hour."

"Frustrating is more like it." I snatched my seed from her palm. "I feel like my everlasting seed is stringing me along behind the thieves."

The last of the blaring ward alarms fell silent. I worked my jaw to pop my ears. Muffled shouts and cracks emanated from Orchardlace Lane. What little I could see of the street beyond the alley didn't reveal the source of the peculiar sounds. What had the female thief thrown?

On my inner map, Daphne wobbled atop the goldsmith's roof. If she was as dizzy as Nimoy, she shouldn't chance flying, but she might risk it to reach me. I needed to get to her first.

"I need to—"

A wall of earth-laced air blocked my path when I turned toward Orchardlace Lane.

Captain Rojas sidestepped to be directly in front of me again. "You believe you saw the person responsible for this mess?"

"*Persons*. There are two of them, a man and a woman. I

not only saw them; Oliver and I would have stopped them if not for the interference of your guards."

Rojas raised a skeptical eyebrow. "Describe them."

"Release Oliver."

She hesitated, then gestured to the guard holding the link. He made a shooing motion to his squad. They took a collective step away from Oliver. The magic binding my friend dissolved. Tail snapping, wings hunched, Oliver stalked to my side. His glare would have made a basilisk proud. I ran a hand down his spine, then rested my palm on a wing. The appendage could have been inert carnelian with how stiffly he held it.

"And the null spell?"

Captain Rojas took longer before motioning the guard again. I drew a deep breath when the elements snapped to me, sharp and sweet. Oliver's boost sang within me, enhancing my strength.

"Ms. Stillwater," the captain prompted.

"The woman is my height, maybe a little heavier. She's the spirit shifter. I caught her inside the goldsmith's. The man is tall, with dark hair. He looks a lot like your under-ling, Haubner." I mentally compared memories of the guard and the thief: They had the same build, same height, same hair color. Had the thief said anything? I didn't recall his voice. Had he intentionally *not* spoken, knowing I would recognize him? "Where is Haubner right now?"

"That's it? I thought you had useful information."

I gaped at the captain. "I just told you there are two people, not one, like you thought. I described what they look like."

Captain Rojas snorted. "A woman of average height and build. A thin, young man. You've narrowed it down to half the people in the city. What about the woman's hair color? Skin color? Eye color?"

"They wore black clothes and masks. The woman had a black cloth covering her head." Dismay at my inability to provide more details only fueled my anger.

"Mmm. Convenient. What about your seed? When did it evolve?"

My fists bunched at my sides. "I don't know. I was too busy trying to stay alive." I brushed a finger across my shoulder, hissing involuntarily when pain flared beneath my fingertip. My shirt was ripped and sticky with blood, but the angle was wrong for me to see the wound.

"But now your seed looks like sunstone ivy."

"Sunstone? That's not . . ." I opened my fist to re-examine my seed. "It's glass, and the plant could be any number of vines."

"It's sunstone," Captain Rojas said. "Follow me."

The guards closed in behind us, as if to prevent us from escaping. I speared another ineffectual glare at all five of them. Oliver's slashing tail clattered across cobblestones, a sharp counterpoint to his deep growls.

We stepped from the shadows of the alley onto a street lit for a nighttime festival. Every lamp and lantern flared with white-hot glowballs, and I squinted against the glare. Dozens of guards rushed along the street, magic flaring around them, blades slashing . . . at light? The entire length of Orchardlace Lane appeared golden, from the cobblestones to the rooftops. Even the trunks of the dogwoods sparkled as if they were wrapped in glass.

Glass that writhed and twisted and spread.

"Sunstone ivy," I gasped. "It was seeds she threw, not sparks."

Already the vines climbed to the rooftops, growing with

such eerie speed they seemed to crawl like tentacles of a vast animal emerging from the cobblestones. Despite its flexible nature, every stalk, leaf, and trumpet-shaped flower resembled chiseled glass or elementally shaped citrine.

"I think Mr. Almasi fibbed about the number of seeds he kept on hand," Captain Rojas said.

I nodded numbly, only now remembering the handful of sunstone seeds Mo said had been taken from the Blue Lotus. No wonder every ward on Orchardlace Lane had responded with full-throated alarms.

Part rock, part plant, sunstone ivy was objectively pretty but dangerously invasive. With climbing tendrils that could wind into unyielding knots and stems coated with delicate, sticky hairs, it could scale any surface, even glass. At night, the ivy remained as supple as a plant, with all a plant's natural vulnerabilities. In sunlight, the entire vine hardened to stone. Any joint or mortar pierced by a tendril would be cracked. Anything caught in its vise would be crushed. A single sunstone ivy plant could consume a house in a night and demolish it at daybreak, if left unchecked. The thief had tossed down enough seeds to tear apart the entire district.

I re-examined my everlasting seed. The shape in the middle—was that Daphne caught in sunstone ivy?

"What was your plan if you caught up with the thieves?" Captain Rojas asked.

"Stop them. That's as far ahead as I thought. Captain, they hurt a gargoyle. I need to heal her."

"Go."

"Oliver . . ." I took in the chaotic street. Ivy crawled everywhere underfoot, and guards swarmed the lane, with more rushing in from side streets. Navigating the mess would be a nightmare for someone Oliver's size and shape.

"I'll meet you," he said, coming to the same conclusion.

He spun toward the alley, where the trees didn't overhang the rooftops. He took one running lunge, then leapt skyward, forcing the guards behind us to scatter to avoid being clipped by his quartz wings.

Serves you right, I thought, as one guard picked himself up and brushed dirt off his pants. But I made a mental note to talk with Oliver. It wasn't in my friend's nature to be so belligerent, and I didn't want this encounter to embitter him.

"Saunders," Captain Rojas said.

"Yes, ma'am."

A second pair of footsteps echoed mine as I broke into a jog. I glanced over my shoulder. One of the guards—a thin, short man with blond hair and an angular, tanned face—fell in beside me. Saunders, I presumed. Captain Rojas had given me a babysitter.

The captain remained behind, conferring with the four other guards who had captured Oliver and me. I doubted they would be getting the skin-flaying dressing-down they deserved for their treatment of Oliver.

Dodging through increasingly dense shimmering vege-tation, I bypassed men and women hacking at the encroaching sunstone with knives and blades of air, water, and earth. The scents of churned soil and bittersweet crushed greenery hung in the air, but the guards' efforts made no visible dent in the glass-like ivy. The invasive vine tunneled roots into the cracks between cobblestones, sprouting snarls of ivy that twined across the lane in ever-bigger tripping hazards. In the loose soil of the planter boxes and open ground around the trees, the ivy grew even faster. The entire lane echoed with the plants' rustles, the cumulative sound louder than people's footsteps and terse conversations.

I thought I chased the thieves only a block, but it had been closer to five, and I was panting by the time I reached the goldsmith's. The thieves had left the door open. The ward remained intact across the threshold, a dangerous weave of fire and air that would pin a trespasser in a scalding net. It had done nothing to stop the sunstone ivy. Glassy vines as thick as my wrist climbed internal display cases and twined across shelves. Thick see-through yellow leaves and flowers as large as my cupped hands refracted the streetlights, transforming the interior into a jungle of sunlight brighter than the goldsmith's wares.

I sympathized with the shopkeeper's misfortune, but I was more concerned about the vines climbing over the roof's eaves. If they reached Daphne's small body, in her dizzy state, she could easily become entangled.

"How long until dawn?" I asked my babysitter. Even a gargoyle's quartz flesh would be vulnerable to the brutal strength of daylight-hardened sunstone.

Saunders grimaced at the sky. "Less than an hour."

"Oliver?" I could sense two gargoyles on the roof. I shaded my eyes against the lanterns' glare, trying to see beyond the dogwood canopies.

"Here." Oliver clawed aside a glassy vine to hang his head over the edge of the roof. "Daphne can't fly, but she can jump. Can you catch her?"

I tested the magic I held, boosted by Oliver. It wouldn't have been enough to catch a gargoyle as large as my friend, but it would be enough for Daphne.

Forming a sturdy net of air, I said, "Ready."

Daphne wobbled to the roof's edge and leapt. Her jade-dark aventurine otter paws flailed against empty air, and her green-speckled wings and oversized fennec fox ears flapped with equal ineffectiveness.

I swooped my net beneath Daphne and lowered her to the ground in one controlled motion. Oliver dropped through the tree, landing hard next to me. Saunders staggered out of the way as my friend nosed between us.

I sank to my knees, cradling Daphne's small fox head in my hands. Her eyes jittered, unfocused. She laid with her paws spread, as if the street might tip sideways beneath her.

"I've got you," I said.

I stretched my magic into Daphne. A familiar vibration ran through her insides, discordant and intrusive. Bracing myself for the baetyl's attack, I soothed the first jangle of energy, then quested deeper. In a blink, my delicate touch morphed into a torrent, the elements transformed into an ice-slick funnel. I scrambled for control, flailing. Failing. My spirit gushed out of me into Daphne.

Tiny ethereal otter paws caught me, cradling me. In this nebulous golden space, physical size had no meaning. Gravity didn't exist. Air was unnecessary. There was only Daphne and me, two spirits in a single body.

Fear trembled in the back of my thoughts. I couldn't hear the baetyl's song. I couldn't feel its powerful presence. I couldn't sense my own body. I could feel only Daphne's shaking form, her spirit quaking against mine.

Time hung suspended and distant, a physical force that couldn't affect us. I stared into Daphne's trusting, glowing eyes. Here, we had no means of communication except one: love. Hers shone from within, flooding me with confidence, chasing away my alarm. Peace took its place, a feeling of utter harmony. This, I sent to Daphne, soothing it down her spirit, countering the vibrations shaking her innermost self.

Daphne stilled. I relaxed, content except for a nagging feeling of forgetfulness, and I waited, filled with infinite patience, to remember.

The cadence of Daphne's love changed. It deepened, pulsing like a drum. Like a heartbeat. Harder. Louder. It shoved against me. I rocked in place, then sloshed more violently. Daphne stared at me, her sharp fox face intent, her eyes rounded with a message I couldn't understand. Had I been wrong? Did she need more healing? Was she still spirit-shifted?

The question burst my tranquility. Urgency flooded in its wake. My body. Where was—?

On Daphne's next thrust, my spirit shot free, punching back into my own skin, my own bones. Gasping, I slumped over my knees. Darkness swamped the edges of my vision.

15

"Mika! Are you all right?" Oliver thrust his face in mine, his eyes saucers of concern.

I lifted a hand to my forehead, willing my consciousness to stabilize. For a terrifying second, my spirit had been entirely untethered. Only familiarity and practice had brought me home to my body.

Goose bumps crawled down my arms. "I'll be fine. I just need a moment."

Daphne rested a small paw on my knee, peering up into my eyes. I gave her a wan smile and cycled the elements, grounding myself in the familiar feel of Oliver's enhancement.

"Tell us what happened, Daphne," I said, eager to divert everyone's attention from my well-being.

The gargoyle crimped her huge ears. "I don't know. I started to feel dizzy. I was afraid my sickness would infect Bashar's magic, so I stopped boosting him. Is he all right?"

"Bashar Brenier?" Saunders asked. "The master goldsmith?"

"This is his shop." Daphne reared onto her hind legs,

peering up and down the street. "Have you checked inside? He was early today. He doesn't normally come in until after sunrise."

I gripped Daphne's raised paw to get her attention. "It wasn't the goldsmith. It was a thief. Someone shifted their spirit to match his."

She dropped to all fours, her sharp canines flashing. "I helped a thief break into Bashar's?"

"They would have gotten in without your help."

She stared forlornly at Traipsing Through Stardust. Sunstone continued to grow with alarming speed and tenacity, coating every surface, including the inside of the window. In another few minutes, it would be impossible to see the interior.

"What a mess," Daphne said.

I agreed.

A cart rumbled to a halt at the end of the street, pulled by a nervous team of mules. A trio of guards spilled out. With deft bands of air, they hoisted a giant copper cauldron from the cart's bed and jogged it up the street.

"Neira, Pozo, Saunders, bring the other," the lead guard ordered as she trotted past.

Two guards abandoned their efforts to uproot sunstone ivy from a nearby planter and ran toward the cart. After a troubled glance at me, my babysitter sprinted after them. With practiced coordination, they levitated a second cauldron and hustled it up Orchardlace Lane, depositing it in the middle of the cobblestones halfway along the block. The driver barely waited for the cauldron to clear the cart's side rail before he gave the mules their heads. The pair lunged away, crushing sunstone ivy underfoot.

"Mika, your seed," Oliver said. "Did it change again?"

I pulled my everlasting seed from my pocket and

showed him its new sunstone ivy shape. Healing Daphne hadn't altered it. "What about yours?"

"You went to the everlasting tree?" Daphne spun to face Oliver, ears on point, wings flared with excitement. "That's such a long trek for someone so young."

"I accompanied Mika."

"You're very brave."

Grinning, Oliver lifted a wing, and I retrieved his seed from the pouch tied to his leg. It hadn't changed either, but Daphne made such a big deal over it that I didn't think Oliver cared, not even when the older gargoyle confessed she couldn't fathom what its shape meant.

When Oliver gestured with a paw, I noticed a chip in one of his claws. He had landed hard tonight—twice. Knowing my friend, he had more injuries he wasn't mentioning.

I reached for magic and seed crystals at the same time, before remembering I had dropped my bag when the thieves attacked. Climbing to my feet, I searched the cobblestones. I had been standing about here . . .

Shiny yellow sunstone mounded either side of the road and climbed the buildings and trees. The semi-clear nature of the ivy provided a distorted view of the stone planter boxes and crushed greenery beneath its leaves and vines. I searched until I spotted a clump of sunstone obscuring a small brown shape.

Grabbing fistfuls of the plant, I yanked, expecting it to rip away. The entire mound shifted, but the snarl of vines was so interwoven and sturdy that I couldn't break it with my bare hands. I knew sunstone ivy was hardy, but I had never encountered it before. I took in the street again, then the lightening sky, better understanding the frenetic urgency of the people working around us.

"Oliver, Daphne, can you boost the others, if you're not already."

"The guards?" Oliver gaped at me incredulously.

"They're trying to spare these businesses. It's for a good cause."

Oliver's expression turned sulky.

"I'm not saying it has to be *everyone*. Definitely not the imbeciles who captured you."

"Not them," Oliver agreed.

"Someone *captured* you?" Daphne asked.

"Caged me in air and earth."

Daphne growled. "Show me."

While I gathered wood and earth into a basic elemental blade, Oliver pointed out the five guards who had been part of the link.

"And not Guard Haubner, either," Oliver said. "That one. I don't trust him."

I spun to look where he pointed. Haubner knelt in front of a store three buildings away, directing magic against the creep of sunstone ivy at his feet. His hair was tousled, but his uniform was pristine. When had he arrived? The nearest residential quarters were too far away for him to have run home, changed, and come back, but maybe he hadn't needed to. Maybe he had stashed his uniform nearby. Or he could have worn his uniform under his thieves' garb, making it easy to duck out of sight, peel off a layer, and transform into a figure of authority everyone would trust.

And the woman? I studied the female guards, discounting those too tall, too large, and too old. Was his partner the guard using an ax to chop her way through a thicket of ivy blockading a broken glass door? Or was she the woman standing atop a roof two blocks away, tossing broken vines down to the street? Did Haubner glance around furtively before he spoke with the female guard slicing ivy from the trunk of a dogwood? Or was his partner a guard at all? She could be among the civilians aiding the guards—or she could be long gone, back to their lair with their stolen goods.

"Do you need help?" Oliver asked. He clawed the tangled vines in front of me. The sunstone ripped but didn't release my bag. Sticky tendrils clung to Oliver's toes. He shook his paw, snapping the thin offshoots before they could ensnare him.

"Let me use the elements. I don't want any of this to get stuck to either of us."

Oliver stepped back as I formed a spelled blade. Hacking at the jumble of vines enveloping my bag was tedious. For every stalk I severed, another grew in its place, though smaller and easier to break. Finally, I yanked my bag free, then spent another minute tearing ivy from *inside* my bag and detangling it from quartz seeds spilled across the ground. By the time I finished, sweat beaded my forehead.

I peeked at my everlasting seed. Still no change.

Groaning, I shouldered my bag and dusted off my pants. My pile of dead plants filled my arms, and I carted the mass to the nearest cauldron. Two guards maintained spinning blades of air within the deep container. When I tossed my armful in, the blades shredded the bundle of ivy to harmless mulch.

I hobbled out of the way and stretched cramped back muscles.

"Mika?"

The man asking had a bald head and round gold-rimmed glasses. He wore loose linen pants with a muted floral pattern and a matching tunic top, both embroidered with delicate, expensive-looking spells. Most important, he cradled Daphne in his arms, an air spell holding the bulk of her weight.

"Yes. I'm Mika." After a half second's hesitation, I added, "Mika Stillwater, gargoyle healer and guardian."

"I've heard. I'm Bashar. I believe I have you to thank for saving my business. Daphne tells me you scared off the thieves and healed her. I'm grateful you were— Excuse me."

He sidestepped me and plucked a message spell from the air, activating it immediately. An urgent masculine voice spilled out.

"Anyone with a shop that doesn't get dawn sun, please assist your neighbor. Send apprentices and extra helpers to the rooftops. Fifteen minutes until sunrise."

Even as the spell dissipated, Bashar crafted his own and repeated the message word for word. The moment he released the spell, he formed another and spoke the same message again, then another. Each spell hopped up the street, diving toward a civilian working to clear sunstone ivy. The recipients listened to his words, then formed new messages, and their spells winged away to those farther up the street.

Turning back to me, Bashar said, "Here, Guardian, please accept this with my gratitude." He pressed a nugget of solid gold the size of my first pinkie knuckle into my palm.

My jaw dropped. "This is too much."

"Nonsense."

Basher kissed Daphne's forehead, then launched her into the air. She flew through the arching tree branches to perch on a roof cleared of sunstone. Bashar hustled toward two younger people slashing at sunstone in his shop's doorway, and he tossed a wave over his shoulder when I called out my thanks.

"Did you see that?" Oliver asked, twining around me, his everlasting seed still clutched in one paw.

"I don't think so." I found it difficult to look away from the chunk of gold. Bashar's gift would cover this month's rent and maybe next month's, too. Reverently, I tucked the gold nugget into my pocket.

"Bashar's spell. It was incredible."

"The message?" I asked, confused. Message spells were more useful than a shout in this busy environment but as humdrum as granite.

"Not just his message; his and all the rest," Oliver exclaimed, practically vibrating with excitement.

"They were all the same. Nothing fancy. Everyone just repeated what they heard."

"Exactly!" Oliver crowed. "Whoever had the original message didn't have to repeat it and send it to *everyone*, one person at a time. Bashar sent it to three people. They each sent it to three people. Those people sent it to three others. I lost track of the spells after that, but, Mika! They got the message out so fast. It was like—" Oliver's eyes rounded with shock. He set his everlasting seed on the cobblestones between us. "It was like this."

I crouched beside him, struck by how much the twenty-sided golden icosahedron looked like solidified sunstone ivy. I pulled my everlasting seed from my pocket, marveling that both now appeared to have been sculpted from the same source.

Oliver looked from his seed to mine, his eyes wide. With a claw, he rolled the icosahedron. Inside, the thin amber lines danced, each branch receding endlessly inward from the edge of the seed.

"I've been going about it all wrong," he said. "I've been spreading messages all by myself, trying to speak with every gargoyle personally. But I don't have to. Other gargoyles can help."

As if Oliver's words were a spell, his everlasting seed shimmered. A glow burst along the amber lines, intensifying until I shielded my eyes with my hand. When I lowered my arm, a plum-sized polished pale rock sat before us. Its limestone sides were shaved into twelve identical pentagons, transforming Oliver's glassy icosahedron into a stone dodecahedron. Simple hieroglyphs were etched on each side, no two alike.

Oliver snaked his head closer to the seed, his gaze going cross-eyed. "I did it! I evolved my seed." He pranced in place without moving his nose. His antics made me laugh.

"May I?" At his nod, I picked up his seed and examined it from every angle. It was uniformly ivory in color, and heavy enough to be solid limestone. The hieroglyphs appeared to be ancient, chiseled by hand and worn by time. I didn't recognize the symbols, but then again, I didn't study archaic pictorial languages. "Any ideas?"

Oliver shook his head, his grin undiminished.

I placed the seed in his paw. "I don't think I understand. Gargoyles can't make message spells."

"But we can fly. We're almost faster than message spells. Every gargoyle I tell about you—or about those horrid thieves—I can ask them to tell a few others. It'll take planning, but if we do it right, every gargoyle will get the message—and it'll be *much* faster than me talking with every gargoyle personally."

Someone nearby made a rude noise. I glanced up. Haubner watched us from across the street, his arms crossed, his eyes narrowed with familiar suspicion. I glared back, then resolved not to allow him to steal the joy from

Oliver's moment. However, my friend's smile was already gone, and it wasn't because of the guard.

"I should have thought of this sooner," Oliver said.

I rested a hand on his jaw. "All good ideas seem obvious after the fact."

"Yeah?"

"*Yes.* You evolved your seed. That's a big deal, Oliver."

His grin returned, lighting up his whole face.

Oliver and I were in the midst of a celebratory hug when the first rays of sunlight speared over the horizon. Shouts of alarm rang along the street, and wards flashed up around individuals and groups.

I crouched within Oliver's embrace, and he tightened his wings around me. Following others' cues, I crafted a hasty quartz-laced air ward around the two of us.

"What's going to happen?" Oliver asked.

"I don't know." Despite everyone's frantic efforts, sunstone ivy grew unchecked everywhere I looked. "I've never seen anything like—"

An ominous report resounded across the street. Another clap echoed from farther away. Crackles and pops punctuated the ever-present rustle of growing ivy, drowning out people's cries. I watched in horror as sunlight touched the tip of the vine across the street. The questing tendril solidified with a pop, its supple curve crystallizing into quartz-hard stone. From its tip to its roots, the vine metamorphosed from vegetation to stone in a rolling avalanche of sound. As each leaf hardened, it lifted, exposing dangling seed pods hidden against the stems.

"Oh no."

I yanked magic through Oliver's and Daphne's boosts. Straining, I crafted a second ward, closing it around Daphne.

Hundreds of seed pods exploded in unison, firing thousands of golden sparks with punishing force. The projectiles pelted my shields, chipping away at my magic. If I had been unprotected, the seeds would have left bruises and welts. They might even have chipped quartz gargoyle flesh.

For a violent, terrifying minute, the world narrowed to our bubble of safety amid the golden bombardment. All around us, glass shattered, brick shrieked and cracked, tree branches snapped, and planter boxes ruptured. Yellow pellets cascaded down the rim of my ward, puddling in the cobblestones' cracks. Tiny vines immediately sprouted, bending and twisting around the air-slick curves of my elemental barrier. I strained under the effort of holding two wards, wishing fervently that I wasn't so tired.

Then the street quieted.

The guards released their wards first, the rest of us more slowly. Like waking from a dream, shop owners and workers gawked at the hardened sunstone ivy, the mounds of seeds collected like drifts of jeweled snow, and the new plants already knotting themselves around any available climbing surface. Then everyone got back to work.

I released both wards, urging Daphne to a safer building farther from Orchardlace Lane. Thankfully, the seeds that landed around her remained inert in the sunlight. It was only those in the shade that posed an immediate danger.

A linked squad of guards marched past, incinerating loose seeds before they took root. Oliver and I scuttled aside. After confirming neither of us were hurt, I tucked Oliver's evolved everlasting seed into his pouch and retied it to his upper leg. My own everlasting seed remained unchanged.

More and more people poured into Orchardlace from side streets, throwing themselves into the battle against the pernicious plant. They crowded along the shaded side of the street, hacking at supple vines, racing ahead of the sun—stopping only to ward themselves when fresh pods burst.

"I'm going to stay to help," I said.

"Because of your seed?"

I shook my head. "Because it's the decent thing to do."

I could walk away, but it wouldn't be right. Every last hand was useful in a catastrophe.

Mindful of my exhaustion, I didn't bother with attacking the vegetation. My strength lay with earth element, and I would focus my efforts there. Turning toward the opposite side of the street, I studied the hardened sunstone ivy crushing a shop under its weight.

By habit, I tested the solidified ivy with quartz-tuned earth magic. The resonance was close. Adding a fiber of wood, subtracting a lick of fire, I found a harmonious match. Hesitantly, I reshaped a sunstone leaf. Quartz would have resisted, but the sunstone bent as easily as gold foil.

"Wow, you've got a knack for this," a woman in a bright-pink dress said. She stood four feet away, painstakingly tunneling a similar spell into the base of an ivy plant, though her threads of earth were substantially weaker. Squinting hard, as if her eyes were doing the work, not her magic, she pulled the plant's roots into a puddle of yellow stone atop the cobblestones. When she finished, her face was as pink as her dress. With a puff of a laugh, she said, "Me, I'm not so adept. But this is my shop."

She cast a sad look at the once-beautiful building. The wood siding was splintered and cracked around hardened stone vines. Shards from the roof's tiles littered the ground, and three out of four of her huge display windows were shattered.

"Let me see what I can do," I said.

I plunged magic back into the earthlike plant. With

Oliver and Daphne boosting me, it was almost easy to peel the ivy from the roof, reshaping it into a crude lump as I collected leaves, tendrils, and flowers. Any plant parts woven through the shop's walls, window ledges, and sign-posts, I melted free and added to my clump, leaving holes and cracked wood behind without adding to the damage. When the hunk of sunstone grew heavy, I broke it off, patted it into a vaguely cubic shape, and lowered it toward the ground.

The woman in pink caught it with a cup of air much stronger than her earth magic. Her smile lit her whole face.

"Good. You do that. I'll pile the dreadful stuff where it can be carted off." She suited words to action and set the cube of sunstone in the middle of the street. The next guard running past us gave the sunstone brick a sharp look, then called for a wheelbarrow.

I finished clearing half the building, passing reshaped sunstone to the proprietor, before I recognized the light feeling in my chest: camaraderie. As a gargoyle guardian, I worked in isolation, a lone individual meeting the needs of many. But in this moment, I enjoyed a kinship with the stranger beside me and the others saving the street. We were all connected by our common goal, and our efforts were coordinated. I had forgotten how fulfilling working as part of a team could be.

I almost wasn't surprised when I felt my everlasting seed shift in my pocket. I knelt in front of Oliver to examine it. It was still sunstone in texture and color, but the detailed ivy had vanished. The animal figure remained frustratingly incomplete and unrecognizable, like one of my unfinished figurines.

"It changed," Oliver said, confused.

Changed, not evolved. Again. I was still doing something

only half right.

I closed the seed in my fist, then shoved it into my pocket. I would worry about it later.

Using earth magic to manipulate a stone so similar to quartz soothed a restlessness deep inside me I hadn't been aware of. I wanted to stay until the street was clean, but I was forced to stop after less than an hour when exhaustion eroded my elemental coordination.

I finally acknowledged Marcus's repeated admonishments: I needed rest.

I owed him an apology.

Admitting as much lifted a phantom weight from my chest. Feeling more clearheaded than I had in weeks, I turned toward home. I took comfort in knowing my departure wouldn't cause a hardship; droves of people had rallied to clean the street. Even Lucy was present, her feather-eared pink-and-purple hat impossible to miss despite the crush of people. Hopefully she could sign new clients for her firm; from what I had seen, she wasn't the best insurance saleswoman, but the widespread destruction might work in her favor.

Haubner watched Oliver and me leave, his gaze hooded. I returned his glare. I had done my best to keep track of the guard throughout the morning, and in doing so had learned exactly nothing to confirm he was—or wasn't—the same man who attacked me.

It wasn't until I reached the airbus stop that I remembered the reason Oliver and I made the early-morning trek in the first place. At my request, Oliver flew to Earthspire Studio. He returned minutes later with nothing to report. The studio was open. No gargoyles were in residence. Whatever had prompted my seed to show a partial logo of the studio remained a mystery.

———

16

I arrived home on a rented flying carpet. It was small, slow to accelerate, and quick to pivot, but it was mine for five days. It also cost nearly as much as Bashar's gold nugget was worth. If I could have put aside the money instead, waited, and saved, I could have eventually afforded to purchase a flying carpet. But I didn't have the luxury of time. The thieves would strike again—tonight, if they stuck to their same pattern. I couldn't let a gargoyle suffer while I plodded across the city on foot again, or worse, let another gargoyle attempt a dangerous, dizzy flight to reach me.

Having a flying carpet also meant the thieves wouldn't be able to outrun me a second time . . . if I stumbled across their location again. Encountering them once had been blind luck. I had no way to predict where they would strike next, or which gargoyle they would harm. For all I knew, I would be chasing down and healing spirit-shifted gargoyles for another week.

A headache pulsed between my temples, and I tamped down my pessimism. Everything would look better after some sleep. For now, I savored the extravagance of floating my way home, my tired feet dangling a foot above the sidewalk, my stomach full after a brief stop at Eilidh's bakery. This was so much nicer than being cramped on an airbus.

A tin of Eilidh's pizazzy pastries sat on my lap, unopened. I didn't need the energy kick right now, but I might later. All I currently wanted was the soft embrace of my bed.

The wind shifted, and I got a whiff of myself. Make that a shower, then bed.

Excited chatter drifted on the air, the words indistinct, the voices gargoyle. Smiling, I shaded my eyes to check the Victorian's roof. Oliver had flown ahead, eager to share his pivotal revelation and everlasting seed's evolution with his siblings. Three beacons glowed atop the roof. I spotted Anya beside Oliver. The other beacon must belong to their smallest sibling, Herbert.

I coasted up the walkway, raising my hand to wave. A screech pierced my eardrums. Fear transformed my spine to ice. *Harpy,* my brain screamed. Predatory, murderous harpy.

Ducking, I fumbled for the elements. Foreign magic hit me first, a wave of wood-laced air that slammed into the carpet and shoved. The ground rushed past, grass and stone walkway flashing beneath me. Before I could form a defense, the attack died. Off balance, I tumbled to the sidewalk. My bag slapped down beside me, spilling seed crystals. Grabbing the carpet, I domed a shield over myself. Then I gawked at the Victorian. An angry ward bubbled the whole building. The spell's surface rippled with a blinding yellow light.

Three gargoyles dove from the roof—Oliver in the lead, Herbert close enough to ride on his back, and Anya with a snarl baring her long panther fangs. They landed in a deafening clatter, stirring dust and whipping my hair into my eyes. Oliver and Anya fanned their wings into a protective stone wall around me. Herbert shoved against my side, half hiding under me, half propping me up with his sturdy armadillo body.

"What just happened?" I asked, dumbstruck. I might have shouted. The ward's initial shriek still rang in my ears, though it was blessedly quiet now. "Is something wrong? Are we under attack?"

"I don't know." Oliver swung his head, his wide eyes searching for a threat. "Everything was quiet, and—"

The screen door slapped against the house. "Who is it, Anya?" Ms. Zuberrie yelled from the porch. "Who dared attack our house with sunstone?"

With a heartfelt curse, I dropped my head into my hands and released the triple-enhanced volume of magic I held. My shield dissipated. The elements bled from me, leaving me jittery with the rapid pulse of my pounding heart. The alarm, the expulsive magic, the ward, those were Ms. Zuberrie's safety measures. If I had been thinking clearly, I would have realized our vigilant landlady would ward our house against the invasive vine.

Breath shaky, I patted Anya and Oliver, letting them know they could relax. They lowered their wings, giving me a clear view of Ms. Zuberrie's furious expression.

"Mika? What is the meaning of this?" Ms. Zuberrie clutched a sturdy kitchen bowl in one hand, sharp sewing scissors in the other. A dense cloud of elements drifted around her, the aftermath of a potent, unraveled weapon or defensive spell.

I pulled an apple-sized globe of sunstone from the depths of my bag and held it up for Ms. Zuberrie to see. Sunlight refracted through its twenty sides, making it appear to glow from within.

"It's inert. The sun already hardened it, and it doesn't contain any seeds."

"What in the name of all the fertile soil in this beautiful land possessed you to *buy* that despicable stone?"

"I didn't buy it. It's a keepsake."

"That's the most nonsensical statement I've ever heard."

"Can I come up there?" It would be much easier to explain when I didn't have to shout.

"With *that*?" Ms. Zuberrie jabbed her scissors at the sunstone. The ward didn't budge.

I resisted the urge to drop my head back into my hands. Herbert rubbed his beak against my calf, leaning his body's weight into me in his version of a hug. Oliver sniffed the sunstone.

"It looks like my seed did, only no lines inside."

"I wanted to commemorate your seed's first evolution and your epiphany."

"This is for me?" Oliver asked. At my nod, he pinched the sunstone between his claws. He swiveled to face the house and our landlady. "Ms. Zuberrie?"

Lips pursed, Ms. Zuberrie glared down at Oliver, or more specifically, at the beautiful stone cupped in his red paw.

"You're positive it's safe?" she finally asked.

Oliver and I nodded emphatically.

"Fine." With a huff, Ms. Zuberrie started to turn away, but she spun back fast enough to flare the hem of her narrow skirt. "Oliver, I don't want to see that anywhere near my garden."

"Of course not."

Ms. Zuberrie gripped the door frame and teased magic into the house's siding. The rippling gold ward dissipated.

Hesitantly, Oliver carried the sunstone across the property threshold. When nothing happened, he gave me a grin.

"I'm going to put it in our room. Thank you, Mika." He reared and launched himself toward the balcony. Anya leapt for the roof, tail snapping in displeasure.

"Thank you," I called after her, squinting against the dual downdrafts. She didn't look back. Stroking a hand down Herbert's wings, I thanked him, too.

"I'll smooth things over with Josephine," he whispered.

As if he were as light as a sparrow, he flitted up to the porch, then pawed the door open to follow Ms. Zuberrie inside. I sighed, then dusted off my pants and began arduously collecting spilled seed crystals scattered like marbles across the yard.

————

TWENTY MINUTES LATER, SCRUBBED CLEAN, I COLLAPSED ATOP my bed. I didn't need more than a lightweight sleep shirt and shorts in the sunbaked room, and definitely not covers.

Outside the window, finches chirped. The murmur of Ms. Zuberrie and Herbert floated through the floorboards, along with faint, comforting sounds from the kitchen. On the roof, Oliver and Anya repositioned themselves atop Kylie's bedroom, where their footsteps wouldn't wake me.

My body hummed with fatigue. I could feel my pulse in my feet. The cut on my shoulder stung from being scrubbed, and the ointment I applied stuck to my shirt.

My eyes drifted shut.

The male thief stood in front of me, hands poised, elemental weapons prepared. Fear shivered through my gut. He had been strong. I could still feel his sharp water shards pummeling my ward. If I met him again, alone . . .

I rolled to my side with a huff. He hadn't been strong enough to break through my gargoyle-enhanced magic the first time; he wouldn't be strong enough the second. But holding him at bay wasn't my goal. I wanted to capture him. Him and his accomplice.

For the hundredth time, I conjured a mental image of both thieves. The woman's eyes haunted me. I could picture her staring at me, but I couldn't recall any specific details. Shadows shrouded my memory of the man, too, blurring his features, his height, his body shape. I concentrated, and he was Haubner. Then he wasn't.

With a stifled growl, I rolled to the other side. Of course it was Haubner. He had been at every burgled site. He knew Oliver and I were warning gargoyles, and he had picked a location far from both our house and the last theft location. Only chance had led me to interrupt them.

And then he tried to kill me, and the woman stopped him. Why?

I replayed the attack and chase. Had she stopped the man when she spotted—or heard—Oliver? Or had it been before? It was all a frustrating blur.

I flopped to my back. Everything had happened so fast, and my emotions had been too high. If I could have run the thieves down . . . If I could have caught them . . .

My molars clenched at the memory of being held help-less by the guards—of *Oliver* being bound—while the thieves escaped. I was tempted to ask Amelia to inform the guard chief about his subordinates' vile actions. The only thing that stopped me was the possibility that another full-spectrum intervention would make our next interaction with guards even worse.

Kicking empty air, I repositioned myself on the bed. Heavy gargoyle footsteps plodded across the far roof, followed by the familiar creak and slap of Oliver's paws on the balcony railing. I sat up as he let himself into my room.

"Everything all right?" I asked.

"That's what I came to ask you." He squirmed into the room, navigating the cramped quarters with practiced ease. When he rested his head on the bed next to me, worry clouded his eyes.

I lay back down and stroked a hand along his glossy mane. Bracing myself, I asked, "How does my beacon look?"

"Dim. You look tired."

I gave him a wan smile. I couldn't ask what I really wanted to: How had my beacon looked when I healed Daphne? How had I looked right after, when my spirit felt unmoored from my body? If I voiced either question, it would alarm Oliver, and I was already scared enough for both of us.

"I need more rest. Marcus was right. He'll be happy to hear it." I tried to make my words light, like a joke.

"You should tell him."

I searched Oliver's eyes, then nodded. Before I lost my resolve, I formed a message spell. I didn't have the energy to make it large enough to record more than a few seconds' worth of sound, so I spoke fast.

"Marcus, I'm sorry. Another gargoyle was sick this morn-ing, and I—I understand what you mean now. I'm home. I'm resting. I just wanted you to know. And I haven't said it lately, so I thought I would remind you: I love you." I pictured him here, holding me in his strong arms. Every-thing was better, every problem more manageable, when he was beside me. "I miss you."

The last came out a whisper, and I sealed the spell before my emotions spiraled. I keyed the spell to Marcus's familiar signature and set it free. It shot through the open window and disappeared over the treetops. Releasing a slow breath, I felt the knots in my neck relax.

Oliver's contented sigh ruffled my hair. "I like it when you two aren't fighting."

"Me too."

I petted his neck, blindly tracing familiar curves in his stone fur. Gradually, my hand stilled, resting where his mane transitioned to scales.

"I'm going to go talk with a few gargoyles."

At Oliver's quiet statement, my eyes popped open.

"Are you sure?" I assessed his beacon, pleased he looked healthy. This morning had been tiring for us both, and he needed rest, but not nearly as much as I did.

"We need to warn everyone not to boost the thieves before they strike again. Anya and Herbert are each talking to three gargoyles, but I want to do my part, too."

I must have dozed off, because I hadn't sensed either gargoyle's departure.

"We can't let another gargoyle get sick," Oliver said, his voice tense.

I patted him reassuringly. "If one does, I'll heal them."

"No one should go through what Nimoy experienced."

If Oliver had been concerned only for his fellow gargoyles' well-being, he wouldn't have ducked meeting my gaze. He was worried about me. I wondered what he wasn't telling me about my beacon. I tried to hide the strain of healing spirit-shifted gargoyles from him, but Oliver wasn't blind. He was in a rush to enact his network so he could spare me.

I thought about pointing out that it wasn't necessary for him to go. If Anya and Herbert each spoke with three gargoyles, and they carried on the message to three more, they were already doubling the number of gargoyles Oliver had been able to contact in a day before he hit upon this idea. But I understood his desire to do the work himself. Hadn't that been part of the reason I stayed to clean up sunstone ivy: to feel productive and like I was making a difference? Oliver deserved a similar sense of accomplishment.

"You won't push yourself?"

"I'm only going to downtown and back."

I nodded my approval.

Oliver trundled to my bag, clawed open the top, and rolled some seed crystals out. "Once you make me quartz bracelets, I'll be off."

I started to gather magic, then stopped. "Why do you want bracelets?"

"In case of an emergency."

"But I won't be with you." I sat up. We were back to Oliver avoiding my gaze. What was I missing? Oliver had been wearing quartz in case I needed more than I could carry. But I would be staying home. "Unless a gargoyle shows up here, I won't be healing anyone today. If they do, it would be better for me to have more seed crystals on hand."

"But if you might have to leave, and I'll meet you. I should have some, just in case. Besides, you have plenty of crystals here. More than you can carry."

"How long do you think you'll be gone?"

Oliver shrugged. "An hour. Maybe two."

"So you're saying you want to lug around extra pounds in case I get called out to a healing in the next hour?"

Oliver nodded.

"That doesn't make sense."

"It does to me," he said.

I padded across the room and knelt in front of Oliver. He used a claw to separate the crystal spheres into four neat rows. I waited until he finished, then cupped his cheek and forced him to look at me.

"Oliver, what's going on?"

He shuffled in place but didn't answer.

"It was a great idea," I said. "Very thoughtful. But in all the time we've been trekking around the city, I've never run short on seeds. You don't have to carry spare quartz, especially not when you're going out alone."

"I do if I want to get stronger," Oliver mumbled.

"Stronger?" Gargoyles were hardy by nature, and Oliver was no weakling. "I don't understand."

"I barely caught you," Oliver whispered.

"When?"

"On the dirigible."

My stomach flip-flopped at the reminder. I didn't like to fly, and our last harrowing airborne adventure had done nothing to decrease my anxiety about riding in dirigibles. I didn't allow the event to replay in my mind, only the moment when Oliver's stone paws wrapped around my wrists, saving me from plummeting to my death.

"But you did catch me." I scooted closer, running my hands soothingly over Oliver's mane and down his neck. His soulful eyes bored into mine.

"I couldn't lift you. You could have died."

"I didn't. I'm right here with you. You don't have to think about that."

"I can't stop. I see it in my mind all the time. I was too weak. I could have lost you."

"Oh, Oliver." I swooped him into a tight hug.

He had been carrying around such a horrible emotional burden. I had been so caught up in the needs of every other gargoyle in the city, I had failed to notice the one struggling right in front of me.

Oliver enclosed me in his wings, his quartz embrace gentle.

"I love you so much," I whispered, my face pressed against his.

"I love you too, Mika."

When we released each other, I rearranged myself into a cross-legged position in front of him.

"I am incredibly grateful for all you do for me, Oliver. I appreciate how much you care. It makes me ache to think you've been tormenting yourself with that memory. Especially since what you fear didn't happen. And it won't," I added louder, when Oliver started to interrupt. "But now I'm afraid for your health. Your stamina might be improving, but I think you're pushing yourself too hard too fast. It's unsustainable."

"But the bracelets don't weigh that much."

"That's my point. Your body is fatigued from how much you've been flying lately, and surplus weight isn't helping." I chose my next words carefully. "Muscle isn't what keeps you airborne."

If wing strength alone were responsible for propelling gargoyles into the air, every gargoyle would be land bound. Even a compact gargoyle like Herbert wouldn't make it higher than he could hop. The problem wasn't even their quartz bodies. It was their stone feathers. No matter a gargoyle's wing size, the limbs would always be too heavy to achieve liftoff. They required magic to keep them aloft.

"Carting around a couple of extra pounds isn't going to alter the way you use magic to fly," I said. "Unless . . . has it? Have you found it any easier to fly with the bracelets lately than you did when you started?"

Oliver's shoulders slumped. "No."

"Good." I smiled at Oliver's confused expression.

"Because that means you're a gargoyle and not a pegasus or a gryphon. Nothing against those two, but I'm a gargoyle guardian, not a pegasus guardian."

Oliver gave me a glum smile.

"I would be lost without you by my side, Oliver. Your presence, your friendship, you sharing your kind heart with me, that's all I ask. That's everything. I don't need or want you to be something you're not."

Finally, I got a real smile from Oliver.

When he departed, he flew with light wing beats, but my heart remained heavy. I had been oblivious to Oliver's ongoing distress. What else had I missed?

I took stock of my bedroom. The toppled piles of paper-work teetering on my table, the dirty clothes mounding the bottom of my closet and the foot of my bed, the library books listing against the baseboards, the crusty plate on my bookcase, and the abandoned, partially finished quartz figurines lumped next to my message bowl—all of it felt like a perfect reflection of my mental state. Disorganized. Scattered. Ineffectual. I was falling behind on too many things, professionally and personally. My health was suffering, and it was affecting my friend's mental well-being. We both needed time and space to recover.

But neither of us would be able to rest so long as the thieves remained free.

Groaning, I reached for Kylie's notebook and map of the thefts. Maybe if I studied it one more time, I would figure out the thieves' pattern. Because they would strike again, and this time, Oliver and I would be ready.

17

I jolted awake at the pressure of unfamiliar magic against my temple. My eyes shot open, my hands flailing. The elements gushed into me. A twist of earth refined the gargoyle-enhanced magic, and a quartz-tuned ward popped into place around me, shoving the foreign spell aside. Searching frantically for the next attack, I grabbed more magic and formed a fist-sized glowball.

"Easy, Mika," Oliver whispered. "It's a message."

I blinked and stilled. The moon hung low on the horizon against a star-studded sky. I was in bed, the light covers shoved to my feet. Oliver crouched, tense, beside me. Only one gargoyle beacon rested on the roof. No others were visible on my inner map.

Heart pounding, I studied the message spell, verifying it was benign before letting my ward dissipate. The intrusive magic rushed me. I caught it with a cup of air and glared at it, then at my message bowl across the room.

"What time is it?" With the windows open and Ms. Zuberrie being a light sleeper, I kept the question low. At least I didn't have to worry about waking Kylie; she was spending the night at Grant's.

"Sunrise is three hours off."

I massaged my temples, a dull headache pulsing to life. At this hour, social norms dictated all messages be keyed to a person's bowl, not to their person.

Unless the message was too urgent to wait until morning.

Dread and anticipation coiling in my gut, I activated the message. Lucy Fishburne's voice hissed through my bedroom.

"Mika, you were right about that guard, Haubner. I'm on a late-night assignment, and I just saw him. Him and a woman. They were dressed all in black and running from Hearthware Spellworks."

I fumbled the elements, belatedly creating a muffling bubble of dense air around Oliver, me, and the unfurling message.

Lucy's trembling voice continued to spill from the unraveling spell. "I don't think they saw me. I really hope not. But you need to come—quick. The gargoyle here isn't looking good. It's stumbling around, and I'm afraid I won't be strong enough to catch it if it falls off the roof. Come to Hearthware. Hurry."

"Wendell," Oliver said as the last strands of the message evaporated into the ether.

I sprang from my bed, picturing the part-pelican, part-dragon gargoyle who lived atop the spellworks studio. Wendell was sweet and cheerful and charmingly chatty. When we met, he had been equally enthusiastic about a new beehive recently relocated to the studio's garden as he was about trips to the nearby Ember Rails khalkotauroi pens to watch the hulking bronze-nosed bovines belch fire.

"Wendell must not have received our warning," I said.

"I was trying to be methodical." Oliver stared morosely toward Wendell's location on the far southeast side of Lincoln River. "I thought starting in the center of the city would make the most sense, but I should have—"

"No. That was the right call. This isn't your fault."

It was Haubner's fault. He had witnessed Oliver's seed-evolving epiphany to set up a network of communication among the gargoyles. Haubner must have chosen Hearth-ware specifically because it was on the outskirts of town, where he had a greater chance of finding a gargoyle not yet warned against boosting people sight unseen. Impotent fury bubbled beneath my skin.

"I nearly had him yesterday. We were this close." I held up my hand, my forefinger and thumb a hairsbreadth from touching. Then my fingers curled into a fist. "And now he's going to escape *again*." Because even with a flying carpet, I would never make it to the spellworks studio in time to catch Haubner.

Now we had a witness, though. Maybe it would be enough to take to Captain Rojas.

I darted to my worktable and slapped the paper-strewn surface, wishing I had taken the time to straighten up. But after I pored over all the information we had about the thieves without learning anything new, my body had given out. I slept straight through dinner. I would have slept the entire night, because somehow, twelve hours of sleep didn't feel like enough.

My hand landed on a lump. I shoved aside a pile of mail and tilted my everlasting seed toward my glowball. An unhelpful animal-shaped lump sat on my palm. Instead of the yellow of sunstone, it looked like clear quartz, but that could have been a trick of the light.

Frustrated, I stalked to my closet.

"Can you let Herbert know where we're going?" I asked over my shoulder.

"Maybe he should accompany us."

"What? Why?"

"What if this is a trap?"

My fingers stilled on a hanger, and I pivoted to face my friend. Concern etched shadows across Oliver's vibrant features.

"The timing. It's too perfect," I said.

Oliver nodded. "What are the odds that Lucy would see Haubner and his partner leaving a crime scene at this time of night?"

"You think he wanted her to see him?"

"I don't know. Maybe."

If Lucy was working at this hour, it would be because a business her company insured had contacted their office, and they sent out their junior agent. As a guard, Haubner would know of any crimes or catastrophes that would warrant a late-night insurance claim. He could have selected a location to burgle specifically to guarantee Lucy's presence.

"He would know Lucy would send for me," I said, catching up to Oliver's logic leap.

"He might be waiting for us."

I shivered at the thought. "We'll be ready for him. Herbert should stay home. I want someone here who knows where we are." And I didn't want to take another gargoyle into a possible trap.

"Anya and Lydia went out this evening to tell more gargoyles about my network, and to warn them." Oliver's claws bunched the threadbare throw rug, his wings hunched above his shoulders. "I asked them to help me, but I should have told them to wait."

I shoved my legs into worn khaki pants, then took a moment before buttoning them to kneel beside Oliver.

"You did the right thing. The sooner every gargoyle is communicating through your network, the better it will be for *all* gargoyles."

Oliver searched my gaze, finding something in my expression that stilled his nervous paws and lifted his chin high. "The network is important."

"Yes." I pressed a kiss to his forehead. "Hurry. I'll meet you downstairs."

I finished dressing while Oliver tiptoed out the side door. The balcony railing creaked when he jumped from it to the roof to speak softly with Herbert. I stuffed my useless everlasting seed into my pocket and slung my bag over my shoulder, staggering when I bent to grab my boots with one hand and the rented flying carpet with the other. Extinguishing my glowball, I jogged on sock feet down the Victorian's stairs.

Seed crystals clacked softly against my back, partially muted by the spare change of clothes tucked at the base of my bag, the water bottle resting on top of them, and the spelled cloth wrapped around three of Eilidh's pizazzies. Tonight, I was going to be prepared.

I didn't stop to stomp my feet into my boots until I reached the walkway at the base of the porch stairs. Then I unfurled the flying carpet with a flick of my wrists and activated its levitation spell. When I sat cross-legged atop the tiny scrap of faded brown fabric, it sank half a foot. Two people would ground the carpet, but it was strong enough for me and my bag. It wasn't the fastest in the rental shop, but it would give me an advantage. Haubner would expect me to arrive on foot and tired.

Memory of the thief's sharp, icy magic pelting my ward flashed through my mind. I formed a message spell keyed to Marcus before I realized what I was doing, but my plea for help stuck in my throat. My message bowl upstairs was empty. He hadn't responded to the apology I sent earlier. Had it been too little too late? Or had he not received it? What did it say about me that I didn't know if my boyfriend was in the city or if he had been called away on FPD business—or if I still had the right to call him my boyfriend at all?

My heart constricted. Rubbing my breastbone as if it would make it easier to take a deep breath, I let the message spell unravel. I could handle this on my own. The thief—Haubner—was strong, but last night he had the element of surprise. This time I would be ready for him.

Settling my bag atop my lap, I took a direct route to Lincoln River, sailing along empty streets. Even the skies were quiet, with only Oliver coasting overhead, staying close and not detouring to chat with any gargoyles we passed.

I slowed as I crossed the Whispering Arch. From dawn to dusk, heavy traffic clogged the bridge, the cacophony of carts and hooves and drivers' shouts making a mockery of the bridge's name. But well past midnight, silence blanketed the stone expanse, and the susurrus of the placid river was audible despite the wind pushing against my ears. I nudged the carpet away from the railing toward the center of the bridge, keeping my eyes on the horizon, not the steep drop to the dark waters below.

A faint red glow lit a trio of roofs to the left. I halted the carpet at the bridge's apex and squinted into the distance. The guttering orange tint to the light was unmistakably a

fire, one too large to be a lantern or a contained bonfire. A
building was on fire.

Again.

My stomach knotted. I didn't know this side of Terra
Haven well enough to identify the faraway structure in the
flickering light, but it was near enough to the location of
Hearthware Spellworks to make me nervous. It couldn't be a
coincidence, either.

Oliver's beacon spiraled overhead, drawing closer. I
waved him off from landing, wanting him to conserve his
strength.

"We'll circle and come at it from the other side," I said
into a message spell, then guided it to him by line of sight.
The spell broke across his nose, and my element-captured
words whispered in the air above me.

Oliver gave me an exaggerated thumbs-up as he pulled
out of his dive. My hair whipped in the downdraft from his
wings. I shoved it out of my eyes, then pushed the carpet
into motion. By the time I reached the base of the bridge,
the hills of Terra Haven and the maze of buildings hid the
burning structure from view.

I swung wide, circling the district along narrow residential lanes rather than main thoroughfares until I
approached Hearthware from the east, the opposite direction of my house. The delay in treating Wendell grated, but I
was afraid of blundering into Haubner's trap. Would it be
another ice-blade assault? Or would it be something worse?
If he had successfully robbed the spellworks studio, he
could have all manner of pre-spelled items at his disposal.
Hearthware specialized in everyday kitchen tools—pots and
pans spelled to maintain a specific temperature no matter
how hot the heat source, ice boxes crafted with air and
water magic to keep the interior frosty, and numerous

specialty items like butter churn barrels and coffee grinders built with air-spin spells affixed to the handles. None of their goods were weapons in themselves, but I could envision plenty of nefarious ways they might be used against me.

My nerves stretched tighter with each passing block. I flew with my head canted against the wind, listening for trouble, my eyes scanning the shadows of alleys and balconies. When a lumbering fire brigade bucket airship sailed over the nearest roof, I startled so hard I had to clutch the carpet to avoid falling off. The ship's downdraft blasted the street seconds later, lifting dirt and dust into an eye-stinging whirlwind and knocking my carpet about like a leaf caught in a current. Cursing, I grounded the carpet. By the time I skidded to a stop—facing the wrong way—the three-story buildings on either side hid the bulky water-bearing ship from sight. I could track it by sound, though.

Powering up the carpet, I pivoted it in a slow circle until I faced the same direction as the airship. If I squinted past the bright streetlamps, I could see a faint glow above the nearest roof. The fire was close.

Wendell was close, too. I had been able to sense his beacon for the last minute, and I compared his light with Oliver's on my mental map. Both looked equally strong and bright. Of course, I hadn't discerned a difference in Carmen's beacon until I was nearly on top of her. At least I was close enough to confirm that Wendell wasn't at the same location as the fire. He was several degrees to the right.

Distant thunder rumbled, so low it barely registered. Tense, I strained to hear it again, eyes shifting over the column of visible sky. Cautiously, I pushed the carpet into motion. The faint scent of burning hay drifted on the air, mingling with deeper notes of roasting nuts. Then the wind shifted, bringing the overpowering acrid aroma of scorched metal. I glanced toward the roofs as I coasted between buildings. The fire's glow was close, the sky bright enough to see plumes of smoke hazing the air above the flames.

A man's shout came from ahead, made indistinct by the tall buildings surrounding me and the wind against my ears. A pair of guards in olive-green-and-black uniforms sprinted past the end of the street. Neither looked my way, focused on the magic stretched between them. They were out of sight before I could identify the spell they held.

I slowed as I approached the intersection. When no one else ran past, I eased into the open.

The crossroad twisted, climbing a short slope lined with old brick and timber workshops. Near the top, flames engulfed the wooden roof of a two-story structure. Flares of white-hot fire billowed from shattered second-story windows and burst out the front doorway. Shadowed figures clustered well back from the gaping opening, water and earth spells surging from them into the building's interior— for all the good they did. The flames leapt higher, licking at the underside of the fire brigade airship hovering over the building. The team floating aboard the ship funneled the water it carried directly through the burning building's roof, again with little effect. It wasn't until I spotted the building's tattered sign that their lack of progress made sense: It was a cotton dye house. Everything inside was highly flammable.

Active wards domed the buildings on every side, preventing the fire from leaping from roof to roof, but the dye house's fire-suppression spells were long since spent. Or perhaps demolished. The wide delivery doors appeared to have been shattered, the ragged edges of its metal frame bent inward and warped by heat.

Had Haubner done this? He and his partner used fire for

distraction before. I slowed the carpet, drifting into the middle of the intersection as I checked my mental map. Wendell was to the left, several blocks away—

Oliver plunged so sharply his beacon flared like a meteor across my mind's eye. He angled away from me and away from the fire. I mentally tracked him, half blind to my surroundings as I gathered magic.

Something rumbled behind me, approaching fast. I twisted to look over my shoulder. A burning wooden wagon careened down the street I had just exited, on a collision course with me. Its broken hitch dragged on the ground, and no one sat at the driver's seat.

Panic speared down my spine as I shoved elements into the flying carpet. The rental gained speed with agonizing leisure. The wagon bore down on me twice as fast. I slammed air into the rudder spell, spinning the carpet uphill. Finally, the carpet's propulsion kicked in. I jolted forward as the wagon plowed through the intersection. It jounced over the corner curb and smashed into the building behind me. The driver's box splintered. The wagon's burning end flipped skyward, flames billowing against a cloth awning. Heat bathed my back. I clapped my hands over my ears as the building's ward ignited with a shriek. Water element shot from the ward to engulf the cart, extinguishing the flames.

I slammed the carpet to a stop, nearly unseating myself to avoid colliding with a streetlamp. Heart pounding, I tried to make sense of the burning wagon. How had it caught fire in the minute since I passed down the street? Was Haubner behind me? Was that a trap successfully avoided or something else?

Thunder sounded again, not so distant this time. I strained to see into the shadowed opening of the street I had exited, but I was too far uphill for a good view. Was it another flaming wagon? I dropped my hands from my ears. The thunder increased, growing louder than the pulsating alarm, until it sounded as if a blacksmith were pounding steel just beyond the street's opening.

Dread dropped my gut to my toes. That wasn't thunder; it was hoofbeats. I fumbled for the carpet's propulsion spell, clumsy in my haste.

The world's largest khalkotauroi burst from the side street with an enraged bellow. Over six feet tall at the shoulder and at least ten feet long, the enormous bull stampeded on bronze hooves as big as Oliver's paws, tearing up chunks of cobblestone with each stride. Terror etched white circles around the normally docile beast's brown eyes, and sweat matted his dark fur. Lamplight glinted off the khalkotauroi's bronze muzzle, but the bull's own fiery exhales brightened its metal nostrils to honey yellow.

The khalkotauroi tried to turn away from the shrieking ward. All four metallic hooves fought for traction and lost. The bull crashed into the corner building. Bricks crumbled and dust sprayed the air. Bellowing his fear and pain, the khalkotauroi unleashed a gout of flame that scorched a three-foot arc in the cobblestones.

Oliver plunged down the side street after the bull. Intent on the khalkotauroi, he didn't look up until he overshot the stunned bovine.

My heart lodged in my throat. Oliver was going too fast and he was too low. If he tried to land, he'd break his legs. If he tried to swoop back into the sky, he'd crash into the brick building. I cried out a warning, but Oliver was already twisting. Fighting against his own momentum, he flapped hard to gain altitude.

It wasn't going to be enough.

I yanked on Oliver's boost and shunted every drop of my magic into a thrust of air beneath my friend's wings. The weight of a living boulder pressed against my magic, so heavy I could feel the impression of his feet in the elements. Oliver climbed vertically, his wings beating inches from the brick wall. Just when I thought my magic would shatter, Oliver seized the lip of the roof and heaved himself into the open air above it.

I released the elements and sagged over my knees.

The khalkotauroi clambered to his feet. He shook his head, heedless of his horn scraping against the building, unleashing a fresh cascade of plaster and crumbling brick. White-rimmed eyes rolled toward the fire up the street, then back to the smoking wagon. The bull snorted, a pop of flame bursting from his nostrils. One monstrous hoof hammered the cobblestones in deafening strikes, carving a divot into the hard stones.

I shoved air into the carpet's sluggish propulsion spells. The low-grade rental sputtered under my magical onslaught, easing forward.

The khalkotauroi's huge head swiveled to track me. Less than a hundred feet separated us. Another forty feet stretched between me and the next crossroad. I sat in the open, without so much as a wayward display stand or cart to hide behind. I didn't risk checking, but I didn't think anyone from the fire brigade had noticed me or the khalkotauroi. Even if they had, no one was close enough to intervene.

"Easy, you're safe. No need to keep running," I soothed the bull, trying to project calm with a trembling voice.

The triggered ward continued to wail. The bull tossed his head again. Flames guttered from his nostrils.

"Easy . . ."

The khalkotauroi lowered his horns and charged me.

I shoved air into the carpet, nearly overloading the propulsion spell in my haste. I didn't care which direction I was pointed. I just needed to move. *Now.*

Time slowed to match my carpet's glacial acceleration. Even with Oliver's boost, I couldn't build a ward strong enough to withstand the impact of a three-thousand-pound bull. The carpet's levitation spell maxed out at five feet—a quality I previously considered a feature. However, five feet in the air or two, either was within prime mauling range. Nor could I outfly the khalkotauroi; even if the carpet jumped to its top speed, it would be too slow.

I shoved the rental sideways, putting all my hopes into the flying carpet's more responsive directional spells. The bull swiveled to follow. Fire bloomed from the khalkotauroi's bronze nostrils. My vision narrowed to the twin flames and the bull's curved horns. I would have to jump. If I timed it perfectly, I could make it clear of the bull's deadly hooves. Probably not the flames, but I had to try.

I gathered my feet beneath me atop the scrap of floating fabric. My left foot tangled in my bag's straps. Crystal seeds clacked and rolled. The bag slid half off the carpet in the wrong direction, then snagged on something. I lurched for balance when the carpet jerked to a stop. The khalkotauroi filled my vision. I shook my foot violently, but I couldn't dislodge the bag from myself or whatever it was stuck on.

A scream climbed my throat. I was going to be trampled to death because I was too clumsy to save myself.

Desperate, I slammed a quartz ward in front of me, knowing it wouldn't be strong enough.

A sheet of ice slapped the khalkotauroi in the face. The bull bellowed flames and sat back on his heels, metal hooves cutting grooves into the cobblestones as he slid to a stop.

I froze in place. Six feet separated us. I crouched, one hand splayed for balance, my bag an ungainly weight dragging on an ankle, and my thighs quivering with the strain of the awkward hunch. I was afraid any movement would spook the khalkotauroi into another charge, but I couldn't hold this pose much longer.

The bull shook his head, snorted twin fists of flame, and started to back up without taking his eyes off me. He kept his head lowered, his horns poised to run me through. Somehow, I had become the focus of the bull's panic, the scapegoat for his rage.

"Hey! Over here!" a man shouted. Footsteps pounded down the hill, and I caught a glimpse of olive green in my periphery. A guard. When the man whistled, the khalkotauroi flicked an ear in his direction, and I risked a glance over my shoulder.

My jaw dropped. My rescuer was *Haubner*?

18

Even as Haubner sprinted closer, waving his arms to draw the khalkotauroi's attention, my stomach sank. All my caution, all my craftiness in my approach, and I still fell right into his trap.

Only, why was Haubner distracting the bull?

I glanced past him, up the hill. No one was looking in our direction. They were all focused on the raging fire inside the dye house.

"Go! Quick, now, before . . ." Haubner's orders died when he caught sight of my face. *"Mika Stillwater?"* His feet slowed and his arms dropped. "What are you—?"

Oliver's beacon plummeted fast on my right. I spun in time to see Oliver tuck his wings to his body, arrowing for the street. Distant firelight glimmered along his square muzzle, down the scales of his stomach, and across his folded wings, transforming him into a fiery ghost. His gaze darted from the khalkotauroi to Haubner. With a snarl, he fanned his wings, changing his trajectory. He sailed over the bull straight for the guard, paws extended as if he planned to scoop Haubner up in his claws.

Haubner dropped to all fours with a strangled curse. Oliver overshot him by inches. The khalkotauroi bellowed his alarm, unleashing a gout of red-hot flame that seared the air above Haubner and engulfed Oliver's tail as he surged skyward. Shaking his head, the bull backed up another stride, panting fire.

Eyes locked on the khalkotauroi, Haubner inched to his feet. I bent in half just as slowly to tug at the strap binding my foot. The khalkotauroi snorted and swung his broad head, unsure who to track.

I gathered magic, waiting for Haubner's attack. This was his trap; all he had to do was set it back in motion. It would be easy enough for him to provoke the khalkotauroi into another charge at me. He could let the bull trample me and claim it was an accident. No one was around to say otherwise.

Abruptly, my foot slipped free, and my bag tumbled to the cobblestones, every seed crystal inside chiming louder than the last. The carpet jolted. My balance tipped, and I fell to the sidewalk, barely getting my feet beneath me in time.

The khalkotauroi whipped toward me, horns lowered. His white-rimmed eyes promised my death. I crouched. The nearest side street was thirty paces to my left, Haubner halfway between me and possible escape. Nothing else on the street was worth hiding behind. Making it to the corner was my only chance for survival, and even then, the bull might be faster.

Cursing, Haubner began flailing his arms again and ran *toward* me.

"Over here! Hey!" He slapped the bull's muzzle with a flurry of ice. Haubner's defense shocked me, but the bull only shook his head and snorted fire. His wild-eyed gaze remained locked on me.

"Stillwater, the alcove," Haubner shouted, pointing.

The recessed door wasn't deep or narrow enough to protect anyone from a khalkotauroi. Did Haubner honestly think I was going to rush right into his trap?

Then again, Haubner was angling for the same alcove, as if he planned to take a stand there *with* me. That didn't make any sense. If Haubner had lured me here to kill me, why place himself in danger, too?

The bull charged. My doubts crumbled, overpowered by raw terror. I bolted.

Haubner met me halfway, grabbing my arm to propel me into the shallow doorway. I slammed into the wall, and Haubner mashed himself against me, pinning me in place. I started to fight him but stopped when I realized he wasn't constraining me. He was protecting me. Magic whirled from him, a dense shield of air and ice and earth swelling to cocoon us.

It wouldn't be enough.

Oliver's beacon dove down the street faster than the khalkotauroi. I pictured how it would look from his perspective: Haubner caging me and the bull bearing down on me, intent on roasting and skewering us both. Oliver would throw himself in the bull's path, and he might try to take out Haubner in the process. I couldn't let either happen.

"Link," I gasped. I shoved magic to Haubner, the bundle of elements clumsy but balanced.

Haubner grabbed my magic. An incongruous tranquility flashed through me as I registered Haubner's serene magical signature. Then a dizzy rush of elements was wrenched from me. The shield around us doubled in strength, covering the alcove opening. I squeezed my eyes shut and willed Oliver to understand. He boosted me. He would feel Haubner using my magic and know we were linked.

At the last second, Oliver's beacon veered aside. I twisted to peer over Haubner's shoulder in time to see Oliver flash between us and the rampaging khalkotauroi. The bull jerked, tracking the blur of carnelian gargoyle but not slowing. Oliver landed fast, half loping, half sliding into a puddle of golden lamplight. Shaking his wings so they shimmered like living flame, Oliver split the air with a shrill whistle.

The khalkotauroi took the bait. Belching a funnel of fire in Oliver's direction, the bull pivoted to give chase—or tried to. Bronze hooves scrambled on cobblestones as the bull strained to alter one and a half tons of forward momentum toward his new, shiny target. His charge curved away from us, but not fast enough.

The khalkotauroi slammed his shoulder and side into the shop front beside our alcove. Heat washed over me, heavy with the earthy scent of hot fur and burnt wheat. The bull's hind foot splayed out, his hip crashing into Haubner's shield.

Haubner thrust me from the link a millisecond before his magic shattered. The bull's legs bunched. He righted himself and tore away from us. I lurched around Haubner's hunched frame to peer up the street, heart in my throat.

Oliver gave his wings one last taunting shake before launching into the sky. He flew low, heedless of the khalkotauroi's enraged fiery bellows that engulfed his tail and hindquarters. Whistling again, this time to catch the attention of the guards at the top of the hill, Oliver led the khalkotauroi out of sight around the bend.

I strained to track the bull's hoofbeats, but I was half deaf from the khalkotauroi's charge, and the buildings and the curve of the slope distorted the sound. I didn't take a full breath until I sensed Oliver's beacon lift skyward. He was safe. The khalkotauroi was the guards' problem.

I sagged against the wall, only then realizing Haubner held my wrist in a vise to keep me from bolting after Oliver. The guard's face was ashen from the backlash of broken magic—a backlash he protected me from by booting me from the link. Again, not the behavior of a man who was trying to kill or entrap me.

I gave my wrist a shake, and Haubner released me. Taking a step back, he leaned against the opposite side of the alcove, breathing harshly. His brown eyes bored into me, suspicion and confusion warring on his face. I held his gaze, letting the truth sink in: Haubner wasn't the thief.

When Oliver landed in the middle of the street, I broke my staring match with the guard and rushed to meet my friend halfway. Oliver loped toward me, his gaze swinging from me to Haubner. I studied his wings, his feet, his stride, verifying with my eyes that he was all right even as I formed a test pentagram tuned to his living carnelian makeup.

"Stillwater, if you're behind these thefts and fires, I'll make sure you never touch the elements again."

My step hitched in shock at Haubner's words. His threat wasn't a ploy of misdirection, as I assumed in the past. No one was close enough to hear his accusation. He wasn't playing to an audience. Haubner genuinely suspected *me* of being the thief.

I would have laughed at the irony if I weren't so affronted.

I spun back to face him, then thrust a hand out to stop Oliver from surging past me to confront Haubner.

"Why do you suspect me?" I demanded. "Why have you *always* suspected me?"

The guard stalked into the street, though he wisely stopped five feet away when Oliver growled a low rumble of a warning.

"You have gargoyles reporting to you from all over the city, keeping tabs on guard locations, keeping you informed on our investigation."

"*What?*"

"Don't bother denying it. That gargoyle tried to lose me the other night, but I followed him right to your doorstep, and then you showed up the next day at the Blue Lotus, same as him. It was too suspicious. So I asked myself: Who better to saunter in and out of gargoyle-guarded locations than the *guardian* herself?"

My jaw locked at the sneer he gave my title. "Who better? Perhaps a guard. Someone everyone trusts, even gargoyles."

"Yeah, I heard you think the male thief looks like me. We have only your word for that, of course."

I flushed and opened my mouth to defend myself, but I let the words die. We could exchange accusations all night, but it wouldn't get us anywhere.

Turning away, I knelt and eased magic into Oliver. Aside from bruised paws, he was fine. The khalkotauroi's flames hadn't so much as singed him. I wove delicate healing through his paw pads to encourage them to mend faster, then withdrew my magic. I would have added a hug for my friend and told him how much I appreciated his bravery, but Oliver hadn't taken his gaze from Haubner.

I straightened and faced the guard. Haubner's expression hadn't lost any of his arrogance, but he no longer looked furious. He worked his jaw, then spoke almost civilly.

"Explain your presence here tonight."

I crossed my arms. "I'm on my way to a sick gargoyle, Wendell, who lives atop the Hearthware building. I was informed the thieves were in the area—"

"Informed by who? Your gargoyle network?"

I shook my head. Oliver growled, and I rested a hand on his mane.

"You realize this"—I pointed uphill toward the burning dye house—"is a distraction, right?"

Haubner crossed his arms, matching my body language down to the quirked eyebrow. "Let's see. The Ember Rails khalkotauroi pens were demolished, two bulls, three heifers, and a calf were whipped into frenzies and unleashed in six different directions, and nothing was stolen from Ember Rails. Of course it's a distraction." He uncrossed his arms, his expression twisting into disdain. Or maybe it was frustration. "Unfortunately, it's a smart one. We've got seven squads working to capture the khalkotaurois and another three coordinating with the fire brigade to contain all the fires they started. The thieves are long gone."

I hated that I agreed with him. With mayhem this sophisticated, the thieves could have struck multiple locations and slipped away with no one the wiser—except for Wendell and any other gargoyles they sickened.

Haubner strode to my wayward rental carpet and shifted it aside, then extricated my bag from a snarl of ornamental shrubbery with an effortless tug. I gritted my teeth. Without the threat of a khalkotauroi bull stampeding at him, of course it was easy to untangle.

The guard grunted when he lifted my bag. Frowning, he set it atop the floating carpet, then flipped the top open as if he had every right to rifle through my belongings.

"Hey!" I stomped to his side and grabbed my bag, staggering when it fell from the carpet. I let it swing to the cobblestones and knelt to close the top flap. My pastries were smashed, but the cloth holding them was still knotted. I could eat the crumbs—once Haubner wasn't watching me.

"What are you carrying in there? A gargoyle?" Haubner asked, but he backed up as he spoke to make way for Oliver.

My friend's tail flicked with annoyance, his quartz scales grinding against the cobblestones in rough rasps that set my teeth on edge. With more force than necessary, Oliver pawed through the soil at the base of the shrub, unearthing a handful of spilled seed crystals. I accepted them, wiping the dirt off on my shirt before tucking them into my bag.

Straightening, I met Haubner's suspicious eyes and forced my words out. "Come with us to Hearthware."

Oliver started to protest, but I overrode him.

"Maybe you'll see something that will lead us to the thieves while I heal Wendell." If working with Haubner meant we could find the thieves sooner, I would stomach my dislike of the man and collaborate.

Haubner studied me, as if weighing my words for hidden meaning.

"I can't leave my team until we have all the khalkotaurois contained," he finally said. "Stay here. I'll accompany you when I'm free."

I shook my head. "The sick gargoyle can't wait."

"A few minutes more won't hurt. The khalkotaurois—"

"I know what to look and listen for." I wouldn't stand here idly while a gargoyle suffered. Reaching around Haubner, I gathered the flying carpet and manually maneuvered it into the open.

"Fine." Haubner's glare should have nailed us to the spot. Maybe he wished it would. "But once you heal the gargoyle, wait at Hearthware. Touch nothing. If you run off, I will find you."

"We'll wait."

I expected Haubner to watch us until we were out of

sight, but he gave me a crisp nod, then broke into a jog toward the fire.

I climbed onto the carpet and sat with far less grace than I intended. It took three tries to get my bag settled on my lap. When I would have pushed the carpet into motion, Oliver stood to plant a paw on the fabric, holding it in place. He didn't lean on the threadbare platform; the rental's levitation spells would have collapsed under even half his weight.

"Are you all right?" he asked.

I brushed a loose lock of hair behind my ear with a hand that visibly shook. My stomach felt little better.

"I'm fine. It's just jitters. That was way too close—for you *and* me."

Oliver pushed his chin against the base of my throat, his wings flaring to wrap me and the carpet in a gentle hug. I curled my arms around his slender neck, hugging him back.

"Far too close," he agreed.

I took a deep breath of his clean, mineral scent, then another. Adrenaline bled from my body, and my trembling stilled. Tipping my chin down, I kissed his forehead.

"Thank you, Oliver."

He folded his wings, dropping to all fours. His smile died when his gaze landed on Haubner. The guard was nearly at the top of the hill, and when he glanced back, I couldn't read his expression.

"I still don't trust him, not completely," Oliver said.

"It would have been easy enough for him to let the khalkotauroi kill me."

Oliver growled.

"I don't think he's the thief," I said.

"That doesn't mean I have to trust him."

"True."

Fatigue pervaded my limbs and ran molasses through my magic. I waited until the carpet was in motion and on course toward Wendell before fishing out the cloth of Eilidh's pizzazies. As I suspected, they were pulverized. I ate the crumbs, using the cloth to funnel every last morsel into my mouth. I stopped myself from licking the cloth clean, but only because the pastries' pick-me-up properties kicked in.

I slowed the carpet when I spotted the Hearthware Spellworks building set back from the road. Twin lanterns marked the short drive in front of the large brick-and-glass structure. Dim light shone through its high windows, and the building's ward looked intact. As it would if the thieves altered their spirits to walk through it.

But Wendell's beacon wasn't at Hearthware.

Had I misread Haubner after all? Had he saved me from the chance encounter with the khalkotauroi only to send me into a premeditated trap of his own design?

Easing the carpet to the center of the road, I peered toward Wendell's beacon. It shone another half a block in the distance, on the fringe of the extensive Onacona Auction House grounds. A long stone wall followed the curve of the road in front of the property, with a wide wrought-iron gate barely visible farther up the street. Every thirty feet or so, the auction house's emblem, a white owl, was inlaid in the gray stone with spell-perfect precision. Ornamental shrubs and winding flowerbeds adorned the space between the wall and road, encompassing the sidewalk. Wendell waited either against the wall or close beyond it. If he was on this side, he was lost among the plants. Lamps were spaced wider apart here than downtown, leaving swaths of darkness large enough to hide wyverns. The mixture of elm and oak trees lining the winding lane added more shadows—and prevented me from signaling Oliver.

I gathered elements to create a message for him, but Oliver's beacon suddenly dropped. He dove over the trees and plunged behind the wall. He banked, landing close enough to Wendell that their beacons merged. I pushed more speed into the carpet, keeping my eyes peeled for a trap.

A harsh clatter of quartz against metal rang through the still night air from Oliver's location. My heart pressed into my throat. The carpet was too slow, the wind against my ears too loud. I strained forward, rushing across the cobble-stones, closing the distance. Heavy thumps emanated from the other side of the wall. It was at least six feet tall, but if I pushed the carpet's levitation spell, I could get high enough to jump over and—

A small wrought-iron pedestrian gate burst open ten feet farther up the wall. No wider than three feet, black, and hidden among the shadows, I hadn't even noticed it. Lucy thrust her head out, her distinctive feather-eared hat quiver-ing, her eyes as big as saucers.

"Mika! Over here! Something's caught Oliver and the other gargoyle." She ducked out of sight, then reappeared looking twice as frightened. "Hurry, Mika! I think they're both hurt."

19

The levitation spell jounced when I sailed over the curb, twisting the carpet's trajectory off course. Rather than fight it, I jumped from the carpet, landing at a run. My bag swung in a ponderous arc in my grip, then I got my arm through a strap. The maneuver nearly toppled me when my boots slid in the crushed granite leading to the gate.

Lucy leaned farther out the opening, motioning me faster with one hand, twisting to glance at the gargoyles and whatever had them trapped. With the grounds behind her more shadowed than the street, I couldn't see Oliver or Wendell.

"Thank the gods you're here," Lucy exclaimed, grabbing my arm as soon as I was in reach. She spun with me toward the auction house, propelling me through the gateway with unnecessary force. My shoulder wrenched in its socket when she jerked me to a halt a step later.

"What are you—?"

Lucy flung her arms around me in a vise of a hug.

"Lucy, let go. I need to—"

The gate clanged shut behind me. An alarm bell went off in my head. Starting to struggle in earnest, I twisted to look for Oliver.

"Hurry, Gralen," Lucy hissed.

Who?

A meaty hand circled my bicep in a crushing grip. Fear sizzled through my veins. I tore free from Lucy. My elbow hit what felt like padded marble. A man grunted, his exhale fluttering the hair on my neck. A scream climbed my throat, cut off when thick arms banded my torso, squeezing the air from my lungs. A cage of earth and water reinforced the physical restraints, and a slap of air gagged me.

Lucy danced out of reach of my flailing feet. I bucked against the thick arms holding me, fighting for freedom. Where was Oliver?

When I spotted my friend, horror hollowed my gut. Oliver lay crumpled on his side, bound tighter than a calf for branding, his chin cinched to his front paw with elementally strengthened rope. An iron band crimped his wings above his back, and another loop of iron pinched his muzzle closed. He couldn't stand no matter how much he struggled. I feared he could barely breathe with the iron mashing his nostrils. His eyes when they met mine were wide and scared.

Wendell lay beside him, his small strawberry-quartz pelican body half lost in Oliver's shadow. The scales of his curved neck shimmered from pink to milky white where they met his triangular dragon head. An ugly ring of iron clamped Wendell's jaw shut, but his snarl revealed sharp quartz incisors. His wings weren't bound, and neither were his clawed feet, but they didn't need to be: Wendell's neck snaked back and forth, and his wings flailed, but he couldn't find purchase in the dirt, as if the ground kept slipping out from under him. His eyes grazed across me, dizziness making his pupils bounce.

"Lucy, what have you done?" The rhetorical question slipped out on a whisper of despair.

I was such a fool, and now we were all trapped. Far, far too late, I grabbed for magic, seizing earth and spinning it into—

Pain cracked across my cheek, splintering my concentration. I kicked blindly, connecting with my captor's shin.

"Luce, I'm going to snap her if you don't—" The man's growl cut off with a curse when I slammed my head into his chin.

Stupid, I chastised myself. The man's chin was sharp and a lot harder than my head.

Before the black static of pain cleared from my vision, Lucy planted herself in front of me again. She held the signature-analyzing pipsissewa in one hand. Fast as a snake, Lucy caught my middle finger with her free hand and yanked it backward. Pain stiffened me. Flipping the pipsissewa over, Lucy jammed its brass ring around my finger, shoving until the metal bit into the soft flesh at the base. Her fist closed over mine, crimping the pipsissewa against my palm. A glowball flashed into existence, illuminating the cheap copper bracelet on Lucy's wrist and casting sinister shadows across her face. When she shoved the glowball beneath the pipsissewa, I tried to jerk aside, afraid she was going to burn me.

The pipsissewa sampled the spell, feeding Lucy's magical signature to me as if we had formed a link. Only, it must have been damaged, because Lucy's signature felt like an echo, a watered-down sensation of a branch of red alder burning fitfully in a cloudy, shallow puddle.

"That was close," Lucy said, talking to the man—Gralen. "Bind her while she's still woozy."

I surged for the elements, readying earth to cut the rope binding Oliver and air to bludgeon—

Magic slipped through my grip. I scrambled for it again. It felt as if I were clawing into a cloud, the elements soft and misty. Not even Oliver's boost had an effect. I could sense magic, but I couldn't reach earth element no matter how hard I strained.

Gralen released me. I dropped to my feet, stumbling at the unexpected freedom. Rough hands spun me, and rope bit into my wrists, binding them together.

"Careful!" Lucy barked. She darted around to cup her hand beneath mine, protecting the signature analyzer.

In the light, with his face uncovered, Gralen bore only a passing resemblance to Haubner. They shared a similar height and coloring, but Lucy's partner was rougher, stockier, with far less grace. Stubble shaded his jaw and upper lip, and his eyes were as hard as black spinel.

Water element trickled to me, the pathetic amount too flimsy to be useful. Something must have shown on my face, though, because Lucy's lips pinched. Her glowball swept beneath the pipsissewa again. Her faint signature tunneled into my brain. I swayed in place, confused and scared, as the elements flickered in my grip and dissipated.

"Protect this as if your life depends on it," Lucy said, squeezing my hand around the pipsissewa to emphasize her words. "Because it does."

Her hat slid forward to engulf her eyebrows, and Lucy gave a huff of disgust. Grabbing the brim with crushing force, she tossed the ridiculous feathered headpiece to the dirt. Her glasses followed. With quick, efficient movements, Lucy gathered her long brown hair into a high ponytail.

In my haste, I hadn't noticed she wasn't wearing her usual frumpy dress. Instead, she was cloaked as she had been last night, in sleek black pants and an ebony top. With her hair scraped back from her face and without her trademark goofy hat, I could have passed the thief on the street and never recognized her. The Lucy I knew was soft, eager, and youthfully naive. This cruel stranger looked right at home next to Gralen.

Bitter remorse burned white hot in my lungs, consuming all my oxygen. I had trusted Lucy, because she seemed harmless. A silly hat and an ill-fitting dress had blinded me to the criminal beneath the disguise. And now Oliver and I were trussed up and Wendell was sick.

"Gralen, tend Oliver," Lucy said.

"Who's Oliver?" Gralen asked.

Lucy shot him a withering look and slashed a hand toward Oliver. My friend growled. Gralen took a step back, but only to swipe a bar of iron from the scuffed dirt. The metal was as thick as my wrist and three feet long, but the thief whipped it through the air as if it were as light as a willow branch. He mimed swinging the bar at Oliver's head. My body went cold, then hot, fear and fury warring for dominance. Not even Oliver's quartz body could withstand a blow from that bar.

I strained for magic, pulling hard on Oliver's boost, but I couldn't cobble more than a trickle of water and air together.

"Stop struggling, Mika," Lucy said. "We both know you're not going anywhere so long as I have Oliver."

"Why are you doing this?" I barely heard myself, more intent on drawing Gralen's attention from Oliver than on what I said.

"Because you're special, Mika." Lucy's feral smile chased chills up the nape of my neck.

How long until daylight? One hour? Two? How long until Haubner came looking for me? When he didn't find me at the spellworks studio, would he think to look here, behind the auction house's tall wall? Would Marcus—

My heart clinched. Three days ago, I would have been certain Marcus would tear the city apart looking for me if I didn't return home in the morning. But I had driven him away. The memory of my empty message bowl haunted me.

I gritted my teeth. I didn't have time to wallow in self-pity or self-recriminations. I had one goal right now: getting away.

Think like Marcus, I told myself. *What would he do to escape?*

The gate to the street was closed and locked. Whatever Lucy had done had reset the auction house's perimeter ward, creating an elemental seal along the entire fence. If I tried to escape through the gate, the ward would send up an alarm. That would be ideal. The alarm would bring guards. But until those guards arrived, the ward would hold me captive and helpless in a net of air. Lucy and Gralen would be free to escape—or to harm Oliver and Wendell.

If only I could release Oliver. Even if I couldn't undo the metal binding his wings, if he were free, he could fight back long enough for me to grab Wendell. We might not be able to escape the property, but we could hide until Haubner showed up.

I cast a glance around, my heart sinking as I realized the futility of my desperate plan. The Onacona grounds resembled a full spectrum's country estate, with sweeping gardens sprawling across acres before reaching the imposing auction house styled to look like a French mansion. None of the shrubs or shadowy clumps of plants grew above waist height. The fountains were uselessly slender, the reflecting pools shallow. Only the mansion itself would hide Oliver's bright red body. Even if I could clobber Lucy and Gralen hard enough with my malfunctioning magic to give us a head start, we would never reach the building before they caught us again.

When I refocused on Lucy, she smiled as if she could read my thoughts.

"I'm not special. There's nothing I can do that you . . ." My words died as I realized what she wanted.

Lucy and Gralen must have used Wendell's boost to enhance their spirit-shifted magic when they infiltrated the auction house's impressive perimeter ward. Now they needed his boost again, only Wendell was in no condition to give it.

"You need me to heal Wendell." This wasn't the first time I encountered someone who saw gargoyles only as a tool and my ability to heal them as a means of repairing them so they could be reused. Every time, it sickened me.

"Who? Oh, the pink one?" Lucy made a dismissive noise. "You're here. He served his purpose."

Bait. Wendell had been bait to trap me. I ground my teeth, choking back a growl to match Oliver's.

"Here. Your job is to open this." Lucy pulled a wooden object from her pocket.

It was a plain hinged box hardly large enough for a seed crystal. As far as I could tell, it lacked a lock; only elements held it closed.

"That's it? Just open the box?"

Lucy nodded.

I considered all the nasty spells that could be set on the

box, and all the reasons why Lucy and Gralen wouldn't want to open it themselves.

"Untie my hands, and I'll do it." The words were sheer bravado. I had no intention of blindly complying, but at least with my hands free, I had a better chance of fighting back.

Lucy snorted. "Here's how this is going to work, Mika." Her sharp nails gouged my flesh when she grabbed the rope binding my wrists, then sidestepped. Her boot struck the back of my knee. My legs buckled, and I crashed to my knees in the soil. Lucy's cruel grip kept me from toppling forward and crushing the pipsissewa. "You'll do what I say, when I say it, because I know your weak spot. I own you."

"Luce is real good at ferreting out people's weaknesses," Gralen said.

Gralen circled behind Oliver, callously stepping on the tip of Wendell's drooped wing as he got into position. Oliver tried to claw himself upright, his snarls rising in volume. Gralen tsked, then jabbed the iron bar into Oliver's neck, driving my friend to the ground. Oliver's muffled, muzzle-bound cry of pain tore shards through my heart.

"Stop it!" I tried to leap to my feet, but Lucy kicked my shoulder. I toppled to my side. A cushion of air protected my hands, but my head bounced against the hard-packed soil. Pain drove a high-pitched whine through my skull. Blinking, I struggled to focus.

Lucy bent in half over me, her hands behind her back. "Pay attention, Mika. Oliver's life depends on it."

A tear rolled into my hair. "I'm listening," I whispered.

"Any stupid move you make, Gralen will punish Oliver."

"Most people think gargoyles are tough," Gralen said, his voice floating from behind me, and I didn't need to turn to know he was looming over my helpless friend. "I find them surprisingly fragile."

"Do you understand, Mika?"

I nodded, grinding dirt into my scalp. Another tear escaped.

Oliver's carnelian scales rustled, then a hard crack made me jump. My friend went still. I shoved up on an elbow, not breathing until I saw Oliver's glowing eyes and the rapid rise and fall of his sides. He couldn't see Gralen from his crimped position, but his glare promised the man would suffer when we got free.

"Right. Oliver, the same goes for you," Lucy said blandly. "Any attempts to interfere, and Gralen will punish you."

My gaze slid along the tall wall. Freedom lay twenty feet away—on the other side of a locked gate and perimeter ward. No one knew to look for Oliver, Wendell, or me here. Rescue wasn't coming, not in the form of Haubner and his city guard colleagues, and not from Marcus. If someone was going to save us, it would have to be me. When the opportunity arose, I would be ready to strike. Until then, I had to play along.

"Whatever you want," I said. "I will do whatever you want."

Lucy pulled me to my knees. In my imagination, I swung my bound hands into her jaw, felling her. In reality, I remained passive. No matter how fast I struck, Gralen would be faster to hurt Oliver, and both he and Lucy still had the advantage of magic.

I rolled my shoulders and shook dirt from my face. The abrupt movement set my head pounding, and I breathed shallowly until the throbbing subsided.

Lucy lifted my hands, shoving the pipsissewa in front of my face. I stared glassy-eyed at the oversized magic-infused flower, realizing it was another lie I had blindly swallowed. Why had I believed an insurance firm would let a junior agent run around with such an expensive, rare device? It had to be stolen property.

"If you break this, I will kill you, because I will have no more use for you." Lucy's voice was matter-of-fact, and all the more chilling for it.

I didn't blink. I don't think I breathed. My brain rebelled in reconciling this hard con artist with the plucky woman I met at the Blue Lotus. She didn't look like she was playing a role now, either. She looked serious. Deadly serious.

"If you *attempt* to break the analyzer, I will have Gralen kill Oliver. Understand?"

I nodded, the motion shaky.

"Open the box." Lucy set the box in front of my knee and retreated a pace.

For a wonder, the elements stabilized enough for me to create a test pentagram. I kept the basic spell small when Oliver's boost would have enabled me to pull twice as much magic. A bit longer, and I might have my full strength back. I ran through wards I knew, but none were strong enough to hold off Lucy and Gralen, not if I stretched it far enough to encompass Oliver and Wendell, too. Oliver's boost enhanced my abilities, but the thieves could link. I couldn't risk failing—the thought of what they would do to Oliver terrified me. Until I was certain I would be strong enough to defend against both Lucy and Gralen, I had to bide my time.

Easing the test pentagram over the box revealed a simple lock of wood and water, with a tiny ward threaded through the elements. A needle of ice was poised to shoot from the ward if broken. A blade of fire would slice through the lock and incinerate the ice needle in the same stroke.

"Oh, I forget to tell you: You can't break the lock," Lucy said.

I let the fire dissipate. "Then how am I supposed to open it?" Brute force wouldn't work; the spell was too strong. If I had Gralen's iron bar, I could shatter the box. But if I had Gralen's iron bar, the box wouldn't be the target of my swing.

"Use the pipsissewa."

"You want me to test the signature of the spells?"

"Use it, Mika. Stop stalling."

Oliver squirmed, his denial clear even through clenched teeth. Gralen jabbed his wing, flaking off the tip of a feather. I ground my molars and looked away from Oliver's pained expression.

Fearful of a trap, I extended the pipsissewa toward the box. The magical signature of the lock struck my mind like a blow, an intense blizzard of icy flakes raging across an isolate tundra broken by jagged spires of brittle gypsum. Goose bumps lifted on my arm. I almost missed Lucy's softer signature beneath it. My test pentagram collapsed, and I swayed in place.

Lucy knelt, bracing a hand on my shoulder and studying my face. I blinked as the shadows behind her slid, then snapped into place when I focused on them.

"Open the lock, Mika."

I gathered the elements. They squirmed and slithered in my grip.

"Remember, if you fail, Oliver gets it."

Drawing on Oliver's enhancement for stability, I wrestled the elements. I needed precision. Destroying the lock, even accidentally, would give Gralen reason to hurt Oliver.

Sweat trickled down my temple as I reached for water. The element gushed to me with uncharacteristic eagerness, a phantom chill accompanying it. Wood element eluded my first two attempts, then trickled to me. I pretended to fumble with the box, positioning it so the needle would fly toward Lucy, not me, if I messed up the counter spell.

"Nice try, Mika." Lucy yanked the box from my fingers and flipped the booby trap back toward my stomach. "Stop stalling and open it already."

Feeling as if I were building a spell for the first time, I bent my magic to reverse the twist of wood and water, holding it against the lock but not activating it. If this were my elemental lock, I could easily unwind the wood from the water without disturbing the ward. But it wasn't mine. The magic didn't have my signature.

Oliver whined, his wings rasping against the dirt. His gaze snagged mine, his blink a fraction too slow, his pupils sliding away before jerking back. He shook his muzzle as much as the binding would allow, then clamped his eyes shut, his breathing gaining a panting pace. His back claws dug into the dirt as if he were preparing to lunge—or as if he were straining for purchase. For balance.

I released his enhancement with a gasp of dismay. He was dizzy, spirit-shifted sick . . . because of me. The pipsissewa felt hot in my hand, and only the threat to Oliver's life stopped me from crushing it against the hard ground.

"This isn't a signature analyzer, is it?" I asked, my voice coming from somewhere remote.

"Of course it is. But I modified it into a signature shifter, too." Lucy's satisfied expression twisted. "If I didn't have to hide my gifts, I would be lauded as a savant spellworker."

How many different ways could I be an idiot? I should have made the connection earlier. I should have paid more attention—to a lot of things.

"The box, woman," Gralen growled. "Open it already."

His gaze shifted from the sliver of street visible through the wrought-iron gate to the sky.

Numb, I brushed magic against the bands holding the box shut, touching them but not asserting pressure. I could sense the twin signatures on the box, but not on my magic. Sensing my own signature was impossible, but for once, I thought I knew exactly what it felt like: a blend of ice and weak fire.

With a soft *snick*, the box popped open. The ice-blade booby trap dissolved. Nothing was inside.

I braced my forearms on my thighs. The garden spun in my periphery.

"You did it," Lucy said, holding up the open box. Her wondrous smile turned smug at Gralen's exclamation.

I cringed when Gralen darted around Oliver to stop beside me. He snatched the open box from Lucy's outstretched hand. His iron club dangled next to my face. If I could grab it . . .

I sat back on my heels—and tipped sideways. Hastily, I dropped to my forearms, careful of the pipsissewa.

"But that was two signatures," Gralen said, opening and closing the box with quick flicks of his wrist. "She matched them both at the same time? I thought that was impossible."

"I told you she could do it."

"Faster than you, too, and you can barely shift your signature to match *one* person's."

"And you can't shift your signature at all," Lucy snapped.

My head floated light atop my stone-heavy body. Slowly, I sank, my awareness dipping into my bones, the ground a mile away. The familiar sensation of my spirit returning home to my body hit me like a physical jolt. Fear stole my breath.

The garden stopped spinning, and Gralen's words sank

in. I had shifted my spirit. Without meaning to, simply by using Lucy's modified signature analyzer, I had altered my magical signature to match the signatures on the box. In doing so, my spirit had shifted to match *two other people's spirits*. In essence, I had copied their spirits and then worked magic as if I were both people.

And I had done so with Oliver's boost.

20

Gralen and Lucy turned to me. A feverish excitement lit Lucy's face, but it was Gralen's calculating, cold eyes that I recoiled from.

"This is . . . incredibly useful," he said. "Think of all the places we can get into with this. We're going to be so rich."

"*After* I get mine," Lucy said.

The elements hiccupped and sputtered in my grasp. Oliver wasn't offering a boost to me anymore. I didn't think he could. But I had to fight while I still had a chance—

Gralen fisted my hair, wrenching my head back. Tears sprang to my eyes, and I lost my tenuous grip on a thread of earth. The thief grinned at the pipsissewa in my bound hands, his expression pure cruel speculation. Finally, Gralen's eyes slid to mine. I struggled helplessly in his grip. He laughed and released me with enough force to snap my teeth together. Ice frosted my knees beneath the signature shifter, and Gralen's harsh signature jabbed through me. The elements I clung to destabilized and vanished.

A whimper pierced the quiet air, and I realized the sound had come from me.

Oliver struggled to rise, fighting the rope and metal binding him. Gralen sauntered to him, then jabbed the iron bar into Oliver's throat, driving him to the soil. Pinned, Oliver could do nothing to stop Gralen from slicing through the ties holding his everlasting seed's pouch to his leg. The thief crumpled the small bag in his fist, then backed away.

"What do we have we here?" Gralen shook Oliver's seed into his palm. The small limestone dodecahedron looked fragile in the man's grubby palm, and I held my breath when Gralen rapped the seed with the iron bar. Lucy stepped up beside her partner, pulling her glowball close to examine the symbols decorating the seed.

"It's a game Oliver likes," I said, stripping my voice of emotion. If they realized it was an everlasting seed, they might be stupid enough to keep it, thinking it would work for them.

"That doesn't look like any game I've heard of," Lucy said.

I shrugged. "It's a gargoyle thing."

Lucy glanced at the horizon, then at auction house. "We'll figure it out later."

Gralen's eyes lit with the same feverish avarice when he took in the Onacona. The auction house was famous for selling coveted, high-priced items. It was equally famous for its security. Thieves had pitted themselves against the auction house's wards in the past, and failed. But those criminals attempted to break, bend, or trick the spells layered throughout the building. None had the ability to simply walk in undetected. In me, Lucy and Gralen possessed the equivalent of a master key. The pipsissewa would shift my spirit again and again to unlock spell-protected treasures until it used me up, and the thieves would get away scot-free.

"Let's get going," Lucy said.

Menacing Oliver with the iron bar in passing, Gralen strode to the wall and pulled two empty black sacks from the shadows. One, he tossed to Lucy. The other he looped across his chest, the inky material blending in with Gralen's black shirt. Oliver's seed disappeared into the thief's sack.

"Why are you doing this, Lucy?" I couldn't fight the thieves with magic or fists, but maybe I could with words. I had to delay them until . . . My plan fizzled out after that, but my only other option was to do nothing, so I kept talking.

"You're smart and quick-witted." I stretched for the elements, but they mutated as I touched them, water turning to ice turning to mist, earth hard and brittle, then soft as clay. "You would be great at any number of jobs and—"

Lucy's laughter cut me off. "Are you trying to compliment me, Mika? I don't want a *job*." Her mirth died. Her eyes narrowed on me with unsettling intensity. "I want my freedom. I want what's owed me."

"Owed to you? By who?"

"By the bastards who tried to keep me small." Lucy slung the strap of her bag across her shoulder with more force than necessary. "Tonight, I take back what was stolen from me. You're going to liberate me, Mika."

She turned to Gralen. "We're done here. Kill the gargoyles. Bring Mika."

The crackle of Oliver's carnelian feathers fracturing against the iron band confining them drowned out my stunned denial. Gralen slapped the bar against his palm, his cruel smile glinting in the moonlight. Skirting Oliver's writhing wings, he raised the bar high over Wendell's helpless body.

"Don't touch him!" I shouted. A burst of adrenaline

launched me to my feet. I staggered to keep my balance on soles numb from being bent beneath me too long. "Don't hurt either of them, or you'll never get what you want."

"You think you can refuse me?" Lucy asked, but she motioned for Gralen to wait.

I tried to breathe, struggling to think around the terror coursing through my body.

"I already told you I would do whatever you asked. But if you hurt them—" If Gralen killed Wendell, my heart would break. If he killed Oliver . . . I shuddered, my heart a frantic rabbit caught in a snare of panic. I wouldn't survive watching my friend be murdered. "The gargoyles are too important. You need them. *I* need them. Their boosts are why I could open the lock." I was talking fast, words tumbling out almost before they formed in my thoughts. "Without Oliver and Wendell, your signature shifter won't work for me. Like it doesn't for Gralen."

Lucy studied me, her head cocked to one side. My knees trembled. I ran through my options—throwing myself across Oliver, into Gralen; running for the gate and screaming for help; smashing the pipsissewa against Lucy's temple—but in every scenario, Lucy or Gralen stopped me with a simple band of air. So I held still and pleaded with my eyes.

"You had no problem using the pipsissewa at the LTs' without any gargoyles present."

"Not true. Carmen and Oliver were both close enough to boost me." I made myself think only of the truth of my words, not of how I hadn't thought to use Carmen's boost or how Oliver had been too far away when I first used the pipsissewa in the tradeswomen's kitchen. I couldn't let Lucy see even a hint of a lie in my words. My friends' lives depended on it.

Lucy squinted at me, running her tongue over her teeth.

Gralen bounced the iron bar against his palm. *Slap. Slap. Slap.* "What's it going to be, Luce?"

She held my gaze, unblinking. "Bring them. Alive."

I sagged under the weight of relief and hate.

Wendell staggered to his feet, his long pelican wings flapping fast for balance. His triangular head swayed on his thick, scaled neck, and his claws dug into the dirt for purchase. Scrapes and gouges marred his strawberry-quartz chest and dragon paws. Wendell's eyes were still cloudy with dizziness, but he appeared to be focusing on me better. Or maybe it was wishful thinking. For a second, I thought he might manage to walk, but gravity tugged him off balance, and he toppled. His chin smacked into the ground, the metal band clamping his mouth ringing against his quartz muzzle. The rest of his body followed in a painful slide.

Gralen laughed.

"Let me heal him, please."

Lucy's fingers dug into my arm, holding me in place. "We're not wasting your energy on that."

"Ugly little thing," Gralen said, giving Wendell a shove with his foot. "This is going to take forever."

"Leave Oliver and Wendell here," I said, trying not to let my eagerness seep into my voice. "They can boost me from here even if we go to the other side of the property." That was a lie, but I suspected Lucy and Gralen had never enjoyed a gargoyle's boost outside of those they stole by mimicking other people's magical signatures. They would be ignorant of gargoyles' limits.

Lucy laughed. "Oh, Mika, you are so easy to read. You think I don't know they'll go for help?"

"How? Wendell is too sick and Oliver can't move." Neither could call for help, either, with their muzzles clamped shut. But Oliver was resourceful. If I could convince Lucy to underestimate him, he would figure out a way to untie himself and bring help.

"Nice try, Mika." Lucy shook her head, still chuckling.

"I don't know, Luce. Maybe she's right. We could stick the ground-beef-looking one in the shrubs. No one could see it from the road. The other, I could *flatten* a bit to make sure he didn't go anywhere." Gralen menaced his iron bar above Oliver.

My breath caught in my throat. "If you harm him, I'll . . ."

"You'll what?" Lucy asked. "You'll refuse to help us? I don't think so, Mika." She tapped her forefinger against her bottom lip, and the cold calculation in her gaze made me want to shrink into my own skin. "You would do anything to stop a gargoyle from feeling pain—or rather, *more* pain. If Gralen were to, say, snap off the tip of Oliver's tail, you wouldn't do anything, because you don't want to make us have to kill your friend, right?"

My stomach roiled, bile splashing up my esophagus. I shook my head, denying the image she put in my head and her threat to murder Oliver.

Lucy turned to Gralen. "Bring the big one."

Gralen planted his hands on his hips, the iron bar held loose in his fist. "Bring it? And who's going to carry it? Because it's not going to be me."

Lucy's nostrils flared in annoyance. "Bind its front foot to its back. Give it an inch to move, but no more."

A band of air slid beneath Wendell and strained to shove the gargoyle toward the hedges, generating more wiggle than lift of the small gargoyle. Wendell's bright eyes focused on me, fear or sickness adding a tremble to his lifted head. My heart ached. Some protection I provided; it was only because of me that he was a hostage.

"Link, Gray." Lucy snapped her fingers.

Gralen extended a balance of elements to Lucy, and the net of air beneath Wendell thickened. The gargoyle floated toward a low hedge.

Gralen loosened the rope binding Oliver's muzzle to his foot. Oliver sprang to all fours. His head swung wildly, clipping Gralen's shoulder. The thief staggered but caught his balance far too quickly. Weapon raised, he rushed Oliver.

I locked the iron bar in a vise of air before it collided with Oliver's fragile head. Yanked off balance, Gralen nearly toppled to his butt. My magic, already weak, fractured beneath the thief's weight. Agony shredded my brain as the elements were torn from me. Before I could recover, a steel ball hit my gut. I doubled over, clutching my bound hands to my stomach.

Cursing under her breath and shaking out the hand she had used to sucker-punch me, Lucy dropped Wendell in a boneless heap and slammed Oliver's head to the ground with a crushing blow of air. Oliver's front legs collapsed, and his bound wings tipped him off balance. He landed hard on his side. Metal grated on quartz, and red rivulets ran like sandy blood to coat the soil beneath his wings.

Gralen scrambled to his feet, not half as quiet in his cursing. Grabbing the loose rope, he tied Oliver's front-right foot to his back left, cinching it tight. Lucy welded the knot in place with twists of wood element. Gralen stepped back, murder in his eyes. Gasping for breath, I seized a trickle of magic. I had to protect Oliver.

Lucy slapped me. My head snapped to the side, and I worked my jaw to clear the ringing in my ears.

"Gray, look at her. She'll do anything for that one."

Gralen's gaze flicked over me. "Yeah, she would. It could make her dangerous."

I forced myself to look away from the challenge in his eyes, my jaw tight.

"Mika? Dangerous? She's got the bleeding heart of a healer. She won't be a problem. We're wasting time. Hide the small one and let's get moving."

Through blurry vision, I watched Gralen lower the iron bar to his side. Oliver's eyes tracked the weapon. Beneath the bronze muzzle, his lips curled in a snarl. Whatever happened tonight, I would make it my life's mission to ensure Gralen paid for his torment of my friend. He and Lucy both.

21

G ralen hooked Wendell with a ruthless vise of air and dropped him into the nearest hedgerow. The gargoyle's splayed wings and writhing body snapped branches as he fell through the waist-high shrub. He hit the ground hard and lay still.

Gargoyles are resilient. Their rock bodies can withstand an incredible amount of abuse. A few scrapes are worth it if it means Wendell will be left here.

The thoughts did little to ease my worry.

Hidden in the dense foliage, Wendell wouldn't be visible to passersby. No one would look in and think to rush to his aid. Or to mine. Wendell was in no shape to fly for help, either.

"We're wasting time," Lucy said. "Get that one on its feet."

Gralen used his iron bar and a wedge of air element to shove Oliver to his feet. My friend splayed his free paws wide, his head and tail flailing for balance. With his wings crimped above his back and his bound legs forcing his spine into a tight arch, he would have struggled to stabilize himself even if he weren't spirit-shifted dizzy.

Gralen circled Oliver, deftly avoiding Oliver's clumsy lunge for him. Oliver toppled. Metal grated against quartz, shearing off another layer of feathers. Oliver's head hit the ground hard enough to chip his beautiful mane. Dazed, he lay panting on his side. My heart broke for him.

Gralen chortled.

Lucy wrenched my arms in their sockets, yanking me into place in front of Oliver. Then she slapped me. I saw the blow coming in time to twist my head with it, but it still felt like Lucy hit me with a hand sheathed in quartz.

"Every time you misbehave, Oliver, Mika will suffer. Stop delaying us and get moving."

I blinked away involuntary tears, quivering with the need to heal Oliver, to tear those dreadful metal bands from his body and the rope from his legs, and to fight back. But since nothing I could do would be fast or strong enough to stop Lucy or Gralen from retaliating, I stood mute.

Oliver must have reached the same conclusion, because his expression was a mask of anguish beneath the iron muzzle.

Lucy shoved me aside as Oliver labored to his feet unaided. As soon as he was up, Lucy set off across the garden, hauling me by my bound hands. She locked her gaze on the auction house, stomping a straight line across the manicured landscape, ignoring the curved gravel paths twisting through the garden.

Oliver hobbled into motion. With his paws hog-tied together, and his crimped wings bumping against his humped spine, his momentum was reduced to a rocking shamble, each truncated step advancing him less than a foot. Gralen prodded him mercilessly with the iron bar, his agitated jabs intensifying when Oliver slowed to navigate a shallow embankment.

Moonlight illuminated the grounds, revealing a depressing lack of bramble fences and lava moats. At best, the flower beds and shallow reflecting pools might present tripping hazards. Even the garden's spells were benign, maintaining soil moisture and cleansing fountain water instead of barricading trespassers from trampling the botanical oasis.

The loamy scent of churned earth mingled with the bitter green of crushed plants as I blundered along behind Lucy. I nearly fell when I finally seized stable magic. Drawing a thimbleful of cool quartz-tuned earth, I held the element like an anchor. The familiar magic soothed my battered mental pathways, clearing my thoughts. When I tried to draw more magic, the element quivered in my weak grip. Pain spiked between my temples. My fantasy of clobbering Lucy and Gralen with a club of earth element died. I would never pull off two attacks fast enough to best both thieves.

I searched the shadows closer to the huge auction house, hoping to spot a guard or worker. In the predawn hush, our progress should have been loud enough to bring the most inattentive watchman out to investigate. When Oliver crashed to his side a third time, and no one materialized, I abandoned my wishful thought. Oliver and I were in this alone. We would have to rescue ourselves.

Lucy tapped her foot with impatience as Oliver struggled to stand. The binding on his ankles forced him to use his wings to leverage himself to his feet, and even with metal clamping his muzzle shut, his pained cry rang through the air. Without thinking, I darted magic toward Oliver.

"Release it, Mika," Lucy ordered.

She swiped her glowball toward the pipsissewa. I jerked my hands away and released the elements fast enough to make myself dizzy.

"His injuries are slowing us down," I said, striving to keep my tone factual and not pleading. "If I heal him, he can move faster."

"I told you, we're not wasting your energy on—"

"Please. Just so Oliver can walk without falling. If he trips out here, he smashes a bush. But if he falls inside, he might set off an alarm. Let me stabilize him."

Since a tripped alarm would bring city guards, I should have been praying Oliver would trigger one. But the possibility of guards arriving in time to save us was too slim to gamble on. Oliver's well-being was more important. Each fall wrenched fractures through his wings. Once we were inside, his falls wouldn't be cushioned by soil, and he could be seriously injured. In fact, I was certain he *would* be seriously injured if he unwittingly activated the building's wards and alerted the guards; Gralen would see to it.

More importantly, one of us needed to be strong. So long as I wore the pipsissewa, it wouldn't be me. I didn't know how many times Lucy would force me to use it, or what it would do to me. I didn't trust I would be able to save either of us. I had to ensure my friend was capable of saving himself when the time came.

"Or you could untie his legs," I added, seeing Lucy waver.

She scoffed. "You have fifteen seconds."

I dove gargoyle-tuned magic into Oliver. I should have used caution. The last time I healed a spirit-shifted gargoyle, I lost control. My entire spirit had fallen into Daphne. But I didn't have time to go slowly. Besides, this was *Oliver*. My spirit was safest with him.

Pain radiated back to me through the connection. I swayed in place, clinging to the elements when they threatened to unravel. Agony blazed from Oliver's wings, with dull aches pulsing from his muzzle and feet, and sharp pinches like dozens of wasp stings pierced his flank from Gralen's repeated jabs.

Forcing myself to ignore the wounds, I pushed deeper. The discordant vibration of Oliver's spirit tried to pull my magic apart. I had done that to him. Guilt sullied my impotent fury, then redoubled it. I trembled, physically and spiritually, caught in a maelstrom of vibrating elements and emotions. Lost, I clung to my magic, striving for serenity.

The baetyl crashed down on me like a silent tsunami, and my spirit tumbled inside Oliver, a piece of flotsam lost in the undertow of the baetyl's omniscience.

Dumbstruck, I witnessed the baetyl reshaping my magic, questing it into Oliver to heal his sickened spirit. Before, when healing Nimoy and Carmen, I convinced myself the sensation of the baetyl was my imagination or a way of processing latent information I had absorbed when linked with the immortal sentience. But this was more than a flashback. The baetyl's power existed here and now. Not all of it—a mere fraction of its full power worked through me.

But it terrified me to my core.

"Nine, eight, seven," Lucy counted.

Panic goaded me into action. Clinging to tatters of my spirit, I reeled myself in. The baetyl fought me, straining to delve deeper into Oliver. The more I struggled, the harder the baetyl worked against me.

Oliver whined. The baetyl and I both froze. By some miracle, I recovered faster, reclaiming control just in time.

"Three-two-one," Lucy finished in a rush. She shoved her weak glowball beneath the pipsissewa.

I yanked my magic from Oliver before it could be tainted. The flare of pain in his eyes barely registered before the spirit shifter burrowed Lucy's signature into me, reshaping my magic. The familiar sensation of a smoldering red alder branch floating atop a murky puddle zinged through me. The quartz-tuned earth element devolved, fire weakened, water turned soupy. With a gasp, I released the elements.

Lucy tugged me forward, and I stumbled on legs that felt like hollow canes. Oliver hobbled into motion, more stable than before but no faster. My friend's gaze collided with mine, full of a message I couldn't interpret.

My spirit hiccupped and oozed back into place. Stomach churning, I fought to stay upright. For better or worse, the baetyl remained dormant.

"Hurry up," Lucy said, tugging me faster as we neared the auction house. I despaired as I took in our isolation—the vast garden stretching for acres in all directions, the wall surrounding us, the empty sky overhead. Terra Haven and all the city guards might as well have been miles away.

From afar, the Onacona Auction House was impressive. Up close, it intimidated. Three boxy turret-topped towers jutted from the tawny limestone building, their spiked tips jabbing the crepuscular sky. Gable windows glared outward from the third floor, flat and empty, and a dozen arched windows on the second floor reflected the garden behind us in watery monotone, like portals into alternate worlds, each bleaker than the last.

Glowballs clutched in black iron sconces cast flickering shadows across limestone figures carved into the facade. A pillared arcade fronted the left side of the building; a rounded solarium bulged on the right. Between the two, at the base of the central square tower, stood gargantuan twin doors. When the polished wood panels were open, a pair of gryphons could walk into Onacona side by side, and their riders wouldn't have to duck.

An empty gravel driveway wide enough to serve as a landing pad for a fleet of dirigibles stretched between the garden's edge and the front of the auction house. Shoulders hunched, Lucy dragged me across the expanse. I scuffed my feet, driving grooves into the otherwise smooth gravel. It was a feeble gesture of defiance on an even weaker chance that someone would fly overhead, see the marks, and investigate.

I would have a better chance of alerting help by "accidentally" triggering a ward. Since every door, window, and walkway sported a spell, all of them tied into the building's main trespassing ward, I just had to bide my time and be ready if the opportunity presented itself.

When, I corrected myself. *When, not if.*

Lucy angled away from the double doors toward the shadowed arcade on the left. I tripped as gravel gave way to stone tiles. Oliver's quartz paws rang deafeningly in the confined space, and I suspected he was stomping. Like me, he was attempting to do anything possible to attract notice.

And like my efforts, his were just as futile.

Lucy jerked me to a halt at a door half hidden against the wall. A lightweight ward sealed the door, but it would blare an alarm if breached. I clawed for magic, desperate to stabilize my spirit before Lucy made me use the pipsissewa on the door's lock.

"Mika, get us in." Lucy positioned herself to one side, her hands on her hips.

I swayed, only partially faking my instability. My spirit still reeled from the baetyl's assault and from my broken connection with Oliver. The elements felt strange in my grip, like wet sand when they should have been as firm as quartz.

"My hands," I said, taking a calculated, clumsy step so my arm brushed the air above the door's ward. Another half inch, and I would have ignited it. The hairs on my arm lifted. I lurched aside, heart pumping. The back of my knuckles banged against the door handle. I curled my wrists to protect the pipsissewa—and to keep it from forcing the ward makers' signatures on me.

"Careful!" Lucy grabbed my shoulder and hauled me back a step.

I let myself fall into her. She staggered under my weight, then jabbed me with an elbow. Pain exploded across my ribs. I sagged over my knees, breaths rasping, as I found my balance.

"Gray, remind Mika what happens when she disobeys me."

I spun, my denial ringing through the stone arcade a half second before Gralen struck Oliver. He grazed my friend's hip with the iron rod, cutting a bright line through Oliver's carnelian flesh. Oliver ducked his head, his eyes locked on mine until Lucy stepped between us.

"That was unnecessary," I growled. "It's not Oliver's fault I am dizzy. You've used this, Lucy." I waved the pipsissewa in her face, and she leaned back a fraction. "You know how it feels. I need my hands untied. It will help me balance."

"You'll do fine." Lucy grabbed my shoulders to spin me around.

"I don't want to break it by accident." I clutched my hands to my chest, cradling the pipsissewa to my body.

Lucy's gaze dropped to the signature shifter, then

bounced back and forth between my eyes, assessing my honesty.

My words were truth: I didn't want to break the pipsissewa *by accident.* I wanted to smash it. I wanted to rip apart every resin-hard petal and demolish the spell in its depth. But most of all, I wanted to increase my odds of surviving until sunrise, and freeing my hands was a step in the right direction.

Lucy yanked my arms straight. Instead of using the elements to cut the rope, she untied the knot by hand, sawing the abrasive hemp across my wrists. When the binding fell away, Lucy kept one hand locked around my wrist.

Leaning close, she whispered, "If you set off an alarm, I have no reason to keep your precious gargoyles alive. Keep that in mind, *guardian.*" She hissed the last like a curse, and goose bumps pebbled my arm at the rush of her warm breath across the shell of my ear.

When she released me, I gingerly flexed my fingers. The pipsissewa sat heavy against my left palm, but I had mobility and magic. Now was my chance to strike.

Except the elements still stuttered in my grip, and Gralen still held the iron bar over my helpless friend, watching me with a chilling smile.

Mindful of the larger spell on the door frame, I braced myself with one hand on the doorknob and aligned the pipsissewa with the door's elemental lock. A whirlwind of sand and embers cut through me, softened by dewdrops drawn into the windstorm from the tips of daffodil blossoms. The signature swept through me, replacing mine. Gingerly, I reached for magic. Earth grated like sandpaper and fire smoldered in my grasp, a pale comparison to its usual texture. Water and wood repelled each other, while air built too fast, nearly overpowering the other elements. I labored for the correct balance to match the door's lock.

"What's wrong?" Gralen asked. "Why is she taking so long?"

"She's just started," Lucy said.

"She was faster than this with the box."

"Mika knows what happens if she stalls."

My fingers tightened on the doorknob until my knuckles were white in the pale light. Sweat dotted my forehead. Finally, my magic steadied enough for me to twist the lock. I tugged the door open. Relinquishing the elements, I cradled the pipsissewa to my stomach, where it couldn't brush against another signature. Lucy shoved me aside and floated a test pentagram across the threshold. When nothing happened, she eased into the dark room. Something sharp prodded my back, and I stumbled after Lucy, as graceless as if I were walking with someone else's feet.

I waited for the familiar sensation of my spirit jolting home. When it didn't come, I quested outward, reaching for it the same way I reached into a gargoyle. My head floated atop my neck like an unanchored dirigible balloon. Vertigo tipped my equilibrium. Frantic, I reversed my mental fumbling. With a snap, my spirit rebounded into me. I dropped from my tiptoes to my heels, then hunched over my knees, breathing through my horror.

Marcus claimed all spirit shifting was the same, but he was wrong. When I intentionally untethered my spirit from my body and anchored it inside a gargoyle, I gave it a home. The gargoyle kept me safe, and I posed no danger to them because my spirit so closely resonated with theirs.

But this . . . This was wrong. The pipsissewa was a perversion of the shifted-spirit healing I performed on gargoyles. Its magic corrupted the user's spirit, shunting it aside—not into anything, not anchored anywhere. It simply overwhelmed it.

I should hurl the pipsissewa to the ground and crush it beneath my boot. It was madness in magic form. I should, but I couldn't, because Gralen would kill Oliver. But how many shifts could I endure before the pipsissewa permanently severed my spirit from my body and killed me?

22

A soft glowball ignited in the middle of the room, the dim light playing off gold filigree on the wall panels and glinting along the strings of a tall harp set in the corner closest to us. Lucy pushed the light farther into the room, revealing two couches, several chairs, and four end tables, as if we had entered a drawing room. Only the wards shimmering between us and the furniture indicated this was a tableau of goods meant to be auctioned.

Lucy spun in a slow circle, stirring scents of wood polish and lavender. Display cases sat against one wall, and warded shelves lined another. She darted to examine their contents while I shuffled to the side to make way for Oliver. His crimped wings scraped the door frame on either side, gouging the wood. Gralen crowded behind him and tugged the door closed. He and Lucy shared a grin.

"We did it," she said, reaching for him. Gralen crossed the room and pulled her into a one-armed hug, his gaze greedily inventorying the shelves.

Careful not to draw their attention, I rested a hand on Oliver's mane. With the cool texture and sturdy lines of his carnelian fur to ground me, I closed my eyes and concentrated on tuning earth element to quartz. It took three attempts, then even longer to match the other four elements to Oliver's familiar makeup.

Jittery with the need to hurry and fearful of what the baetyl might try, I eased magic into Oliver. Energy elongated and shrank inside him, the shift of his spirit a slow slosh. The baetyl gathered itself, a predator at my back. Prioritizing speed over gentleness, I pressed Oliver's spirit smooth.

The ominous energy of the baetyl receded. I released a shaky breath. Floating inside Oliver, I savored a sublime sensation of wholeness. His boost flowed into me, anchoring my spirit. His love cocooned me in safety.

"It's not here," Lucy said.

My eyes snapped open. My magic unraveled, severing my connection with Oliver.

"I'm sorry," I whispered—sorry I cut our link so abruptly, sorry I couldn't heal him. Sorry I had gotten us in this terrible situation.

My spirit flexed, then settled back into my body. Delicately, I held a pebble's worth of quartz-tuned earth element. Every time I had healed a spirit-shifted gargoyle, I used earth magic afterward, and it helped restore my equilibrium. Clutching this minuscule amount of quartz magic would have to be enough.

The door was two steps behind me. When Gralen shut it, the ward resealed the entrance. With one touch, I could activate the alarm. However, since I was still too weak to keep Oliver and myself safe until the guards arrived, I considered my other option: the pipsissewa. If I could open the door, Oliver and I could run out, then trap Lucy and Gralen inside. But using the pipsissewa would take a minute or longer—an eternity in which Oliver and I would be vulnerable.

Lucy stalked the room like a caged cactus cat, stopping in front of me. She glared at my hand on Oliver's neck. Grabbing my bicep, she yanked me away from him. I let my weak magic unravel, fighting not to give in to despair.

"Look at the gold on this tea set," Gralen said, pointing with his iron bar to a top shelf. "I say we take those with us. And this silverware."

"No. We find the Sannino bitch's items first. Everything else can wait." Lucy tugged me across the room toward a narrow doorway. Oliver followed.

"Where are you going? The main showroom is this way." Gralen pointed to the wide doorway on the opposite wall.

"Use your head, Gray. It's not going to be with the big-ticket items. It'll be in the back."

"But this way lets us scout the place, decide what we're taking with us—"

"My freedom is more important than any piece of junk out there," Lucy spat. "I'm going this way, and Mika is coming with me. You need to keep the gargoyle in line."

Gralen slapped the iron bar into his palm, scowling at Lucy, then Oliver. My friend glared back with open hate, and I prayed he wouldn't give away his new clearheaded state.

Stalking across the room, Gralen raised his iron bar to take his frustration out on Oliver. I jerked free of Lucy to block him, pipsissewa raised. Gralen's lips twisted.

Lucy lunged for me. "Don't do—"

An icy fist of air punched my side, and I crashed to a knee, then toppled. Lucy screamed. At the last second, I curled my hand to my chest, protecting the pipsissewa. The floor slammed into my shoulder, but I didn't feel the impact, lost in a piercing blizzard of ice and gypsum as Gralen's signature spiked through the pipsissewa.

When my head cleared, Lucy stood over me. Her fist wrapped my wrist, and she twisted my arm high so she could examine the signature shifter. I gasped at the sharp wrench in my shoulder.

"Damn it, Gray." Lucy's tiny glowball lit sparks in her brown eyes as she straightened. "You could have broken the spirit shifter."

"You saw her, Luce. She was trying to—"

"I don't care. This is my *one* chance, and you're not going to blow it. Don't touch her again." Lucy kicked my thigh. "Get up, Mika."

I crawled to my hand and knees, not having to fake the effort the simple act took. I must have lost some time, because my spirit was back, jumbled and weak, but my own.

Oliver inched closer. Trickles of carnelian sifted from freshly broken feathers. He must have strained to break the metal band when Gralen knocked me down. I feared he was dangerously close to snapping his wing muscles. I couldn't allow that—not just because of the pain it would inflict on Oliver, but because broken wings would catastrophically inhibit his ability to escape.

"So we're clear: I'm not leaving with an inch of empty space in my sack," Gralen groused.

Lucy sashayed toward him. "We're going to have it all, baby, power and money."

"The world at our fingertips."

"The elite under our thumbs."

Their words sounded rehearsed, like promises they made to each other time and again.

Pretending to use Oliver's shoulder as a prop, I sank a thready collection of gargoyle-tuned elements into him, afraid I had been holding his boost when Gralen attacked. Pain reverberated through my fragile magic, but Oliver's spirit resonated with the tranquil stability of his gargoyle nature.

In my relief, my mental muscles relaxed. My battered spirit surged forward, rushing down the narrow conduit into Oliver. Into safety. I snatched my hand from my friend, clamping down on my magic.

My awareness stretched across the empty space between us, inhabiting quartz and flesh at the same time. If I withdrew my magic, I could tug my spirit back into my body, but I hesitated, an idea forming.

Oliver twisted to look at me, worry shrouding his eyes.

"Remember Focal Park?" I whispered.

Oliver nodded, his whine almost subvocal.

In a desperate bid to save the lives of Oliver and his siblings during a magical cataclysm at the park, I had split my spirit among them. Once they were safe, they returned my spirit to me. It had been the first time I shifted my spirit. I hadn't known what I was doing, acting instead on instinct. I had a lot more practice now.

Cautiously, I severed a portion of my spirit, leaving it inside Oliver. Then I retracted my magic. I braced my free hand on the floor. Gravity had tipped, no longer directly below, now several inches to my right. I could feel Oliver's body around me, like a ghost cloaking my skin. At the same time, I existed in the disorienting void of the gap between us.

"Is this all right?" I mouthed. I hoped that by housing part of my spirit in Oliver, he could keep it safe. No matter how much the pipsissewa twisted the rest of my spirit into new patterns, at least the portion Oliver held would remain pure.

Oliver's solemn nod and the pat of his unbound front

foot against my knee told me an explanation was unneces-sary. My friend understood exactly what I was doing, and he approved. Gratitude welled up in my chest, choking me.

"What are you two conferring about?" Lucy demanded. She pinched my ear in her fingers and lifted.

Pain lit across my scalp, and I scrambled to my feet. When she released me, I swayed toward Oliver, overcor-rected, and tottered two steps to the left.

Lucy grabbed my arm with an exasperated tsk. "Stop being dramatic, Mika."

She shoved me into motion, scrutinizing Oliver as he followed. Did she suspect Oliver was no longer dizzy? What would she do to him—or let Gralen to do to him—if she realized Oliver had regained his coordination?

Oliver's bound paws caught in the carpet, and he tripped. The jerky motion rippled through his contorted body, forcing him to whip his head and tail to maintain his balance. Satisfied, Lucy clamped her slender fingers in a bruising vise around my wrist and marched into the next room. As soon as she turned her back, Oliver steadied.

He had faked it.

I bit down on my fierce grin, proud of my smart, resourceful friend.

Lucy's steps quickened through the next three rooms even as Gralen lingered. She didn't pause to examine spelled gowns dripping in jewels the way her partner did. She didn't hesitate over the collection of pocket watches so orna-mented in gold and silver I hardly recognized them as time-pieces, though Gralen remained transfixed until the darkness swallowed him and he was forced to form his own glowball for light. Only Gralen slowed to peruse a room staged to look like it had been transported straight from a bazaar on another continent.

Oliver struggled to keep up, his truncated steps no match for Lucy's determined march. When Gralen noticed, he ruthlessly jabbed the iron bar into Oliver's hindquarters. Oliver's harsh, labored breathing ate at me. I yearned to tear the dreadful band from his muzzle so he could take a full breath.

"What are we looking for?" I asked, dragging my feet on the soft carpet.

Lucy laughed, short and sharp. "Why? You want to help me?"

"I want you to get whatever you came for so you'll release me and my friend."

"Release you?" Gralen chuckled.

Lucy shot him a glare.

"We're here for my freedom," she said. "I'm here to reclaim my true signature."

"I don't understand."

"See this?" Lucy shoved the hand that caged my wrist in my face, forcing my arm high. With her free hand, she pushed aside her shirt's black sleeve, revealing the plain copper bracelet I had noticed before. The thin band looked as if it had been welded to conform to the oval of her wrist bone, fitting so tight it couldn't be twisted. If it hadn't flexed when she moved her wrist, I might have assumed Gralen grafted it onto her like the bands he inflicted on Oliver.

"What is it?" I asked. With the bracelet inches from my nose, I spotted something I missed before: the faint smudge of a spell embedded in the metal.

"I'll show you." Lucy released my wrist, then swept the bracelet beneath the pipsissewa's petals.

A murky swirl of chaotic magic whipped through the spirit shifter and slapped my brain, each spiraling fragment a claw shredding my thoughts. My spirit shuddered, caught in a maelstrom of pain.

I screamed and swung the pipsissewa away from the bracelet, disengaging it. Nausea climbed my throat, and blackness darkened my vision.

Slender fingers pinched my neck, shoving my head toward my knees. I stared at the maroon carpet fibers through the pinprick of my tunneled vision, breathing hard, until the urge to vomit subsided and my vision cleared.

"This is a prison," Lucy said, thrusting her wrist into view.

I jerked the pipsissewa as far away from her bracelet as I could stretch. When I straightened, all the blood rushed from my head, and I held myself rigid until the threat of passing out receded. Oliver watched me with worried eyes, but he made no move toward me. I gave him a small nod, letting him know he had made the right choice.

"This is jealousy given form." Lucy glared at the bracelet. "Its twisted magic is designed to keep me small and weak. I was born with full-spectrum strength, but these"—Lucy revealed a twin copper band on the other wrist—"these won't let me draw more than a trickle of any element. They've mutated my abilities."

"But why?" I genuinely wanted to know. If I understood what drove Lucy, maybe I could use it to convince her to let us go. But even more, I wanted to keep Lucy talking. Any delay increased our chances of being caught.

"You know how full spectrums are, Mika. Look around. None of this finery is getting into the hands of anyone but the most wealthy, *powerful* people. Their power is how they stay rich, and when they see someone new—someone like you or me—gaining power, they feel threatened."

I nodded, because it seemed wiser than arguing. People

weren't nice or mean based on how powerful they were. It wasn't that simple. Not even for Lucy. More than hatred and envy of full spectrums had to be driving her.

"Sannino," I said, remembering the name Lucy cursed. "Did they put those on you?"

"The bitch didn't wait twenty-four hours after my parents died to clap these manacles on me."

"Luce, dawn's coming," Gralen said, gesturing impatiently toward the next doorway.

Lucy's jaw clenched, and she yanked me into motion again.

"I'm so sorry about your parents," I said, repeatedly tripping to slow Lucy. Pain radiated through my shoulder at her brutal manhandling, but my suffering was negligible compared to Oliver's.

"They died in a freak accident. I was thirteen. My aunt took me in, but she always resented me. The first thing she did was drag me to see Joan Sannino." Lucy's voice changed, her next words high-pitched and nasally. "'She's a renowned healer, Lucy. She'll help you, Lucy.'" Lucy made a test pentagram and jabbed it across the shadowed threshold to the next room. Her fingers dug into my wrist so tightly that it felt as if I were held by a skeleton, her bones grinding on mine.

"The 'healer' did this, curtailed my powers before they could fully develop. All because my aunt was jealous. I was more powerful than her. More powerful than anyone in my family. More powerful than Sannino herself. And none of them could stand it."

If what she claimed was true, Lucy would already be free of the bracelets. Any court in the country would imprison the false healer and destroy the bracelets the moment Lucy reported the crime. So what wasn't she telling me?

"Today, we're freeing you, darling," Gralen said, his voice floating from behind us. "You'll be a power to be reckoned with. No one will deny us anything."

"We'll walk among full spectrums and look down our noses at *them*." Lucy's smile was obsidian sharp.

No full spectrum would have such a lackluster signature. When the full import of Lucy's bracelets sank in, I couldn't keep the horror from my voice. "The healer altered your magical signature, didn't she?"

"Ironically, it's the only gift the charlatan gave me," Lucy confirmed. "I saw how she reshaped my signature. When I got my hands on the analyzer, I knew exactly how to alter it to make it a signature shifter."

The healer hadn't only altered Lucy's signature when she curtailed her magic; she had shifted Lucy's spirit. For more than a decade, Lucy had lived with a spirit that didn't quite fit her body. It was a wonder she could function. It also explained how Lucy had repeatedly used the pipsissewa without the extreme consequences Marcus and Captain Rojas predicted. Her loose spirit made her vulnerable to the signature shifter's magic, but the copper bracelets and their magic tethered Lucy's altered spirit to her body. After each use of the pipsissewa, the bracelets reinforced and reinstated Lucy's spirit.

I had no such protection. Only my experience with shifting my spirit into gargoyles had saved me from losing hold of myself completely. Even sequestering some of my spirit in Oliver was a flimsy backup plan. Already, the thread connecting my split spirit to the portion residing in Oliver felt as tenuous as gossamer. When it snapped, would I survive?

Would my sanity?

23

Lucy dragged me through a library filled with rare books—Gralen didn't give them more than a bored glance—to a plain door at the back of the room. A discreet ward sealed it.

"Open it."

Soft bands of air wove through the spell, the kind designed to seize and hold a trespasser in place. No alarm would sound if I bungled this spell. No painful magic would attack me. But if any of us were caught in the web of air, we would have to destroy the spell to free ourselves. *That* would ignite the auction house's clamorous ward.

I peeked over my shoulder. Lucy was close enough to be caught in the door's trap with me, but Gralen was too far away. He would be free to harm Oliver—and to save Lucy. To save himself, too. It hadn't escaped my notice that he let Lucy take all the risks, while he traipsed along in our wake, poised to reap the rewards.

"Focus, Mika," Lucy said. "Or do you need motivation?"

Gralen mimed shattering Oliver's wing. I turned to the door.

With insensate efficiency, the pipsissewa forced a kaleidoscope of signatures into me. Pain, sharp and short, sliced through my head. Oliver and I both cried out. Then I was lost to heat blasting from a blacksmith's forge, cotton fibers hanging like a cocoon from a sycamore, towering pines surrounding a barren basin of clay, and snow flurries that became starlight reflected on a turbulent sea before morphing into a dewy, sun-drenched grassy plain.

Magic fractured and disintegrated in my grip, molten and frozen, fecund and sterile. I glommed it together again: more earth, less air. And again: more fire, less earth. Finally, I got the texture of each element right, cobbled together the correct ratio by sheer luck, and shoved the magic clumsily into the door's spell before any element drifted.

The lock snapped open. The spell unraveled. My spirit devolved with it.

I scooped the ether with frantic mental hands, straining to corral the intangible mass. A signal of pain spiked up my arm to my brain, and I fell through the doorway, crashing into Lucy's back when she stopped with a pleased gasp. Gralen prodded Oliver in behind us, then pushed past Lucy.

"Eureka," he whooped.

I closed my eyes, all my attention focused inward. My spirit slipped and slithered around me. Then, like a ghost taking possession of my body, it coalesced. I opened my eyes. I felt hollow, as if the smallest movement would tear my fragile connection with my spirit, and it would dissipate forever.

We stood in a storage room. Lucy's and Gralen's glowballs illuminated rows and rows of warded shelves cluttered with auction items, the aisles disappearing into the darkness. Lucy waved her hand in the air above the nearest shelves, not quite breaching the protective spells. Gralen darted down the adjacent row, shouting excitedly.

"Caladrius rings! We've got to have these. Silver leviathan dice? And another set in gold? One to keep, one to sell . . . Oh! A firebird feather fan. That'll bring a fortune."

Fingers trembling, I reached blindly for Oliver. He nudged his muzzle against the back of my hand, careful not to jostle the pipsissewa. For every item Gralen and Lucy wanted to steal, I would first have to bypass the ward guarding it. My spirit would be shifted and shifted and shifted into oblivion.

I fumbled for the tether between Oliver and me, searching for the reassuring connecting thread between the two portions of my spirit.

It was gone.

Wild-eyed, I met Oliver's scared gaze. The pain just before the onslaught of signatures . . . Had that been my spirit tearing? Was any part of my spirit still safe within him?

"Stop messing around, Gray. Look for Sannino's items."

Lucy grabbed my chin and jerked me to face her. Her gaze darted from my left eye to my right and back, then she locked my forearm in a vise, yanking me down an aisle. I floated before landing hard on my right foot. My left foot came forward faster, falling farther to reach the tiled floor. I teetered, then caught my balance.

"Stop lallygagging." Lucy's hand shifted to clamp my bicep, her fingers as sharp as talons. I high-stepped, feet landing clumsily. My eyes told me the floor was flat, but I felt as if I were walking a crooked staircase.

Cautiously, I gathered earth element, fearful of drawing Lucy's attention. I shouldn't have worried: My spirit was too fragile to draw more than a flicker of magic. By rote, I tuned it to quartz. The magic wobbled and collapsed on itself. I closed my eyes to help focus and found myself looking at the mental map of gargoyle beacons. Oliver's beacon glowed as faint as moonlight on mist and equally as insubstantial. I would have wept with fear for his life if he weren't beside me. I could confirm with my eyes that he wasn't at death's door. The fault was in my perception, a flaw brought about by my weakened spirit.

I followed the sickening logic. My spirit defined me. It gave my magic shape. It made me *me*. Without it, was I still Mika Stillwater? Was I still a gargoyle guardian?

Desperate to reinforce my ability, I stretched my senses farther. Wendell was well within my normal range. Yet even knowing where to look for him, I missed seeing him the first three times, and my ability was so warped he appeared in echo, two beacons sitting side by side.

Lucy gave my arm a vicious shake. "Open your eyes, Mika. Help me look."

"There's a box of anchors here," Gralen shouted. "Spells intact."

"Look for Sannino."

"I *am* looking, Luce, but we shouldn't waste this time."

"None of it matters as much as removing these bracelets."

"He sounds like he cares more about money than your freedom," I said.

Lucy turned to me with eyebrows raised.

"Maybe he's not eager for you to be a full spectrum," I continued, my voice soft enough not to carry beyond the two of us. "After all, that will make you stronger than him."

For a moment, I thought Lucy was considering my words. Then she smiled, all teeth and cruel mirth. "Are you trying to manipulate me?"

"Just observing. This whole time, Gralen's let you take all the risks. Did you notice how far back he stood from the door wards? He makes sure he's safe, but he's not doing the same for you."

"Too heavy-handed, dear." Lucy patted my cheek condescendingly. "Instilling doubt is a subtle art, and you're, well, you're like a gargoyle: too earnest and honest." Holding my gaze, she raised her voice and said, "Gray, put Mika to work. We're leaving here with everything we can carry."

"Lucy, I don't know how many more times I can use the pipsissewa. You don't want me to run out of energy before we get what you need, do you?" I was talking too fast, and I forced my mouth closed.

"No, *you* don't want to run out of energy before I get what I need, because that wouldn't bode well for Oliver. Why don't you keep that in mind?" Lucy gave my cheek another pat, this one hard enough to sting.

I squeaked when Gralen grabbed my arm in a meaty fist. He set off at a jog, and my teeth clacked together as I jounced along behind him. Oliver thumped after us, and Lucy disappeared in the opposite direction.

"One wrong move, gargoyle, and you're leaving here without a tail," Gralen growled when Oliver bumped a shelving unit in an awkward, hobbled turn.

"That would weaken his boost," I lied. "Each time I use the pipsissewa is harder. I need Oliver's full strength."

Gralen shot me a quick, narrow-eyed glare. "Not my problem. This one. Open it."

I caught my balance against Gralen. He flashed me a leer that made my skin crawl. Not wanting to give him the satisfaction of seeing my fear, I pivoted to face the shelf. A trio of bird statues sat at eye level—one ruby, one emerald, and one fire opal. Each was small enough to fit in my palm, but their combined worth exceeded my yearly rent. A single ward domed the figurines. The spell was simple, meant to be lifted with a touch.

I hesitated, tears blurring my vision. I wished I could run with Oliver and not stop until we were safe, preferably with Marcus's arms wrapped tight around us.

"Stop stalling." Gralen reached across my body and yanked my left hand up, pointing the pipsissewa at the statues.

A magical signature plowed through me, the heat and strength of a blacksmith's forge nestled in a tree-ringed basin of clay, like a bowl made for a giant. My spirit crumbled like shale. I cried out at the loss, and again in confusion when the new shape of me sank into my bones, warm and earthy.

"Unlock the gems," Gralen said, giving me another shake.

I blinked at him, assessing his magic. I knew his signature as intimately as if we had linked, and he was no match for me. His weak gypsum earth magic would be pulverized beneath my clay; his brittle water magic would melt and evaporate in the face of my forge's heat.

I gathered the elements, drawing them deep—

Fire speared my skull and seared my synapses. With a gasp, I released magic and clutched my temple. The pipsissewa punched my nose, startling me. Dazed, I stared at the spirit shifter. How had I forgotten I wasn't a full spectrum? The pipsissewa had altered my magical signature and my spirit so thoroughly, I felt as if I possessed the same magic as the person who made the spell protecting the statues. But I wasn't that strong. My attempt to draw a full spectrum's level of magic had nearly fried my brain. My fingers shook. I could have nullified myself with a mistake like that.

A sharp icicle of magic jabbed my side. "Get busy, woman."

Hesitantly, I lifted the pipsissewa to the statues. The forge-and-clay-bowl signature echoed through the mutant analyzer, seeming to come from me and the ward at the same time. With a twist of fire and a pinch of wood, the ward dropped.

Gralen released me and pawed the statues into his bag. Then he grabbed my arm and hauled me to the next item—something gold and silver—and forced my left hand and the pipsissewa up to the ward protecting it. My spirit atomized and blew away, replaced by a woodsy cocoon of cotton and sycamores buffeted by gentle snow flurries. Another familiar signature, but I couldn't place from where. The ward collapsed beneath my touch. Gralen dragged me to the next location.

Music played faintly inside my skull. I canted my head. The thready tune was familiar but fading. I grasped for it. The baetyl. It was within me, singing to me. If I could listen, it would guide me and help restore my spirit.

Gralen lifted the pipsissewa to a new target. A summer's late-night breeze blew across a creek lit by floating lanterns. The beautiful melody disintegrated.

I opened the ward in front of me and dropped my hand. A tear splashed across my wrist. When Oliver nudged me with his bound muzzle, I ran the back of my hand along his jaw, trying to make the awkward stroke soothing. He nudged me again, harder, his eyes telling me something I couldn't decipher.

Gralen yanked me to another shelf, this one empty except for a set of five kraken ink bottles. The bottles themselves were ornate enough to be works of art, but the ink was the real treasure. I didn't wait for Gralen to lift my arm. I didn't want him touching me more than necessary.

The pipsissewa read the spell domed over the bottles. My spirit shifted, snapping back to the shape of the hot blacksmith's forge. The transformation happened as fast as the pipsissewa fed the signature into me, but I pretended it took longer. This signature had an affinity for metal.

"I need to touch the gargoyle," I said, giving my voice a breathless, slurred quality that was alarmingly easy to fake. I wiggled my arm in Gralen's grip, emphasizing my words and my weakness.

"Why?"

"Power," I said, swaying dangerously close to the active wards.

Gralen cursed and wrenched me into the center of the aisle. I blundered into him and fumbled to regain my balance. Oliver whined, and I tried to reach for him.

"Touching him makes his boost stronger. I can't—I can't go on this fast unless I have more power."

Gralen's suspicious eyes bored into mine. I let my gaze go distant, as if I were attempting to maintain eye contact but too dizzy to focus on him. I was gambling on Gralen's ignorance of gargoyles and his greediness, but my reasoning wasn't a complete lie: I couldn't continue shifting spirits so fast. I was fragmenting, bits and pieces of me drifting away with each shift. I had to get Oliver out of here before I forgot who I was.

"Fine. So long as you work faster." Gralen released me with a negligent shove, sending me stumbling into Oliver.

My friend caught me with his muzzle, stabilizing me as I made a production of finding my footing. Meanwhile, I clamped my empty hand on the metal band cinching Oliver's mouth. I could feel the structure of the iron, the way the metal fibers aligned, the crude seam where Gralen had elementally welded the ends together. With this signature, I could work metal as easily as I could quartz—

A flare of panic shattered the thought. I couldn't remember how to tune earth into quartz. I couldn't even conjure up the sensation of quartz. The clay texture of this signature's earth magic didn't match up.

I met Oliver's eyes, swallowing hard at the alarm reflected in my friend's bound face. I couldn't remember how to heal him, and he badly needed healing.

One step at a time, I silently promised us both. First, I had to free Oliver. Until I achieved that, nothing else mattered.

"The ward," Gralen said, giving me a bruising jab to the breastbone with his metal rod.

Air caught in my throat and I coughed, gripping Oliver's neck to stay upright. Gralen struck Oliver's wing, cracking off a feather's tip. Fury burned molten in my chest. With a snap of magic, I disengaged the ward caging the kraken ink. Gralen swiped the glass bottles from the shelf, then pointed to the far end of the aisle.

"Get going, woman. You said you'd be faster touching the gargoyle. Prove it."

I planted a hand on Oliver's neck and shuffle-stepped with him toward Gralen's next target. Keeping my magic small, I trickled iron-tuned fire and earth elements into the metal muzzle. It stretched and thinned. Oliver's nostrils flared, and his sides expanded with his first full breath since we were captured.

Gratitude made me lightheaded. I wouldn't have been able to do anything to the metal with my spirit, but this one could help Oliver. I longed to work the same magic on the band around Oliver's wings, but I didn't dare while Gralen watched so closely.

The next spell shifted my spirit again, but the one after brought it back to the blacksmith's forge. It made sense to repeatedly encounter the same signature; the person who set these spells must work at the auction. With a bit more fumbling, I weakened twin lines through the iron muzzle on either side of Oliver's face. I stopped before I loosened it far enough to slide off, but I was certain Oliver's powerful carnelian jaw could snap the band when we were ready.

Before Gralen could become suspicious, I tapped a spell guarding a pair of elemental anchors, opening it.

Gralen started to shove past me, and I let my magic flare as if it were out of control. My ruse became reality when fire built too fast and brushed against the shelf. Cursing, Gralen sliced ice through the wayward element before the protective magic in the oak could react. My magic fractured. I was too slow and too weak to release the elements to avoid the backlash. Pain overloaded my brain.

When I blinked my vision clear, I was on the floor, my cheek pillowed against Oliver's hard ankle. My left arm was bent behind me at an excruciating angle, the pipsissewa cradled by Gralen in a vise of air. Groaning, I rolled to my back to take pressure off my shoulder.

"Gray. I found it. I found it!" Lucy shouted. "Bring her. Bring her *now!*"

My stomach flip-flopped. We were out of time.

24

Gralen tried to rush me across the storeroom. Weak and dizzy, I tripped and slid in his grip. At the end of Lucy's aisle, I buckled my knees, forcing Gralen to support my full weight. He cursed and staggered into the wall. Pain seared through my wrenched shoulder, but with his sack of loot tangling in his legs and one hand locked around the iron bar, Gralen couldn't lift me. We ground to a halt.

"Let me breathe," I panted. "I need to regain my magical strength. I need to touch . . ."

Oliver scooped his head beneath my empty hand, and I took an exaggerated breath. As if Oliver infused my muscles with strength, I climbed to my feet.

Gralen watched me with narrowed eyes. "You try anything stupid, you both get it." He slapped the iron bar against his palm. The threat would be tiresome if it weren't so effective.

I nodded and took a limping step. Oliver scooted forward beside me.

"Look, Gray, no one's touched it," Lucy called.

Gralen menaced the air between Oliver and me with the bar. When we both shied away, he laughed and jogged up the aisle to Lucy.

Staying hunched, I built iron-tuned fire-and-earth magic fast, shoving it artlessly into the metal binding Oliver's wings. A molten-orange line flared across the silvery metal. If Oliver's wings had been flesh and feathers, it would have burned him horribly, but I trusted his carnelian body to protect him from the intense heat. The metal thinned, stretched—

Gralen's and Lucy's attention snapped to me at the same time. I released the elements so fast it spiked a backlash of pain through my head. A metallic taste filled my mouth. I hoped it was blood and not the scent of flash-heated iron.

Oliver and I hobbled forward. I didn't dare turn my head to check if Oliver could free himself, terrified of drawing the thieves' attention to my handiwork. Oliver's gait remained as stiff and pained as before. His wings didn't drop a fraction of an inch. Maybe I hadn't done enough.

"This one," Lucy said, pointing to a ward covering an inch-high marbled-green soapstone figurine of a bluecap, the humanoid sprite hugged by artistic flames. "Open it, Mika."

I shuffled closer, discreetly signaling Oliver to hang back. I wanted to tell him to make a run for it the first chance he saw, but I didn't dare try to communicate my hopes with so much as a glance, not while Gralen tracked me with his raptorial eyes. For once, he stood beside Lucy, too far from Oliver to threaten him. I needed to use this to my advantage. I just couldn't see how.

"I thought you needed to touch the gargoyle for strength." Gralen's gaze shifted to Oliver, and his glowball expanded.

I squinted against the light and made a show of tripping over nothing to draw his attention back to me.

"I recognize this signature. It will be easier." It was the truth, and I didn't care if he heard my frustration. The ward Lucy wanted me to open had been created by a familiar dew-dappled grassy signature—a spiritual makeup with no affinity for metal.

I searched the nearby wards for a spell created by my blacksmith-forge signature, spotting one three shelves away. As soon as I unlocked the figurine, I would use the pipsis-sewa to shift my spirit back to this signature so I could finish breaking Oliver's bindings.

Caution prodded the periphery of my mind, distant and easily ignored. This was the longest Gralen had let me rest between shifts. My true spirit, if it were going to reinstate itself, should have done so before now. But it no longer seemed important. If this was the insanity Marcus warned of, I couldn't bring myself to care. With the blacksmith signature, I could work metal; without it, I couldn't. So long as I could reclaim this spirit, I could free Oliver. His escape was all that mattered.

I eased the pipsissewa toward the ward above the soap-stone bluecap. Lucy, impatient, grabbed my wrist and thrust my hand up to the spell.

The meadowy signature tunneled into my skull, the blades of grass razor sharp, the sun blistering hot. I clenched my free hand to my temples as agony spiraled down my neck into my chest.

"Breathe."

Lucy poked stiff fingers into my midsection. I gasped in air, blinking as black dots receded from my vision. Lucy swung me around by my limp arm, pushing her face inches from mine.

"Don't screw this up, Mika."

With the elements trembling in my grip, I unlocked the spell caging the figurine. I started to retreat, but Lucy's grip on my wrist brought me up short, her smile feral.

"Are you ready to see true power, Mika?" Not waiting for my response, she yanked the pipsissewa from my finger.

I hissed as the ring scraped skin from my knuckle. When Lucy released me, I stumbled two steps before catching my balance. She didn't seem to notice. I curled my fingers toward my palm, fighting the urge to snatch the pipsissewa from her. I couldn't let on that I needed the signature shifter. I couldn't let Lucy or Gralen suspect I had an escape plan for Oliver.

Licking my lips, I took another hesitant step toward Oliver.

"Stop." Gralen's icy magic collared my neck.

I froze.

Lucy let her glowball dissipate, cutting off half our light. She slid the pipsissewa's ring around her finger and lifted the spirit shifter to the bluecap figurine, holding it steady. The soapstone carving held an easily recharged warming spell. If the healer Sannino had possessed the bluecap figurine through a single winter, she would have renewed the spell multiple times, reinforcing her signature on the tiny object. The pipsissewa should have read Sannino's signature in a flash, but Lucy's brow furrowed as if she required concentration. Silence stretched. Lucy twitched and trembled. Pain pinched her lips. Still, she remained locked in place, signature shifter extended.

This was how long it took Lucy to shift her spirit? She made it seem like I was slow, but even matching my spirit to multiple signatures hadn't taken half this long. No wonder she and Gralen had been so eager to capture and use me.

The pipsissewa didn't have to work to untether my spirit; I had done all the work for it.

Oh, Marcus, I should have listened to you. How many times had I shifted my spirit into a gargoyle? I had seen it as a strength, an extension of my healing abilities, but I hadn't recognized the toll it had taken on me. Marcus had. He had seen the dangers, and he tried to protect me. Rather than listen, I pushed him away.

Belatedly, I reached intangible feelers into the ether, searching for my spirit. A shiver twined down my spine as I quested into a void.

"Luce, you all right?" Gralen asked.

Lucy made an indeterminate sound. Gralen shifted his feet. The contents of his bag clanked. Finally, Lucy lifted the pipsissewa clear of the figurine. Magic lashed out from her, cutting into the bracelets. Lucy convulsed. Teeth gritted, she altered the elemental composition, then attacked the bracelets again. Her body bowed. She toppled, and Gralen caught her against his chest.

The icy vise on my throat vanished. I backpedaled until Oliver's muzzle pressed against my hip.

Lucy hacked at the bracelets with more magic. The bands stretched. A long, agonizing scream tore from Lucy, escalating into a roar.

Oliver's lips closed on my shirt, and he tugged. I took a slow, silent step backward. This was our chance to escape, but Oliver couldn't run, not with the rope hog-tying his legs. He couldn't even turn around in the tight aisle. If he moved, his quartz paws scraping against the tile would give us away.

The bracelets clattered to the floor. Lucy's chin sagged to her chest, only Gralen's grip beneath her armpits holding her from a complete collapse.

I flexed my magic. Loose earth and soft water formed

easily. Fire was dimmer, as was air. Wood overwhelmed it all, supple and full of potential growth. With this spirit molding my magic, I could grow a better garden than Ms. Zuberrie, but my attempts to form sharp weapons crumbled.

Lucy's eyes opened, her pupils huge in the bright light. Straightening, she slid the pipsissewa from her finger and into a pocket. I watched it disappear with a mix of dismay and relief.

Magic unfurled from Lucy, forming a seething knot in the air between us. She parsed it into individual elements, holding all five clumps simultaneously. The globe of fire made Gralen's glowball look like a candle.

"I'm doing it, Gray," she breathed. Awe softened her features as she twisted the elements into a thick test pentagram. When the tips of the star threatened to touch the shelves on either side of the aisle, she pivoted it from horizontal to vertical and kept adding magic.

I shrank against Oliver. Without the bracelets capping Lucy's abilities, she was terrifyingly powerful. Marcus might be a match for her—if he were boosted by Oliver and all his siblings. Lucy wasn't just a full spectrum. She was something stronger.

"You're amazing," Gralen whispered. He wrapped an arm around Lucy's waist, drawing her against his body and pressing a sharp-lipped smile to her neck. "Nothing can stop us now."

"Link with me, sweetie." Ecstasy shone from Lucy's eyes as she pulsed the elements, flexing bands of magic as thick as my thighs with frightening ease. "I want you to feel how incredible this is."

Gralen's gaze flicked to Oliver and me, then to the massive pentagram. His grin said clearer than words that he expected Lucy's overblown power to keep us in check. He extended a paltry balance of elements to Lucy.

She swallowed his magic in a single bite.

Gralen stiffened, exhaling like he had been sucker-punched. "Luce, it's so much. Too much."

"It's everything I'm due."

Fire seethed along one arm of the pentagram, audibly crackling. Heat fanned down the aisle, and I staggered backward. Oliver retreated with me. Lucy's gaze snapped to us, and a whip of air burst from the pentagram. It struck my shoulders, and I crashed to my hands and knees. Oliver snaked his head over me in a futile attempt to protect me.

"Luce, pull back."

Lucy hummed and spun the monstrous pentagram.

I scanned the shadowed shelves, searching for some means of defense.

Glass bowls spelled with dancing gryphonettes.

Silk fabrics and ceremonial mantles.

Ceramic glowball lanterns.

Nets of leather and twine.

Oil paintings.

Where were the element-wrought swords and ceremonial daggers? I would give all my remaining magic for a simple sharp knife.

"This feels wrong." The horror in Gralen's tone drew my attention. His lips were contorted in a gruesome, pained snarl, and veins bulged in his flushed neck. "The elements aren't right. They're rancid, Luce. It's all wrong."

Lucy smiled dreamily. "Nothing will ever be wrong again, my love."

Lucy pried Gralen's fingers from her waist, not noticing when he dropped to one knee and his bag of stolen goods crashed to the tile.

"This is freedom, Gray. It's like standing in the sun after a lifetime of darkness. It's incredible."

Gralen moaned and clutched his head with both hands.

I dug my fingers into the rope knotted around Oliver's ankle. We had to get out of here while Lucy was preoccupied with her own power—before she thought to turn it on us for more than a disdainful swat. Rough hemp fibers cut into my flesh, but the rope didn't budge. The knots, already elementally hardened, had cemented in place with Oliver's steps. I would never be able to pull them apart.

I considered triggering a ward—*any* would activate the building's anti-theft and trespassing spells and bring guards running—but I froze with my hand inches from the nearest shelf. The moment I set off an alarm, I would have Lucy's full attention. No rescue would arrive fast enough to spare Oliver or me from her wrath.

"The things I can do with air, with water, with any element—full spectrums everywhere will bow to *me*. We'll be royalty." Lucy frowned when her ponderous pentagram wobbled. The branch of water flared and collapsed, and the clap of displaced air rattled the shelves and jostled their contents.

"Let me go, Luce. Release the link. I can't— I— *Lucy, please*."

Gralen writhed on the ground, one hand feebly plucking at Lucy's bootheel. Blood trickled from his nose. Lucy didn't take her eyes from her magic.

"I don't know what's happening, Gray. It's not supposed to do this." Her magic bowed and flexed again. Fire bubbled into turbulent flames that popped and snapped at the air, and Lucy released the element with a cry.

I had to get Oliver out of here. *Now*.

The lantern. Like most nearby items, it sat beneath a

ward created by the grassy signature—my current signature. Before I could second-guess myself, I unlocked the spell. Easing a hand around the lantern, I drew it to my body, then crafted a feeble glowball within it. The lantern's internal magic amplified my flimsy offering, transforming it into a ball of fire bigger than my fist. Hiding the light with my body, I thrust the flame beneath Oliver's rope hobble. The hemp caught fire, smoldering more than burning.

A gurgling sigh emanated from beyond Lucy. I didn't want to look, but I couldn't stop myself. Gralen spasmed on the floor, his eyes staring sightlessly at the ceiling. Blood ran freely from his nostrils, but his expression was oddly peaceful.

Too late, Lucy glanced down. With a cry of dismay, she dropped to her knees. Three new glowballs sprang to life, haloing Lucy and her broken lover.

"Gray?" Lucy sounded small and confused. "Gray, sweetie. Gralen!" She gave his shoulders a shake.

"It's gone, all gone," Gralen said, his words too wet. "So empty."

When Lucy shook him again, his eyes remained locked on something none of us could see, and he didn't respond. His chest rose and fell, but I wondered how much of the man still existed behind those vacant eyes.

"I don't understand." Lucy touched Gralen's face, blotting clumsily at the blood. "It was just a surge. I'll get better. That's what I told Sannino. What happened with my parents, that was an accident. It won't happen again. I won't let it, not with you. I'm powerful, but I need practice. Wake up, sweetie. We'll work together."

Horror immobilized me. Lucy didn't lack training. She lacked control. The flames that formed on her pentagram, her startled reaction—Lucy hadn't done it intentionally. It was as if her powers were mutating the elements in her grasp. Except that wasn't how magic worked. The elements were steady. It was our spirits that shaped them. But if a spirit was warped . . .

The bracelets. Lucy's explanation hadn't made sense. A healer wouldn't impede someone's abilities *unless they had reason*. The spelled bands hadn't been a malicious imprisonment. They had been a protective aid to prevent Lucy's malformed magical abilities from killing her.

Or from killing others.

Oliver flexed his legs, straining against the rope. With a series of pops, the frayed twine snapped. Oliver's freed paws jerked apart, his carnelian claws screeching on the tile. He wedged a claw between his jaw and the metal band muzzling him. The weakened iron snapped, ricocheted against the shelves, and clattered to his feet. He kicked it behind us with a snarl.

Lucy's head jerked up. The vulnerability in her expression hardened, her chin tilting imperiously. "Mika. You're a healer. Heal Gralen."

"I can't heal humans."

"Liar!"

I flinched away from the madness in her eyes. Gripping Oliver's ankle, I gave him a push. He obligingly eased back. I talked louder to draw Lucy's attention away from his slow retreat.

"I'm a gargoyle healer." I *was* a gargoyle healer. I didn't know what I was anymore. "My magic is different. That's why I'm so good at using the pipsissewa. I'm faster than you. You said you can't shift to multiple signatures, but I can. It's because my magic is shaped for gargoyles. Here." I rose slowly, extending a hand, willing her to place the pipsissewa in my palm. I didn't move my feet, though. Logically, I knew the distance separating us didn't make me safe, but I couldn't make myself step any closer to the madwoman. "Let me have the shifter. I'll open any ward you want. You'll be the richest woman in the world when you walk away from here."

Lucy folded her arms across her chest. "You're doing it again, Mika. So earnest. So *transparent*. So clumsy in your attempt to manipulate me." Her gaze dropped to Gralen's face. "But if you're not a real healer, you're useless to me."

When she looked up again, I read my death in her cold stare.

25

L ucy gathered magic, forming a wobbly wad of fire
and earth. The underlying spell twisted in her
grip. I didn't wait for her to get control of it.

"Run, Oliver!"

Unable to turn around in the tight space, Oliver shuffled
into a clumsy backward lope. His spine knocked into his
bound wings. His glossy feet slid on the tile. The harder he
tried to increase his speed, the slower he seemed to go. He
would never reach the end of the aisle in time.

I snatched up the glowball lantern and hurled it at Lucy.
Blistering pain seared my fingers. Lucy swatted aside the
flaming clay container with a band of air, shattering it and
extinguishing the flame inside. Her wobbly spell unraveled.
Cursing, Lucy glommed the elements together again.

I grabbed for magic. A dizzying rush of fertile earth and
dew-touched wood swelled inside me, the shape of the
magic both foreign and familiar, all of it too soft for the
defensive spells I knew. Given another day, another hour,
another ten minutes, I might have patched together a
protective shield, but I had seconds. Lucy's spell was

coalescing, all jagged lines of ice and air far more powerful than anything I could block.

Backpedaling, I searched the shelves for another weapon. It was beyond time to activate the auction house's central ward, but I still couldn't risk it. The protective spells on the shelves would ensnare me, leaving me helpless. If only one of the premade wards was large enough to hide behind . . .

I pounced on the idea. Still stumbling backward, I spotted a ward tuned to my stolen signature that spanned half a shelf of goods. Using pinches of air, I picked up the spell like a stiff sheet. It shouldn't have worked. I had never attempted anything like this before, and if I thought about it too hard, I would lose control.

Wielding the elements with blind instinct, I stretched the ward across the aisle, anchoring it to the floor, to the shelving's struts, and to the ceiling. The magic of the original spell thinned but held. The defensive measures built into the ward—viscous bands of air and wood that would have caged a raging minotaur in place—now looked hardly strong enough to hold a fly.

Lucy climbed to her feet and studied the spell, then me. Her eyes gleamed feverishly in the bright light of her glow-balls. Gralen's blood glistened on her cheek, smeared from her fingers when she brushed her hair from her face.

"You keep surprising me, Mika."

Oliver crashed into the back wall. "Mika!" he called, a warning and a cry to hurry all in one.

Hesitating, I fed more magic into the protective barrier spread between Lucy and me. It quaked. Lucy's lips curved in a wicked smile.

I spun on wooden feet and lurched after Oliver.

"Go! Find a door!"

Oliver sprang into motion. Magic built behind me. I hunched my shoulders to my ears and ran faster. Slamming a hand against the back wall, I shoved myself around the corner of the aisle. Heavy thumps pelted the wall behind me. A dozen icy spikes pierced the wallpaper at chest height. One step slower, and I would have been skewered.

Oliver loped into the darkness, not slowing. Behind me, Lucy closed the distance between us far too fast, the sound of her footsteps lost beneath the clatter of Oliver's quartz paws, but her progress easy to track by the light of her glow-balls. I would never be able to outrun Lucy, but I had to buy Oliver time.

I ducked down the next ink-black aisle. Oxygen burned like acid in my esophagus. Haphazardly, I flung wads of wood element over my shoulder, afraid Lucy wouldn't see me. I needed her attention on me.

A chunk of spiked ice whipped overhead, whistling through the air. I ducked. It hit the tile in front of me, chipping the limestone and exploding into a puff of ice crystals. I abandoned my weak elemental lobs and concentrated all my energy into running.

Lucy's next frozen projectile crashed into a shelf behind me. Cracking wood rent the air—a protective spell activated. I didn't look back, afraid nothing short of nullification would stop Lucy. Rounding the end of the aisle, I sprinted left, away from Oliver. Lucy's light faded, and I cut down the next cavern-dark aisle.

Between one step and the next, lava replaced my bones. Agony pierced my heart and expanded, driving spikes into my skull and lungs. I crumpled, clamping my hands to my head. Fire licked through my body as an unseen force ripped muscle from bone. Frantically, I cast about for some means of defense, yet no spells, malicious or otherwise, touched me.

"Mika!" The thunder of Oliver's footsteps drew closer. "To me!"

The glow on the wall was getting brighter again. Lucy was advancing. Whatever ward she had triggered, it hadn't been enough to stop her formidable magic. Any second, she would round the corner and find me vulnerable.

Vision swimming, I shoved into a shambling run. Pain cleaved my skull when I reached for magic, and I gave up. I was no match for Lucy's freakish strength. After a handful of staggering steps, the consuming agony shrank to a throbbing pain. My legs wobbled, or the ground did. I wanted so badly to collapse, but I had to keep moving. For Oliver.

The aisle abruptly brightened, flinging my shadow out in front of me. I didn't need to look to know Lucy stalked behind me. I willed more speed from my legs. My skin crawled in anticipation of the next deadly attack.

"You can't escape, Mika. I have all my power now. I'm unstoppable."

A familiar whistle shrieked through the air. I dove for the tiles. An ice axe larger than my torso blasted overhead and exploded against the far wall, carving a hole in the plaster.

Lucy launched another spinning ice blade, this one twice as big and utterly unavoidable. I scrambled on all fours, skidding around the end of the aisle. Cold air whipped across the back of my neck, then the blade shattered against the wall. Razor-sharp ice shards pelted my bare arms. I shook off the sting and clambered to my feet.

Oliver skidded to a halt three aisles away. My plan to martyr myself crumbled when I caught his expression.

"Stay close, no matter what," he said.

Rearing on his hind legs, he performed a twisting turn, landing in the opposite direction. The maneuver knocked his bound wings into the wall, sifting a fine rain of carnelian from shattered feathers as he burst into a lope. I raced after him.

We reached the end of the room. Oliver took the turn at full speed. I registered the bend of his torso, the flick of his tail disappearing into a black corridor, but I slammed into the wall before my body caught up with my brain. The impact rattled my skull. Bouncing back half a step, I swayed in place.

"Mika!"

I lumbered toward Oliver's voice, my brain screaming for me to run but my legs failing to comply. A wild bolt of Lucy's malformed magic streaked around the corner, ice-tuned water element biting the backs of my arms and thighs before disintegrating.

Oliver shoved open a door. Weak light spilled through the opening, illuminating the crackle of fractures across his muzzle. He peered over my shoulder, his face compressed with anxiety. Lucy's sprinting footsteps pounded behind me, far too close.

"Go," I rasped, urging Oliver to safety.

He waited until I reached his tail before springing through the doorway. Straining for magic, I leapt after him. Pain exploded my earth magic into shale shrapnel. Half blind, I flung the fragments into the storage room, not bothering to aim. Elemental shards pelted every spell in sight.

Wards pinged to life, delicate domes of wood and earth, mists of water and air, all of them useless.

"Fire," Oliver urged.

I couldn't distinguish the element from the pain, so I flung it all into the storage room. A cloud of firefly-sized flames hit the protective wards. With a sound like hammers on steel, inch-thick vines burst from the shelves. They struck my magic, pulverizing it. Scorched vines snapped free, and the spell flared brighter. In a cascade of unleashed magic, hundreds of wooden vines burst from the shelves, the cacophony of their eruptions echoing out of sight down the aisle. Like an angry arboreal beast, the elemental branches seethed in the air, questing for an intruder.

Lucy yelped, and something heavy banged against the wall. A cluster of vines speared through the open doorway, angling for me. I fell backward, landing hard on my butt. Oliver surged over me and slammed the door shut. He jerked aside when intricate ribbons of air and earth knitted the door frame, sealing the opening better than any physical lock.

My arms gave out. I collapsed and stared unseeing at the sky, relishing each lungful of fresh air that cooled my burning lungs. We made it out. We were safe, and Lucy was locked inside, where she couldn't harm us.

Oliver took two truncated steps away from me. With a snarl of pain, he flexed his bound wings. Metal grated against quartz. Bright red carnelian feathers crumbled beneath the strain. Then the iron band confining Oliver's wings snapped along the side I had weakened. With a bruising *thud*, his right wing sagged to the flagstone. His left remained pinched in the metal band.

I rolled toward him, but Oliver didn't wait for help. He hooked his teeth into the metal. Jagged iron screeched across his feathers, cutting deep, when he wrenched it from his body. Oliver's left wing sagged to the ground. Whipping his head, he flung the metal band. It landed with a clatter beyond my line of sight, but I didn't look for it. I couldn't tear my eyes from the carnelian shards splayed across the flagstones.

"Oh, Oliver." I reached useless fingers toward him.

Oliver tried to stretch his wings, whimpered, and let them sag again. Ugly fractures ran through his overtaxed wing muscles, and too many feathers were broken or missing for him to be able to fly.

Grief sat leaden in my chest. I couldn't remember how to shape the elements to match Oliver's unique quartz composition. I couldn't heal my friend.

The flagstone vibrated beneath me like the deck of a dirigible in flight. Bands of water, wood, and fire spiraled from the auction house's door toward the roof. Pulses of air followed, swelling and ebbing in expanding waves up the side of the building. Finally, far too late, we had activated Onacona's central ward. Unless we wanted to be snared in it, we needed to move.

Would it be so terrible to let the magic capture me? A respected establishment like this wouldn't have anything harmful built into their wards. Most likely, it would simply confine me until the guards arrived. What was the point of moving, anyway, since I couldn't do anything useful?

Oliver jumped and shuddered when the building's magic rolled over his long tail. His whine pierced my self-pity. He wouldn't leave me behind. Unless I wanted him to suffer further, I had to get up.

I rolled to my hands and knees, hissing when sharp carnelian shards scraped my burned fingers. The world continued to turn around my head, and I tipped toward my left shoulder.

Oliver shoved his forehead against me, stabilizing me. Lifting an arm, I grabbed hold of his neck behind his mane. Standing took two tries, and I remained upright only because Oliver propped me up. Together, we stumbled away from the building and through a shallow courtyard. Putting one foot in front of the other took all my concentration, but I would have had to be comatose not to flinch every time Oliver's drooping wings scraped against the flagstones. When we finally reached a dirt path, we sighed in unison.

Lawn stretched in front of us to a high hedge. Black iron posts peeked through the greenery, defining the property's fence. Spears of entwined water-and-earth element arched from the building toward the fence posts. The perimeter ward burst to life. Fire element in the form of blinding light pulsed down the fence, then shot skyward. If the building's alarm hadn't notified the city guards, the flares would bring them running.

Swaying, I fought to make sense of the view. The gardens were missing. All the flowerbeds we trampled on our way in were gone. The shrub hiding Wendell was nowhere in sight. Neither were the gates that would let us escape into the city. I craned my head to look behind us. The building sprawled in both directions, blocking the view, but my brain finally put together the logical pieces.

"We came out the back," I said, the words slurring across my tongue. I swung left, feet dragging. Wendell was out front, needing help. We had to keep going until we reached him.

I tripped to a halt when Oliver stopped.

"Mika."

The urgency in his voice pierced the exhaustion wrapping my brain like wool. I teetered when I tipped my head to look at him, inordinately proud when I caught myself before falling to a knee. Something in his expression told me it wasn't the first time he had said my name.

"We need to keep going," I said.

"Mika, you have to take your spirit back."

I blinked, struggling to process his words. "You still have it?"

"I have it. But it's weakening. So are you. Mika . . ." His eyes pleaded with me, filled with an emotion I didn't have the energy to interpret. "Mika, I think you're dying."

What? Oliver wasn't making sense. I wasn't dying. I was just tired. So very tired.

"Wendell needs . . ." He needed a guardian, not whatever I was. I shoved the thought down. "If I don't keep moving, I'll collapse."

"Mika, you won't make it to Wendell. Neither of us will."

I stared into Oliver's eyes, wanting to weep. "Does it hurt?" I whispered, knowing he would understand I wasn't talking about his physical injuries.

At his infinitesimal nod, I sank to my knees on the lawn. Moisture soaked my pants, chilling my shins, and I shivered.

Oliver's wings carved arcs in the soil as he circled to face me. Deep cuts bisected his muzzle. I yearned to heal his wounds, but I no longer remembered how. I couldn't even caress his mane; my arm muscles refused to lift.

"What do I do?" I asked, feeling small and lost.

"I'm going to push your spirit into you. You have to catch it."

If I failed, what would happen? I didn't voice the question, though. Now that I wasn't moving, I could feel the brittle flutter of my heart against my rib cage. Oliver was right. This wasn't the lethargy of exhaustion.

"I'm scared, Oliver."

"Me, too." His earnest expression broke my heart.

Lifting a paw, he placed it over my heart. Long carnelian claws curled over my shoulders, and I shivered as the dew clinging to his foot soaked through my shirt. Oliver's quartz flesh radiated the same cold as the lawn, but I leaned into his touch anyway. With the last of my energy, I cupped a trembling hand around his paw and closed my eyes.

"Ready?" Oliver curved his neck, resting his stone forehead against mine. His exhale fanned my breastbone.

"Ready," I croaked.

The cessation of Oliver's breath was my only indication that he was doing anything. Nothing else changed between us. Nothing stirred within me.

Nothing but fear.

"I can't feel it."

"Reach for it," Oliver said, his voice strained.

Reach for what? I wanted to wail. I pawed at the empty ether with mental fingers.

"Here," Oliver said, flexing his claws, pushing his paw harder against my chest.

I sank my awareness into the pressure, feeling the definition of each toe and the solid pad connecting them. Only the thickness of my shirt separated us physically, but my grasping mental fingers stretched much farther.

Something thin and squirming brushed against me. Startled, I recoiled. The fragile tendril mirrored me, flinching away. Oliver groaned. I quested forward again. The substance met me halfway. In a flash, it coiled around me.

I gasped and jerked back, but I had nowhere to go. Heavy veins of earth weighed me down, cinching fire and wood in tighter bands around me. Splotches of water and air glommed onto me. I shook myself.

This couldn't be my spirit. I was . . . I was . . . I cast through my memory, recalling soft soil and a blacksmith's forge, an icy storm and dewy grass. This spirit was too heavy and stiff and unforgiving and utterly foreign. I gave another forceful shake. Something was wrong. This wasn't me.

"Take your spirit," Oliver said, his voice a pained growl. "Please."

His *please* broke through my frantic resistance. I stilled. I trusted Oliver. He wouldn't lead me astray.

Tentatively, I closed my grip around the misshapen spirit and pulled. Oliver made an encouraging sound. The spirit stretched taut as a bowstring.

"Careful," Oliver said.

A barrier gave way. The bowstring morphed into an arrow, and my spirit shot into my chest. My eyes flew open, my lungs compressing in an airless gasp.

I stood inside the cocoon of a giant geode, sparkling clear-quartz columns jutting from the curved cave walls around me. The tips of dozens of hexagonal crystals brushed against me, sharp but not hurting. Steam swirled, thick and warm, rising from a hot spring at my feet. I could smell the minerals in the water and hear the whisper of wind rustling through vines of white clematis.

The cave blurred and disappeared. I sucked in a cool breath that tasted wrong, like damp soil and crushed grass.

Had that been my magical signature? Was that what my spirit looked like? Like—like a miniature baetyl?

Oliver's head snaked into view, his carnelian eyes blazing. The star-speckled navy sky framed his face. I was on my back, his paw pinning me to the wet lawn.

"Hold it," he ordered. His claws flexed, tenting his paw above my breastbone, as if he were trying to cage something. Fear added gravel to his chiming voice. "Grab your spirit, Mika. Anchor it inside you."

The elements of the geode—the sturdy quartz and resilient vines and steamy warmth—were fading, dispersing into the ether around me. Frantically, I cobbled them into the shape of my spirit and hugged it to my body. It was like trying to press air through my skin.

"Open your inner self and pull it in," Oliver said, his voice distant, hypnotic. "You are the guardian and the gargoyle. Seek out your deepest, truest self. Show your spirit the way."

I thought about how I quested into Daphne and Carmen, Nimoy and Lowell. Soothing their shifted spirits from the outside in had been simple. There had been only one direction to go, one path toward their inner selves. But I was already *in* myself, and the same diving, delving action wouldn't work. My spirit was *out*, and I had to let it in. I had to relax, but I was afraid that if I released my tentative grip, I would lose my spirit completely.

"Find your core. Find the spark that makes you *you*."

Oliver's words conjured an image of a small woman huddled in the center of my chest. She glowed with the same golden light of the inner gargoyles, only so faint it was almost hard to see her. I clung to this image even as I despaired at the truth of it. I had done this to myself, weakened myself. I had whittled away at my core until I was a frail, fragile shell.

With ephemeral hands crafted of compassion and atonement, I cradled the small golden woman. She stretched, turned, looked at me—

My perspective flipped in a blink. I floated, weightless, bodiless in a void of pure peace.

"Call your spirit to you." Oliver's voice rumbled through every particle of my being.

I looked for him and found my spirit instead. It shimmered in a nebulous cloud, hovering close. My flickering fingers brushed the edge of it. Then, trembling, I spread my arms wide, welcoming my spirit home.

It struck sharp as a needle, vast as the sky itself.

Pain engulfed me. It burned through my golden body, lighting me up from the inside, until I glowed like a sun. My spirit exploded outward, filling my body.

Gasping, I burst to the surface of my awareness. Energy surged through my limbs, tingling in my fingers and toes. Cool air rasped down my throat. I opened my eyes . . .

And the baetyl looked out.

26

The song of life thrummed through me. It echoed in the world around me: a soft chorus murmuring among the growing grass blades; a piping lilt of air currents swirling and weaving across the open gardens and through the distant hedges; a glissando of temperature fluctuations between sand and grass, sky and brick. The pattern of existence was everywhere, visible, audible, tastable, and touchable.

I shrank away from the sensory onslaught, and the baetyl expanded into the gap I left in my retreat.

"Mika?" Oliver stepped back, wings dragging.

The baetyl sat my body up, carrying me with it, a passenger in my own skin. We examined our hands, prodded our stomach, tested our soreness in our shoulders and arms. With each probed body part, I slipped deeper into the recesses of my own consciousness. The baetyl's power was too strong, its presence too vast. Simply by being, it overwhelmed.

The baetyl looked up, assessing our surroundings. It used my eyes, but it perceived so much more than I ever had. The ward around the auction house no longer seemed complex. A bit of wood and fire applied to the interlocking knots at the eaves, and it would fall apart. The perimeter ward was no better, with obvious elemental flaws to be exploited. All it would take was a pinch of misty water along the seam, and the whole spell would evaporate.

These weren't my thoughts, but they felt like they came from me. I could see the truth of the baetyl's assessments, but what it considered a *bit* and a *pinch* of elements would require five linked full spectrums to achieve.

Or a flicker of a baetyl's full strength.

This was what the gargoyles deserved, what a guardian should be. Powerful. Knowledgeable. Competent.

So unlike me. I was weak. I made mistakes. I messed up and got gargoyles hurt.

I forgot how to heal them.

My inner map blinked into focus, overlaying the auction house grounds. A dizzying array of lights twinkled against the limestone building and flickered among the hedges when the baetyl turned my head. This wasn't how my inner map worked. It existed in my mind. It didn't project onto the physical world.

Disoriented, we closed our eyes. A constellation of golden lights glittered across the back of my eyelids, dozens where before I had sensed only Oliver and Wendell. Awed, I focused on the farthest gargoyle. He had to be at the edge of the city or beyond, out in the country. More wondrously, I could distinguish the gargoyle within the beacon. He was a canine-avian blend, with jasper and smoky quartz markings. Twin scratches ran down his tail. The third nail on his back-right paw was chipped.

Eagerly, I switched my attention to a closer gargoyle, an agate-and-amethyst feline cervid with stripes of bright citrine along her tiger body and abraded paws in need of soothing. The next gargoyle had a strained wing. Another, a chip out of her tall rabbit ears.

The baetyl shifted our attention to a cluster of lights almost on top of us. Too fast, it assessed three gargoyle beacons, leaving me with an impression of wings and paws and bodies held statue stiff in surprise before the baetyl focused on the next closest gargoyle, a small pelican dragon with an injured snout.

Wendell, I told the baetyl.

This gargoyle was sick. He vibrated with disharmony, out of tune with the song of existence. A small fix. An easy one.

The baetyl's attention landed on Oliver. This gargoyle had a multitude of injuries—a scraped and cut muzzle, sprained wings, missing feathers, broken claws, spinal stress fractures, chipped spine ridges, a scuffed stomach, a cracked mane. The baetyl cataloged his injuries impassively, shunting aside my horror.

We would heal him—we would heal all of them.

I relinquished more control to the baetyl, making myself even smaller. It seized a thimbleful of magic. I sensed the elements remotely, as if through a link, though no magical signature radiated from the baetyl. It didn't possess a spirit through which to grasp magic. Instead, it used mine.

The baetyl refined earth element to quartz. Memory sparked, and I wanted to weep. I remembered how to layer the elements to create an exact match to Oliver. I didn't need the baetyl's help. I could heal him myself.

The baetyl didn't give me a chance. With my magic, it reached into Oliver and—

Liquid fire immolated my brain.

I spasmed, collapsing to my side. Raw elements blasted

from my grasp, tearing funnels into the soil on either side of Oliver. Tears leaked from my eyes as the agony waned to a pounding headache.

Oliver whined. I tried to reach for him, but I couldn't so much as twitch a finger. I expected him to rush forward to help me. But Oliver didn't move, leaving a five-foot rift between us.

The baetyl's awareness turned inward. My body was feeble, my magic fragile. This vessel wasn't strong enough for what was necessary—but it could be.

Fear drove me forward, an airless denial echoing inside my head. The baetyl possessed the knowledge of life itself. It wouldn't be difficult for it to reshape my body in whatever form it desired, and it wouldn't care if I were eradicated in the process.

Wendell first, I reasoned. *We can heal him. He'll be easier than Oliver.*

The baetyl took the bait, shifting its attention to the beacon I indicated. The pelican dragon. The simple solution.

It started to reach for magic, as if it could heal Wendell from here, despite the hundreds of feet and stone building between us. Maybe it could. But *I* couldn't.

Closer.

I pushed myself back to a sitting position, or I pictured it. The baetyl was the one who leveraged my arms and lifted my body to my feet. We swayed in place, then took a deliberate step. My boot landed hard, jarring my vision. The next step was smoother.

"Mika?"

The gargoyle paced us, his flawed wings dragging on either side of his body. His hind leg hitched, disrupting his stride. These imperfections needed to be corrected.

Wendell first, I insisted even as I ached for my friend. Guilt distanced me farther from my lurching body. Oliver wouldn't be suffering if not for my actions.

"Mika, try to hold on until help arrives."

No one could help us. No one's help was necessary. Waiting was pointless. The pelican dragon needed us.

We locked our attention on the distant gargoyle and shuffled our clumsy body around the building and across uneven soil, trampling flimsy plants in our path, kicking through vines that tangled our cumbersome feet. An assault of organic scents billowed around us, bitter and resinous and musky. Repulsive.

The baetyl's awareness delved beneath the topsoil. Silvery lines burst across my inner vision, as bright as gargoyle beacons, spearing outward in every direction and *down* so deep beneath me that vertigo prickled when I focused on their farthest tips. Between thin lines and thick, soft starry silver flecks and coarse glowing knots dotted the emptiness.

Quartz. This was a quartz map. Every vein, every pegmatite, every speck caught in granite and feldspar beneath Terra Haven glistened in my awareness, ripe for manipulation. Not ten feet below, a thick rope of quartz snaked across our path.

Magic gathered on the periphery of my awareness. Earth element—so much earth element—coalesced at my fingertips, all of it tuned to a crystalline quartz so refined it made my cowering spirit tremble with joyous envy. The baetyl reached magic toward the quartz. Plants contaminated the soil with their foul matter. They decayed and died. We would cleanse our path with quartz and beautify this land.

Magic built faster, pushing against the tiny space where I clung, threatening to rip me to pieces.

No! The gargoyle is more important.

The baetyl's awareness swung to me, pressing heavier than the magic it held at bay.

If we reshape the earth, we won't have any energy left to heal the gargoyle. Shoving the thought toward the baetyl was like ramming air through granite. *Gargoyle first.*

GARGOYLE FIRST, the baetyl agreed.

Earth element dispersed. The quartz map disappeared. I panted, breathless, lungless, clinging to the last thought like a lifeline.

Gargoyle first. Gargoyle first. Gargoyle first.

The jolt of our knees slamming into soil rang through me. The pelican-dragon gargoyle sprawled in front of us. Snapped branches and waxy green leaves fanned around his akimbo wings, and furrows pocketed the soil behind him. A hole existed in the hedge, the ragged edges a testament to his struggle to escape. A grotesque bar of metal pinched the gargoyle's mouth closed. Sickness radiated from him, a discordant tremble that grated on our senses.

Wendell. His name is Wendell.

The thought splashed against an impassive consciousness. Names were insignificant.

Familiar quartz-tuned earth element sprang to my fingertips, threaded through with fire and air and whispers of wood and water. The magic poured from me into Wendell, and a crystalline gong reverberated in my head, a single pure note of all-consuming pain.

———

COPPER TAINTED MY TONGUE. MY EYELIDS FLUTTERED OPEN. I stared up at the sky. Only the brightest of stars remained visible in the steel-blue expanse. This long night clung as tight as I did, refusing to let go.

The thought didn't feel right. Neither did my body. My arms—our arms?—twitched but didn't cooperate when I tried to sit up.

A physical heaviness settled on my thigh. I rolled my eyes down my body. A narrow milky-quartz dragon's chin rested atop my leg. The band that had clamped Wendell's mouth shut was missing. His muzzle bore no sign of fractures. His eyes were clear when they met mine, but exhaustion radiated from his glimmering white-and-pink irises. The baetyl had healed him before I lost consciousness.

Or after.

A tear trickled down my temple. The baetyl had used my body to do what I hadn't been capable of.

It hadn't stopped with Wendell, either. It continued to work the elements inside me, *on* me. With preternatural delicacy, it manipulated threads of elements so thin that a hundred combined wouldn't equal the thickness of a cobweb. I couldn't discern the baetyl's pattern, but I could feel their results. I was getting stronger. Already, the pain throbbing inside my head abated.

I should have been grateful, not terrified, but the baetyl wasn't acting out of kindness or generosity. Right now, I was too weak to carry on. I couldn't sit up, let alone heal another gargoyle. The baetyl saw me as a means to an end. It possessed the patience of a mountain reshaped over an eon and the single-minded determination of a being who had one sole reason for existence. The baetyl repaired my mental pathways because doing so served its purpose, not because it cared for me. It was shaping me into a superior gargoyle-healing design. More surely than the pipsissewa had altered my spirit, the baetyl was deftly remaking me—and I was helpless to prevent it.

A whisper of relief and guilt ghosted through me, chased by a sadness so deep it hurt to even brush up against it.

I had pushed myself to the brink of exhaustion, and then further still, in an attempt to be someone worthy of being called a gargoyle guardian. Repeatedly, I had battered myself against the limitations of my mind, my body, my *spirit*, and I had come up short.

But I didn't have to any longer. Maybe I wasn't good enough to be a gargoyle guardian . . . but the baetyl could change me. It could make me better. Less like me, more like it.

So maybe . . . maybe I should stop fighting and let it.

27

An explosion concussed the air. A trio of gargoyle beacons launched from the auction house. I surged to my feet, and I couldn't say if it was me or the baetyl who operated my limbs.

The massive front doors of the auction house lay in splinters across the wide driveway. A foot-deep trench cut from the front steps to the garden's edge, hazed by a cloud of wood fibers. Lucy stalked through it in a bubble of fiery air, incinerating splinters in bright pops of light. Her eyes locked on me. A cruel smile curved her lips.

"Mika Stillwater. That was a mean trick you pulled back there. Did you think this place's paltry wards could hold me?" Over an acre of ornamental vegetation separated us, but she didn't yell. In the still morning air, she didn't have to.

The gargoyle on the right dove. I couldn't make out more than a blur of black against the shadowy bulk of the auction house, but the baetyl's extraordinary senses filled in the rest. She was an onyx fox, about fifteen inches tall, with a hawk's head and wings. Arching bands of blue lace agate glistened across her shoulders and sides. She speared through the air, angling for Lucy's head.

A lightning-fast club of wood element whipped from Lucy, bashing the gargoyle in the side. The fox tumbled through the air, twisting frantically to right herself. Her front feet struck the ground. The impact sounded like twin shovels slamming into dry clay. Chills ran down my arms. Through the baetyl, I witnessed hairline fractures crackle through the gargoyle's paws. A millisecond later, a sprain tore along her left wing when the tip clipped the hard driveway.

Fury roared through me, a molten furnace caged beneath the cold weight of the baetyl as it dispassionately assessed the gargoyle's injuries—and the source of them.

Lucy flung a hand, and a fireball burst from her fingertips. It splashed across the downed gargoyle, breaking along her spread wings. For a breathless moment, the gargoyle was engulfed. Then she launched skyward, shedding flames. The red heat hadn't hurt her, but beating her wings did.

"I'm not letting you escape, Mika. Spare your gargoyles. They can't protect you." Lucy advanced, forming another fire spell. Her magic flared wild and hot, unraveling at the seams. With a frustrated cry, she pitched the rebellious elements skyward. A dozen melon-sized fireballs arced on chaotic trajectories, unraveling midair. Before they finished dissipating, Lucy seized water element. It built around her, the magic swelling to levels that should have been impossible without gargoyle enhancements.

The element pulsed, flexing and twisting in Lucy's grip, dangerously close to whipping out of control. She wrestled it into five bands and braided them into a malevolent spell peppered with razor-sharp ice shards rotating around a central blade.

A compact opossum gargoyle with thick wings and a horned lizard's face dove in front of Lucy. The madwoman startled, and her spell tore apart. Too fast, she reshaped a fist of water element into ice. Snarling, Lucy punched it into the gargoyle. The stone opossum crashed to the ground, a bruise blossoming two inches deep in her orange agate stomach.

I screamed for Lucy to stop. And then I simply screamed as pain cleaved my skull in two.

Magic ripped through me, dense earth, suffocating air, and petrified wood shredding my mental pathways as the spell formed. The baetyl's intention burned the prescient image into my mind of Lucy caught in the magic's crushing power, her breath suctioned from her body, her bones and flesh replaced with hardened silica. Once Lucy was alchemized into a statue, she would be incapable of harming another gargoyle.

The baetyl's logic chilled me. It saw nothing wrong with committing murder.

I surged for control. Agony sliced black daggers through my vision. Magic so vast, each element inhumanly refined, crumbled in my grip. I shoved it all from me, forcing it *up* instead of *out*. The mutated spell smashed into the dome of the Onacona's perimeter ward and split open. Silica tentacles lashed out from the baetyl's spell, sinking crystalline tips into the ward. Wood burst from the ward to counter the attack—a tactical error of a spell never designed to combat magic crafted by a sentient immortal force. What should have been destructive counter-magic became constructive fuel. The baetyl's spell devoured the dome, morphing it into the hardened mineral composite of petrified wood. In a thunderous rush, the petrification swept from the dome's apex to the ground, sealing us inside in utter blackness.

The gargoyles dive-bombing Lucy spun in disparate directions, their beacons bright in the void. In rapid succession, they landed, two with soft thumps in the pitch-black garden and the third—the fox—crashing into something that snapped and rattled. Scratches chafed her chest and wings, then she was free.

Silence fell, as oppressive as the darkness.

I curled my fingers into gritty soil. Closing my eyes, I quested for earth element. It brushed against my mind, smooth as polished quartz. Searing pain accompanied the magic, and I let it go. I wasn't nullified, but I should have been.

"Mika?"

Oliver's whisper came from a great distance. I opened my eyes. The world remained inky, the air motionless. Cave-like. The baetyl approved of the enclosure—we were meant to be within the earth—but not the darkness. Gargoyles needed light to navigate by.

Pain pinged through my temples, and a peach-size globe of light materialized above my head. Wendell lay at my feet, his strawberry-quartz body a dreamy pink in the warm light. His eyes were wide open, but he hadn't risen from his slumped position. Oliver crouched out of reach on my right, worried eyes glowing as they examined me.

I tried to form his name, but the baetyl crashed over me, a tidal wave of dominance that stole my speech. With a flick of air, it levitated the glowball to the apex of the petrified dome. A pentagram of elements sliced through it, then inverted. My brain vibrated like a struck gong. The glowball imploded, metamorphosing into a new, unfamiliar spell. Firelight as soft as sunrise struck the petrified wood. It expanded until the entire silica dome radiated light as if we stood inside a giant balmy glowball—or inside a baetyl.

Lucy gaped at the dome. I crouched, one hand braced on the ground, chest heaving, my throat a column of hot coals. The baetyl gathered itself to crush Lucy, its only hesitation my fragility. If it struck Lucy now, it would kill us both.

The baetyl receded to the back of my awareness, resuming its gossamer modifications on my brain. Healing me. Changing me.

Giving herself a shake, Lucy broke from her trance. She hoisted the strap of the black sack hanging from her shoulder and stomped through a bed of dahlias. Soft metallic clinks and chimes sounded from within her bag of stolen goods.

I forced myself to my feet, placing myself between Lucy and Wendell. The baetyl gathered itself to strike. Oblivious, Lucy closed the distance between us to ninety feet. Forty.

"Stop," I begged, my voice a scratchy whisper.

Lucy tried out her guileless junior-insurance-agent smile. It didn't work, not with her eyes glowing with madness and greed. "I'll stop if you link with me, Mika. Together, we can do incredible things."

The baetyl lined water and wood element down my throat in a spell that tasted of greenthread and chamomile when I swallowed. The heat in my esophagus abated. My next words projected almost painlessly.

"Give up, Lucy. Please. Stop where you are and give up."

"You were holding out on us, Mika. On Gralen. If you can make this"—she gestured to the petrified dome—"then you can heal him."

"I can't."

"Liar!" Lucy shrieked.

I shook my head. Like most people, Lucy confused

strength with ability. It didn't matter how much power I wielded, none of it would help Gralen, because I didn't know how to configure it correctly. If anything, my ignorant magic would do more harm than good.

The baetyl, though . . . The baetyl could heal Gralen. It understood the building blocks of life. Mending the man's nullification and his physical injuries wasn't beyond the baetyl's capabilities. It wouldn't even tax it.

But the baetyl wouldn't help Gralen. If I got anywhere close to Lucy's partner right now, the baetyl would kill him for what he had done to Oliver. I didn't think I would be able to stop it—or that I would want to.

"You're no better than a full spectrum," Lucy hissed. "Hoarding your power. Selfish and miserly. So full of your own superiority."

Magic burst from Lucy. It wasn't a spell, but it wasn't raw, either. Rage powered it, shaping it into a mass of molten spikes and frostbitten blades. The baetyl surged for control. We should smash the human. Pulverize her bones into the soil. Eliminate the threat to ourselves and the gargoyles.

I was ready this time. I shoved a new idea in front of the baetyl, one closer to our natural tendencies. It hesitated a fraction of a second that lasted a lifetime. Then, the baetyl plunged earth element into the soil, dragging a ring of quartz to the surface as easily as I might reshape a seed crystal. Pain pounded through my skull in a distant accompaniment to the earth quaking beneath my feet, but all I felt was shock.

I had done this before. I had pulled quartz from the earth. Loads of it. *Tons* of it. I had done it on instinct out of desperation to save myself and Marcus. It had nearly killed me, and I assumed the trauma had been the reason I couldn't remember much of the magic. Now I saw the real reason: I hadn't just altered earth on instinct; I had borrowed the baetyl's power on instinct, too.

Quartz speared to the surface, displacing soil and plants, until it circled Oliver, Wendell, and me in a foot-high wall of white rock. Lucy's malignant magic bore down on us, more than six feet high and equally as wide. The minuscule barrier wouldn't protect us.

I tried to yank the quartz higher, but the baetyl had other ideas and all the control. Fire and water whipped into the stone wall. I barely had time to flinch from the heat— had the baetyl tuned fire element to *lava*?—before a ponderous clear crystal speared from the quartz. It shot eight feet into the sky and swelled three feet wide.

The heart of an avalanche would have been quieter.

Deafened and dazed by the rush of magic—too much, too fast—I stood flatfooted as Lucy's deadly magic collided with the crystal pillar. The glommed-together elements warped and flattened against the crystal. The unrefined ice blades shattered. The fiery spikes rebounded.

Lucy cried out, clutching her temples from the backlash of her broken, primitive magic. Her legs crumpled. She barely managed to lift a shield in time to deflect the blazing barbs that ricocheted in her direction. They pummeled the soil all around her, inflicting death upon the nearby plants.

Lucy didn't rise. I couldn't tell if she breathed.

The baetyl didn't give me a chance to check. It pulled more crystals out of the quartz ring. Agony raked white-hot needles through my skull. I gagged on sulfur and chlorine and the flat, burnt-ozone scent of overheated water, and I wondered distantly if it was the smell of my brain melting. My vision darkened. My legs disappeared.

I caught myself on my hands and knees and blinked black motes from my eyes. My pulse powered a pendulum of pain inside my skull. Sitting back on my heels caused my vision to narrow again, and I took careful, deep breaths, until I was certain I wouldn't pass out.

Four new crystal pillars stood equidistant around the ring. None were as tall as the first, and all four were so slender that I could circle each with my hands. They were a far cry from the enormous first pillar the baetyl had attempted to replicate.

I stared up at the rock dome as soft magic soothed my aching head. The baetyl's repairs ghosted through me, so delicate I wouldn't have known elements worked inside me if I weren't part of the magic. As it replaced pathways the latest spells had scathed, it tweaked each, altering me. The core of me, the part that made me *me*, was being reshaped by the baetyl's inexorable advance.

Nothing about its actions felt inimical. The baetyl didn't change me because it was frustrated by my weakness, just as it didn't heal me because it felt compassion for my pain. It saw me as a tool through which to care for gargoyles, one it could commandeer and remold to better suit its purpose.

And yet.

If the baetyl was lurking inside me all this time, why hadn't it taken over sooner? I had been teetering on the brittle edge of exhaustion for weeks. It had plenty of opportunities to usurp my body and magic. But it only roared up from my subconscious when I was using my spirit inside a gargoyle.

The truth struck like a viper, stunning me.

I was a fool.

The baetyl reacted not when gargoyles were in danger, but when *I* was in danger. It wasn't attempting to take over me. It was filling in the missing pieces of me.

Somehow, when I fled Reaper's Ridge after healing the

broken baetyl, I did so with a piece of the baetyl embedded within me—and not just the part that gave me the ability to see gargoyle beacons: with a part of the baetyl itself. Or maybe the two were the same thing. It didn't matter. What mattered was that I kept extending myself too far, wrenching my spirit to and fro, and weakening myself. I made myself vulnerable, and the baetyl stepped into that opening to fill it up. It worked to fix the holes in me, as I had fixed the holes in it.

So long as I kept tearing myself apart, the baetyl would keep remaking and reshaping me according to its own design, until I no longer recognized myself. Until I was the human equivalent of a baetyl.

"Fight it, Mika," Oliver urged.

I shook my head, immediately regretting the movement. "I can't."

"You must."

Oliver huddled as far from me as he could get within the baetyl's quartz ring. His wings drooped to the ground on either side of his stiff body. Pain shouted from him as if with its own voice, but his eyes reflected only love—and fear.

Tears blurred my vision. The baetyl saw Oliver's injuries as flaws, but it didn't recognize his suffering. It cataloged his crackled muzzle and sprained wings, but it didn't ache with empathy. It didn't feel the pride that swelled in my heart at my friend's bravery. It bore no love for my companion.

The baetyl's elemental intelligence vastly exceeded mine, but it was emotionally vacuous.

"I need you," Oliver said. "I need you to remember who you are."

"I'm Mika Stillwater, gargoyle guardian."

"You're more than that."

I heard Marcus's bitter words replay in my mind. *You're*

pretending you are your work. That's a pretty narrow definition of yourself.

It was the definition the baetyl would give me.

It was the definition I had been attempting to achieve. Being a guardian was a gift, a calling, and a privilege beyond any I believed I deserved. I thought the only way to make myself worthy of the honor was to sacrifice everything about myself that wasn't a guardian. But in doing so, I had nearly undone the very essence of myself that shaped me into a guardian. My spirit was in tatters. I had to fix this. I had to fix myself, before the baetyl made it impossible.

I held Oliver's eyes, and I focused all my being on my love for him. The baetyl paused. It tested the repairs it had done on my mind against the repairs this gargoyle needed.

He needs a hug. He needs comfort. He needs a friend.

The baetyl's hesitation lengthened. Heartened, I quested into myself the same way I quested into gargoyles, looking for my spirit. I found the baetyl instead. It filled me, a glistening sphere of quartz crystals. Every facet of it glowed golden, but I could discern variations in the quartz that hinted at a pattern too complex to comprehend. Gently, I cupped the baetyl's spirit in my ethereal hands and sent it my gratitude for all it had given me—for the map of the gargoyles and their ability to sense me as a guardian, for the knowledge it embedded in my subconscious, and for keeping me alive when I should have been dead a dozen times over. Then I wrapped the baetyl's spirit in love, flooding it with emotion. *This is my infinite power, and I give it to you. I love you as I love myself.*

The baetyl stretched into the emotion, absorbing it, expanding, merging with me until it revealed the fragile human form at its heart. Her outline wavered at the edges, held together by gossamer strings tethering her to the baetyl's crystals.

I sent this deep, inner core of myself love in the form of forgiveness. I had done what I thought was right. I had made choices detrimental to my own welfare, but I had done so out of love. It was a good place to start, but now I knew better. I would look after gargoyles *and* myself with the same compassion and dedication.

The glow of my spirit intensified. It called to me, pulling me deeper into myself until I could no longer sense my body. I was light, pure and radiant and serene. On my exhale, energy breathed from me down the tethers, flowing toward the baetyl's crystals. I accepted its changes as a part of me, harmonizing with each connection. Anchored, safe, my spirit settled.

As I rose to the surface of my consciousness, my mental map of gargoyles shrank, the details of each beacon unraveling like a dream upon waking. I scanned the five beacons under the dome, now reduced to generic, near-identical lights. The loss of knowledge was bittersweet. I would always want to exceed my limitations, but I was grateful for my current powers, too.

I was small, but mighty in my own way. I was whole.

I was enough.

28

"Oliver." I blinked my friend into focus.

Whatever he saw in my eyes brought his ears up. With two limping strides, he closed the distance between us. I ran my hand across his carnelian mane and pressed my forehead to an uninjured patch of his scales, marveling at the pleasure of being in control of my own body. Breathing deep, I grounded myself in his familiar dry scent. Oliver arched his neck to rest the tip of his muzzle on my shoulder, his breaths stirring my hair.

"Is it gone?" he whispered.

"No, but it's safe. I'm safe."

Oliver inhaled deeper, then nodded.

I would explain more later, when each thought didn't feel as if it were stretched a mile long and traveling at a turtle's pace.

"Boost me?"

Oliver pulled back so he could study my face. "Why?"

"I think it will strengthen my spirit."

Magic unfurled inside me, a sum more vast than my own and pathetically small compared to the baetyl's. I tapped earth and tuned it to quartz, drawing lightly on Oliver's boost. It felt like coming home. Watching Oliver closely, I increased the magic I held, ready to release it in an instant. His eyes remained clear, troubled only by worry, not sickness.

When I realized he was monitoring my well-being with equal intensity, I smiled, but I couldn't hold the expression.

"I want to heal you—"

"I won't let you," Oliver interrupted.

I sighed but nodded. "I won't let me, either."

We could both feel it: The baetyl had pushed me to the cusp of nullification too many times. I needed real recovery before I could safely work complex magic again.

"Can you get us out?" he asked.

I eyed the petrified dome. "I would need a chisel." And the energy to lift it.

I tested the elements again. Sleep sang like a siren song, but I refused to listen. Eventually—*soon*, hopefully—someone would break through the petrified dome. When they did, I wanted all of us protected from any fallout.

"Everyone," I called, raising my voice to be heard by the three gargoyles out in the garden. "Come to me."

"What are you going to do?" Oliver asked.

"Create a shelter."

Oliver hummed a note of distress, and I assured him I would be careful.

"Can I help?" Wendell's enhancement sank into me, doubling my available magic. It was more than my element-seared synapses could currently use, but just the shape of his boost was enough. It thrummed a harmonious chord with my spirit, connecting me to the larger song that murmured at the edge of my awareness, providing another anchor for my spirit.

"Thank you, Wendell."

"You saved me." He waddled on dragon paws to my side and sank down, exhausted, against my thigh. "I knew you would."

I ran my fingers along his slender muzzle, and he closed his eyes. The baetyl had healed every nick and scratch on his strawberry-quartz body. I wished it could have done the same for Oliver.

Three additional boosts pressed against my awareness as the gargoyles who had distracted Lucy drew closer. One by one, I accepted their enhancements. The inrush of available magic dizzied me, and I dug my fingers into the soil beside my hip to steady myself. Like with Wendell, I didn't draw on the wealth of elements their boosts provided, savoring instead the way their enhancements bolstered my spirit.

When my equilibrium stabilized, I painstakingly pulled a simple quartz-hardened ward through the crystal pillars, doming it across the tips of the crystals above our heads. By the time I finished, my head pounded, and I released the elements gratefully. The other gargoyles joined us, passing through my ward with ease; I designed it to withstand a cave-in, not to bar gargoyles.

I slumped over my knees. The spell would hold even if I passed out, which sounded like a fine plan.

"Mika, she's moving."

Oliver could mean only one person. I braced a hand in the churned soil and peered over the shallow quartz wall.

Lucy swayed on her feet. Dirt flaked from her black pants and dusted her black top brown. In the last hour, she'd aged a decade. Shadows grooved her eyes above sallow cheeks. Her ponytail hung askew, and snarls of hair framed her face, some of it singed.

Dragging her bag of loot with one hand, she lurched

toward us. Magic sputtered around her. On her third step, she managed to create a crude icy slurry, but it imploded before she could fling it at me. She stumbled to one knee, then kept coming.

I climbed to my feet. My limbs were granite. I locked my legs to stay upright.

Cold determination burned in Lucy's eyes. Lips pinched white, she gathered magic. The earth element crumbled and the water evaporated. Her magic fizzled.

Oliver growled. If he decided he needed to protect me, he would leap through my ward. I reached for him, holding him in place with a light touch on his mane.

"You should stop before you hurt yourself, Lucy," I said.

Her bag caught on a low bush, and Lucy fell twice before she tugged it free. I couldn't summon sympathy for her.

"You need help. Your magic is broken."

"There's *nothing* wrong with me," she snarled.

"Is that why you nullified the man you love?"

"Don't talk about him!" She teetered to a stop five feet from the ring of quartz. Sweat beaded her forehead and matted her hair despite the cool morning air.

"You can't even grip the elements," I pressed. "Your spirit is too unstable."

"Not for long." Her hand trembled when she released her white-knuckle grip on her bag. Flexing her fingers, she glared at the crystal towers. Then she reached into her pocket and pulled out the pipsissewa.

A chill ran down my spine.

"No, Lucy, that's a terrible idea."

"Afraid, Mika?"

Yes, but not for the reason she believed. I wracked my sluggish thoughts for logic that would penetrate Lucy's mania.

"You'll still be trapped. That dome—"

"Will let me pass." Lucy shoved the pipsissewa ring onto her finger. "My strength, your spirit. I'll be unstoppable."

Lucy assumed my spirit would be like any other. She had no way of knowing a piece of a baetyl was curled inside of me. Lucy's spirit would never be able to shift to match mine, because I wasn't fully human. Even if her spirit wasn't already weakened—even if she were like me and compatible with the baetyl's energy—I would still be terrified for her. The baetyl didn't hate. It didn't love. But it possessed a dispassionate desire to squash Lucy for what she had done to me and Oliver and all the other gargoyles she knowingly sickened. I wasn't sure what would happen to Lucy if she invited that into her spirit through the pipsissewa, but it wouldn't be good.

"Don't, Lucy. This is far more dangerous than you realize."

Dropping her bag, she shuffled forward, the toe of her right foot dragging.

"Gralen! Think of Gralen. He's going to need you here. He's going to need you when he recovers."

"I told you not to speak his name."

"Then stop!"

Oliver's paw wrapped around my thigh, exerting pressure. I stood inches from my barrier, my hand lifted. With a touch, I could break my magic. Lucy couldn't shift her spirit to a spell that didn't exist.

But doing so would leave Oliver and Wendell and the other gargoyles vulnerable.

I let my hand drop.

"If you value your life, please don't do this."

"Earnest Mika, still thinking you can manipulate me with words." Two and a half feet of air and my thin quartz ward separated us. Holding my gaze, she lifted her arm, pipsissewa extended.

"Oh, Lucy . . ." I took a step back, closer to Oliver.

The pipsissewa sampled my magic. Triumph sparked in Lucy's eyes. Her free hand lifted to shove through my ward.

She froze on a sharp inhale. Terror rounded Lucy's eyes, and her pupils blew black. Her head snapped back. Lucy fell in a boneless heap. Magic convulsed from her, wild and twisting. It burrowed into the soil around her body, setting the ground seething. Gnarls of misshapen quartz bubbled forth, mounding around her arms and legs in mutant piles pocked with sand and gravel. Body rigid, mouth open on a soundless scream, Lucy sank into the freakish quartz. The ugly rock oozed over her biceps and ankles, encasing her limbs.

Lucy lost consciousness before it could swallow her whole. It took another thirty seconds for her magic to fizzle out.

I held as stone-still as the gargoyles, all of us frozen in horror. Lucy's face protruded from the loathsome quartz. I stared at her closed eyes, her pallid cheeks, her open mouth. Her indrawn breath wheezed loud in the silence.

She was alive. I waited to feel relief, but I couldn't summon more than hollow ambivalence, not after the harm she had inflicted. But for the junior agent I met on the steps of Mo's florist shop, I felt genuine sadness. I liked that Lucy. If she had recognized her curtailed magic for the gift it was instead of bitterly striving for more power, she could have been happy. She could have become a friend.

A loud crack brought my head up. Across the gardens, a hole punched through the dome a person's height above the ground and wide enough for an air cart. Marcus burst through the opening, a ball of muscle and magic. He landed lightly in a crouch, a ward wrapped around his body. His FPD uniform gleamed with activated spells. In one sweeping glance, he assessed the grounds. Then his gaze locked on me.

He started running.

Behind him, four more FPD warriors leapt through the opening, fanning out. Marcus's whole squad had arrived. Magic flowed along the underside of the dome, supporting the massive petrified spell. It was over. We were safe.

Almost.

I banished my ward. Relief had replaced my muscles with molasses, and I couldn't manage to walk, so I crawled over the low quartz wall. Oliver came with me, his injured wings scraping the quartz.

"You don't have to—"

"I'm not leaving your side."

Lucy's eyes were closed. Her chest rose in shallow breaths. Splatters of misshapen quartz flecked her cheeks and knotted in her hair. Larger clumps of the grotesque, dirty rock encased her shoulders and biceps. A swath splashed across her ribs like dingy water frozen in place. Another minute, and she would have entombed herself alive.

Careful not to touch any of the mutant quartz, I reached for Lucy's hand. A tug, and the pipsissewa came free in my grip. Lucy would never, ever use this dreadful magic again. *Now* we were safe.

I rolled away from Lucy, onto my back. I intended to keep going. To get up and start running and not stop until I was in Marcus's arms. But I couldn't muster the strength. The ground hugged me. Its rich aromas of disturbed dirt and trampled grass wafted over me. Oliver lay down beside me, and I breathed in his clean, cool scent—the best smell in the world. Voices shouted and footsteps thumped, but all of it was distant. Unimportant.

Marcus dropped to his knees beside me. Worry grooved his forehead. His lapis lazuli eyes skimmed my face and body, snagging only an instant on the pipsissewa. He assessed Oliver's injuries, then Lucy's imprisoned body. The air around him seemed to shimmer from the amount of magic he held.

"Can you move?" he asked.

"Help me?"

Oliver made room, and Marcus scooped me into his arms. A dozen aches flared down my body. I ignored them, nuzzling into Marcus's chest. He smelled like fire, warm and comforting. A close second to Oliver's scent.

I protested when Marcus laid me gently on a patch of grass less than twenty feet away. He positioned himself where he could see Lucy, the opening, and the auction house.

"How bad is it?" he asked, his voice a rasp. His gaze tracked Oliver, who limped to catch up, his wings dragging, his body so badly in need of healing. "Are you—?"

"I'm not nullified," I said. "My spirit . . . I'm too weak."

Marcus's hands balled into fists, but his magic was whisper soft as he assessed my injuries. Oliver hobbled the last two steps to my side, then sat as close as his stiff wings allowed and wrapped his tail across my hips. Wendell coasted low to the ground, landing at my feet.

I lifted a hand to trace Marcus's jaw. He had come for me. Despite how terribly I had treated him. Despite how I had ignored him and pushed him aside. I didn't deserve him—

I shut the thought down. The sentiment too closely echoed my old belief about the baetyl's gifts. Somewhere along the way, I got it in my head that I had to achieve a state of human perfection to be worthy—worthy of calling myself a gargoyle guardian, worthy of the abilities bestowed upon me by the baetyl, worthy of the love of this impressive man.

But no gargoyle ever doubted I was a guardian. The baetyl gave me its gifts freely, believing I would use them well.

And Marcus loved me *as I was*. I didn't have to change to be worthy of him, and believing I needed to do so only insulted Marcus's judgment.

"I should have listened to you," I said. I let my hand drop to rest atop his, too tired to keep it lifted above my head but needing to maintain contact with him.

"I should have listened to *you*. Clearly, this was more than city guards could handle." The disgust in Marcus's tone could have been for the guards, but I suspected it was directed inward.

"I shouldn't have pushed you away. I'm sorry. I don't know if you got my message . . ."

Marcus's smile was as tender as the kiss he brushed across my lips, but his eyes remained worried. "I love you, too."

"Mika!" Kylie tore across the gardens, blond hair streaming out behind her.

While I had been distracted, someone had widened the hole in the petrified dome, opening it to the ground. People poured in, most of them in guard uniforms, but my friend raced ahead of them all.

Kylie collapsed to her knees beside Oliver, her hands fluttering over both of us. "Oh, Oliver, your wings. Mika, are you all right? How can I help?"

Quinn landed several feet away and loped to us. Anya was right behind him, her blue-and-green panther body a sleek echo of his heavier lion form. Lydia and Herbert landed closer, rushing to my side. Lydia hissed at Wendell, then settled right next to him, her plump swan body pushed against his pelican side. Herbert squirmed between Marcus and me, tucking his round armadillo body into the curve of my waist. All their boosts were open to me, and I gingerly connected with each of them without touching the elements they enhanced.

"You can start by letting her breathe," Marcus said.

Kylie nodded and leaned closer, brushing hair from my face. Tears shone in her eyes.

"I'm so glad you're safe," she whispered.

The guards' shouts and footfalls echoed strangely against the dome, and the haze of elemental currents suffusing the air exaggerated their numbers. Discombobulated by the commotion, I closed my eyes.

I opened them on a gasp. Dozens upon dozens of gargoyle beacons gathered outside the dome near the opening, so many that the glowing lights appeared to make a solid, curved line on my mental map. The first beacon swooped inside. Another followed, and another, the stream of lights becoming a cloud as the gargoyles fanned out. I twisted to watch as a gray-and-red agate bear with a sheep's head and owl wings flew into the dome, followed by an amethyst alpaca-headed heron, then a citrine-and-tigereye hedgehog with barbed wings. More and more gargoyles kept coming, some that I recognized—Lowell's compact raccoon body with his distinctive bands of orange, brown, and white sardonyx; Carmen's impressive kraken form with her eye-catching iris agate spots—others I had never seen before. Most flew to the Onacona's roof, lining its peaks and turrets, but several landed in the garden, perched on statues and fountains. Every gargoyle faced me, silent but attentive.

"They've come from all across the city," Marcus said quietly. "When I couldn't get a spell to lock on your signature, I tracked them. Then Quinn got the message, and we got here as fast as we could."

"The message?" I echoed, confused.

"Oliver's Network," Wendell said, and I heard the capital N.

"My network?" Oliver swung his head to take in the riot of gargoyles atop the Onacona. "It worked?"

"When Sosha found me trapped in the hedge"— Wendell indicated the lizard-opossum gargoyle who had saved us from Lucy's baneful spell—"she left to warn others, then returned to help. Sosha only told two others, so . . ." Wendell smiled at Oliver, sharp teeth flashing.

"It worked!" Oliver crowed.

"What did she tell the others?" I asked.

"That you, Guardian, and Oliver were captive here and needed help."

"Every guard house in the city got the same message from a gargoyle," Captain Rojas said, striding up to join the crowd around me. "I also believe we have you to thank for all this help." At my confused look, she waved a hand through the air.

I realized it wasn't my muddled mind exaggerating the amount of magic being wielded under the dome. Considering the sheer number of spells and the magnitude of the elements in use, multiple gargoyles must have been enhancing every guard present.

"Ah, no. That's the gargoyles' doing."

Guard Haubner strode up behind the captain. His brown eyes swept over my gargoyles, narrowing on Kylie and Marcus. Even though he saved me from the khalkotauroi and knew I wasn't responsible for the thefts, he still

assessed me with a trace of suspicion. I finally realized it
wasn't personal. Haubner didn't distrust me in particular; he
needed to be convinced of everyone's innocence—gargoyles
included.

"What happened here?" Captain Rojas asked.

"Mika needs a healer—" Marcus said, on top of Kylie's,
"Questions can wait—"

"The thieves happened," I said, overriding them both. I
wanted to sleep. I wanted to be healed so I could heal Oliver.
But first I had to be sure Lucy couldn't hurt anyone else. I
glanced from Marcus to Kylie. "I can't leave until they're
arrested."

Marcus helped me sit up, and he kept a hand against my
spine to steady me. I didn't have the energy or inclination to
ease into my retelling of the night's events, so bluntness
would have to suffice.

"They forced me to shift my spirit."

"They? They who?" Gravel was softer than Marcus's
voice.

"Gralen and Lucy. Gralen is inside, in the storage room.
He needs a healer, if it's not too late."

Captain Rojas spoke into a message sphere, ordering
three guards into the building, and sent it flying. She
turned back to me before the spell disappeared over her
shoulder.

"How does someone force you to shift your spirit?"

I uncurled my fist, revealing the pipsissewa. "Lucy made
it. She's been using it to slip through wards, like you
suspected."

The captain leaned in for a better look, her hands
clasped behind her back. Haubner's expression tightened
with skepticism.

"Isn't that a spell analyzer?" Kylie asked. She reached for

the pipsissewa but let her hand drop when I twitched it away from her.

"It is," Haubner said.

"It was. Lucy's modification is in the ring. That's the part that forces a spirit shift on the wearer." Saying it so clinically made it sound benign.

The captain speared Haubner with a look. He shrugged.

"When Lucy let me inspect it, I didn't use the ring," he said.

"I did."

Every eye returned to me.

"That's when Lucy discovered I had—have a...weakness that makes it easy to shift my spirit. They lured me here tonight to exploit me."

"They hurt Wendell and used him as bait," Oliver said, his voice a near mimicry of Marcus's growl.

"Then they imprisoned Oliver and used him to force me to comply." I wanted to sound equally as tough, but my voice gave way on a quaver. Oliver had suffered so much.

I recounted Oliver's bravery in the face of Gralen's cruelty, but I glossed over most of my spirit shifts after I explained how we got into the auction house. My memories of the series of torturous shifts in the storage room were already jumbled and getting fuzzier; I had no desire to strengthen them by reliving them.

No one interrupted me until I explained Lucy's broken magic, unharnessed once she destroyed the bracelets curtailing her twisted power. Captain Rojas peppered me with questions—most of which I was happy to let Oliver field—and Marcus sent a warning to Grant. The FPD squad erected a containment barrier around Lucy's unconscious body. If she woke and her magic lashed out, they would ensure she didn't harm anyone.

"How did you escape someone that powerful?" Captain Rojas asked.

"We fled, but we weren't fast enough to escape completely." My eyelids were heavy. I was afraid I would say too much, so I jumped to the end. "We barricaded ourselves there, inside the quartz. Lucy tried to break through by shifting her spirit to mine, but she lost control of her magic again, and . . ." I trailed off, glancing toward Lucy's repulsive quartz prison, then away.

"You're saying you didn't attack her?" the captain asked.

Oliver growled. I patted his foot, and the small gesture took effort.

"I didn't attack her. I made my ward and hid inside it."

"Your 'ward.'" Captain Rojas pivoted to examine the perfect circle of quartz.

As if they timed it, the city guards dismantled the eastern arc of the petrified dome. Sunlight spilled through the opening, sparking off the crystal pillars. Light danced across the gardens, and diffuse rainbows refracted against the remaining curve of the dome.

"Most people simply hold the elements. What possessed you to build *that*?" the captain asked.

"It seemed safest."

Captain Rojas settled into her stance, her wrinkled face devoid of expression as she decided if she was going to accept my answer.

"You haven't mentioned the dome," she finally said.

I considered blaming it on Lucy.

Marcus must have seen something in my expression, because he said, "It feels like your magic, Mika, but not wholly."

Everyone listening knew I didn't have the skill necessary to create a petrification spell, especially not at this scale. But

Marcus had been linked with me when I pulled a quartz wave from the ground to save our lives. He had been with me inside the baetyl when I healed it.

He knew I had come out changed.

Marcus wasn't suggesting I tell the truth, though. Baetyls were the gargoyles' most closely guarded secret. We would both go to our graves with the knowledge of their existence. Instead, his words were a warning. If he recognized my magical signature in the petrified dome's spell, the captain would, too.

Captain Rojas glared at Marcus. Her instincts must be telling her he had given me a signal, but she couldn't pinpoint what it was. I picked my next words quickly but carefully, and I was pleased when they distracted the captain.

"I don't understand how I did that to the dome." Truth. "My spirit was unstable when it happened." Truth. "I guess my mangled magic warped the auction's ward." Lie. Such a big lie. I took a slow breath, not rushing. "I wanted to send out a beacon for the guards. Instead, that happened." A truth and half-truth woven seamlessly.

"There's so little we know about spirit-shifted magic, since the practice is so dangerous," Marcus said.

The simple statement gave weight to my shaky explanation. I could have kissed him.

Captain Rojas squinted at the dome, then back at me. "It had nothing to do with all the gargoyles?"

"Using their boosts would have made them sick."

"I think the captain has everything she needs to make her arrest, right?" Marcus looked from me to Captain Rojas, receiving a nod. "Then, Mika, let's—"

"Wait." I tried to raise my hand but only managed to twitch my arm. "Two more things. This must be destroyed."

I uncurled my fingers from the pipsissewa.

"I will see it's handled properly," Haubner said, gingerly collecting the dreadful device.

"Not 'handled.' *Destroyed.*"

Marcus laid a warm hand on my shoulder to soothe me. "Grant will keep an eye on it while the city guards complete their investigation. After that, the FPD will see to its safe destruction."

I relaxed against him. My eyelids fluttered closed, and I fought to peel them open again.

"You said there were two things," Kylie encouraged. Her fingers closed on my hand, squeezing softly. "Can the second wait?"

"Oliver's everlasting seed."

Oliver started to speak, but I kept going.

"Gralen stole it. It's in the bag near Lucy."

"I'll make sure he gets it," Kylie said.

The captain and Haubner had more questions, but I couldn't seem to follow along. Marcus said something, too, his voice a pleasant rumble against my back.

Oliver's cool paw settled on my thigh. "Go gentle on her," he said. "She's still fragile."

Before I could ask who he was talking to, cool elements slid through my head, clumsy only compared to the inhuman delicacy of the baetyl's magic. Pain lifted, and I floated with it into a welcoming void.

EPILOGUE

With a hook of quartz-tuned earth element, I stretched the orange agate seed crystal in my hand, attempting to replicate the shape of Greta's large-nosed face. I sat cross-legged on the floor of my room, Oliver sprawled in a sinuous coil in front of me. Kylie perched at my worktable, addressing envelopes in her neat handwriting, and Herbert helped, licking and affixing stamps with surprising dexterity. Sunlight spilled through the bay windows, but a gentle breeze alleviated the afternoon heat. I smiled to myself, savoring this peaceful, ordinary moment.

"Make the face blunter," Oliver said, when I held the seed up for him to inspect. "That's more like a badger."

"Good point." I softened the nose and added small groves to define it. A subtle resistance tugged against my magic, as if I pulled the elements through a sieve. I decided to leave the delicate work of creating eyes and ears until later, when I was more rested. Instead, I elongated the seed into the approximate shape of Greta's body, then gave the figurine blunt legs.

When I released the elements, it felt as if an overtaxed fist of mental muscles unclenched. I sagged against the bed frame with a soft sigh.

"How do you feel?" Oliver asked, scooting closer to rest his head on my lap.

"Tired but better." Each spell strengthened my spirit and my magic in tandem, but I still needed frequent breaks.

I spent five days in a healer hall before they released me. I no longer suffered an instant headache when working magic, but I was far from fully recovered. The healers warned me it would take time. How long, they weren't sure. They had never seen anyone with a spirit as weakened as mine who was still sane.

I set my project on the floor next to three finished figurines, each a variation of Greta's scaled body and wombat face. None were quite right. The head was too large on the first, the wings too thin on the next. I would keep at it until I crafted a flattering replica of the little gargoyle. After word of the thieves' capture hit the newsstands, Amelia and Greta had shown up at the healer hall with an armload of adventure books to keep Oliver and me entertained while we recuperated. Amelia insisted I owed her nothing, but I thought a figurine of Greta would make a nice thank-you gift.

Every paper in the city had covered the petrified dome, Lucy and Gralen's thefts, and the guards' response. Few mentioned gargoyles except to note how they flocked to the site. Fewer still mentioned me, and then only as a victim in a footnote. As much as I cringed at the thought of drawing attention to myself, I decided I needed to tell my side of the story. I had learned that being a gargoyle guardian involved more than healing and protecting. It included a lot of advertising and educating the public.

Kylie had been too concerned about my fragile state to care about missing out on the story of the season—a truly alarming sentiment from my ambitious friend. However, after I explained my desire to capitalize on the free press, she finally agreed to leave my side long enough to write an article. When she brought me her rough draft, I knew I had made the right call. Part interview, part exposition, Kylie's piece balanced attention-grabbing details with useful information regarding gargoyle health and safety. It ran a day later on the *Terra Haven Chronicle*'s front page, above the fold, complete with a picture of Oliver and me. If anyone harmed a gargoyle again, the citizens of Terra Haven knew who to contact.

I stroked my fingers across Oliver's smooth muzzle. Clear quartz striated his carnelian nose and jaw like liquid splinters, filling in and mending all thirty-two fractures. I had counted.

All told, it had taken fifty-three seed crystals to heal Oliver's mangled wings and battered body. Tending his wounds filled my waking hours the first two days at the healer hall—a process slowed by my own limited abilities as I recovered. Like me, Oliver had days of rest ahead of him before he would be back to full strength, and at least another week, maybe two, before his repaired wings would be capable of flight.

"How do *you* feel?" I asked him.

"Grateful."

My smile went wobbly at the love in Oliver's eyes.

"Yeah," I said softly. "I know what you mean."

We were alive and together, safe at home with friends and family. Life didn't get better than this.

I closed my eyes and assessed Oliver's beacon. As my spirit strengthened, so did my certainty that the baetyl had changed me—gifted me—again. When I focused on Oliver's bright golden beacon, I could sense his carnelian makeup and body shape within it. It wasn't only because he was sitting close enough to touch, either. A hint of Herbert's shape shimmered within his beacon, and on the roof, it was easy to pinpoint Quinn from Lydia. Only time would tell if I would be able to sense their injuries at a distance as the baetyl had.

"There, that's the last of them," Kylie said, stacking the sealed envelopes into a column nearly as tall as Herbert. Each envelope contained my trade card and a typed letter of introduction detailing my services. Tomorrow, they would be sent out to families who lived with gargoyles.

"I can't thank you enough for addressing all those for me," I said. "And for typing up so many copies."

"You did the hard work."

"Signing them?" I asked, eyebrows raised.

"Writing the first one. That's a well-crafted letter. And long. I can't believe you've been hand-copying it every time."

I flushed. I had wasted a lot of time trying to make every letter feel personal by handwriting each. Kylie's plan of typing them was faster, and smarter, and I should have thought of it sooner.

"When you have the funds, you should consider hiring a typesetter for a day to make copies. But for now, I think we're done." She sat back and admired my worktable with a satisfied smile.

The surface was clean and the paperwork organized into actual stacks instead of a daunting sprawl. Better still, the bulk of the table was bare. It had taken the entire morning to weed through my mess, and it would have taken even longer to clean my room if Kylie hadn't gotten a head start. While I was still at the healer hall, she washed my laundry, remade my bed with fresh sheets, and gave every shelf and surface a polish. I owed her so much more than thanks.

Footfalls pounded up the porch step, audible through the open windows. A burst of excitement flipped my stomach. *Marcus.*

Oliver sat up.

"He's here!" we said in unison.

Kylie grinned at us. "Looks like we finished just in time."

She helped me to my feet, and I pulled her into a tight hug.

"Thank you for everything," I said.

"Promise to never scare me like that again," she said when I released her enough to breathe.

"I promise to be as safe as you from now on."

She narrowed her eyes at me, then nodded as if I had made a solemn vow. I hid my smile. Kylie ran toward danger if it meant getting a story. My statement was the equivalent of promising not to stick my hand in fire unless my fingers were cold.

"Say hi to Marcus for me." Kylie let herself out through the balcony door, holding it wide for Herbert to fly through to the roof. She peeked back inside. "And remember not to do anything *too* strenuous. You're still recovering."

I widened my eyes at her. "What are you implying?"

Laughing, she disappeared into her room and shut the door behind her.

One ear tuned to the deep rumble of Marcus's voice a story below, I set my figurines on a shelf. I wanted to run down to greet Marcus, but I made the trek downstairs less than an hour ago, and I wasn't sure I was up for a repeat journey.

Unexpected nerves danced in my midsection. I ran my fingers through my loose hair, then smoothed the wrinkles from my pants. I couldn't wait to see Marcus, but I kept thinking about our last argument. Although Marcus had spent hours with me each day at the healer hall, neither of us had brought it up—at first because I didn't have the energy, then because it hadn't been the right place. But I couldn't put it off any longer. I didn't want to.

Marcus knocked softly, as if he thought I might be asleep. I tugged the door open, then forgot how to breathe.

He wore casual clothes: charcoal trousers that hugged his thighs and a sapphire shirt unbuttoned at the collar, the sleeves rolled up to expose his tan, corded forearms. His black hair was so glossy it looked wet and just long enough to reveal a wave in its length that I longed to thread my fingers through. When his gaze settled on me, his entire face softened, and my heart tried to beat out of my chest.

When he smiled *that* smile, the one he saved just for me, warmth suffused my entire body.

"Hi," I said, far too breathlessly.

Marcus's smile kicked up, and his gaze dropped to my lips, his pupils dilating. He stalked into my room, crowding me without touching me. Negligently, he pushed the door shut behind him. I pounced before the latch clicked home.

Marcus caught me against his chest, lifting me off my feet. His lips pressed to mine, our kiss a reunion and a benediction, sweet and raw.

"I've missed you," Marcus said, when he set me on my feet. He kept a hand around me, his palm a warm support against my lower back.

I laid my cheek against his chest, breathing him in. "You saw me yesterday. And the day before that."

"And the day before that, but it's been a while since I got a greeting like this."

I tipped my head up to meet his gaze. "I know."

His eyes searched mine, his smile tentative. He gave me another quick kiss, then released me to greet Oliver. I scooted out of the way so Oliver could wrap his friend in a quartz-winged hug.

"So what's the plan?" Marcus asked.

I had sent him a message when the healers released me, asking him to meet me here this afternoon. I hadn't specified why.

"I thought we could have the meal we promised each other days ago," I said.

Marcus tilted his chin and lifted a brow, assessing me. I knew how I looked: frail and a bit haggard—which was how I felt.

"I brought my carpet, but it can't fit all three of us," was all Marcus said.

I smiled and shook my head. "I'm not up for going out, but I was hoping you wouldn't mind a picnic right here."

His smile returned. He glanced around the room. I took it in, too. The last time Marcus had seen it, the place resembled the aftermath of a disaster. The chaotic mess had accumulated gradually, and I hadn't realized how much it reflected and magnified my tense, tired, and overwhelmed mental state until it was gone. Now, seeing my figurines aligned on the bookcase, my worktable a usable surface, and the floors clean and tidy, I felt confident and tranquil. There would always be more gargoyles to heal and gargoyle families to contact, and I was ready for it, secure in my own competence and in the knowledge that I would do my best.

"I like what you've done with the place."

"Me too."

We laid out a blanket in the center of the room, then I resumed my cross-legged seat with my back to my bed while

Oliver fished the picnic basket out from under my work-table. Marcus knelt to pull out dishes.

"You can cook turnovers?" Marcus asked, holding up a spell-wrapped platter of roasted-sweet-potato-and-brie-stuffed puff pastries.

"Only if you wanted to eat something both burned and soggy. Thankfully, Ms. Zuberrie is a much better cook."

Marcus laughed.

We ate and talked of nothing important. Marcus indulged in every excuse to touch me—a hand on my thigh when he reached for his drink, a brush of his thumb across my lip to catch a crumb, the drape of his arm around my shoulders to tug me closer—and I did the same. Each contact helped ground me, mending pieces of my spirit no amount of magic could rebuild.

"You were right, you know," I said after we finished the meal and set the dishes aside.

"Yes. But you're going to have to be more specific."

I smiled like he wanted me to, but I sobered too quickly. Seeing it, Marcus shifted to face me. Our knees brushed against each other, and I reached for Marcus, interlinking our fingers.

"What was I right about, Mika?"

"About me. About how I was behaving." I took a deep breath and released it slowly. "I'm a gargoyle guardian, but it shouldn't define my whole life. It can't. I need more."

Being a gargoyle guardian was an incredible gift. To say I needed more seemed greedy and selfish. I took another deep breath, waiting for guilt to swamp me, but it never surfaced.

"Ah, about that." Marcus rubbed the back of his neck with his free hand. "I could have been more compassionate in my wording."

"I needed to hear it. I wish I had listened better. All that happened to Oliver—and to Wendell and Nimoy and all the other gargoyles—it was because of me, because I was weak—"

"Now, Mika," Marcus began, but Oliver's trilled denial drowned him out.

I shook my head at both of them, waving aside their protests. "I'm not saying I'm responsible for Lucy and all the evil she engineered. I'm saying I didn't take care of myself, which meant I couldn't take care of gargoyles. It meant when gargoyles needed me, I was more of a liability than a guardian. *You* knew it," I said to Marcus. "You could see how run-down I was. So could my everlasting seed. It was trying to heal my spirit to make me a better, stronger guardian."

I had given this a lot of thought, and I explained it to Marcus now. Again and again, my everlasting seed pointed toward ways for me to strengthen my spirit through the use of earth magic. The first iteration of my seed had shown the Stone Sworn ruins, an earth elemental's haven; if I had worked magic within its concentric circles sooner, I would have been more physically and metaphysically fortified when Lowell crash-landed on my doorstep.

The second shift of my everlasting seed had pointed toward the League of Tradeswomen's craft show, which would have been a great place to showcase my figurines— and a reason to make more, thus strengthening my spirit. But I really should have put it together when my everlasting seed showed the Earthspire Studio logo. Using magic in a facility dedicated to my element would have grounded my spirit.

Battling the sunstone ivy was the only thing I had done right, according to my seed's clues. Doing so had stabilized my spirit after I weakened it healing Daphne, though I hadn't recognized it at the time. I also hadn't recognized my seed's evolution into an unfinished figurine as yet another nudge to encourage me to work more with earth element.

"My specialty in quartz, all the time I spent perfecting it before I healed my first gargoyle, that's what shaped my spirit. That's a core part of who I am. But I've been neglecting it for weeks, throwing everything into building my business. Even healing gargoyles—not spirit-shifted ones, but gargoyles with normal, physical injuries—even that couldn't fully restore my spirit. My energy was already dangerously depleted, and I just kept pushing myself further."

"That make sense," Marcus said slowly. "But that doesn't explain why your seed kept drifting between half-formed shapes."

"I think I'm to blame. I tried to trick the everlasting tree. I asked, 'How can I best fulfill my role as a gargoyle guardian today and every day for the rest of my life?' But the only one I fooled was myself. Trying to be everything to every gargoyle *today and every day* is impossible. It didn't help that each time my seed would start to form an answer, I would shift my spirit and make everything worse."

Marcus's eyes narrowed. "You're talking in the past tense. You figured out what your seed's clues meant, so does that mean it evolved?"

"It did." I reached behind me, pulling my seed out from under my pillow. I kept it hidden in my cupped hands. "My seed's muddled shapes perfectly reflected how I had diluted my abilities and weakened myself. When we escaped Lucy, I vowed I would never do that to myself again—for gargoyles' sakes, but also for my own. I deserve care, too. I think that was when it evolved."

I tightened my fingers around my everlasting seed. This

clue represented a gargoyle in need. The urge to throw myself into researching it was overwhelming, but that was my old way of thinking. Meeting Marcus's eyes, I asked, "Does the offer to spend time at your friend's place still stand? If you think it's the kind of rest I need to restore myself, I want to do it."

"Even if it means being away from Terra Haven?"

"Yes." The thought of leaving my home for somewhere unknown scared me, but not as much as staying put and becoming a liability to the gargoyles I swore to protect.

Marcus shot Oliver a guarded glance. My friend smiled. Oliver and I had already discussed this, and he approved, too.

"What about the gargoyles here?"

"They will understand. And when I return, I will have the strength to heal them. Right now, I can barely take care of myself."

Marcus pulled me into a hug, his embrace crushingly strong in all the best ways.

"I can't tell you how happy it makes me to hear you say that. You had me so worried," he whispered.

"I was certain I was doing the right thing."

"It's that warrior heart of yours, Mika. You throw yourself into every battle." Marcus leaned back. "So how much longer are you going to keep me in suspense?"

I grinned and opened my hands.

A two-inch-tall jade pixiu sat on my palm. If not for its small wings barely longer than its shoulder blades, the feline could have been mistaken for a panther. Its fierce green eyes glared at the world, its spine straight and proud, and its long, slender tail curled around its front paws. If it had been quartz, it could have been one of my creations.

"I know a pixiu trainer across town," I said. "When I get

back, I'll look her up. She might . . ." I trailed off when I caught sight of Marcus's expression. "What?"

"I don't think I ever told you what my friend does, did I?" he asked.

I shook my head.

"She trains pixiu."

My jaw sagged open. "You mean, if I had listened to you a week ago . . ."

Marcus shook his head. "No. If you had left the city when I wanted, Lucy would still be sickening gargoyles. For all we know, she could have escaped Terra Haven and gone on to plague other towns and hurt other gargoyles. You needed to be here to stop her."

I let out a constricted breath, accepting the truth. I had been weak, and my weakness had gotten gargoyles hurt, but I had still been a guardian. I had stood between gargoyles and those who would harm them.

Marcus brushed my hair behind my ear, then cupped my cheek. I tried out a smile, not surprised when it trembled.

"I'm going to miss you," I said, turning to kiss his palm.

"Well . . ." Marcus dropped his hand to caress my arm, then twined our fingers together again. "There's something I've been wanting to tell you, too. My aunt recognized my everlasting seed. Her ex-husband used to make toys just like it. Still does, we think."

"Really?"

"The last time anyone saw him, he was living on the coast, not far from where you're heading. If you'd like, we could travel together."

My heart lifted. I shared an excited grin with Oliver. "I would love that."

"Me, too," Oliver said, prancing happily.

"Wait." I held up a hand to forestall Marcus's next words. "You don't plan to fly, do you? Because we can't. Airships aren't good for recuperation. But trains are. A healer told me that."

"Interesting." A twinkle lit Marcus's gorgeous eyes. "Would this healer also happen to be a gargoyle guardian?"

I nibbled my bottom lip. "Maybe."

"She sounds wise."

Laughing, I snuggled into Marcus's arms.

The flawless notes of an almost-remembered melody rose from my spirit, a harmonious counterpoint to the joy singing in my veins. I smiled to hear it. Then I kissed Marcus and let the baetyl's song unravel, choosing to concentrate on my version of perfection instead.

Celebrate the holidays with Mika, Kylie,
and their beloved gargoyle companions
in three heartwarming festive stories.

MAGIC BY STARLIGHT
TERRA HAVEN HOLIDAY CHRONICLES
BOOKS 1–3

AVAILABLE NOW!

Turn the page for a sneak peek.

EXCERPT: MAGIC BY STARLIGHT (BOOKS 1-3)

TERRA HAVEN HOLIDAY CHRONICLES

The Stolen Solstice
(Book 1)

I hummed an upbeat tune as I sank quartz-tuned earth element into a brilliant green aventurine seed crystal. The solid stone stretched like clay, forming a multifaceted star larger than my hand. I blunted the tips of each point, then pushed a small hole through one spoke and threaded a red ribbon through the opening. Lifting the ornament by the ribbon, I studied my handiwork. Muted midday sunlight refracted off the quartz's angular planes, chasing green light down the white sleeve of my angora sweater. The shape of the ornament was simplistic compared to my normal gargoyle-inspired figurines, but it was more fitting for the winter solstice party Kylie, Ms. Zuberrie, and I were hosting today.

"Oh, that's beautiful, Mika!" Kylie said.

She pushed through the Victorian's back door, balancing a platter of food in each hand. The delicious aroma of warm cheese, rosemary, and butter swirled into the crisp air, making my mouth water. Kylie bustled to the wooden table off to one side of the yard and arranged her cheesy herb cookies and a tray of assorted fruit among a growing selection of celebratory foods.

"I really like the way they're turning out too," I said, spinning in a slow circle to admire the decorations.

Yesterday, Marcus and Grant had strung cables in a zigzag pattern across the backyard above our heads—an easy feat for my boyfriend and Kylie's fiancé, since they both stood over six feet tall and could enhance their reach with platforms of air when needed. I had spent the last hour adding decorative lanterns and my own quartz artwork, using a step stool to reach the cables since I didn't possess the same elemental strength as the men.

I climbed atop the stool once more, tied the latest star in place, and then hopped to the grass. Seed crystals clacked in my skirt pockets. Brushing my hands across my hips, I marveled at the transformation of our ordinary backyard into a solstice wonderland. In addition to the decorations suspended overhead, cedar garlands threaded with silver ribbon and strung with brass ornaments and a few of my quartz creations hung along the walls. Red velvet banners draped among the garlands, artistic renditions of amaryllises, hellebores, and poinsettias stitched down their lengths in golden thread. Once I finished adding another dozen or so ornaments to fill in the gaps in the cables, and a couple more to spruce up the dormant plum and apple trees growing along the fence, the yard would be party ready.

"I think you could sell these." Kylie plucked a hollow rose-quartz sphere from a garland, rolling the ornament in her palm. The thin carnelian piping spiraled around the quartz seemed to dance as the light hit it. "Anywhere that sells your current work would be delighted to add these to the mix, especially in the months leading up to the solstice. Something to think about next year."

"I put a few samples out at the Eclectic Emporium," I confessed. My calling as a gargoyle guardian and healer paid my bills these days, but quartz artistry remained a passion. Besides, working with delicate quartz every day kept my skills honed.

"Good for you! Why only a few, though?"

"I ran out of time."

Kylie snorted. "We've had a busy year, haven't we?"

"Busy but wonderful." This year had brought Marcus into my life—and Grant into Kylie's. It had also pitted us against more danger than either of us had encountered in the twenty-some-odd years we had lived prior, but I wouldn't change a moment of it.

"Speaking of wonderful"—Kylie tipped her head back to check the peaks of the Victorian's roof—"where are our gargoyles?"

"Lydia and Anya are attending the midday winter solstice ceremonies at the capitol, and Oliver, Quinn, and Herbert wanted to fly around the city and take in the sights."

"They know the party starts in . . ." Kylie checked her pocket watch. "Oh crap! Less than two hours? We've got to get the sourdough in the oven, and I wanted to soak the cherries in bourbon for at least an hour." Her hand went to her head, where a soft braid held her white-blond hair mostly in place. "I still need do my hair, and—"

"The gargoyles will be back soon. No one wants to miss the party. And you look . . ." I scrunched up my face as I eyed her up and down, unable to resist teasing her. "Well, it's nothing a cleansing spell or three won't fix."

Kylie's eyes widened. "It's not that bad, is it?" She rushed to the nearest window, using the faint reflection to examine herself. Her fingers fluttered around her hair, but she stopped herself before touching the berry-stained tips to her white tresses. Her eyes narrowed at me in the reflection. Planting her fists on her hips, she turned the full force of her glare on me.

I grinned. Kylie loved a good solstice party, and she always cooked too much, but this year had her wound extra tight. I couldn't tell who she wanted to impress more: her new fiancé or her parents, who would both be attending.

"You look beautiful," I reassured her. "Fit for a high-society party."

She made a face, but I was right. Her hand-tailored navy tunic with its embroidered pale-blue flowers that perfectly matched the aquamarine of Kylie's eyes looked as if it had been designed specifically for her. Soft brown pants and navy suede boots completed her outfit. The cranberry-stained yellow floral apron protecting her clothing and a dusting of flour across her chin added charm.

"You know, Grant would probably prefer you like this," I said. "Smelling of cookies, cheeks flushed from the stove's heat, hair tousled."

A blush flashed up Kylie's neck to her cheeks, and she lost her imperious posture. I burst out laughing.

"I'm right, aren't I?"

Kylie patted her cheeks with the backs of her fingers. "No comment. Now come on. We've got more dishes ready to come out, and we could use your help."

I trailed after Kylie into the house, my skirt swishing around my ankles, my stomach growling at the savory and sweet aromas wafting from the kitchen. A wall of heat enveloped me, and I propped the back door open. I didn't make it fully into the kitchen before Kylie loaded me down

with a pie-sized quiche and a tureen of mashed sweet pota-
toes, both wrapped in warming spells.

"Come right back. I've got more for you," Kylie
instructed, then disappeared behind the kitchen door.

"Remind me how many people we're expecting," I said
over my shoulder.

"More than we invited. Everyone's curious about what
goes on in this house," Ms. Zuberrie said, and since it was
just the three of us, my landlady didn't bother to hide the
satisfaction she derived from being the talk of the neighborhood.

"It looks like we're feeding a village," I said, mostly to
myself. The table outside was already crowded. How much
more were they making?

"People can't resist a well-thrown party," Kylie shouted.

"Maybe a few will," I whispered to the quiche as I snuggled its ceramic dish between an apple-shaped kettle of
mulled cider and a vase of yellow and blue pansies. I
preferred small, intimate parties, the kind where I knew
everyone and didn't have to make small talk with strangers.
Kylie and Ms. Zuberrie thrived on social interactions. At
least Marcus would be coming, and maybe we could sneak
away after we ate.

I pivoted toward the house, then paused to take a second
look at the table. Something was off. The cheesy cookies
hadn't been so haphazardly arranged when Kylie brought
them out, had they? She was a talented cook, but she didn't
have an artist's eye for design. Nevertheless, she wouldn't
have bunched them into a pile on one side of the platter.

I rearranged the cookies into a pleasing fan—sneaking
one that didn't fit right—and hustled back inside. When I
returned with honey-and-ginger roasted turnips and a
basket of garlic bread rolls, half the cookies were missing.

I plunked the turnip platter and basket onto the table and frowned at the cookie plate. Then at the ground. Three cheese-and-rosemary morsels appeared to have leaped off all on their own. More crumbs sprinkled the grass. I circled the table, checking the yard. Everything appeared to be in place and nothing—

There. The garland on the southern wall hung askew. The tigereye ornament nestled among the decorative cedar boughs was missing. I remembered that particular ornament because it had been hard to position in a way to be visible. The stone's natural brown-and-gold pattern camouflaged it, and I had decided against making another ornament with tigereye.

A rosemary bush grew beneath the garland, and I gently rummaged through its branches, double-checking that it hadn't simply fallen. When I didn't find it, I formed a quartz-tuned pentagram, refined it to tigereye, and swept it back and forth above the soil. Nothing.

"What's taking so lo— What are you doing?" Kylie asked. She set down a pitcher of orange juice and stalked to my side.

I didn't want to voice my suspicion out loud, but quartz ornaments—and cookies—didn't walk off by themselves.

"I think we have a thief."

———

Keep reading *Magic by Starlight*. Pick up your copy today!

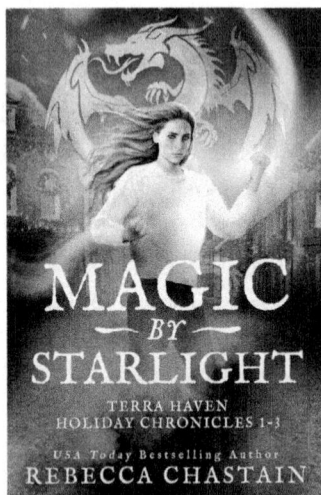

ACKNOWLEDGMENTS

For your patience, for your continued support, and for picking up this book and reading this far, you have my heartfelt gratitude. Mika (and I) have come a long way thanks to you!

Specifically, I want to thank Leiah Cooper for naming the Blue Lotus and influencing the shape and personality of Mo Almasi. For helping me refine the final draft of the book, a huge thank you to my beta readers: Amy Lynn Rosen, Susan Cook, Katie Lee, Debbie Mumford, Seana Waldon, and Jillian Cori Lippert. You enabled me to see the book with fresh eyes again, and your feedback revitalized my energy when I needed it most.

For the final polish and for making me look like I know what I'm doing grammatically, thank you to Crystal Watanabe and Carla Pinilla.

To my friends Kate, Des, Cari, Ned, and Tamara, thank you for humoring my rambles about character motivation and for being wonderful sounding boards.

Cody, I know this book brought up a lot of self-doubt, and it was (*I* was), frankly, exasperating. Thank you for your empathy and compassionate pragmatism, and for reminding me I'm not here to check items off a list; I'm here to experience emotions, and happiness is a worthy goal. So long as you're close, happiness is always in reach.

The theme of this book came about organically—in other words, with me fighting it the whole way. Mika had to learn that her self-worth is intrinsic, just as I did. It was a long process for us both.

In case you're in the same place, Dear Reader, take a moment to celebrate your self-worth with me:

Place your hand over your heart, close your eyes, and say to yourself, "I love you."

You are enough.

ABOUT THE AUTHOR

REBECCA CHASTAIN is a feminist, animal advocate, and nature devotee. She believes empathy is a hero's trait and love is a motive, an inside job, and a transformative energy that shapes each person's world. She is the *USA Today* best-selling author of the Gargoyle Guardian Chronicles and Terra Haven Chronicles fantasy adventure series and the Madison Fox urban fantasy series, among other works.

If given the opportunity, Rebecca will befriend your cat.

Visit RebeccaChastain.com
for free stories, bonus materials, updates, and so much more!

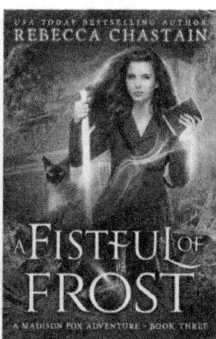

– NOW AVAILABLE –

Don't miss a one-of-a-kind hilarious adventure
from *USA Today* bestselling author

Rebecca Chastain

TINY
GLITCHES

Dealing with her electricity-killing curse
makes living in modern-day Los Angeles
complicated for Eva—and that was before
she was blackmailed into hiding a stolen
baby elephant and on the run with Hudson,
a sexy electrical engineer she just met.

"I laughed out loud too many times to count."
–Pure Textuality

RebeccaChastain.com

Printed in Dunstable, United Kingdom

71549676R00241